# BOUND

## AN MMF GARGOYLE MONSTER ROMANCE

## TRISH HEINRICH

BEAUTIFUL FIRE

# CONTENTS

# Author's Note

Seattle was the city I came of age in. It's where I met some of my dearest friends. Where I met and married my husband. Where I brought my children home from the hospital. I have thousands of fond memories of eating greasy food at Minnie's Cafe late at night, of getting drunk at the local dive bars with my acting school friends. Of eating nachos at Mamma's Mexican Kitchen until I almost burst. Of waiting to get into improv in the middle of the night while simultaneously being grossed out and mesmerized by the gum wall.

The city I made these memories in really doesn't exist anymore. Gone is Minnie's with it's take your life into your own hands bathroom and sticky menus. Mamma's insanely good and cheap food and famous Velvet Elvis room was demolished, along with dozens of restaurants and bars that held some of my fondest memories. Even the gum wall fell to "progress" and was steam cleaned. Every time I go into the city now, there's one more place that has fallen to real estate developers looking to make big money in a city that has become unrecognizable due to big corporate money. If that money was going toward real improvements (such as affordable housing and help for the homeless) then I don't think I'd mind my old haunts being destroyed. But that's not the case, and it breaks my heart.

So, the Seattle you will read between these pages is not the Seattle of today. It's the Seattle of my yesterdays. I did this as a homage, but also because I can't quite picture this 'new and improved' Seattle being atmospheric enough to house a serial killer with Jack the Rippers Knives. Or to be suitably old enough to make Gargoyles giddy with anticipation of perching on the city's buildings. I took the story, and hopefully you, back in time and I hope you'll be alright indulging me in that.

If you're curious about the ghosts, I did my homework on that and the ones I mention are actual ghosts that have been sighted in Seattle. Pike Place Market in particular has a rich history of hauntings and if you love ghosts stories as much as I do, then I encourage you to either do a ghost tour or look up some of the documentaries, etc. that have been done on Seattle's rich paranormal history.

I definitely also took some liberties with The Smith Tower, but this is, after all, fiction. And if I haven't convinced you that the penthouse at the top of the tower really could be glamoured and somehow much larger than it actually is, then I haven't done my job as a storyteller very well at all.  I sincerely hope that's not the case and that you are able to sink between these pages and lose yourself for a few, wonderful hours.

# CHAPTER ONE

## STELLA

I didn't mean to punch him, I really didn't.

But when you think about it, what kind of idiot shakes a woman who's passed out on her couch in her underwear? It's only logical that I would think it was an intruder and choose to defend myself.

Of course, it might've also had something to do with the nightmare I was in the middle of and the half bottle of Jack I'd consumed prior.

"Damn it, Stella!" my fellow detective and partner Isaac yelled, rubbing his jaw.

It took me a second to realize who it was and that I wasn't in danger. And when I did, anger coursed through me, hot and sour.

"What the fuck are you doing here?" I demanded as I stumbled from the couch.

No mean feat considering the empty take out containers, bottles and newspapers strewn around.

"Well, it certainly isn't for the ambiance," he answered.

"Fuck off, I didn't invite you."

Isaac gave his jaw one last rub before turning his baby blues onto me, the gaze appraising in a very unsexy way. Usually Isaac wore a grin, as if he knew a secret about you that you weren't aware of, and his gaze was just shy of lascivious. It was nice actually, having a Gargoyle check me out on a somewhat regular basis. Yet, this look was anything but sexy. This look was worried.

"Jesus, you're worse off than I thought you'd be," he said with concern.

"Aw, you thought of me these past weeks? Couldn't tell from the absolute silence."

I'd been told to take some time off from the special Supernatural branch of the Seattle PD after an "altercation" with some of my fellow officers. It hadn't been my first, and chances were that it wouldn't be my last. No matter how the captain and the sheriff said they cared about the lives of the Supernaturals in Seattle, their lack of proper storage for evidence and slow response times all said otherwise.

I winced and pushed the memories away with a swallow from the bottle I found under an empty Pad Thai container.

"You should lay off that," Isaac said.

"And you should mind your own damn business. What are you even doing here? You decide to commit professional suicide?"

"No one could get a hold of you."

"That's what happens when I turn off my phone."

I brought the bottle up to take another swig when Isaac's hand yanked it away.

"What the fuck, man?"

"You're needed."

I snorted.

"For what? The captain knows I'm not a boot licker, so if he's looking for someone to back him up with the inquiry, he can suck my balls."

Isaac's gorgeous lips quirked up at that.

"While I rather like the image of anyone sucking your balls," he glanced at where my tits were half out of my tank top, "that's not why I'm here. We got a body. Two, actually."

Bile rose in the back of my throat and I swallowed it, along with the images of body bags that still haunted my dreams from that case the other officers had botched.

"Get someone else."

"I need you."

The words were thick with the double entendres that had haunted our professional relationship since day one and I ignored it. The glamour that Isaac wore out in the world to hide his Gargoyle form was supermodel pretty, with strawberry blond hair, a square jaw that always had the perfect smattering of stubble on it, an honest to god dimple when he gave me that devastating crooked smile of his, broad shoulders and the most lickable pecs and abs I'd ever seen on anyone. He was everything that anyone would want in bed and then some. If he hadn't been one of my coworkers, I'd have banged the shit out of him a long time ago.

His face softened the longer I stared at the ground and he nodded.

"I get it, I wouldn't want to come back either."

The simple understanding was nice. More than that, it was a balm, one I hadn't even known I needed until now. Everyone else had either been pissed as hell, wary of me or avoiding me because they just didn't know what the hell to do with me. To be fair, I'd been a whirlwind of anger and pain those first few days after. It was a wonder I hadn't been fired, though I assumed that I'd scared the higher ups enough that they thought I'd go to the press if I had been.

"Did the captain sign off on this?" I asked.

"Yes."

"Did he choke on it?"

"Oh, he turned about five shades of red and then had one of his lackeys tell me to get you."

I laughed and wiped my eyes, which had gotten wet with this unwanted trip down memory lane.

Isaac reached out and took my hand, and I froze. Everything between us had been heating up just before I'd been put on leave. He was starting to show up in my sexy dreams, the object of my fantasies on a nightly basis. And from the way he was looking at me now, I knew that he hadn't been thinking pure thoughts about me either in the past few months. Still, I needed to hold onto some level of professionalism. And banging him, unfortunately, was a violation of my personal rules around that.

"Please, Stella? This one is...it's different. I need my partner."

"Well, how can I refuse when you beg?"

It had been a joke, a verbal poke in his ribs. We'd verbally spared dozens of times. But this time something different happened. Instead of returning it, or laughing, Isaac's pupils flared, his face flushed and lips parted.

I had just turned him on.

*I wonder what it was exactly?*

While I had a suspicion about the answer to that question, I shoved it away and focused.

"Okay," I said. "Just lemme clean up real fast."

"Good idea."

I glared at him and he shrugged.

"Sorry, you know most of us have really good sense of smell and...yeah, I'll even wait for you to shower."

I flipped him off as I went and did just that.

I took a swig of the coffee Isaac had insisted I drink, and had to admit, the man knew how to make just about anything taste like gourmet. Even my shitty off brand coffee.

As we drove through the wet, dark streets of Seattle, I was struck for about the hundredth time with how perfect this city was for Supernaturals. Old and riddled with Ghosts, the whole city felt like a place that simultaneously loved and loathed the modern. We were the city of Microsoft and hemp festivals. Of sports teams that could not catch a break, and musicians that set off a music revolution from underground clubs. It rained or was at the very least overcast most days, giving the city a noir feel that every resident took pride in. Old buildings weren't torn down but renovated and preserved so that we remained old and new all at the same time. Yeah, we had the Seattle freeze, but at least we were upfront about not wanting to make new friends.

Seattle was the second largest Supernatural population in the country but most humans, or Mundanes as we were called, didn't know that due to the glamours every Supernatural wore. I had no idea how the glamours worked. It was a closely guarded secret among Supernaturals and not even Mundanes who married Supernaturals knew all the magic that went into the damn things. But when a Supernatural was born, a Witch was always summoned, and the new child was given a glamour to hide it's true nature from a world that wasn't ready to know that Mundanes weren't the predominant species on the planet.

And if the number of homicides in my department alone was any indication, Mundane's wouldn't be ready for that revelation for a while yet.

"What's the situation?" I asked just before we got to the scene.

"Two bodies, one male presenting, the other female presenting. The male is an Orc and the woman is Mundane. They were found in Post Alley near the market."

"Cause of death?"

He swallowed and I frowned at that. Isaac was not squeamish, which was necessary for this job. In the year he'd been with the special branch, we'd seen our share of dead bodies. So the fact that he was hesitant to tell me meant that this was going to be a stomach churner.

"That bad, huh?" I asked.

"To be honest? I've never seen anything like this."

"Great. You don't call for almost a month and when you do it's to drag me to a gruesome murder scene. Some friend you are."

I was mostly joking, trying to lighten the mood a little but I couldn't get rid of the hurt that was still there. Isaac and I had worked together almost exclusively for the past year and when I needed a partner most, he'd ghosted me.

"Stella--"

"Forget about it."

"I should've called. Come by, something. But I just didn't think you'd want to see any of us after...after what happened."

I let it go, not wanting to dig all of that up. Right now I just wanted to be *here* with Isaac, pretending like our jobs were straight forward. That there weren't piles of shit we had to wade through on a daily basis just because we worked in the Supernatural Branch.

By the time we pulled up to where the other squad cars were, it had started to drizzle. Even in the middle of summer, the nights were cool in Seattle, and I pulled on my UW hoodie. The sickly yellow tape was up and I bit down on the way it affected me. I had been on the Supernatural team for close to six years, and before that I was a detective with the Seattle police. I'd seen some heinous shit in that time. I'd gone to plenty of mandatory therapy sessions for it and developed a rather aggressive love for Jack and coke as a result. And yet, the previous home invasion and triple murder had been the one that broke me.

*I suppose that should be a comfort. Proof that I still have a heart.*

But it wasn't. It wasn't even cold comfort. Just gnawing rage and grief that had nowhere to go.

*Although, maybe I can channel it into this. Yeah, that's fucking healthy.*

I almost laughed at myself until I saw two of the officers I'd punched three weeks back. One of them had the faint proof of the broken nose I'd given him, while the other had obviously gotten a bridge to replace the two teeth I'd knocked out.

"Boys," I said with a smirk.

"Bitch," one of them said.

Isaac lunged for him and I held him back, though between the two of us, we could've taken these two shit stains. I was not a short woman. Freakishly tall was one favorite descriptor from my youth and honestly, I'd gotten a thick skin about it. Dating men and women I could bench press wasn't a big deal to me; if it was, I'd be living like a nun. But Isaac was still about half a foot taller than me and half Gargoyle. While he may have allowed me to stop him, Isaac let out a low growl and flashed his purple eyes at the two.

"Fucking freak," the one with the dental bridge said.

"Come on, let's leave them to piss themselves in peace," I said.

"You watch your fucking back, you bitch," broken nose said. "Snitches tend to retire early."

"And cowards like you stick around. Yeah, I know the drill. Now if you'll excuse me, I have a job to actually do, not just *pretend* to do."

Isaac muttered under his breath as we made our way toward the mouth of alley.

"They been like that all this time?" I asked. "I've never heard them say something like that to your face."

"The captains inaction has made them bold," Isaac admitted. "But he's also made sure his men and the Supernatural team aren't ever at the same crime scene. I didn't expect them to be here, though I guess it makes sense."

I stopped just before we rounded the corner where I assumed the bodies were.

"What do you mean? What aren't you telling me?"

Isaac looked down at his hands.

"The reason captain gave me permission to get you was because the mayor asked for you specifically."

"What...? Why?"

"Because this is the second set of bodies in three weeks. Same MO, similar post mortem mutilation."

I swallowed at that.

"And was the other couple a Mundane and a Supernatural?"

Isaac nodded.

"And, there's one more thing..."

"Fuck, what else?"

"We got word an hour ago that Scotland Yard has sent someone to investigate."

"Um, why? Was one of them a member of the royal family or something?"

"No, it's a cover for--"

My breath hitched and I felt sick.

"No, no fucking way."

Isaac nodded.

"Secret Archive."

The Secret Archive was an organization that dated back so far no one really knew how old it was. They saw themselves as the guardians of any overly powerful and dangerous physical objects they called "artifacts". For hundreds of years, agents of the Archive would scour the globe, collecting these artifacts and storing them. They operated outside of any government, and were supposed to be neutral. Of course, through the years there had been more than a few power hungry directors; the one that just died was probably the worst. But from what I've heard through the grapevine, Francesca had been replaced by a level headed woman by the name of Angelica Dearborne.

Everyone in the special branch knew about the Archive. Not only was it a necessary part of our job to alert a local representative from the Archive if anything artifact-like came up, but most Supernaturals were raised with a healthy dose of fear and respect for the secret organization.

My father had been the police liaison to the Archive, and the captain of the special branch of the sheriff's office. I grew up around the complicated politics and dangers that happened when the supernatural community and artifacts intersected. And, considering how skittish much of the supernatural community had become when it came to the Archive, I was probably the most knowledgeable about the group. If the Archive was suddenly involved, that could only mean that an artifact was potentially responsible for these murders.

"So, we have a probable serial killer targeting Mundane and Supernatural couples and an artifact thrown into the mix for shits and giggles."

Isaac nodded.

"That's an accurate summary, yeah."

"No other surprises waiting for me?"

He had the decency to look sheepish before we continued to make our way down the alley.

It was a spot in the market I knew well. A long curving section that was barely lit and went downhill. The wall to my right was covered in about twenty years' worth of gum, a Seattle underground point of pride that many a person had added to over the years. I remembered making out with my girlfriend or boyfriend against the wall before going to an improv show or concert. This was a part of the market cloaked in shadow, and it felt like a different world from the main road that ran through it. The distant scent of brine from the water mixed with the thick, coppery tang of blood wafting to me from just down the slope of the cobbled ground. There were plenty of dark places in the market at night. It wasn't like the interior of the place was all that secure if you were bold enough to break through the security gates between walkways.

*Although everyone in the supernatural community knows that the Ghosts here are chatty as hell so it's pointless to commit a crime in the market proper. Which means this person might be a Mundane.*

When we got down the slope of the alley, I spotted members of our team, who gave me a nod but thankfully didn't ask me how I was or give me looks of pity. I needed to pretend that all of that was in my rearview, even if it wasn't the truth.

The smell of death was more pungent here, and I had a moment of panic as memories flooded me. I shoved it back, forcing my brain to click over into that space that made me the best at what I did. That distance that had me wondering, more than once, if I just didn't have a soul anymore; I could look at the deceased as if they were just a mystery waiting for me to unravel their secrets and nothing more.

I was finally coming to realize, as the bodies came into view, that this wasn't a failing, but a blessing.

Especially in this moment because Isaac was right. The sight that met me as my team stepped out of the way was unlike anything I'd ever seen.

Blood coated the spaces between the cobblestones, running down the slight incline to pool a few feet below the bodies. They were laid out side by side, fingers entwined in a way that made my stomach twist. Was it posed post mortem, or did they do that as someone hacked their bodies apart?

I edged closer, the murmurs of those around me fading into the background. The Orc wasn't tall for his species, which might mean he was only half or quarter Orc, but his skin was a dark green, his features very typical with tusks, violet eyes wide open, dark hair cut short. His throat had a gash, probably the cause of death, though the slashes on his face that tore his mouth into an obscene rictus and had dislodged his jaw from his upper mouth might've also contributed if he was alive at that point. The fingers of his left hand were missing, his chest was carved up and his...

*Fucking hell, did they castrate him?*

I swallowed back bile and tried to find that distant space where I could simply take in the facts. But the more I examined the Orc male's body, the harder it became. The killer was brutal, obviously wanting to send a message or make the Orc suffer or both. And it really was all about the Orc because if not for the precise cut across her throat, I would've thought the killer had been downright gentle with the Mundane female. The woman's eyes were closed, her body lying in repose with her blond hair spread out like a fan behind her, clothes in place, neat even. Whereas the Orc, in addition to having been brutally carved up, had his eyes open, mouth gaping and clothes torn. Somehow, the contrast made the whole thing even more disturbing.

The forensic photographer was snapping away and I tugged gloves on my hands to begin examining the bodies.

"What was the coroner report on the other two bodies found three weeks ago?" I asked Isaac.

When he didn't answer I glanced up at him. His face was contorted with anger and sadness. Out of the two of us, my little boy scout was the more sensitive one, and I'd be lying if I said I didn't like it.

"Sorry," he murmured. "I haven't had the chance to look yet. The only reason I know this is the second is because Jack told me."

Jack was the only Mothman on the team, and a damn fine detective, if not a little too much of know it all.

"Jack, what was the sitch on the other murders?" I asked as I got a little closer to the Orc.

"Two victims," he began, his deep voice quiet as usual, "one of them a Harpy and the other a Mundane female. Throats cut, Harpy's body mutilated, Mundane barely touched."

"I'm gonna need to see that file when we get to the office," I said.

"It's already on your desk."

I grinned up at him.

"Someone was confident I'd be back."

Jack's glamour was almost as thin as his true form and his long face split into a wide grin.

"I knew you wouldn't be able to resist a case like this."

"Does that make me more or less of a fucked up individual?" I asked as I peeled back some the Orc's blood soaked shirt.

"It makes you special."

"Yeah, specially fucked up," snorted Sal, the enormous Orc on the team. His glamour gave off serious mob enforcer vibes but he was a total cinnamon roll.

I flipped him off playfully and he clutched his chest.

"Don't tease me, Stella."

"Oh, come on Sal, you know your wife would kick my ass if I let you hit this," I said.

"Only cause she wants to first."

"Hey, Mary wants a piece of me all she has to do is call," I shot back, trying not be bothered by the fact that the Orc victims testicles were also missing.

The joking came to an abrupt halt the more I examined the Orc. Even with all the fucked up shit my squad dealt with, for us this was still pretty gruesome.

Very carefully, I turned the Orc's head and that's when I noticed the missing ears.

"Possible trophy?" Isaac asked behind me.

"Maybe. But there's several missing parts...Jesus."

"Yeah."

I looked up at Jack.

"You get anything from the Ghosts around here?"

As a Mothman, Jack had spectral sight and since the market Ghosts were often nosy as hell, they loved giving him information.

"Yeah, Mae West saw something but she's not sure exactly what."

Mae West was the Ghost of a woman who used to ask the merchants if she could help out by watching their stalls as they took breaks and such. She got her name from her outlandish clothing and her raunchy humor. To this day, no one told a dirty joke like Mae, or at least, that's what I've heard since I can't see or hear her beyond a silvery-purple shimmer in the air. Her ashes were scattered in the market and now her spirit is tied here, not that she seems to mind like some of the other local Ghosts.

"So, she actually gave you info instead of talking your ear off?"

Jack winced and I chuckled.

Mae loved to chat about the merchants to anyone who could actually hear her, and these days it was her fellow Ghosts and anyone with spectral sight, like Jack.

"Eventually," he said, "she admitted that she saw someone in head to toe black, wielding a set of knives. When I asked her to elaborate she actually clammed up."

I frowned, stomach turning.

"That doesn't sound like Mae."

"No, it doesn't. Something about those knives or the perp or both scared the shit out of her."

Ghosts didn't tend to scare easy. Unless someone was a Witch with Necromancer powers, there wasn't much that could actually harm them. And Mae was supposedly one of the most brash Ghosts at the market. If she was scared, that really wasn't good.

"Okay, thanks, Jack. Try and see if any of the others  will talk and let me know if you get anything."

He nodded and walked away.

I continued to examine both of the victims as much as I could, but it soon became clear that the Orc was too cut up for me to be able to do much without ruining any evidence that might be in his wounds. I moved on to the woman, and that's when I saw the puncture mark in her neck. I had the photographer get a picture and Isaac made a note. It wasn't until the coroner's office began to move them into body bags and separated their hands that I saw the stamp on their wrists.

"Hold it," I ordered, when I saw the sword and heart stamp.

"Holy shit," Isaac whispered beside me.

I glanced up and was surprised to see recognition on his face. The stamp was for one of the most exclusive and famous sex dungeons on the West Coast. I had worked there as a sub, and eventually a Dom, for several years. At first, it had been to pay for college, and eventually it became a need. The other subs, Doms and the woman who ran the place, Queen Dawn, had become a family to me. Even though I hadn't worked there in years, I would still go to the club on occasion when I needed a release or to forget things for a few hours. Although, that hadn't happened in quite some time.

"How do you know that stamp?" I demanded.

Isaac blushed, eyes darting down for a moment in a way that made the air in my lungs rush out.

I recognized that look, even if he only did it for a second. I'd seen it on the faces of too many subs over the years. The knowledge that Isaac, in some capacity, was not only a pretty boy sub, but also knew this club, had heat rushing through my body instantly, despite the fact that we were still surrounded by blood and had two dead bodies cooling at our feet. But was it just knowledge, or had he actually gone into the club and participated? And was it wrong of me to hope that he was a bit new to all of this in the off chance I got to be the Dom that guided him through it?

"Look at me." The snap of my Dom persona was easy to slip into my voice and I kept it quiet, just for him.

Isaac's gaze jumped to mine, pupil's dilated and lips parted on a sharp inhale.

"Good boy," I murmured. "Now, we'll talk later about how you know that mark. Alright?"

He nodded.

"In the meantime call the dungeon and see if we can get a meeting with Queen Dawn. Tell her you're calling for Mistress Magdalena."

Isaac gulped and nodded briskly.

"Yes, Mist-- I mean, Detective."

Damn, the thrill that shot through me at almost hearing my Dom name come out of his lips! It stole my breath and I leaned into Isaac, wetting my lips with the tip of my tongue.

"Yeah, we are definitely talking later."

"Talk?" his voice was laced with disappointment.

I looked up into his eyes and the need there nearly took my legs out from under me.

"Yes," I said. "Talk."

With great restraint I turned my back to him and tried to focus on the crime scene. We'd had close calls in the past where professional and personal lines had started to blur. But this shared knowledge of a secret life was by the far the most intimate thing that had ever passed between us. It tempted me far more than I wanted it to, and I realized how dangerous my friendship with Isaac had suddenly become.

I had never, ever fucked a coworker, no matter how much we may have wanted to. I had seen what that had done to my father, ruining his marriage to my mother, and then the pain of losing that woman to a case gone wrong. It had been one of many brutal lessons my father's line of work had taught me, and I swore I'd never make the same mistake.

Yet here I was, pussy wet just thinking about making Isaac kneel in front of me with a collar around his neck.

*Focus! You've got a serial killer, Queen might be involved and then there's that Scotland Yard douche coming. Maybe they'll be a pushover. I mean the Archive isn't what it used to be and...*
Then I saw him come around the corner.

I hate the expression "time stood still" but in this exact moment, it was the only explanation for why everything around me faded into the background and the only thing in focus, in color, was the man who'd broken my heart twelve years ago.

He'd visibly aged, something you don't see every day since full blooded Gargoyles seemed to age at a snail's pace. But the salt and pepper strands in his dark red-brown hair and the faint lines around his warm brown eyes only made the son of a bitch that much more gorgeous. His glamour was very tall with light brown skin stretched over high cheekbones and a square jaw, and he had a body that most movie stars killed themselves to get. Broad shoulders, washboard abs and pecs that were so perfect they looked airbrushed.

James used to love to fuck with people about where he was from since most assumed he was from a Spanish speaking country even though he spoke with a clipped, British accent. He would never tell anyone the whole truth, and sometimes his fabricated back stories were so outlandish he'd have me in stitches as people tried to figure out if it was true or not.

My dad and I were two of the only people who really knew the truth.

Hundreds of years ago, James' family had been the personal guards of the Spanish royal family. As Gargoyles, their fierce visages and powerful bodies ensured that no one fucked with the powerful family. But during the reign of Isabella, she bent to pressure from the Catholic church and banished them. James' family went to England, hiding as the Inquisition tore through Europe. It was only with the creation of permanent glamours that James and his family came back into a semblance of regular life. It always pulled at my heart whenever I used to think about the pain his family must've felt, being tossed aside after centuries of service and devotion.

He grew up hearing the stories of his ancestors and their struggle to hide their true forms during the Inquisition. It made him slow to trust anyone with who he really was but it also made him fiercely loyal to those he did let in. And when he finally let me see the real him, his Gargoyle form, James turned out to be every dark, sexy dream I'd ever had come to life. Over seven feet tall, dark purple skin, with massive wings and hands that could cover my entire head. His jaw was even more square as a Gargoyle, with cheekbones that could cut granite, and deep set eyes that were just as intense as his glamoured ones. His hugely muscled body made mine feel petite by comparison. And that fucking tail of his! Oh how I'd wanted to know what that long, ribbed tail would've felt like inside of me, but we never got that far. Though the memory of the fierce, primal look in his eye when he fucked me up against a wall twelve years ago sent shivers down my spine even now.

He scanned the area with a hard frown and I held my breath, suddenly becoming that horny twenty-year-old I'd been the last time he'd seen me. I stood still, waiting, as I always had, for him to notice me.

When he did, my mouth went dry and the hard-won confidence I'd gathered over the years dissipated like fog on a sunny day. I stood there, rooted to the damn spot as he stared at me. From the way his eyes widened and his lips pressed into a thin line, I surmised that it was just as much of a surprise for him to see me.

But the emotion passed quickly, and before I was ready, James began to saunter closer. There was the barest hint of warmth in his eyes as he drew near.

"Detective Wright." His voice wasn't just deep, it resonated with authority, sensuality and a hint of humor that had my body unsure whether to be turned on or annoyed.

I chose to go with the latter.

"I guess it's true what I heard."

He arched an eyebrow.

"Archive's really scraping the bottom of the barrel."

He opened his mouth to respond but I beat him to it.

"I'll take a coffee with cream and a croissant from the bakery around the corner, they should be opening in about five minutes. You boys want anything? Douche from across the pond is paying," I asked my team.

They laughed and yelled out a few coffee orders.

"Don't let me keep ya," I shot at James as I headed for the coroner's van.

"Good to see you too, Stella," he called after me.

And god damn him to hell, my stomach actually fluttered.

# CHAPTER TWO

## JAMES

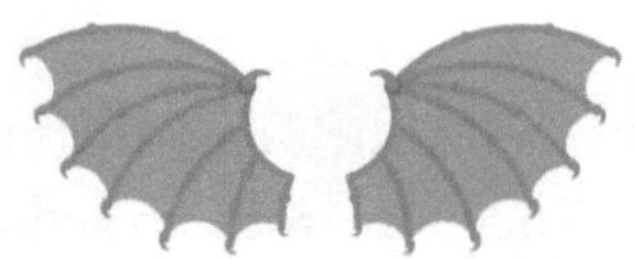

I didn't know Stella would be here, though it shouldn't have surprised me. Her father had started the Supernatural branch, she'd grown up here and swore she'd never leave. Hell, I'd kept tabs on her until she graduated from the academy just to make sure she was okay.

Or that's what I told myself anyway.

If I was being honest, I would have to admit that I *liked* seeing her there, doing the job she was meant to do. Her father had always said that Stella was smarter than all of us and twice as stubborn. It was the bloody truth but now I could add "carries a grudge like a champ" to the list.

And who could blame her really? I'd treated her abominably that night. By the time I realized that it wasn't her I'd been running from, it was three years and thousands of miles too late.

Still, I'd tried to numb the pain of leaving half of my heart behind with the damn woman when I'd fled. It took hundreds of faceless sexual dalliances, and dozens of dangerous missions, but up until ten minutes ago, I thought I'd killed that longing for her.

Yet one look at her, maturity having graced her body and face with a painful kind of beauty, and that place in my chest that had ached for years after I'd left her, gave a lurch that almost had me bending forward.

Now it was throbbing away inside of me, reminding me of why I'd stayed away to begin with.

*That was a long time ago. I'm here for a mission, a vitally important one that could cost more innocent lives if I don't accomplish it. My personal wants have no place here.*

A voice in the back of my head called bullshit and I ignored it. That damn voice was what had me fucking Stella against a wall, hours after her father's funeral twelve years ago.

Just coming close to the memories of her tight, wet heat had me biting back a groan. This was going to be a long mission if I didn't get my cock under control and fast.

As I came around the corner, I saw her partner, the pretty one with the strawberry blond hair and the very strong Gargoyle imprint on him. My horns could sense Supernaturals when they were near and I'd honed the skill to be able to see through glamours if I wanted. This male was clearly half Mundane; his Gargoyle features under his glamour far more Mundane than a full blooded Gargoyle. But that didn't mean he wasn't breathtaking. He was like carved gray marble, hard edges and square body with massive muscles that I suddenly wanted under my hands.

*Well, now. That's a possibility. Maybe it's just been too long. A good fuck with a male like Isaac could be just what I need.*

Then I saw the way he and Stella looked at each other, all of the suppressed lust that was burning in every glance. An insane jealousy spiked through me and a quiet growl rolled up from my throat.

*Fucking get a grip! The knives, you're here for the knives!*

I took a deep breath, and started to recognize  each species on her team below their glamours as my horns flared and filled my senses with the knowledge. They all seemed comfortable with one another, in the way long time colleagues in a high stress job did, and it made me lonely for the good ole days when Stella's father and I could know what each other was thinking just with a look.

He'd been one of my best friends, one of the few Mundanes I'd ever trusted. Which made falling for his daughter complicated in the extreme. Not to mention the fact that I was almost two hundred years old the last time I'd seen her.

*Though, if actual age was a true impediment to sexual partners I'd be severely limited. Maturity was the issue...she wasn't mature enough. I had taken advantage of her grief.*

It was a thin repetition of the things I'd said to her the last time I'd seen her. And while I believed they had been true, they most certainly weren't now. Which left me defenseless when she turned those cold, wary baby blues my way.

I extended my hand to her partner, ignoring Stella for a moment.

"I'm Agent James Carmichael."

"Detective Isaac Garret," he said, manner guarded as he gave my hand a brief shake.

Our hands didn't touch for more than a few seconds, but a warmth spread like a comforting embrace through my skin. I hid the surprise under the guise of glancing at the crime scene, but Isaac's eyes widened and he practically recoiled from me in shock.

*Well, now that's...interesting.*

"Now that we have that out of the way," Stella said, "what the fuck are you doing here?"

"I think you know." I hid the way she affected me under a smirk.

"Yeah, an Artifact--"

"Could you keep your bloody voice down?"

"No one is paying any attention to us with the carnage that's still being cleaned up," she said. "What I want to know is, what exactly are you looking for?"

"You know I can't disclose that."

Stella froze, two spots of color rising to her pale cheeks.

"Okay," she replied slowly. "Have a nice flight home empty handed. Isaac, let's go."

She started marching off, Isaac following her like a guard dog that was completely enamored of his master and suspicious as hell of me.

I took off after her, already annoyed that she was planning on making this difficult.

"You can't freeze me out of this," I said.

"Watch me."

"Stella-- "

She spun around so fast that I almost collided with her.

"Detective Wright to you, *Agent*. And I'm not going to let you swoop in here and potentially compromise our investigation because you have a skyscraper sized stick up your ass about how important you are!"

"That's not what I'm asking, but you know how this goes. You know I have a sacred duty to--"

"Fuck your sacred duty! I have a probable serial killer having a grand ole time carving up Supernaturals and you want me to just what? Let you walk all over us while you look for some magical screw driver or whatever that may or may not be involved? You either share or leave. Those are your choices."

I glanced behind her, where her team was glaring at me, arms crossed or hands resting not at all subtly on their service piece. They loved her, were loyal to her and as a result they would freeze me out. I could go over their heads to the sheriff, but from what I read about recent events, that would cause a whole different set of problems that would only create more obstacles to finding the knives.

Time was of the essence, I knew that. The longer someone was in possession of the knives, the further they slipped into psychosis. I'd seen it before, and the end results were usually as terrifying for the killer as those he killed.

"Fine," I sighed, "but only you."

"And Isaac."

The Gargoyle crossed his arms, flexing a rather impressive set of biceps that were monumentally distracting. Still, no matter how pretty he was, could I trust him?

"He's my partner, I'm gonna tell him anyway so you might as well save me the trouble."

I growled, low in my throat, and was surprisingly pleased to see Stella's pupils widen at the sound. The fact that I could still affect her as easily all these years later was both an advantage and a dangerous temptation. I'd have to watch myself.

"Fine," I ground out.

"Good. You can ride with us," she said as she started to walk away. And then over her shoulder, "In the back, of course."

I exhaled long and slow through my nose before following her. As I passed the rest of the team, I swear I heard one of them wish me luck and another ask me if I wanted a last meal.

*Bloody hell, what have I gotten myself into?*

I followed them up the steep slope of the cobblestone alley, admiring the aesthetic of Seattle's old time charm, even as I wondered why the hell they allowed an entire wall to remain coated in twenty years' worth of chewing gum. The car was thankfully a large gray SUV, without the sheriff's logo on the side, and I slid into the back without having to bend myself in half as I normally would.

"Queen Dawn said that they're closed and she'll call to let you know a good time to come by," Isaac said as I closed the door.

Stella sighed.

"She hates talking to cops but I thought she'd make an exception in my case."

"How long...I mean, are you two close?" Isaac asked.

My eyes narrowed as I focused on the way he asked her the question. It was respectful, but there was also something specific about the tone of his voice, the way his eyes were downcast. It all added up to something that I couldn't quite put my finger on.

From the way Stella paused, studying him, she saw it too, but I got the feeling that, unlike me, she knew what it meant. Then she looked at me in the rearview mirror and I realized that she was weighing how to answer because I was in the car. If I wasn't here, she'd be spilling whatever the truth was to this male. But with me present, she hesitated.

It hurt, I couldn't ignore that. There was a time when Stella told me everything; to the detriment of our relationship, that was true, but still. Being on the outside of her trust shouldn't be this hard to swallow, not after all of this time and yet, it very much was.

"Yes," she finally answered. "She's like a mother to me."

"What are you two talking about?" I demanded.

Stella hesitated again before answering.

"Hearts and Swords Club. Both vics had the stamp on their inner wrist."

"I know the club by reputation," I said, eliciting an arched eyebrow from Isaac.

"Oh really?" she asked.

I knew what they were both thinking, but in spite of my private proclivities for enjoying Dom kink in my sex life, I had never sampled the offerings at the elite club. However, I did wonder how Stella and Isaac had secured an audience with the elusive Dom that ran the place. Were they members? Was Stella?

The thought sent heat rushing to my dick, and I shut it down as fast as I could. That ship with Stella had sailed a long time ago, and I was the one that made sure of that. I wasn't going to complicate my life, and hers, by allowing myself a single moment of wishing it were otherwise or wondering about what could be now. It was done, in the past. I had made my peace with it and so had she.

So why was there an annoying spasm of doubt in the back of my mind? Why did the moment my eyes met hers in the rearview mirror send a jolt of want shooting through me like a lightning bolt?

I grit my teeth and pushed it all aside. Maybe I did need a down and dirty fuck, and after all this was done and behind me, I'd put in for some leave, find a resort and take care of my needs.

"I want to get back to the precinct and look at the file Jack left for me," Stella said. "Isaac, I'm going to need you to contact the coroner's special branch office and tell them to expedite the autopsies."

"Got it."

"And as for you, Scotland Yard," she said with a smirk, "spill. What are you looking for?"

I rubbed my hand over my face and let a grunt of frustration leak out.

"I wish you'd just let me do my job."

"And I wish you hadn't come back. We both don't get what we want, I guess."

Isaac frowned as he followed the back and forth and I realized that she probably never even mentioned me. That shouldn't have hurt either, but it did.

I took a deep breath and slipped into what past partners called my professor voice: firm, and full of a "just the facts ma'am" dispassionate tone.

"Three weeks ago the murder of the Harpy and the Mundane female set off an alarm in the world wide hub that monitors all law enforcement offices around the world. Usually, we would need a bit more information than just one murder, but this set off a class five alarm which warrants immediate investigation."

"Class five is...?" Isaac asked.

"The most dangerous," I answered. "Potentially catastrophic."

"And what do you think this class five artifact is?" Stella asked.

"Jack the Ripper's knives," I answered, the words bitter in my mouth.

"Holy shit," Isaac gasped.

Stella, for once, was rendered speechless.

"They are one of the most dangerous and elusive artifacts known to the Archive," I continued and pushed as much seriousness as I could into my words. "No agent has ever been able to bring them in."

"Why not?" Stella asked.

"Because the agent is either killed by whoever is wielding them or they're driven insane by the time the knives are transported."

"And how will you avoid that?" Isaac asked.

"They don't affect Supernaturals. And I've brought a special containment unit with me. It should be in my penthouse as we speak."

"Oh my god, you kept it? In this economy?" Stella gasped.

I couldn't help laughing at that.

"You have no idea how much I love that place."

"Doesn't a single mother and her daughters live there? And you're kicking them out essentially just to stay there for a few days?"

"What am I missing?" Isaac asked.

"James owns the penthouse at the top of Smith Tower."

Isaac turned wide, bright eyes on me, flashing that damn dimple as his grin widened.

"You're shitting me?"

"Nope."

"Damn, you Gargoyles and your love for old buildings," Stella said with a shake of her head. "It's not even big enough for your true form. And it doesn't have places for you to perch and be a weirdo."

"There's totally a place to perch," Isaac interjected.

"And how do you know?" Stella turned a questioning gaze at him.

"Well...I mean, I've flown over the city a lot and I've landed on a lot of buildings and..."

"It's got a nice feel to it," I interrupted. "And the penthouse is glamoured to look smaller than it actually is. The real penthouse is three times the size it appears to be to Mundane eyes."

"That's cheating!" Stella teased with a laugh.

"But in a fucking *brilliant* way," Isaac grinned at me.

And bloody hell, he was adorable.

"Glad you think so," I answer.

"Do you two want to be left alone at the penthouse so you can perch and glower down at the Mundanes?" Stella asked with a bite to her tone.

Isaac cleared his throat and turned around but I couldn't seem to wipe the remnants of the grin off my face.

"I didn't kick her out, by the way," I said after a moment. "They know that I sometimes need the place so I sent them on a lovely vacation to Hawaii for the summer."

"Generous," she murmured. "But back to these knives. Why do you think that they're being used for the murders?"

My brain switched back to the task at hand, though I'd much prefer to fly over to the penthouse and try to get Isaac to smile again.

"The post mortem mutilations," I said. "It's a trademark of the knives. No matter what else the killer does, no matter what his reasons are, they are compelled to carve the corpse up in various ways. And...well to be frank, there was something about the crime scene photos...I just knew..."

The one other interaction I've had with the knives was one I'd much rather forget, but the scar on my left arm won't let me.

"What aren't you telling me?" Stella asked.

It would be useless to try and put her off. She'd just go digging for the truth, or she'd annoy the shit out of me until I told her. In the past, I rather enjoyed the second option, but I couldn't afford such things now.

"When I was a young Archive agent, my mentor and I had an encounter with the knives. A serial killer in Australia was carving up young women. We found him but..." I stopped to take a breath as the sound of screaming and the smell of blood tried to overtake me.

"Easy, Agent," Stella's voice was firm but not unkind this time. "You're not there."

A simple enough statement but I clung to it all the same and focused on the two of them in front seat. Isaac passed me a bottle of water and I gulped it down gratefully.

"Sorry," I said after a moment.

"No need," Isaac said, "we all have demons."

The simple statement overflowed with regret and frustration, and I had a gut feeling that he wasn't referring to his time with the special branch.

But before I could see anything more, Isaac's gaze became shuttered and he turned around.

"As I said," I cleared my throat, "we found him but he was too far gone in the thrall of the artifact. He stabbed my mentor twenty times before I was able to get to him. And when I did, he managed to slash me with one of the knives before I subdued him. As it turns out, being wounded by the knives, but not killed, has a rather unfortunate consequence that it seems even Supernaturals can't escape. And that is that I can sense them, their handiwork, their proximity. I can't pin point it with enough accuracy to know who has them, but I can *feel* the malevolence of the knives. I felt that when I looked at those photos. And then tonight, being near the bodies. Someone has found those knives, and they're using them to kill again."

"What happened to knives? Why didn't you get them then?" Stella asked.

"When I put them in containment, the unit wasn't strong enough. One of the intake workers at the Australia branch stole them and the knives haven't resurfaced until now."

"They didn't turn the thief into a Ripper...um, rip off?" Isaac asked, cringing at the wording.

I chuckled as Stella snorted a laugh.

"We don't know much about them," I said as we pulled into the precinct parking lot. "We don't even know if the knives made the original Jack the Ripper or if the Ripper made the knives. There are a few possible stories about the knives before the 1888 killings, but nothing we can either discount or confirm with any certainty. All we do know is that Jack used these knives and they've been showing up in connection to gruesome killings ever since. And they don't always drive someone to kill others. Sometimes they simply coax the person to harm themselves. But they always end up finding their way into the hands of someone with a tendency toward this kind of mass violence."

"You make it sound like the One Ring," Isaac said. "Do we need to find a huge lake of lava to throw them into?"

*Good god, just when I thought he couldn't get any fucking sexier, he makes a Lord of the Rings reference.*

"While I wish it was as straightforward as the Fires of Mordor," I smiled as Isaac's grin widened, "it's not. I have the strongest containment unit I could transport here, and if that's not enough...well, I don't know what will be."

"God, you two are dorks," Stella said, though the smile she gave Isaac was affectionate enough to make me feel the burn of jealousy in my chest once again.

I glanced at the small, square building we were currently driving to the back of and realized that we hadn't gone to the expansive police station downtown. This was a non-descript, and rather ugly, gray building on fifth, the sign on the door reading "IRS, authorized personnel only". Even inside the SUV I could feel the crackle of a repelling spell on the place. Only those that were supposed to be there would want to open the door. There was a small parking lot behind it that we were currently pulling into, and a few construction signs that made it seem that the building was under repair. Even with how unattractive the place was, it was a far cry from the tiny two offices that Stella's father and I had when this branch was started.

"Could we please keep this all between the three of us?" I asked. "No disrespect to your team, but the more people who know--"

"The harder it could be to actually find them," Stella finished.

"Yes, exactly."

"Sure, I think that would actually be best. I'm not sure I want anyone on the team near this. Except for you, of course," she shot Isaac a playful grin, "cannon fodder that you are."

"Oh, c'mon," Isaac said, flashing her that dimple and twinkle in his eye, "you'd be devastated if something happened to me."

Stella pretended to think about it and shook her head.

"Nah."

"You wound me!"

"Poor, baby," she crooned and patted him on the head.

The touch lingered a little too long, her fingers threaded just a little deep through the waves of his hair. I had a sudden, visceral image of her taking a handful of that hair and guiding him down between her thighs, his moans mingling with hers. I wondered if they had ever been together, if perhaps they were now. He did have hints of her scent on him but I assumed that was from being partners. What was confusing was that I wasn't sure who I was actually jealous of. Stella? Or Isaac?

"If you two are done flirting, maybe we can get inside and take a look at the evidence?" The words came out harsher than I had intended, and Stella gave me a glance with an arched eyebrow.

I was relieved that Isaac simply shrugged and left the car.

"Sheesh," Stella said as she opened her door, "someone a little jealous? I swear I haven't fucked him. Yet."

# CHAPTER THREE

## ISAAC

The sexual tension between Stella and James had me confused as hell.

On the one hand, I was territorial when it came to Stella. She was *my* partner, the one I'd fallen for months ago even though I knew she'd never cross that line with me. And when she commanded me with *that* tone in her voice at the crime scene?

Gods above, I wanted to fall to my knees on the dirty cobblestone and beg her to let me brush my cheek against her leg. She was always a sexy-as-hell female, with her strength and take no shit attitude, long legs and strong physique. But finding out that she was a Dom for one of the best sex dungeons on the West Coast? That made her something altogether different. Something I could easily become enthralled by.

Not seeing her the past three weeks had been torture. I'd awakened in the middle of the night with a throbbing pain in my chest, as if someone had carved something out. The moment I'd seen her passed out on her couch, that ache had eased. I wasn't sure what it meant, or that I really wanted to know. Stella would never cross that line with me, so what was the point of letting myself long for her?

Then there was James.

My situation here was already starting to become untenable before the agent of the Archive showed up, one that had history with the woman I was in love with, and had me feeling things that only confused everything further. To say I had a weakness for Dominate partners was a laughable understatement, but it had never been this bad before. Being in the car with the two of them, all I wanted to do was make them both happy, to hear that I'd pleased them. The times I'd been able to get a smile out of James was a high that was only matched by the times I'd managed to lighten Stella's mood.

I checked my watch, and the tension in my shoulders became tighter.

I was late for my check in, something that my handler had been getting increasingly impatient about these past weeks.

*Damn it. I'm gonna have to come up with an excuse.*

We'd been going over the slim file that Jack had found about the other two murders for the last hour. Both James and Stella were getting increasingly frustrated at how that case had been mishandled and she was currently fighting with the coroner's special office about where the hell the bodies had been sent since half the autopsy photos were missing.

James was pacing around the small office, his long legs eating up the short distance between desks, as he stared at two of the pictures with a deep scowl as if silently demanding they reveal all the secrets to the case.

*I'll tell them I'm getting some decent coffee and some food. We could all use it.*

My phone pinged with a text from my Aunt Laura, which was a cover for my handler, letting me know that it was past time to meet with them. My stomach twisted and I tried very hard to school my features to hide the truth. I was shit at it, but Stella and James were too distracted to notice as I told them the stupid excuse for why I was leaving.

The early summer air was cool, as I darted out of the building and began a brisk walk to the coffee shop three blocks away. I could say that it had the best coffee, that I was craving their vegan oat bar, but that wasn't at all the truth.

I wished I could've enjoyed the sunny morning, the scent of the water brushing against my heightened senses and the painfully blue sky dotted with fat, soft clouds. Seattle really was a gorgeous city with so much character and history. The Ghosts here were fun as hell and the buildings really were great for Gargoyles, since for us it was about the history of a place more than the look of it. I could settle here, be a part of something. Maybe even convince Stella to give me a chance.

If I wasn't a lying piece of shit, that was.

What no one knew was that, while I did used to work at the Special Supernatural Branch of the Chicago PD, I hadn't left simply for a change in scenery. I'd been frustrated with the ways my hands had been tied there, jaded, discouraged and ready to just throw it all in, when I was approached by someone promising me that I could do some good in the world by hunting for artifacts. They'd been very convincing, telling me that there was more for me to do than solve crimes, only to have the perps get off in a court that was stacked against the Supernaturals.

I thought I was joining the good guys, the ones that would truly protect the world. Hell, it was in their sanctimonious fucking name, the *Protectors*.

But it became clear very fast that it was bullshit. That the only thing the leaders were interested in protecting was their own power, along with increasing it at every opportunity. Which was why I was sent here a year ago.

They'd gotten intel that Jack the Ripper's knives were spotted along the West Coast, so they dispatched a dozen of us to infiltrate law enforcement to keep our eyes open for the artifact. There had been brief flickers of possible sightings in the past year, but nothing concrete.

I had started to think that maybe they'd forgotten I existed and it had been a relief. Until three weeks ago when the Harpy and the Mundane woman turned up dead and mutilated. Then I got the ping. My handler had ordered me to steal evidence and give it to him, keep my ears open, get to any new crime scenes first, pocket any evidence I could. It was against everything I believed in as an officer of the law, everything I wanted to *be*. But the moment I balked at the new instructions, the bastard had threatened every member of my team.

"And when you've watched the last one die, then we'll make sure you follow them, but not for many, many days," he'd said.

There was no warmth or proof of humanity in the man's eyes. He would do it, and it would be just as gruesome as he promised. It was then I knew that I'd never escape them. I'd sold my soul to the wrong people, for the wrong cause and there was nothing I could do about it. So, I stole the evidence with shame burning in my chest and gave it to him. But now we needed that information, if for no other reason than to stop this person from doing any more harm.

I pulled open the glass doors to the cafe and nodded at the barista, who was sporting a lime green mohawk today. The scent of espresso and pastries hit me and I breathed in deeply. I'd been to a lot of places and I had to admit, nothing measured up to really good Seattle coffee.

"Hey, man," he said as he steamed some milk, "your usual?"

"Yeah, and I'll need two drip coffees, two slices of the quiche, a couple of espresso chip coffee cakes and two vegan oat bars."

"Got some hungry friends waiting?"

"Yeah, we pulled an all-nighter."

The barista nodded and laughed.

"Man, I hear that. Be right up."

The cafe was still mostly empty since it was early Saturday morning, so it wasn't hard to spot my handler reading a newspaper near the back corner of the shop.

"Hey, I see a friend. I'm just gonna go say hi and I'll be right back for all that."

"Cool man," the barista said as he prepped my drink.

My handler, a balding, white Mundane male in his late fifties, didn't even bother looking up from his paper when I flopped into the chair opposite him. He was angry, I could see it in the tension of his jaw, but I really couldn't care less.

"You're late," he hissed.

"You want me to find this thing or not? Investigations don't work on your time table," I shot back.

"That better be the reason, Isaac, and not some silly fit of pique about your duty as a detective."

I clenched my jaw and looked away. My hands itched to squeeze the man's neck, to show him my true form and watch the terror unfold in his cold eyes as he realized what kind of beast he had poked. But I couldn't do that without endangering the people I'd grown to care for here. So I took a deep breath and calmed the fury of my anger.

"Why are you suddenly using me anyway? Don't you have other agents around here to do your work the way you like it?"

His lips twisted and I got the very distinct impression that he did indeed have someone else, and something had happened to them.

"You don't need to know the whys and wherefores," he snapped. "My superiors are keeping a very close eye on this operation. So there's no room for mistakes or second thoughts. Do I make myself clear?"

"Crystal."

"Very good."

"And if that's true," I said, "I'm going to need that evidence back."

He sat back in the chair, eyes narrowing.

"Why?"

"Seriously? You want me to find this thing then you have to let me do it *my* way and that doesn't include only having half the information at my disposal. I need all of it in order to track this down."

"You had a visitor last night. He still hanging around?"

He meant James and the bite in his voice had a chill racing down my spine.

*These guys really hate the Archive.*

"Yes. All the more reason to let me do this the right way and not raise anymore suspicion."

I held his stare, daring him to deny me. It struck me that I'd never actually pushed back before, and I wondered how much I could before they decided to retaliate.

"Fine, it will appear to have been misfiled."

I frowned.

"How? I thought--"

"That you were our only operative? No, not nearly. So make sure you keep your nose clean, Isaac. I'd hate to lose such a young, promising agent like you."

The barista gave me a wave, letting me know my order was ready and I waved back at him. The knowledge that there was someone else in the special branch working for the Protectors had my stomach in knots. Any thought of dissenting was now fraught with difficulties that I had no idea how to overcome. It was smart to not rely solely on me, and if it had been any other operation, I would have admired it. But not this time.

"Be good, Isaac," he said, gathering his trash. "I'd hate to have to let you go."

By the time I got back to the precinct, the last thing I wanted was to eat any of the delicious pastries I'd purchased.

Regardless, I plastered a smile on my face as I walked through the small entryway lobby, and to the front desk manned by an old female Werewolf who smiled at me when I set a piece of Espresso chip coffee cake in front of her.

"You little charmer," she cooed. "If I was younger..."

"Who says I don't like older women?" I said, winking at her.

"I have eyes, don't I?"

She winked back and my stomach did a flip. She meant Stella, but I played it off with a laugh.

"You know you're the only one for me."

She waved me away and took a bite of the pastry as I walked on. The space was divided into offices big enough for two desks and I went around, delivering some of the food before entering the office that belonged to Stella and me. When I didn't see her behind the messy desk I peered through the glass walls in an effort to track her down.

"She's in the gym," James said as he strolled into the office.

My mouth became dry as he came near, my eyes focused on the file in his hand. Though I was used to Stella's large presence taking up all the air in the room with her intelligence and restless energy, James did the same but with a much more subtle, quiet vibe that was no less intense. I found myself wanting to ask him dozens of questions to try and see the workings of his mind behind those sharp eyes. But at the same time, it felt too dangerous. What would I reveal as I tried to get closer to this male? What would I be creating other than one more person to become collateral damage when I failed to do what the Protectors wanted?

Still, I couldn't stop a quiver racing through me when James' hand grazed my arm as he reached for one of the coffees. A strange pull in my chest made me take a deep breath and hide it under the guise of blowing on my coffee to cool it down.

*What the fuck was that?*

"Thanks for this," he said.

"Sure."

I turned away, pretending to look for something on my desk while James studied me.

"Out with it," I said, unable to stand the way he looked at me much longer.

"You've been her partner a while?"

It wasn't quite what I expected. In fact, I had been wondering if the Gargoyle was able to see right through me to the traitorous heart beating in my chest.

*Though I suppose I should've expected him to wonder about Stella. The way they looked at one another...*

Those conflicting feelings were back and I let out a long breath to try and steady myself.

"About a year," I answered.

James nodded.

"What about you?"

He startled at that.

"What about me?" he challenged.

"C'mon, I'm not stupid. You two have history."

He snorted and took a pull from his cup.

"That's one way of putting it," he finally said. "But it seems you do with her as well."

A nervous laugh flew out of my mouth.

"Not the way you think. Stella has rules about that sort of thing."

"Yeah, she learned that the hard way I suppose." The last bit was said almost to himself, and it only piqued my curiosity that much more.

"What happened between you two?" I asked, unable to keep the acid out of my voice.

Now it was James' turn to let out a long, slow breath. He closed his eyes and I swear I saw a flash of deep regret mar his beautiful visage. It was gone fast, replaced with his stoic mask that revealed next to nothing.

"I hurt her," his voice soft, "and she's never forgiven me. It was for the best, at least I told myself that but...well, it doesn't matter. I did it, she's still carrying it around and we have to work together. So, if you care for her like I think you do, help her while I'm here. Maybe give her someone to punch."

I looked up to see Jack limp by and raise a hand to me.

"Or maybe not," James said with a chuckle. "Wouldn't want that pretty face all messed up."

Was he flirting with me or was that just wishful thinking?

Either way, my cheeks flushed and I looked down. He'd been playful in the car, or at least I had thought so, and from the way Stella had reacted,

I got the sense that she wasn't any surer than I was about what to make of it. I swore one minute he wanted to eat Stella alive, and the next that he wanted to fuck me until I couldn't walk. The fleeting thought that both could be true was a terribly tempting one. But if the waters of this situation were already muddied, all three of us ending up in bed together would make them infinitely more so.

"I should go check on her," I said, needing to get some space from him.

"When you do, see if she'd be willing to take a trip down to the coroner's office when she's done. I think we might need to shake the trees a bit."

I swallowed, knowing that what they were looking for wasn't there, but I nodded all the same.

The gym was in the basement of the building, a state of the art place that the sheriff's office had reluctantly given us as a way to keep the primal tendencies of all of us in check. If we were "training" here with one another, the thought was that we may not be as inclined to pick fights with the Mundane officers. The only problem with that was it didn't take into account the fact that the Mundanes picked the fights half the time and no amount of lifting weights and beating the crap out of one another was going to stop us from snapping when too much shit was thrown our way.

I got to the door and heard the tell-tale grunt and impact of someone beating the shit out of a punching bag. Without pausing, I took a right into the locker room and changed into a pair of shorts and no shirt. I knew that my glamour was beautiful, and I took a healthy measure of pride in the way Stella had started looking at me right before she'd been placed on mandatory leave. Whether it was new or she'd just been hiding it really well, I didn't know, or care. I wanted the fire in her gaze, wanted her to look at me like she wanted to throw me down and mount me, even if she would never take that step. Call it a childish need for my ego to be stroked, but I didn't care.

When I walked into the gym, Stella was beating the hell out of a punching bag, her hands in a pair of sparring gloves, face red and dripping sweat from the exertion. I should've been used to seeing her in skimpy workout clothes; Stella preferred to have little for someone to grab if she was sparring. But the site of her pink tinged chest, stomach and legs was tantalizing. She really was an exquisite Mundane with her long, well-muscled limbs, and the way she reveled in her inherent athleticism. I knew that a lot of Mundane males preferred women smaller than them, petite and skinny, but I couldn't understand how someone could look at Stella and not see an otherworldly sensual creature. Hell, half the appeal was the fact that she could beat the shit out of me in a fight, even with my Gargoyle strength. Granted, I was inclined to not put up as much of a fight as I usually would, because I liked the thought of Stella dominating me and leaving her mark on my skin. The thought sent tingles down my spine and my dick stirred.

*Fuck, dial it back!*

I turned away and pretended to find a pair of gloves as I adjusted myself in my shorts. There was no one else in the gym at the moment, and even though Stella looked like she'd been at it for close to an hour, I knew she wasn't quite done yet.

James had been right, as annoying as that was to admit. Stella needed an opponent, someone she could hit and bounce things off of.

*And it's me, not him.*

I grinned as I turned around, and was hit with a fist to the face.

"Fucking hell! Twice in one day?" I cried, only half angry at the sneak attack.

Stella grinned up and, fuck me, if the delighted little look on her face didn't make me want to throw her down and see if maybe I could finally tempt her into pulling down my shorts and having her way with me.

"You shouldn't have turned your back to me."

"But you like my backside," I lobbed at her, flashing my dimple.

Was I imagining it, or did her flush deepen?

"It's okay," she shrugged as we circled each other. "I've seen better."

"You haven't *seen* it at all."

"Would I be speechless in the glow of your perfect ass?"

She feinted to my left and I acted like I was going to fall for it when she delivered a kick to my side. I blocked it and struck out at her this time, as Stella grabbed my wrist and attempted to spin me into a hip toss. But I hooked my foot around hers and sent us both to the mat. I ended up on my back, Stella's legs tangled with mine and holding her arm across my chest.

"You would be speechless," I chuckled. "Blinded, even."

"Only if I paddled it cherry red."

I groaned and started to roll her onto her front when she twisted in my grip and managed to put me into a shoulder lock.

"Don't tease me," I grunted and tapped out before she dislocated my shoulder.

"You'd like that?" she taunted as she jumped to her feet. "Letting me spank you until you cried?"

I was on my hands and knees, about to get up, and I knew that she saw the way my head dipped almost into a bow, the flare of my pupils as desire struck me. I had so few partners I'd ever explored pain play with, and of those, none had really taken the time know what I wanted. Something told me it wouldn't be that way with Stella.

"Is that what you would do at the club? Are you a good little subbie?" she asked, letting her nails scratch the stubble along my jaw.

My breath hitched and I bit down on a moan. This wasn't fair in the least. She was teasing me, wanting me to be vulnerable without offering anything in return. And yet, I wanted to submit to her. So damn bad.

Wanted to let her rule me.

Wanted to let her rake those nails down my back and have the sweat sting the cuts.

Wanted to worship her with my tongue and make her come.

*But I'm not going to show her mine and be left the only one baring my soul.*

So with great effort, I got to my feet and put some distance between us. I knew I wasn't imagining the bright flame of lust in her eyes, the way her face hardened into a look of domination that made my throat dry.

"If you're part of the club," I said, unwrapping my hands, and turning my back to her, "you know that this isn't how it's done. You don't get to just ask me that like it's some joke."

The words came out harsher than I'd intended, and I realized just how hurt I was that she'd do this here and now, as if it were just another one of our playful sparring matches.

Behind me, Stella took a sharp inhale and I could feel her move even before her hands ran down my shoulders.

"I'm sorry," she whispered. "That was unfair of me."

I nodded, not quite trusting my voice to be able to hide the way her touch was affecting me. Why was it suddenly so difficult to keep myself from giving in to the desire I'd been holding onto all these months? Was it just that I'd finally gotten to a breaking point, or was it the knowledge that, here was someone I cared for that could share this part of my life with me? Whatever it was, the temptation to throw caution to the wind and kiss her stupid was growing by the second. As was that dull throb in my chest, like a pulse that was burning with her touch.

*This can't be what I think it is...can it?*

I pushed that thought to the side as Stella began to speak, not sure I wanted the answer just yet.

"I wanted to ask you about how you knew about the club," she continued, "but I should have found a different way to ask."

"You weren't asking. You were...I don't know what you were doing."

"Me, either."

The confession was soft, as if she didn't mean to say it but that didn't matter. Stella sounded lost, hurt, as if she were a little afraid. And that was the one thing I didn't think I'd ever seen from her.

I turned around and she was so close that I didn't have to reach at all to put my hands on her hips. She rested her hands on my chest as if it was the most natural thing in the world.

"What's wrong?" I asked.

She shook her head and drew little circles with her fingernail on my skin. Either she was clueless as to what that was doing to me, or she knew and couldn't help herself. Either way, it was getting difficult to concentrate beyond the way her body felt against mine, the bright, spicy scent of her skin.

"Is it *him*?"

Her blue eyes snapped to mine and I had my answer.

"He said he hurt you," I said.

Anger flashed and she crossed her arms, though she didn't push me away so I kept my hands where they were.

"He should've kept his mouth shut," she hissed. "It was a long time ago and I was stupid and young."

"Young maybe, but you're never stupid."

She gave me a crooked grin and shook her head.

"See, there's the problem. If I ever let you in my pants, you'd be constantly inflating my ego and there would be no living with me."

"Oh, I think I could manage," I said, easing my arms around her. "And I think you'd like it."

Instead of pulling away she ran her hands up my arms to my shoulders.

"Really? You're that good, huh?"

"Only one way to find out."

It would be so damn easy to lower my head and take her mouth, to unleash all the months of pent up frustration and fruitless flirting. But I knew Stella well enough by now; she had to be the one to cross this line. There was no hiding how I felt. My feelings were always right there for her to see. It was up to her whether or not she would trust me.

"We really do need to talk about the club," she whispered, her breath skating across my skin.

"Yes, we do."

"Would you trust me with that part of you?"

My breath hitched and my arms tightened around her.

"If you could trust me in return? Yes, unequivocally."

Her eyes drifted down to where her hands rested on my body and she nodded.

"Well then--"

"I hope I'm not interrupting," James said from the doorway.

I bit back on a growl and released Stella as she took several quick steps back from me.

One look at the tension in his tall body, the way his eyes darted between the two of us and I could swear he was two seconds away from joining us. The thought made me harder than ever before and I had to turn away from him. I should've been angry that he'd interrupted us, but all I felt was disappointment.

*And a raging case of blue balls.*

"What do you want?" Stella asked, running a towel over her face and neck.

"I think we need to talk about a leak in your precinct," he replied handing Stella a thick folder.

My heart stalled and I wondered if James could sense the fear that had gripped me at the sight of that file. It was the one I'd handed off to my handler, the one that was supposed to appear like magic.

"What's that?" I asked after I'd managed to get a grip.

Stella frowned as she flipped through it and looked up at James as if I hadn't talked.

"Where the hell did you find this?" she demanded.

"It was delivered by a courier from the downtown Seattle precinct."

"Fucking bastards, they had this whole time?"

"The note that came with it said it was misfiled and they apologized."

Stella and I both looked at James, who didn't look like he believed that line in the least.

"Bullshit," Stella hissed. "They love fucking with us and now they're doing it about a serial killer!"

She shoved the file into my chest and started pacing around the sparring area. I knew that she was thinking about all the times they hindered us from doing our jobs, the resources that would mysteriously go missing or the evidence that was tampered with. And now they were doing it with this case.

*Or at least that's what she thinks. Fuck! I'm hurting her with secrets even as I'm trying to keep her safe.*

"We have it now," I said, trying to bring Stella back from her fury. "And they won't try this again, that's for sure. Not with James here."

"That might not be true," James said.

"What are you saying?" Stella asked.

"There's another party interested in the artifact, a rival group. They may already be here, or have people in place."

My pulse quickened and I took a slow, deep breath, hoping he didn't notice.

"Not in my team," Stella said. "I know them. They're solid, trustworthy."

The words were a stab with a hot poker to my insides. Stella didn't trust easily, but she was going to the mattresses for us. For *me,* and I didn't deserve it.

"But what about every person that comes through here?" James asked, pitching his voice lower. "What about the other officers? It could be anyone. And these guys aren't dicking around, they're bloody ruthless. We need to be careful, not just keeping the knives out of their hands but so that we don't die finding them."

Stella let out a long breath, I could practically hear her mind working as she turned over everything James had just said.

"Okay, so what do you propose?" she asked.

James met my gaze and I noticed a moment of doubt, a second where he saw all the secrets I was trying so hard to keep. But it passed and he took the file from me.

"We take everything back to my penthouse and work from there."

"The chief will never go for it," I said.

"He doesn't have a say in it," James replied. "My credentials supersede his jurisdiction on this."

"And you don't think that this leak, if there is one, will notice us walking out with files?"

Against my will, my body warmed as James' beautiful lips spread in a cocky grin.

"There are tunnels that run under here and most of the city. No one is going to see a damn thing."

"I didn't think the underground was safe," Stella said.

"That's what the Supernaturals want you to think," James replied. "That's our territory. Or at least it was. I'm not sure many use it as extensively as they used to in the days before glamours were more widely available."

"We'll have to get permission from the Ghosts down there," I said.

"Already done."

I wasn't sure whether to be relieved that we were going to be able to investigate without someone from the Protectors constantly watching us, or if I was more nervous about this new plan. My handler might panic if we suddenly disappeared with the evidence. Telling them would soothe their worries, but it would also make James and Stella unsafe.

*I need time to figure out the best path forward. One that will bring the killer to justice, keep the knives out of the Protectors' hands and save Stella from retribution. There has to be a way.*

"I think we should do it," I said. "We need a safe place to work and find this guy fast."

Stella nodded.

"Okay, just let me go home and shower first."

# CHAPTER FOUR

## STELLA

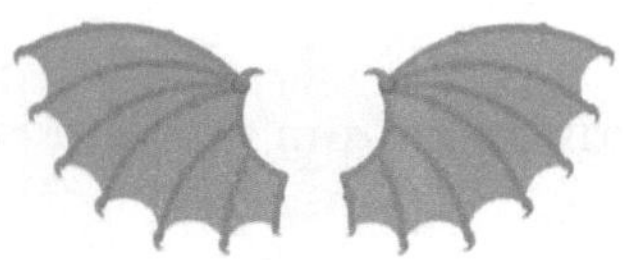

The shower back at my place was a blessing. I needed to get some space from Isaac so I could process what the hell I'd been thinking in the gym. Never, in all my years in this career, had I ever been so tempted to throw my rules out the window and dive head first into a fuck fest. I'd realized while sparring with him how much I'd missed Isaac these past few weeks. He wasn't just a partner, he was a part of my life in a deep, intimate way. I hadn't even noticed it happening and it scared me. After James broke my heart, I'd decided that there had to be limits to how much I let people in. It had worked for a long time, until now.

I finished up fast, not bothering to dry my hair, and slipping on a pair of shorts and a Nirvana T-shirt; not "professional" but I didn't really care. I needed to be comfortable if I was going to be able to concentrate on the case and not the two males that made my emotions spin and twist.

James shouldn't have affected me this much, not after all this time. And yet I had to constantly stop myself from feeling like that twenty-year-old that was left crying in the rain as he ran away from me.

The memory was sharp even as I tried to push it away and I closed my eyes, unable to stop the stab of pain it caused.

My dad had died from cancer when I was still in the academy. James had been his partner for a while, and I'd fallen in love with him hard. I'd confessed it to him when I was eighteen, full of the bravado indicative of that age. James had put me off, gently, and rightly so. Looking back, I was mortified that I'd even thought he would have taken me up on the offer. I was a child.

And while it was true I wasn't much more mature two years later when James came to my father's funeral, that had been the time he crossed the line he'd drawn in the sand when I was eighteen.

Maybe it was because I was hollowed out by having watched my dad, the biggest, strongest man I'd known, become emaciated and unable to even get up and go to the bathroom. I'd had to arrange his hospice care, sit at his bedside day after day and watch him wither away until there was nothing left.

Even now, all this time later, I could still smell the death in his room, hear his raspy breathing.

So when James was there during those days after dad died, when everything was so hard and painful, I needed someone to keep me from falling apart. And he had at first. He'd wrapped me up in his big arms and cradled me against his cool Gargoyle skin. I don't remember who kissed who first, but it didn't take long once it started for us to tear at one another in desperation to feel something other than our grief.

It had been rough, both of us leaving marks on the other, but I had wanted that. I'd only just started to realize how much I liked kink, and I wanted to have that with James more than I'd ever wanted it with anyone. He'd fucked me hard, and I'd begged for more. By the time we'd both come out of the fugue of our passions, I could see the regret plain as day on his face. He could barely stand to look at me.

I'd tried to tell him that I was old enough for this decision. But he didn't believe me.

"You're grieving and I took advantage of you. I left marks on you," he'd said.

"And I want more," I had insisted. "I'm not a child and this isn't just about losing my dad. It's about--"

"You *are* a child, Stella! Too young for me, too inexperienced in the world. This was a stupid mistake!"

I'd slapped him hard enough to sprain my wrist. He'd walked out of my life, taking my broken heart with him. For a long time after, I felt like someone had carved a hole in my chest and left only anger and pain. It had taken years for me to make any kind of connection with other people and the Hearts and Swords club, the people I'd met there, had been the ones to help me through it all. Queen Dawn had been the mother I'd never really had, guiding me through discovering who I was, showing me the strength I had. But I still didn't fully trust or give all of myself to anyone. I always made sure to hold something back so that when they left, and they always did, I had something to use as a life raft.

I ran a hand over my face and let out a long breath, trying to put all of this back into the box in the back of my head where it belonged but it was too late.

*How did I let myself go down this fucked up memory lane? Usually that takes at least a bottle of Jack.*

But I was stone cold sober, a fact that felt quite unfair considering the muck my mind was currently hurling up at me. I glanced at the half drunk bottle on my coffee table. Isaac hadn't gotten around to clearing it off when he'd been here this morning and it would be so easy to just take a pull, let the warmth soothe the ache in my soul.

"No," I whispered to myself and closed my eyes. "I don't drink when I'm working a case, that's the rule and I'm not going to break it."

I dug my nails into my hand and went to look for my keys and wallet so I didn't give in to the temptation. If I started drinking during the day, during a case, then that would be it. I might as well sign myself up for AA because I would become a full blown alcoholic. Some days, like right now, it seemed like the only thing keeping me from crossing that line was this one rule and so I clung to it.

And when I opened my door and saw Isaac standing there, sunlight glinting off his hair and his dimple calling to me like a siren song, I knew that even if I didn't break my rule about drinking, I was pretty sure I'd be breaking all my other rules before this case was done.

"James is waiting out in the SUV," Isaac said. "He thinks we should head over to the coroner's office before heading to his place."

I nodded, grateful to be talking about work. I needed to get my mind back on track and hopefully my libido would follow.

"Great, we can get some answers on the bodies. Did those photos have any more clues?" I asked as I followed him down the path from my ground floor apartment to the street.

"Some," he said, not looking me in the eye.

I waited for him to elaborate and when he didn't I poked him in the arm.

"Explain, please."

"Let's get in the car."

I slid into the back seat this time, James in the driver's seat and Isaac once again as the front passenger. I was about to ask about what he'd discovered from the crime scene photos when Isaac handed me a thinner file that had been inside the larger one that had been couriered over.

After all this time, I didn't bother to really prepare myself for the gruesome sight of dead bodies anymore. Which, in this case, was a mistake.

The two bodies were side by side, just like the Orc and the Mundane in Post Alley. The Harpy's wings were cut off, laying to her side, and her chest had been brutally carved open showing portions of her lungs and stomach. Her face was cut in sloppy arcs, along with her arms and legs. The Mundane woman had her throat slit but that was all, just like the one this morning.

I flipped through the photos, noticing that the blood was more widespread with this one, as if the killer had slashed and hacked in a way that had produced more splatter. The couple's hands were clasped just like the couple from this morning, indicating that this was likely a post mortem positioning by the killer.

When I pointed that out to Isaac and James they both agreed.

"It's part of their calling card," James said, handing me a magnifying glass. "Look at the Mundane's inner wrist."

I already knew what I'd find and held my breath.

It was the same stamp from this morning from the Hearts and Swords club.

"He's targeting people from there," I said, my stomach twisting.

"It looks that way," Isaac agreed.

"It's the only club to specialize in Supernatural and Mundane coupling in the state," I said, trying to move past the panic that was starting to build inside of me. "And the two pairs of victims are exactly that."

"We've found how he's choosing his victims and what part of his requirements are," Isaac said, a grim set to his lips.

"And since the Supernaturals are different in each pairing, it's not focused on a particular type," James said.

I frowned at the clasped hands, the side by side staging. There were no signs of struggle; the victims looked as if they simply laid down and allowed the killer to carve them up.

"There was a needle mark on the neck of the female victim this morning," I said, using the magnifying glass to look at the neck of this woman. "And there's one here too. Do we have the toxicology report from the first two?"

"It's back at my penthouse," James said. "While you cleaned up, Isaac and I took the files there."

I nodded and scoured the photos for anything else. The feathers on the Harpy's neck made it impossible to see any needle marks. And the Orc from this morning was too bloodied for me to detect anything.

*It has to be some kind of paralytic or drug. Probably a different one for each since it would have to be extremely strong to take down a Supernatural. Of course, if they used the same one on both then the Mundane would likely die from that and not the cut throat, making that a post mortem wound...*

I glanced up at the sound of Isaac chuckling and saw that James also had the glimmer of smile on his face. My cheeks turned red and I huffed out a laugh. I hadn't realized I was talking out loud.

"You're adorable when you talk to yourself as you work on a problem," Isaac said.

"Shut up," I said with a lopsided smile of my own.

"The fact that both Mundane bodies had just one deliberate wound when the Supernatural bodies were mutilated speaks to a possible hatred for us," James said.

"And the Mundane women are simply collateral damage?" Isaac asked.

"No," I said, frowning at the picture of her. "She's as deliberately posed and used as the Harpy is. She's part of it. Even if the killer may not want her brutalized, he still wants her dead. Besides, if he just wanted Supernaturals, why target couples from the club?"

"That's another good question," Isaac said as we pulled up to the coroner's office. "Is it convenient because there's guaranteed Supernaturals there or does it have to do with sex work?"

"Who says any of the victims are sex workers just because they came from there?" I asked. "They may be members, not employees."

"Good point," James agreed, "and we won't know the answer until we have more information about the bodies and talk to Queen Dawn. Any word on when that may be?"

"We're still waiting on a call back," Isaac said.

James nodded.

"And we may need to pull long hours getting everything set up at the penthouse. If either of you would like to stay, I have plenty of room."

It was said casually enough, and with a good reason. James was right, this case was going to consume every waking hour, and then some. And since we were making the penthouse home base, it made sense to just stay there and try to get this all solved as quickly as possible. But the thought of being in close quarters day *and* night with both of these

Gargoyles made my stomach do strange, flippy motions and I didn't know whether I wanted to flatly refuse or agree eagerly.

Instead, I shrugged and didn't look either of them in the eye as we walked toward the entrance to the coroner's office. I've always hated the way the place smelled; not necessarily like a bunch of dead bodies were in freezers, but more like they were desperately trying to cover up the fact that there a bunch of dead bodies in freezers.

The Mundane at the front desk nodded at me and waved us to the door that read "Authorized personnel only: No admittance without special permissions."

This was the Supernatural wing of the coroner's office and they kept it locked up as tight as possible. I tried not to think of all the times I'd been here with family members after they'd had identify a loved ones corpse. Grief was a universal language that gutted me every single time I had to hear it. A wife losing her husband, a mother her child, a grown male his father. It didn't matter the combination, I'd seen it all and these halls were haunted with those memories. Some days I was just fine walking in here. Others, like today, I couldn't seem to breathe the specters were so thick.

I whimpered and squeezed my eyes shut. It was all hitting me at once. The walls were closing in and I slumped down to the floor. The sounds and smells, the words, all of it was speeding up, dragging me down so fast that I didn't even have time to do anything about it.

I heard someone call my name and heavy hands were dragging me.

"No," I whispered. "No...stop...Stop!"

I flung my fist out and connected with someone, though I knew I hadn't put enough force behind it to hurt them.

"Stella," a voice, familiar and dear. "It's me, come on...you're safe..."

"Stop it all," I breathed, trying to get everything to slow down.

Then something hard pressed into me, and bands surrounded my body, holding me tight. There was the smell of ozone and something else, spicy and clean.

*Oh...these are arms. James' arms. James is holding me.*

I concentrated on his warmth, the unnatural hardness of the muscles against my body. I let myself sink into his embrace, let him stop the spinning of panic in my chest. There was nothing but James' arms, his low, smooth voice in my ear, telling me that I was safe, that everything was going to be alright.

"I couldn't save them," I whispered, tears thick in my voice. "James...I tried so hard."

I tried to take it back but it was all out there now. The reason I was falling apart, the memories that would forever haunt me.

"I know," he said, his hand ran up and down my back. "You can't stop all of them Stella, but you can help me stop this one. I need you to help me stop him. Can you do that? Can you help us stop this one?"

His words punctured the swirling mass of memories and it began to dissipate until the shaking in my body had stopped and I could take a deep breath without it feeling like I was sucking on glass. I pushed away from him and put a little distance between our bodies. He kept his large, strong hands on my upper arms and looked me in the eyes.

"Thank you," I whispered. "I'm sorry--"

"Don't you dare," he said. "I know what it's like to have memories that haunt. There's no shame in needing a helping hand when it overwhelms you."

I looked away and nodded.

"You good to continue?"

I took a deep breath, wiped my face and got to my feet. Isaac was right there, his hands in tight fists as if he were holding back from touching me. I appreciated his self-control; the last thing I wanted was to be treated like some kind of fragile thing.

"I'm alright," I told him and gave a shaky smile. "I swear I'm alright."

"I'm here for you," Isaac said. "You know that right?"

"I do," I assured him, "but right now, I need you to be my partner so we can catch this asshole and not worry that I'm going to fall apart every five minutes. Because this was...unexpected, but I'm good now."

Isaac gave me a short nod and led the way down the hall. I could feel James' eyes on me as he brought up the rear, but I didn't dare look back. That moment we'd just shared was too much like the way things had been before we'd both ruined everything. He'd always been able to pull me out of dark moods, had been the one I could count on. The fact that he still held this power over me was as comforting as it was confusing. I didn't want to rely on it, or even like it. James wasn't going to be here that long and I'd be damned if I let myself fall apart again because of him.

# CHAPTER FIVE

## JAMES

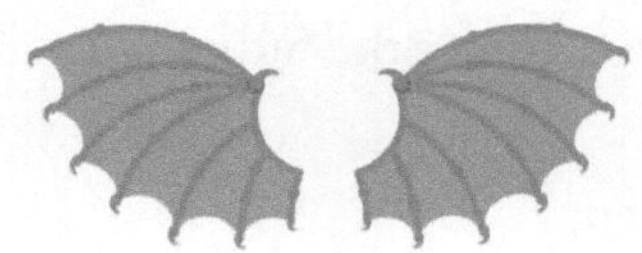

There were few things that I'd ever seen that could bring Stella to her knees. So when she'd crumpled to the floor, my heart jumped into my throat and I'd stood there, dumb struck. It wasn't until Isaac had spoken that I remembered the article I'd dug up this morning, and the rumors I'd heard from the other officers.

Stella had been standing in the breach for her fellow Supernatural officers and the community at large for a long time. And she'd done it with the courage and compassion that made her not only a good cop, but one of the best people I'd ever known.

Now she was paying the price for that action, not just in her career but in her mind too.

It was pure instinct that had me pulling her body against mine, a protective need to soothe the heartache and pain. The moment I'd done it, I realized the mistake.

While my only purpose was to comfort her and pull her out of the panic attack she was drowning in, the feel of her in my arms was like seeing home after years of being banished. Stella fit too well against me, the strong planes of muscles under my hands that helped her protect the soft heart she carried around inside of her made my body ache with repressed need. Memories of the one time I'd let my desire for her get the better of me began to fill my senses. If we'd been alone, if this wasn't work, I would've been tempted to brush my lips against her skin, drag her into a supply closet and drive away her demons in the same way I had that night so long ago.

The fact that it was even a thought at all, much less such a strong temptation, meant that this woman still threatened to become my one weakness even after all of these years, and I couldn't let that happen. Just like I told her, we had to protect the Supernaturals and Mundanes at risk by getting these knives.

Nothing else mattered.

Not my yearning to keep touching her.

Not the way she'd looked at me as if I were still the most important thing in the world.

Isaac glanced back, but instead of looking at Stella, his bright eyes snagged mine and a rush of heat pulsed through me. If not for the way my body ached for Stella, this wouldn't have been all that surprising. Isaac was exactly the kind of partner I craved. Intelligent, sweet, submissive. And then there was that damn dimple, and the geek reference he'd made in the SUV. He was like a decadent dessert: I'd probably regret it afterwards but it would be so sweet in the moment.

*And maybe I should. The way Isaac was acting after getting coffee this morning...he's hiding something. I can't risk that he might be working for the Protectors or some black market criminal intent on selling the knives. If I seduce him, I may be able to figure out if he can be trusted. It would keep him close, not to mention be fun in the process. But does he want me? Or is it all about Stella?*

And then Isaac's eyes skated to Stella and I had my answer.

There was a tenderness there that wasn't present within the fire I saw when he looked at me. To be honest, I wasn't the kind of male that had to have monogamy. I'd had plenty of open relationships through my many years. The thought of sharing Isaac with Stella, smelling her on his skin, licking her juices off of him...

Desire hit me like a physical blow and my steps stumbled.

"You okay?" Stella asked, glancing back.

I took a deep breath and nodded, trying to collect myself.

"Fine."

Her frown deepened but she didn't question me, for which I was grateful.

But Isaac's gaze lingered a bit more and his nostrils flared. He could sense my arousal and when a flush of red bloomed in his cheeks after glancing down at my groin, I only became harder.

"Why don't you go inside," Isaac said to Stella as we reached the door. "I need to ask James a couple things."

Stella sighed.

"If you two start fighting, take it outside, and I don't want to hear one complaint about aches and pains."

Isaac smirked at her, dimple on full display.

"Don't worry, if I do kick his ass, he won't be too badly bruised."

She shook her head and muttered something about territorial Gargoyles before jerking open the door to the receiving room and going inside.

Once the door had closed all the way, Isaac turned to me and, no matter how much I tried to reign in my feelings, I knew that it was useless. They were already out there. Since I was intent on seducing him anyway, I decided to meet all of this head on and didn't wait for him to speak.

"I want you," I said, without any preamble. "And I think you want me."

Isaac choked on a breath, his dick visibly hard in his pants.

"Well, that was...I mean, that answers my question," he finally managed.

"I know you have feelings for Stella, but I also know that you want me," I said, unnerved at how my voice shook a little on the edges.

"You two are complicated."

"Yes. And I know that getting involved with me may complicate things with the two of you, but I don't need to be exclusive."

My voice had gotten a bit raspy at the end, and lust slammed back into me just saying it. Instead of being put off by the statement, Isaac's pupils dilated and his lips parted. He was as affected by the image as I was.

"Jesus fucking Christ," he murmured, running a hand through his hair.

"Indeed."

"You sure know how to throw a wrench in things, don't ya?"

"It doesn't have to be that way."

"But it would be if she's not on board. And please," he held up a hand as I tried to speak, "don't tell me she's over you. We both know that's bullshit."

"I didn't actually," my heart stuttering in my chest.

He frowned at me.

"Seriously? It's pretty damn obvious."

"I...I suppose I assumed she had put all that behind her."

"Oh what, like you did?"

I huffed out a breath.

"I have."

"Let's not lie to each other, not in this moment. I'm not blind. The way you two look at each other? I don't know whether you want to fuck each other or beat the shit out of one another. Or both."

"Hey!" Stella poked her head around the door. "You two coming or what? You can work out your issues after we've seen the corpses."

"Yeah, coming," Isaac said, giving her a smile.

Stella's eyes flicked to me and back to Isaac, and I finally saw what Isaac might've been talking about. There was heat there but it wasn't anger, at least not entirely.

*She's jealous and I'm not sure it's just about Isaac...huh.*

When Stella went back inside, Isaac arched an eyebrow and gestured to where she'd been.

"Well?"

"Yes, I see it now."

"So, this," Isaac gestured back and forth, "as tempting as it is, can't happen. And believe me, I want it to. If she wasn't here, I'd already have your dick in my mouth."

I growled and advanced on him, backing Isaac into the wall. Some Gargoyle males have very strong primal tendencies when it came to mating, but I had learned to control them through the years. So the fact that it had roared to the surface so fast and strong was disconcerting. Though that didn't stop me from indulging in it some.

"Do not say such things unless you intend to follow through," I let my claws pierce through my glamour and ran one slowly down his cheek.

Isaac leaned into the touch and I felt his cock harden against mine.

"James," he breathed, "you know we can't hurt her."

"I do," I admitted even as I pressed my groin more against him.

Isaac gasped and arched his head up, exposing the tempting column of his strong throat.

"We could ask her," he rasped as I ran a claw down his neck.

"Yes. And you know she wouldn't say 'no'."

I wanted to follow the line of my claw with my tongue, to torment and tease this gorgeous male for hours until he was crying, begging me to let him come.

I groaned at the image it painted and I was a hairsbreadth away from finding that damn supply closet when I remembered Stella's face the night I'd broken her heart. For better or worse, she had a piece of me that I'd never gotten back, never wanted back truthfully. And if I hurt her again...

With great effort, I released Isaac and backed away. We stared at one another, chest heaving, eyes bright and cocks hard as rocks in our pants.

"But she would still be hurt," I finished the thought.

Isaac nodded.

"And that's something neither of us will ever do."

I shook my head.

"No."

Isaac closed his eyes and let out a slow breath, obviously trying to calm himself. But that wouldn't do for me, not with as worked up as I was.

"Tell her I'll be right there."

I didn't wait for an answer before bolting to the bathroom we'd passed down the hall. The second the door was latched, I had my dick in my hand and was brutally jacking myself off. But it wasn't just images of Isaac that invaded my mind and made me gasp with sharp arousal.

I pictured Isaac eating Stella's pussy as I pressed just the head of my cock between his firm ass cheeks, my tail circling his cock as I kept him on the edge of coming. I'd allow her orgasm after orgasm from Isaac's mouth before letting him fuck her hard as I pushed them together with my cock filling Isaac's ass. My thrusts would push him deeper into her until all three of us came with cries that would shake the foundations of my penthouse.

Hot cum spurted on my hands and I did my best to get it into the toilet and not my slacks. The release was hard, the pulses thrummed through me and yet it was deeply unsatisfying.

I stood there, sweating and panting while trying to get a grip on my primal urges. I'd always prided myself on self-control, on discipline, and yet here I was, longing to throw all of it out the window because these two had infected my soul within a matter of hours.

How was that even possible? How was I letting myself be tempted by this?

I'd had threesomes before. Hell, I'd had orgies that would make Caligula weep. It was necessary to blow off steam if I was going to be an effective agent without the distractions of a relationship or dry spells. Every time, I'd been able to disengage, to be present with my partners, but always distant enough to not let my emotions become involved. And now here I was, *want* scraping my gut like a beast demanding to be let out.

I wanted them both, together, separate, all of it. I wanted them with a fire I'd never felt before.

*It doesn't make sense. Stella, perhaps, there was more unfinished with her than I thought. But why Isaac? How has he worked his way so firmly under my skin? I barely know him!*

I had no answers as I cleaned up, and it unsettled me deeply. But I did my best to put on an unaffected expression as I made my way back to the office where Stella and Isaac waited for me. The room was a depressing mix of gray and dark green, the smell of antiseptic and heavy cleaners hung in the air like a thick fume. It tickled my sensitive nose and I sneezed.

"It's awful," Isaac said, his eyes watering.

"We'll get used to it," I said, plucking a tissue from the old, utilitarian desk to my right.

The lights were bright and fluorescent overhead, a faint sound of dripping water coming from somewhere. The whole entry room was bleak, which I suppose fit a coroner's office.

When I could focus past the smell, I spotted Stella pacing back and forth near the double doors that would lead us to where the autopsy had been performed. She always had to be in motion, that was nothing new. But the way her lips pressed together, the tight curl of her hands all spoke of a woman who was trying her best not to let her emotions get the better of her.

*I'm such an asshole. She just had a panic attack about this place and here I am, dragging out the stay with my stupid libido.*

"Sorry," I said to her. "I didn't mean to make you wait."

"It's fine," she waved her hand, a gesture that I knew was nervous more than anything else. "They're still getting the bodies for us."

Isaac and I purposely avoided one another's gaze and it was a testament to how shaken Stella still was that she didn't notice. Barely two minutes later, a Goblin in a lab coat with glasses perched on his snubbed nose came through the double doors and motioned for us to follow him. I breathed out a sigh of relief, desperate for something to take my mind off the two people following me through the double doors.

The Goblin led us into a sterile room with brighter lights, and cabinets lining a wall to my right. It was cool in here, the gray tiles along the walls shining and spotless. The dripping sound was coming from a large industrial sized sink against the far left wall. The Goblin walked up onto a ramp that elevated him enough that he was looking down on a large table where the Orc lay. It looked like the coroner had attempted to cover the Orc's exposed organs with the carved away flaps of skin but it that had been rather pointless in places.

"Okay," the Goblin's voice was hoarse, "I need to preface this with a quick disclaimer. There were some missing parts, and I went through two morgue techs who couldn't handle the condition of the body before finally deciding to just do it myself. This is probably one of the most gruesome murders I've ever seen, the Harpy that came through here a few weeks ago the only exception."

"Understood, Vandal," Isaac said to the Goblin. "We just need whatever info you can give us."

"Did you do a tox screen on them?" Stella asked.

"I did and I asked for a rush. It came in right before you got here," Vandal snagged a clipboard from a nearby table and flipped through two pages. "There was a potent paralytic in both their systems. It was developed to treat delirious Supernaturals who could harm their physician if not restrained. In small doses, it wears off in a few minutes, half hour at most. But the Orc had twice what I've ever seen used on anyone before, which would've left him completely helpless for a long time, indicating that the killer wanted him awake but unable to move as long as possible. And while the Mundane had a much lower dose in her system, it would've been enough to paralyze her throughout the ordeal. Both would've been awake for a good portion of what was done to them."

"Oh my god," Isaac whispered.

"No shit," Vandal agreed. "I don't remember what the tox screen on the Harpy said, but I'm sure you've got that record."

"If we don't, we'll call you," I said. "Anything else? Any hair or skin cells?"

"No. Whoever this person is, they left nothing."

"How easy to get is the paralytic?" Stella asked.

"You can purchase the ingredients from any witch's supply. They're actually pretty common," Vandal indicated the carved up chest of the Orc. "He's missing his heart, his lungs and small intestines were cut up with jagged motions, and the directions of the cut make no sense to me. There was no reason I could see to cut those organs unless they were just trying to hurt the Orc if he was still alive at this point, or just wanted to mutilate him as brutally as possible. He's also missing his ears, his testicles, penis, and fingers of the left hand as well as his tongue. The Harpy from three weeks ago was also missing her tongue and the fingers of the same hand. Her genitals were intact, but her heart was also carved out."

My stomach twisted. This was all in line with the knives and their influence on the killers. Organs were always taken, bodies were always carved up, as if the knives were thirsty.

A chill raced down my spine and Stella put a hand on my arm.

"You okay? Need some air?" she asked.

"No."

She nodded and, for a moment, I thought about grasping her hand, soaking up the strength and warmth. But I let it drop and ran a finger over my forehead as I went deeper into thought. None of this was particularly surprising, not even the paralytic. The killers that used the knives tended to have an uncanny ability to find a way to kill silently. Whether that was just a coincidence or something the knives inspired, I didn't know.

*There's always a personal flair that the killer has. But so far, nothing stands out to indicate who this person is.*

Just when Vandal was getting to the end of the list of things that had been done to the body, and which ones were likely post mortem, I was starting to despair of finding anything that would help us figure out who this person may be.

"There's one more thing," he said, "if one of you could help me turn him on his side."

Isaac stepped up, though the poor guy looked a little green around the edges. When they were able to get the Orc turned, Stella and I both gasped in surprise.

The Orc's back was carved up and, at first, it appeared to be random slashes. But as I stared at it, I could see the barest outlines of a shape.

"At the top," Stella said, taking out her phone and snapping pictures. "The lines there are more precise, as if the killer were trying to make a shape and got frustrated half way through."

"Does the woman have a similar mark on her back?" I asked as Isaac laid the Orc down.

"No," Vandal answered. "With the exception of the slash across her throat, which was honestly so careful it could almost be described as surgical, she is without physical wounds."

"Anything else that stands out to you?" I pressed.

"No, and I hope you catch this guy. I don't want to see another one like this, ever."

We thanked the Goblin and got out of there fast. The second we were back in the car, Stella got her phone out and began studying the pictures she'd taken as if they held the answers we were looking for. The car ride back to my place was absolutely silent, and I couldn't help feeling like half the reason for that was what had happened between Isaac and me.

He kept his gaze outside, chewing on his bottom lip, forehead wrinkled in thought. I wanted to ask him what was going through his mind, to see if he had any clues or thoughts. But I didn't because what if that wasn't it at all? The last thing I wanted to do was reveal anything to Stella.

I pulled up to the building's underground parking garage and found the spot reserved for my penthouse. I couldn't wait to shed my glamour inside my home, to stretch my wings and maybe take a flight to clear my head.

*Maybe Isaac would come with me. But that would defeat the purpose, I suppose.*

"You're staring at that pretty hard," Isaac said to Stella in the elevator.

"I think I've found something," she said, her voice thick with worry.

"What?" I asked.

Her blue eyes flew up to mine, and there wasn't just worry making them shine. It was fear too.

"The Pacific Heights murders," she said.

I swallowed, memories flooding back to me that I would've much rather left forgotten.

"How do you...I mean, what's the connection?" I asked, mind reeling.

"I'll show you when we get to your place."

The elevator opened and we all three departed into my entry way.

"Oh, wow!" Stella said, coming to a stop as she looked around. "Was it always this big?"

"Yes," I said, impatience on the edges of my voice.

"Name of your sex tape," Isaac said at the same time.

And in spite of the gruesome sight we just left, in spite of how I was desperate to know what Stella had discovered, I barked out a full, throaty laugh. Stella joined me, snorting at the end and punched Isaac on the shoulder.

"You're such a dork," she said, her tone loving.

Isaac's gaze softened into something warm that had my chest aching as I looked at the two of them.

"I think you meant *cute* dork."

Stella flushed and turned away, tucking a strand of hair behind her ear. It was a moment like any couple might have, and I was on the outside looking in when I wanted to be right there in the middle. The thought startled me and I shook my head.

*Focus. Solve the case, get the knives. That's the mission.*

But, for the first time in my life, I was starting to not give a damn about the mission. And that unsettled me more than my growing attraction for Isaac or the feelings I still carried for Stella.

She looked around with wide eyes while I tried to deflect the warmth Stella's smirk gave me by striding over to the dining room table and getting to work. Stella took in the entry way, living room, dining room and kitchen, which were all open concept, with a wall of windows looking out into the Puget Sound. I kept the colors neutral in cream and light blue to make it feel even more airy and light. The three bedrooms also had views of the Olympics and the city, with enormous beds that barely put a dent in the square footage of the rooms. All of my furniture was special ordered to fit my Gargoyle frame, which meant it was inordinately big.

I motioned them over to the dining room table where Isaac and I had spread out all the files. Two special laptops were also set out with direct connections to the Secret Archive's database and their round-the-clock agents who were available for requisitions. The Archive had emergency offices with supplies in every major city in the world, and Seattle was no exception. I could put in an order, and within the hour two members of the supply team would be delivering my items.

In the far corner of the living room by the hallway that led to the bedrooms, was a large silver box with intricate runes carved into it. It was the outer shell of the most powerful containment unit anyone at the Archive had ever created. I hadn't told them that this was technically still in its testing stages, that it had never been approved for agent use until now. If something went wrong and the artifact reacted poorly to the unit, I would somehow make sure that I was the only one in the line of fire. Losing either of these two was out of the question.

My skin tingled as I shed my glamour and I cracked my neck, and rolled my shoulders. Stella's sharp intake of breath had me turning around to catch her wide eyed stare. I was big, even for a Gargoyle. Nearly eight feet tall and my shoulders were wide enough that fitting into most doorways was difficult. It was only one reason why I rarely had my wings out. My skin was a dark gray-purple that helped me blend into some buildings if I wanted to. The buzz emanating from my horns alerted me to Isaac shedding his glamour and I couldn't help glancing over to see what he really looked like.

If Isaac's glamour was beautiful, his Gargoyle form was lovely enough to make me ache. He had a slightly lighter shade of skin as me, but his height and breadth were more in line with his glamour, though still a bit bigger. He was bare chested, like me, wearing only a pair of loose athletic shorts to cover himself. Still, I could see well-muscled thighs and large, clawed feet at the end. His tail twitched from side to side, a bit smaller than mine, but I supposed that was due to his Mundane parentage. Where I had dark brown eyes, Isaacs were violet, bright and startling.

We stared at one another, while Stella glanced between us both. It was awkward and wonderful all at once, to not hide behind my glamour, which sometimes felt like an ill fitted suit. But also to see Isaac as he truly was.

"Wow," he said, his grin revealing small fangs, "this is...well, this is--"

"Interesting," I supplied.

"Hot," Stella said at the same time.

Her eyes widened and she visibly swallowed as if she hadn't really intended on speaking.

"Oh wow, look at that," she said, motioning to her phone, "a clue for the case we're working. Guess we better get back to it, huh?"

"Smooth," Isaac said, giving her an indulgent grin.

And bugger me sideways, he even had a bloody dimple as a Gargoyle!

*Someone in the heavens obviously hates me.*

My clawed feet clicked along the hard woods, which were spelled to not scratch from my sharp claws, and I cleared my throat.

"Okay," I said, determined to get us back on track. "What's the connection?"

"And what's Pacific Heights?" Isaac asked.

Stella nodded and I could see her putting her feelings away, bit by bit. I disliked it immensely, but I also wanted to move on, so I forced myself to let it go and focus on what she was saying.

"There was a family that lived in gated Pacific Heights community, very rich, some shady business dealings. The father double crossed the Supernatural mafia and so one night, assassins were sent to their home. Three children and two adults were slaughtered. There was one survivor, a ten-year-old boy who swore that monsters killed his family."

"Did they?" Isaac asked.

"Yes," I answered, the memory painful. "But there was no special branch at the time, no one to believe him. Everyone dismissed it as the ramblings of a traumatized child. And while Stella's father and I *did* believe him, our hands were tied. We could only investigate so far before exposing me to Mundanes that could be a threat to me. Add in the fact that the deal gone wrong involved an artifact, and the whole case became entrenched in far too much red tape to do anything about."

"So the killers got away," Stella continued, her voice softer. "The kid was put into his aunt's custody. But he couldn't let any of this go, especially, I think, because no one would believe him. He was in and out of institutions until he turned eighteen, when he got his trust fund and disappeared. No one knows what happened to him. And the aunt also disappeared off the face of the earth at the same time. No body was ever found, and the assumption was that they simply went off the grid for a fresh start. The media frenzy around them was horrible."

"Okay, tragic, but what does this have to do with the carvings on the Orc's back?" Isaac asked.

Stella brought up one of the photos and enlarged the top portion. When she handed it to me, her eyes were lit up with the excitement of finding a good clue.

"Recognize it?" she asked.

I frowned at the image, thinking about that case at the same time. The family had been brutally murdered, the parents tortured and on the bodies were carved--

"Bloody hell," I breathed, "it's the top part of the symbol!"

Stella nodded and turned to Isaac.

"There was a symbol that the killers had carved into the bodies, a kind of warning to anyone else who would betray the mob boss. This is the top part of the symbol."

"And the fingers on the left hand were cut off all five family members," I said, clapping a hand to my mouth and staring at Stella. "This could lead us to the killer."

"You think it's one of the assassins?" Isaac asked.

"No," I replied, "they're all dead or in jail. And even if it could be, the knives don't work on Supernaturals, remember? But the boy...he may be our guy," I turned to Stella. "Your father kept tabs on him, are you sure he didn't know what happened to him?"

Stella shook her head.

"It was one of his biggest regrets, letting that kid suffer like he did because he couldn't prosecute the real killers. My dad visited him when he was in the institutions as often as he could, but had no idea what happened to him."

"A boy that traumatized," I said, "with that much anger toward the Supernatural community, he would be the perfect host for the knives to manipulate."

"In what way? We still don't know much about these things" Stella asked.

I took a deep breath. I wasn't supposed to be revealing this much to anyone not in the Archive, but that didn't matter, not when an artifact like this was out there killing people.

"As I said," I pulled out a case file from one of my file boxes, "no one knows which came first, Jack the Ripper or his knives. But what we do know is that the Ripper killings made the knives stronger, possibly exponentially darker. After the Ripper killings, everywhere the knives went, there were brutal, serial killer style murders."

I threw the files on the table as I talked about them.

"New York 1891. Brothel murders of 1906 in San Francisco. The Salt Lake City murders of 1922. They disappear off our radar for about fifty years until the 1970's sees two different men using them, the Zodiac Killer and Derek Brown. Then the knives bounce around the globe. Australia, New Zealand, Germany, South America, Rwanda, until they finally made their way here. Everywhere the knives go, they attach themselves to men with not just a tendency toward violence, but a hunger for it. At a base level, the knives tap into that need, that drive that a serial killer has and they amplify it, feed it. And sometimes they stop because the knives help the killer to become satisfied, as in the case of the original Ripper. But sometimes, as in Derek Brown's case, they never are. The knives become the only kind of accomplice a serial can have, the kind that cannot become the victim and in fact, helps the killer accomplish their goals."

"An imaginary friend for a serial killer?" Isaac asked, his lips curling in distaste.

"In simple terms, I suppose so," I said. "Only instead of encouraging the killer to steal cookies out of the jar, it tells them to carve people up. But the truly terrifying part of this artifact--"

"*That* wasn't terrifying?" Stella murmured.

"-- is that with each killer the knives are in the possession of, they receive the imprint of that killer's darkness. Their prejudices, their hatred, their creativity and ability to evade capture. To make a dark artifact like this one, it takes a great act of terrible evil. The Ripper was indeed evil, but the fact that he escalated as he did makes us think the knives must've had a previous owner, one that used them in similarly gruesome ways. Once an artifact is created in this way, and then used again and again, that darkness is compounded. It grows, like a cancer, until it takes on a life of its own."

"And now," Isaac said slowly, "it looks like it's in the hands of a man that has a significant hatred for the Supernatural community and a mountain of untreated trauma."

Silence descended in the room as each of us tried to digest the terrifying implications of all this. I had decades to come to terms with an artifact that contained this much compounded evil, and I was still chilled by the knowledge. I couldn't imagine what Stella and Isaac were thinking.

"Okay," Stella let out a long breath and nodded. "Well first thing's first, who wants pierogis for lunch? I'm starving."

# CHAPTER SIX

## STELLA

We worked until late into the night, combing through all the coroner's reports on both the new killings and the ones from the Pacific Heights murders. When I finally couldn't keep my eyes open, I asked Isaac to fly me home, ignoring the hard look James shot my way. I know it might make sense to just stay, but being around the two of them messed with my head in ways I just couldn't deal with right now.

Turns out being pressed against Isaac's hard, warm chest wasn't exactly a better alternative. The way his claws just barely dug into my ass and hips, the beat of his heart under my palm, the rhythmic beat of his wings, all had me wishing I could just cross that last line and ask him to stay with me. One look into his eyes as he set me outside my apartment and I knew he was just waiting for one word from me.

And when I opened my mouth to give it, the words stuck in my throat. So I went to bed horny as hell and frustrated that I couldn't predict whether or not riding Isaac like a stallion was going to ruin everything or simply open up our relationship to wonderful new places.

I woke up late in the morning, cranky and in need of coffee, of which I was out.

"Damn it all to hell," I grumbled, tripping over an empty box by the recycling bin in my kitchen.

I snarled as I broke it apart and stuffed it in the can before going to shower. It helped some, but I was no happier and I realized that it was probably because, even after three orgasms with my favorite toy, I was even hornier. I didn't want battery operated, no matter how many settings it had. I wanted a warm, real dick with a hot Gargoyle on the other end that would fuck me hard and thoroughly.

*Of course it could also be the fact that I wasn't just fantasizing about Isaac last night.*

I ran a brush through my hair and tried not to think of the downright filthy things I'd imagined James doing to me. We'd had one time together, and in spite of the fact that he'd taken me against a wall, it was pretty vanilla. I wanted to know if he'd like being called Daddy, if he would hold me down and tease me with that beautiful Gargoyle dick of his. If he'd make me beg, make me crawl to him.

I closed my eyes and tried to breath, my hand trailing down even as I tried to take hold of my thoughts.

Being around James for twenty-four hours had been quite the mind fuck. I'd thought that my feelings for him had been sufficiently drowned in all the whiskey and sexual experiences I'd had since him. I'd barely thought about the son of a bitch the last five years. And now here he was, shaking everything up like it had only been months instead of years since he'd walked out of my life.

*Maybe, I should just go for it with Isaac.*

I cringed at that. I wasn't an angel, but I wasn't enough of a bitch to use Isaac just to slake my desire for James.

*Then again, I do want Isaac too. Oh my god, I'm screwed.*

And then I snorted at my reflection in the mirror.

*No, actually I'm not. That's the problem.*

My phone buzzed, saving me from any further thoughts of sheer stupidity and I blew out a breath of relief when I saw that it was Queen Dawn.

"I was getting worried," I answered. "Isaac said you'd call yesterday."

"Apologies, my darling," her voice was deep and smoky, like whiskey soaked cigars, "there were...shall we say *obstacles* to overcome."

The hair on the back on my neck stood up at that. Very little kept Queen Dawn from things she wanted. Especially when it came to her club.

"What's going on?" I asked.

"It's complicated. Can you come by now? I realize it's short notice, and I apologize, but--"

"I'll be right over."

"Thank you, my dear. The door code is five-three-zero-two."

I threw on some soft, faded capri jeans and a loose fitting shirt that said "I got a Tini bit sauced at Tini Bigs", my favorite martini bar in the city.

I'd met Queen Dawn two months after James left Seattle. I was angry and confused about my life, who I was, what I really wanted. And college expenses were killing me. I had wandered into her club one night with a friend of mine that thought it would be good for me to blow off some steam. But that night, a part of me that had been locked away under layers of shame and pain was liberated. And I'd wanted more.

Queen Dawn had seen that in me and so much more. She'd taken me under her wing personally and I never looked back. She offered to teach me about this world, and after a few months, had offered me a job as a sub. Within a year, I was training to be a Dom. I had to leave once I made detective; it was too risky to keep moonlighting as a Dominatrix while being a cop. But the years I'd spent there had given me a family, and a firm knowledge of who I was and my own power. If not for Dawn, I know I wouldn't be the woman I was today. I may have taken myself in hand eventually, but Dawn made sure I did it with a safety net and unconditional love.

Thankfully, there wasn't much traffic and I made it to the gate of the club in about ten minutes, which was pretty reckless considering the way the roads near the club curved and wound around, a holdover from Seattle's past as a logging town. The club itself was tucked behind tall trees and down a steep road that ended at a wrought iron gate. The mansion was just beyond the gate, which was adorned on the top with a sword and a heart, hence the name of the club. The door code and the gate code were the same, so I typed it in and the gate swung open to me. Memories hit me like warm drops of sunshine. I'd driven through this gate thousands of times, but coming up to the mansion still took my breath away.

The siding was such a dark gray it was almost black, with stark white trim on the wrap around porch, columns and around the door, which was the only spark of color on the house itself. Blood red with a fat, sensuous heart for a door knocker, which was just for show since no one could get in without giving the password to the enormous bouncer Dawn usually employed.

I was halfway around the building before the sensation of being watched ran down my spine in a rush, cold and chilling. I put my hand on my service piece, ready to draw if needed, and took a look around the perimeter. But the only things I saw were the immaculate grounds that Dawn always kept, the grass a perfect emerald green, the red roses full and brutal in their beauty.

Still, as I got to the back door of the club, I couldn't shake the feeling that someone was indeed seeing everything I did.

Once inside through the back entrance, I slammed the door shut, my heart beating fast and my palms sweating. Not much spooked me, except knowing that someone was able to get the jump on me.

"Magdalena?!" squealed a voice behind me.

I jumped a foot in the air and spun around, only to be engulfed in perfume scented lace and feathers.

"Oh my god, where have you been?!" asked the six and half foot-tall drag Dom named Lady Sugar. "I never thought I'd see you around here again!"

Lady Sugar had gorgeous dark brown skin and always loved to dress in old time boudoir get ups. Garters, lace bustiers, long robes trimmed in feathers. Her wigs were big and beautiful and her make up flawless. If not for her, I'd have no idea how to apply liquid eyeliner, not that I wear it much these days. Today she was in fluffy slippers, satin lingerie shorts and matching camisole with her signature robe. It was hours before she would need to be decked out for her patrons, so her face was devoid of makeup, and she wore a fancy head covering to hide her shaved head.

I gave her a tight hug and released her.

"I'm here to see Queen Dawn," I said with a smile, "but it's good to see you, Shug."

"You too, babe," she hooked her arm through mine and led me from the costume area where the back door let out into. "There has been so much going on! Especially in the last year. I'm married now, don't know if anyone told you."

"What?"

"I know! She is just the cutest little thing, and totally on board with my polyamory. She said, 'Sugar, I just want to be with you. The rest, we'll figure out.'"

"Congratulations!"

"Thanks. Now what about you?"

I snorted and looked at her like she was crazy.

"Mm-hm, that's what I thought."

"What's that supposed to mean?" I tossed back.

"You have sexual frustration written all over you, honey."

"Bullshit."

Sugar just gave me the side eye and led me down the hall toward Dawn's private rooms.

"I'm surprised Dawn wanted to meet you here actually," Sugar pitched her voice low.

My skin prickled.

"Why?"

Lady Sugar opened her mouth to respond when Dawn came around the corner, her long dancers body clad in her usual black satin robe, her red hair flowing down around her shoulders. She was also without makeup, as usual this time of day, and held a saucer and cup in her hands like a Duchess who had just risen from her bed. Faint lines were visible around her eyes and mouth, but they only added to the stark beauty she had always possessed.

When Dawn's blue eyes met mine, a sob caught in my throat and all I wanted was to be hugged by her.

"I think I'll let her explain," Sugar said, planting a kiss on my cheek. "Don't be a stranger, Maggs."

"I won't," I promised, guilt pricking me at how long I'd been away.

Dawn waited for Sugar to walk out of the hallway before she sauntered over to me. She took her time, eyes raking down my body as she sipped her coffee.

"You look good," she purred, "though, you've been drinking too much."

"I know." I never lied to her.

She hooked one long, red tipped finger under my chin and examined my face.

"You take too much onto yourself," she murmured. "Always did. Be careful, my darling, don't let this consume you."

I frowned up at her, wondering at the sharper warning underlying her words. What was she trying to tell me? Dawn wasn't always straightforward; sometimes she spoke around things and it used to make my head spin. I'd often yell at her to just speak plainly to me, but she'd always tell me that sometimes a lesson was more powerful in hindsight. And she was usually right.

*But this...this isn't one of her life lessons. It's a serial murderer case and I can't afford her riddles. Not right now.*

She ran the back of her hand against my cheek before turning on her heel and walking away. I knew without her saying that I was supposed to follow, though after that last piece of advice, my legs were weak and my heart was trying to escape through my throat.

When I stepped into her suite, it was like going back in time. It hadn't changed in the least. Well, perhaps a few more vinyl records, and more light than I remembered. But other than that, the black and red furniture, the dark rugs strewn across the oak hard woods, the way the air smelled of a spicy perfume, and the curtains separating this room from her bedroom. Dawn lived and breathed her life here, Queen Dawn was more than a Dom persona, it was who she was down into her core. I knew that Dawn did have an apartment away from the club so she could get away from the responsibilities of things, but she was rarely there and no one knew where it was. Nor did any of us know her real name, or much about her past. One night, when she'd imbibed a bit too much, Dawn had confessed that she used to have a brother, but he, his wife and his family had died tragically, the killers never brought to justice. In my need to please her back then, I'd tried to get more information out of her so I could look up the case on the police database, but she'd caught on fairly quickly and shut it down. I let it go after that, realizing that some things were better left alone.

Dawn waved at the black couch, not leather but instead a soft fabric that was velvet to the touch. Dawn was not a leather kind of Dom. She was more soft and smooth, until she wasn't.

"Coffee?" she asked.

"Please."

I waited and watched Dawn make coffee in a stove top percolator and assemble an old fashioned coffee service made out of silver. Her movements were deliberate and graceful, much like a dancer. Her red nails flashed in the low light and she only glanced up at me once during her preparations. I waited, hands folded, eyes attentive, slipping back into the discipline that she'd taught me. Dawn may not have ever scened with me, but she had guided some of my first experiences with other Doms, had trained me on how to act, how to respond, and, most importantly, how to advocate for myself in a scene. She helped me explore the edges of my kink and dare to claim my own power. But, with her in this space, I slipped effortlessly back into the dynamic that had formed the foundation of our relationship. It was comforting. I didn't have to think about what to do next, or wonder if I was making the right decision. My mind was quiet and calm here, with her taking control.

I sighed, muscles relaxing and tears burning my eyes, by the time she set the coffee tray on the low iron and glass table in front of me.

Dawn ran her fingers across my cheek, claiming one of my tears for herself before planting a kiss to my forehead. It only made me cry harder and when she lowered herself into her throne-like chair beside the couch, and I slipped to my knees and laid my head in her lap. She didn't say a word, simply ran her nails through my hair, the light scrape against my scalp soothing.

I didn't bother to count the seconds I stayed that way, or worry that I was taking too much time. That wasn't what this was about. And I wasn't in control anyway, in spite of the fact that I'd just knelt before her. Dawn was the one guiding my ship, and I couldn't stop her if I wanted to.

"Your friend said that some of the victims of this killer came from here," she whispered. "So that's why you're here?"

"Yes."

"Not because you turned your back on us when you became detective?"

There was a bite to her words and I looked up confused. Dawn had supported my decision to leave and yet, it seemed now that she felt rejected.

"No," I breathed. "I didn't turn my back on you. It was just that everything I did was scrutinized, and you know how everyone views this place. It's like a home to me, and it killed me to not have it in my life."

"But you had to make a choice."

"Yes."

Dawn nodded, a flash of something angry in her blue eyes that sent chills down my spine just before it vanished.

"I'd hoped when you became head of the special branch you'd come back," she said.

"I wanted to, but it turns out running that place is its own kind of blessing and curse."

Dawn's lips turned up into a tight smile.

"I am familiar with the concept."

"Dawn," I said, my voice raspy, "is there anything you can tell me? Any new members that are causing problems, crossing lines? Anything?"

She turned away from me and I thought perhaps she wouldn't answer.

"There is something...I should've told you before but..."

I got to my feet slow, my legs tingling.

"Shug mentioned that she was surprised you wanted to meet me here, why?"

Dawn's head whipped around, eyes blazing.

"She should've kept her mouth shut, it's going to get her into trouble."

There was genuine worry behind the fury and I frowned.

"Dawn," I pushed a hint of Dom authority into my voice, "tell me."

Her eyebrow arched.

"Impressive attempt, darling. But wasted on me. I would tell you regardless of whether you commanded me to or not."

Just at that moment, a brisk, hard knock echoed through the room. Dawn turned to her door and swore under her breath.

"I had hoped he would give me a little more time," she murmured.

"Who?"

"I'm sorry, my dear, but further explanation will have to wait while I introduce you to my new business partner."

Just as her hand clasped the handle, a rush of foreboding hit me and I almost called her back. When the door was fully opened, I saw why.

All the air rushed out of my lungs, and what little I'd had to eat this morning turned in my stomach. I knew the handsome man who gave Dawn a cold grin, and I wished I didn't.

"I heard we had a visitor," his smooth, all too friendly voice made my stomach twist.

But it was nothing compared to how my entire body wanted to flee the moment his hazel eyes locked onto mine. There wasn't as much surprise as there should've been in his gaze, as if he already knew I was here. But there was a lust, a possessive gleam that I recognized very well. Suddenly it was five years ago and the sense of being trapped was choking me.

I would never forget the face of Ben Harper, the last man I'd ever let have any control over me. We'd dated seriously for over a year and, when I refused to marry him, Ben had started to become abusive; separating me from friends, coworkers, chipping away at my self-esteem. I'd managed to extricate myself from him before he succeeded in completely isolating me, but I'd still had to threaten legal action when he began stalking me. That part only lasted a few months, but it was enough to forever stick with me. I'd had to move three times before he left me alone, and in the end, it was only when my fellow coworkers in the Supernatural Division had started to stake out my house around the clock that he'd backed off.

No one had ever made me feel so weak, so unsafe in the city I'd called home my entire life. I hated and feared him in equal measure, and now both swirled in my gut, a sickening mix that had my hands shaking.

"Stella," my name dripped off his lips, and made my throat tighten, "what a pleasant surprise."

I wanted to be the strong woman I knew myself to be. To tell him to go to hell, to rip his fucking balls off and feed them to him like I'd imagined countless times before.

But all I could do was stand there and stare at him. My entire body seemed to shut down, to do what it had been trained to do around him: be small, be quite, be agreeable.

*No...No! I won't do this. Why can't I fucking speak?*

Dawn's hand on the small of my back snapped me out of the paralytic fugue and I just barely managed to step back in time to avoid Ben's outstretched hand. He wasn't reaching out to shake, he had been on his way to touching my shoulder.

Everything inside of me recoiled at the thought of his hands on my body, his presence in my city, in this club.

"Are you alright?" he asked, concern thinly veiling his delight at my discomfort.

"She's fine," Dawn said, a soothing tone to her voice. "Now if you'll excuse us--"

"Has Dawn told you that I'm now part owner of this wonderful place?" He moved just enough over the threshold to keep Dawn from being able to close the door.

The words stole the breath from my body and I gaped at them both.

"Calm down darling, it was unavoidable," Dawn murmured.

"It kinda was," Ben agreed. "I made some very difficult circumstances go away for Queen Dawn, didn't I?"

Dawn's eyes tightened for a moment, a warning flashing in them and then it was gone, replaced by her cool, calm exterior.

"I don't understand this," I said to her.

"I know it's a shock seeing me again," Ben said, taking a step toward me, "but I assure you that I mean you and this place, no harm."

It was only by the very thinnest margin that I held my ground and didn't retreat from him. He would *not* take this place from me, I wouldn't let him.

"Stella actually is here in an official capacity," Dawn said, her voice holding a warning, but for which of us I had no idea.

"Official?" Ben frowned. "How so?"

Something in me didn't want to tell him a damn thing. In fact, I wanted to hide the entire case from him though I didn't have a logical reason as to why.

*And if we want to watch the club, it looks like I'll need his buy in, as well as Dawn's.*

So, in the fewest words possible, I told him what was happening and that Isaac, James and I wanted to stake out the place and see if we could determine who it was.

Ben listened with a concerned look on his face that made me want to scratch his fucking eyes out. He was one the most heartless assholes I'd ever met, he just hid it well and this was nothing else but just that. Though from the way Dawn looked at him she wasn't fooled in the least.

"That's terrible," he said. "We'll get some additional security around the place, discreetly of course. But I'm afraid I simply cannot allow you and your partners to be on the grounds during business hours."

"I could get a warrant," I said. "I could go through official channels. I could also stake out the street outside the gate and there would be nothing you could do about it."

"That's true. But official channels would take a while, correct? And outside the gates probably won't get you what you really need. Of course, if you wanted to visit as a returning guest," his grin made my stomach twist, "I wouldn't stop you."

Dawn didn't force anyone to do anything, or be with anyone, they didn't want to. But I highly doubted Ben would see my return here, even as a visiting Dom, as anything but an invitation.

*But it might be the only way to get access soon. Son of a bitch!*
"I'll consider it."

Ben nodded.

"It was good seeing you again, Stella."

When he closed the door, I fell onto the couch and tried to breath.

A few seconds later, a cold wash cloth was being pressed to the back of my neck.

"How could you?" I rasped. "You knew what he did to me!"

"Sometimes we must make hard choices my darling," she said.

I looked up, confused.

"But *him*?"

"He's a very accomplished businessman. And he came in with an offer I simply could not refuse."

Ben had always been a shark when it came to business dealings. He was rich when I knew him, but had likely gotten even more so in the five years since I sent him packing. Many of his decisions didn't make sense to me when we were together, but he'd always tell me that it was about the long term goal and that I just didn't understand these things.

*What's the long game with the club? What could he possibly want with it? Other than to get at me? But there's no way he's still wanting me after all this time, right?*

The thought made me shiver and I shoved off the washcloth.

"I should've told you on the phone," Dawn admitted. "But I wanted to see you and I thought I had some time before he got here."

"What else can I do?" I asked. "I can't let something happen to the beings here."

Dawn took a deep breath, eyes searching my face.

"Are you sure you want to do this?" she asked. "This investigation? Stella, I haven't seen you this unsettled since you first came here. Are you up for this?"

I stood up, lips parting on a gasp of confusion.

"I don't mean to make you feel incapable," Dawn continued. "I just worry, that's all."

"Well, don't," I said, my spine straightening. "I'll find the killer, you don't have to worry about that. I've got some extra resources at my disposal on this one."

"Really? The police department finally cares about crimes involving Supernaturals?"

"Oh, I wish. No, this is something different. A guy from London, Scotland Yard."

Her eyes widened and she cocked her head to the side.

"Interesting. Scotland Yard? That's unusual."

"Yeah, I'm actually not supposed to say much, but I have faith that, with his help, I can catch whoever this is."

"Well, considering all of that, I suppose there's no way to talk you out of this. What will you do with the limitations Ben has placed on you?"

I took a deep breath, trying to steady my pulse. There was an appeal to coming back, maybe doing a scene. I had missed this place more than I thought. When Ben and I were together, I never, ever brought him here. I'd mentioned it a few times, told him what I liked. But even before the abuse started, I'd never trusted him enough to do an actual scene with him, or let him have any control over me in the bedroom. Now, if I did come back as a Dom, even if it was undercover, I would be letting him see this part of my life that I had protected from the taint of our relationship.

*But it could save the lives of people who work here, people I care about.*
I closed my eyes and sighed.
"I'll be here tonight."

# CHAPTER SEVEN

## ISAAC

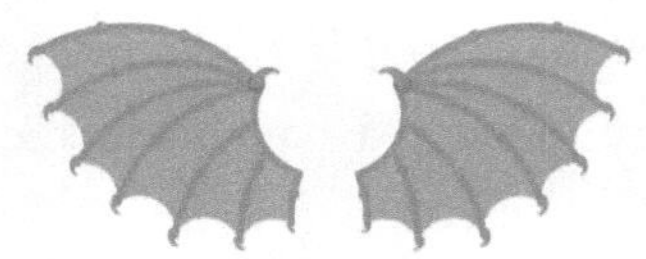

"Un-fucking-believable!" I muttered as I slammed a lid onto the pot of bubbling sauce. "She's being reckless, but will she listen? No, of course not. She has to be the hero every single time."

I was in James' chef-quality kitchen, stress cooking homemade marinara for a lasagna, while banana bread cooled on the counter. It had been three hours since Stella had come over to tell us about her meeting with Queen Dawn and her plan to go undercover at the club.

She'd tried to hide the detail about Ben, but James and I both knew she was holding something back. It didn't take long before she was spilling the situation with her former stalker being Dawn's new business partner and how he'd backed her into a corner about investigating the club's connection to the killer.

We'd both tried to talk her out of it, told her we'd find a different way but all it had done was cause a fight and Stella had stormed out. James and I were supposed to be working on the case but after that I couldn't concentrate on anything, and asked James if I could use his kitchen. Truth be told, I'd been itching to get in here since I'd walked in yesterday.

Most kitchens weren't big enough for me to cook in my true form but James' was a beautiful chrome and white Gargoyle sized sanctuary where I could lose myself in the simplicity of recipes and maybe find a way around this plan of Stella's.

But, after making the bread, the noodles for the lasagna, and now the marinara, I was no closer to a solution.

James huffed and flung a folder across the table. I glanced back and was once again struck by the sheer size and savage beauty of him. I was half Gargoyle, so while I was larger than Mundanes, I was small compared to others of my kind.

But James was a full blooded Gargoyle and it showed. His back was a tempting expanse of purple skin stretched over thick muscles that flexed and rolled with each movement. His arms were currently crossed, making his biceps and pecs bulge in a way that had me longing to run my hands over them just to feel how firm he was. And then there was his perfect ass in those tailored slacks he insisted on wearing, even in his true form, which had an opening for his long, ribbed tail that twitched and undulated like something out of my teenage wet dreams. I'd always wanted to explore tail play with a Gargoyle but I'd never actually had a Gargoyle partner before.

The lurid fantasies that James had planted in my mind yesterday were stirring to life and I wanted to give them full leave to run rampant. And let James Dominate the shit out of me.

The thought made my knees weak. He was so much bigger than me, I'd be completely at his mercy.

"You having any luck?" his voice jolted me out of my fantasies.

"Hm?"

He nodded at the kitchen and smirked at me, as if he knew full well what I'd been distracted by.

"Are you having any luck clearing your head by making a mess of my kitchen?"

"Oh, uh...no. Nothing yet."

I turned away and tried to focus on assembling the lasagna when I felt his presence in the kitchen.

I was also shirtless, but instead of fancy slacks, I wore sport shorts because they were more comfortable on my thick legs. But now I was regretting that decision; my dick was stirring to life at the close proximity of this male who was confusing the fuck out of me.

I wanted Stella. I knew that and nothing would change it. But I also wanted James in an achingly brutal way that had my pulse racing. Where my desire for Stella was a strong, hot thrum under the blood, constant but also quiet, my growing need for James rushed through me, aggressive and demanding. And I wasn't imagining the physical sensation they each stirred in my chest. The pull and the ache, as if there were strings tied to my heart that were connected to the two of them. With each passing moment, those sensations were growing stronger, as were my suspicions about what they meant.

"It smells good," he said from behind me.

"Thanks," I managed, hands stilling in the middle of spreading ricotta on the homemade noodles.

"Am I making you nervous?"

"Yes."

Why lie? James' senses were twice as strong as mine so he already knew how he was affecting me.

I jumped when his hands skimmed the sides of my body and ran up my back to still on my shoulders. It was quietly possessive, especially when he gave me a brief squeeze, and it soothed the edges of my nervousness while stoking my lust.

"You know," he whispered, "I came across your record with the department while I looking at the history of the Supernatural Branch in King county. It's very impressive to advance as fast as you have."

I swallowed, knowing it wasn't impressive so much as the Protectors using their influence to put me right where they wanted me. Was James digging for information? Was his seduction merely a way to find out if

I was loyal or a traitor? With great effort, I managed not to flinch at the stab of guilt these questions produced.

"I wanted it bad enough," I said, finishing the final layer on the lasagna.

"Do you always go after things you want bad enough with such single-minded focus?"

He'd layered a very simple question with so many different possible meanings that I had to stop and consider how to answer. If he was asking this in relation to Stella, then the answer was yes.

If he was asking this in relation to the case, the answer was also yes.

If he was asking this in relation to him...

I turned around. James was standing behind me, close enough to touch but his arms were crossed. His dark eyes were hooded under an intense frown but still I saw the embers of a fire lurking there. It warmed something inside of me, and that tug and pull snapped to life. I was starting to have a suspicion about what the hell this could be, but it was too damn crazy. It had to be wishful thinking on my part, so I tried to shut it down enough to be able to think.

"Yes," I said in answer to his question.

"Me, too," James hesitated, his body tense as if he were on the edge of lunging for me. "If you wanted to be with Stella and also me, I would be fine with that you know."

I sucked in a breath and tried very hard not to let my arousal start to think for me. It was so fucking tempting to just fall to my knees and do what I'd been thinking of since day one. But my feelings for Stella were there, holding me back. I owed her a conversation first, to find out if she would be hurt by this. If she would, then that was it, I was done with this and I'd just have to deal with the longing clawing away at my insides. But if she was alright with it...

*Nope, don't go there yet.*

I took a deep breath and looked him in the eye. That pull beat against my ribs and I ignored it.

"I want you, too," I said. "I can't explain it and I don't want to right now. I want you both. But before anything happens between us, Stella and I need to have a conversation."

His mouth quirked up.

"That seems reasonable. Just let me know what the verdict is, Isaac."

My name rolled off his tongue like he was savoring it and my cock stirred. He seemed to know it too because his smirked widened just before he turned away and sauntered back toward the dining room table.

"Changing the subject?" I posed, clearing my throat.

"Please do," James said.

"She's walking right into Ben's hands. I can feel it."

I know I wasn't imagining the snarl that rolled, deep and jagged from his throat.

"Me, too. But she's also right. There's no other option."

I bit back my own growl of frustration.

"I know. Doesn't mean I'm happy about it."

"Me, either. Which is why we will be there, backing her up if she needs it. Stella is tougher than she looks, and while I don't think she should be alone with that bastard, I think we need to trust her."

"I do trust her, completely. I don't trust *him*," anger shot through my blood once again.

"It does seem like he's got some kind of angle," James admitted.

"What are you thinking?"

"I'm thinking that we dig into Ben a bit, see what we can find. It might be that his interest in the club was purely business. But it might not."

I wiped down the counter top, my shoulders relaxing and my mind finally not spinning into dreadful images if everything were to go wrong.

"I think that sounds like an excellent plan," I said.

We settled at the dining room table and began to do some searches on James' insanely powerful database. The Secret Archive had some of the most sophisticated cyber resources I'd ever seen and I had a feeling that this was just the tip of the iceberg.

An hour into researching Ben, and I was drowning in articles about this businessman that had seemingly come out of nowhere at age twenty. Something about the backstory he'd given the press wasn't setting well with me. It was too clean, too perfect. Parents that died when he was a week away from graduating high school, working three jobs to pay for college, graduating from a small university and then miraculously getting hired by a real estate mogul that mentors him and then in a few years he's making million dollar deals, living the life of the nouveau riche. It was all a little too Cinderella for my taste. It seemed tailor made to evoke both wonder and empathy and keep anyone from digging too deep.

"How easy would it be to fake college records?" I asked.

James glanced up from the lap top he was working on.

"Depends on the resources he would have. I can have a couple friends look into it."

I nodded.

"Do that. His entire backstory feels fabricated."

"It is," James turned his laptop to me. "Ben Harper technically didn't exist until about six months before his big splash in the business world."

My heart lurched. Ben wasn't just an asshole stalker, he was fake. But why? What was he hiding? Why make up a whole new identity?

"We're missing something," I said, frowning at the information I'd collected.

"I feel that way too, but I'm not sure what."

I glanced at the white board James had set up with pictures of the victims, the relevant details of the murder written in stark black marker on one side. It helped to see it laid out, and gave us all a way to see the flow of things.

"We need another white board," I said, hitting print on the articles I'd found.

James' eyebrow quirked up.

"You don't think Stella is going to have a fit when she finds out we're investigating her former boyfriend?"

He said the last word with a distinct growl that made heat flash through me and hit me in the gut. The evidence of his feelings for Stella was growing by the hour. It should've made me jealous, but instead I was oddly hopeful.

*Put it aside, bigger fish to fry right now.*

"I think," I said slowly, "that she's going to want to protect her friends at the club. And if we can dig up proof that he's shady, it could give her an edge to force him out."

"I'm not completely convinced, but let's give it a shot."

I grinned at him and James' lips twitched as if he were tempted to return the smile. As I went to grab the articles off the printer, my phone buzzed. I dug it out of my athletic shorts and my stomach sank at the text message.

*Aunt Laura: I need your help moving a bookcase. Can you come by?*

I glanced at James, who was reading something on the laptop that made his eyes even more hooded as his frown deepened. He was smart, and I had a bad feeling that there was a kernel of suspicion where I was concerned, even with the loaded conversation in the kitchen. I wanted to tell Aunt Laura to go to hell, that I was out and they could just deal with it. But Stella was in enough danger with Ben now in the picture, and with this serial killer still at large I couldn't risk the possibility that they would hurt her and make it look like the killer. Not only would that muddy the waters of the investigation, it would mean that Stella had gotten hurt because of me.

*Shit!*

"I have to go run a quick errand," I said, pushing as much levity into my voice as I could muster. "Elderly aunt needs help with something."

"Hope it's nothing serious."

"Nah, just a quick thing. I'll be back in an hour."

James nodded and went back to the laptop as if he really did believe me. So why then did I feel like I had a neon sign above my head flashing

"Traitor"? As I slipped my glamour back on I felt him studying me, but when I glanced up, he was still reading the screen of his device. I shrugged it off as my own paranoia and headed to a coffee shop down by the market that was indicated by the mention of the bookcase.

The walk helped to calm my racing heart and give me some clarity on things. I wanted out of this, that was nothing new. But the how still eluded me.

I knew that the Archive wanted information about the Protectors, and there were rumors that they were accepting defectors, which was why the only way out tended to be in a body bag these days. But here I was, working with an agent of the Archive, one that appeared to like me more than as just a friend.

*He might be more amenable if I take him as a lover but that feels gross. I need to come clean and hope that I don't hurt Stella too bad with the confession.*

I winced at that, and for the thousandth time wished I'd never heard of these assholes before.

I ordered a coffee from the surly barista, wished we were at the coffee shop I favored and made my way to the back of the room. This place had an underground feel to it with all it's dark paneling and even darker furniture. There were macabre paintings hanging around the place; skulls and bleeding hearts placed on canvas next to images of dying flowers. I liked art, even angsty dark art, but there was something about these that left a sour taste in my mouth.

It could've been the case we were on, or the ferret faced man coming my way with a deep scowl etched into his pale skin.

"Aunt Laura," I said with a sarcastic twist to my lips.

"We aren't happy, Isaac," he hissed.

"What else is new?"

He leaned forward and I instinctively jerked back. The cold glint of his eyes reminded me of a shark, remorseless and deadly.

"Have you forgotten the consequences of failure? She's very pretty. It would be a shame if the serial killer somehow hurt her."

I had a second to wonder if they were mind readers since this had just been my fear not twenty minutes ago. But then I realized that it was just logical. Threaten the person I cared for the most with something that would be horrid and all my fault. My blood heated as I narrowed my eyes at this asshole.

"Where are the god damned files?" he demanded.

"What files?"

He dug a phone out of his pocked and set it on the table opened to a picture. I glanced at it and realized it wasn't a picture, but video of Stella leaving the club this morning.

"I know where she is all the time," he whispered. "I know how she takes her coffee, the garbage she eats, how much she drinks. I know how many people she's pissed off. I can convincingly frame any one of them, or none of them. Many people drink and drive. Then there's her ex at the club. Maybe he just got out of hand one night."

My hands clenched and claws appeared, my canines extended and I let loose a low growl.

"You are so predictable," I snarled. "How many times will you leverage the people I love to keep me in line?"

"Until I don't have to anymore. Or until I've run out of them."

I grabbed the front of his shirt and pulled him down until his beaked nose almost touched mine.

"I'll shred you if you hurt her. You know that right?"

"Not before I've shredded her though," he pried my fingers off his shirt. "Now where are the files on the case? They aren't at the precinct anymore. Where did you and that bastard from the Archive have them moved?"

"No idea," I said. "He doesn't exactly trust me and I don't blame him."

"You expect me to believe that you're working the case without the files?"

"You're going to believe whatever the hell you want whether I tell you the truth or not. He doles out info as he sees fit, it's pretty frustrating and I'm about ready to walk away."

"You'll do no such thing," he snapped, "but you will send us daily reports on the progress of the case."

"And how do you propose I manage that when he's watching me like a hawk?"

He shrugged.

"Figure it out. That's your job."

And with that helpful nugget, the bastard got up and left.

I sat there a while longer, digesting all the bullshit and trying very hard to not let the gruesome images that the handler planted in my mind get the better of me. It was a frustratingly effective way to keep me in check and I needed to neutralize it as soon as possible. Which meant solving this damn case, taking away any power Ben may have to hurt Stella and convincing James to do everything he could to keep her safe.

*Even if that means that I sacrifice my own safety. I may just have to reap what I've sowed here, but Stella doesn't deserve the consequences of my actions.*

I mulled this over as I made my way back to the penthouse. While I didn't have much of a plan to get myself out of this mess, a solution on how to protect Stella from Ben came to me, and I had to stop in my tracks. It was so damn obvious, how had it taken me this long to come up with it?

*Because I'm in love with her, that's why. I'm in love with her and lusting after James at the same time. And their shared history is going to make this complicated but fuck it. I'm done hiding what I feel.*

It was a thin hope, but I'd take nonetheless.

# CHAPTER EIGHT

## JAMES

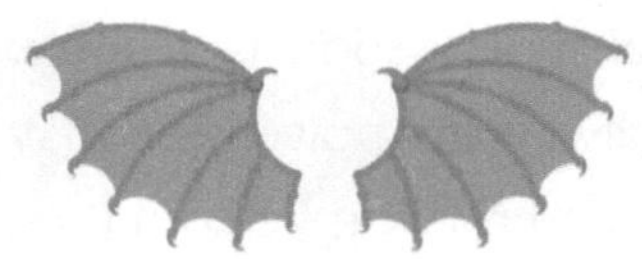

As soon as the door closed behind Isaac, I was messaging Marcus at the tech department of the Archive. I had asked him to put a tracker on Isaac's phone that would be able to tap into whatever messages and emails he received. So far, they were all normal and appropriate.

But the look on Isaacs face had told me plenty when he'd seen that text.

*If he is working with the Protectors, he's a terrible choice for spy. He can't lie worth a damn.*

And I had to smile at that.

At the way his light skin showed a pink tinge when he was aroused, and the delicious pheromones that wafted from his body as his sizable dick became hard. Isaac really was sweet and adorable, his penchant for stress cooking just the latest proof of both things.

My secure messaging system pinged with a response from Marcus.

*Message from an aunt Laura, except Isaac doesn't have an aunt Laura. Probable meet with handler or buyer.*

I huffed out a breath and willed myself to find that distant, logical place that had helped me bag so many artifacts over the years.

*Never get emotionally involved, never let the mission get complicated. It's about the artifact, that's all I'm after. Not the one using the damn thing. Except Isaac might also be after the knives...and for some reason, I want him even more now. It was a mistake to think I could just seduce the truth out of him when I had honest desire for the male.*

Then, as if my head wasn't already spun, the other object of my complicated desire barreled into the room, blue eyes blazing, pale skin flushed and sweaty. She was wearing tight running shorts and a midriff-baring sports bra work out top combo that showed off the muscular cut of her incredibly strong body. I had a sudden image of holding her thighs apart while I tongue fucked her within an inch of her life, and those perfectly sculpted arms manacled over her head as she cried out a devastating orgasm.

But the sharp tone of her voice brought me back to reality and I was grateful, even if it meant I'd get the brunt of her fury.

"I am angry with you," she declared, hands on hips.

It was so simple, honest and full of heat that my confused dick didn't know that this wasn't the best time to go half-mast.

"Oh really?" I asked, sitting back and crossing my arms over my chest.

The way her eyes took in my own well-formed body had me grinning and shifting to show it off even more. I couldn't help it, I liked seeing her a bit off kilter by me, just as I was by her.

"My eyes are up here."

Hers snapped up to mine and narrowed.

"Asshole."

"About what? Not wanting you to walk into a situation where you could be in serious long term danger? Or for the fact that I caught you admiring my assets?"

"I can handle Ben. I've done it once and I can do it again. As for the other," she gave me a wicked grin, "yours aren't even the best assets I've seen in my life."

The temptation to lunge for her, drag that gorgeous body onto the table eat her cunt until she was screaming and begging me to stop had my pulse rocketing. I kept it hidden under a stony facade, the only indication that I was aroused by Stella's biting foreplay was my now fully hard cock in my pants.

*Thank god for the extra-large table to hide the fact.*

I still hadn't quite come to terms with the fact that things between Stella and I weren't in the past like I'd thought, for either of us. But if Isaac and I were messy, Stella and I were a full on disaster. We each dragged the wreckage of our past behind us, whether we wanted to admit it or not. And right now it was causing me no end of problems trying to keep my distance from her while doing my job.

I should have shut this down, brought it back around to the case, kept it professional.

I should have.

But I didn't.

Instead, I chose to lean forward, forearms on the table as I pinned her with a look and give her a smirk that brought a different kind of flush to her face.

"We both know that's not true," I purred.

Her jaw clenched and she actually growled at me. The sound was sexy as hell and I had to tense every muscle in my body to keep from tackling her to the floor.

"You are such an arrogant fuck," she ground out. "You and Isaac both. I didn't get to where I am without being able to handle guys like Ben and here you both are trying to sideline me when I'm our only way into the club!"

*Ah, deflecting with the case. Fine, that battlefield is far less treacherous.*

I stood up and didn't bother to adjust my dick in my pants because I wanted Stella off balance. She was right, she could handle herself. But she was also being impulsive and trying to prove something to herself because of her past with that asshole. I had to make sure she let us back her up in the way that was best for both the case and her.

*Especially her.*

The thought sent a shock through my body as I realized that I was, indeed, perfectly willing to put her safety above getting the artifact.

*Interesting...and disturbing.*

Her gaze flicked down to my crotch, the pink in her cheeks darkening. A memory of the way her skin pinked so beautifully just before she came with my tail in her wet, tight cunt...

If the rush of scent from her was any indication, she was remembering something similar. The knowledge had my hands aching to circle her wrists, to feel her pulse as I slipped the tip of my tail below the top of her shorts and played with her clit...

*Shit! She's supposed to be the one off balance not me!*

But as fast as everything had started to spiral out of control, Stella's face shut down and she shot me a cold, narrowed eyed glare.

*That at least hasn't changed.*

I'd seen that look hundreds of times when she was feeling too vulnerable and wanted to take back control of a situation. If she wasn't truly in danger and in need of a pause to think this all through, I would've felt guilty for making her feel this way.

"You're not thinking this through," I accused, crossing my arms across my chest.

"What is there to think through? We need to get in there, to observe and I have our only invitation. He won't touch me in there, Dawn will make sure of it."

"From what you said, she seems to trust him."

"Yes, but that won't matter when it comes to me. She'll burn that place to the ground to protect her people, that's not going to change because of an asshole like Ben."

"You don't have to prove anything you know," my voice went low, gentle. "Least of all to us."

She swallowed and her eyes became wet.

"I'm not," her protest was hoarse. "I just..."

Stella wasn't a crier, even at her father's funeral she hadn't shed a single tear. It wasn't until we were back at their house that she let loose with wracking, screaming sobs that fractured my heart. To see her now, fighting back tears, scrubbing her hand across her eyes and inching toward the table as if she wanted the comfort of my presence but was afraid to be rejected, it all broke through my last shred of restraint. I went to her without a word and wrapped her up in my arms.

She did nothing at first and I worried that I'd miscalculated. But just as I was about to withdraw, she threw her arms around my waist and buried her face against my chest. Stella let out a long, ragged breath as I ran one of my hands up and down her back, claws just barely scrapping her skin.

I'd done it to comfort her, but the second I had her against me, that throbbing pain in my chest that had been awakened the second I'd laid eyes on her was quieted. As her muscles unwound, so did mine and I found myself curling around her.

It didn't escape my notice that this was the second time in twenty-four hours that I held her while she panicked. It had always been this way with us, even when she was younger and my growing feelings for her were out of the question. She would show the world a strong, capable young woman who couldn't be touched. And then with me, only with me sometimes, she'd let all of that go, and reveal the tender heart that she guarded so carefully. I had cherished every moment of it, knowing that this was special. When I left, I assumed that all of that was sacrificed, that she would never let me in.

But here I was, once again the special one she let in even though I'd hurt her. I savored every second my arms were around her, every glimpse at the part of herself so few ever knew existed.

I pressed a kiss to the top of her head and bent low to lean my cheek there. Stella nuzzled me just a little, her hips pressed to mine and I bit back a moan. She was scared, forced to face trauma from her past this morning in a shocking way and I would not take advantage of that, no matter how the press of her body was affecting me.

"I have to show him that he didn't win," Stella whispered against my skin. "I know you'll say I don't have anything to prove but...I do."

I nodded.

"I do understand that," I pulled back so I could look her in the eye, "I just want you to let us help you so that it's safe for you to do that."

"So you're not trying to stop me from going in there?"

"No," I tucked a strand of her hair behind her ear. "You're right, it is the only way."

"I'm sorry, can you say that again, I'm not sure I heard you."

I chuckled, the ease of this moment with her soothing some of that ache around the edges.

"You *are* right. But so are Isaac and I."

"Shit, I've got two partners now?"

It was said with such playfulness but the underlying possibilities of her simple statement hit us both at the same time, smiles fading as we took one another in.

"If anyone could handle us, it's you," I whispered.

Damn the person or deity or whomever that created hope. It was a terrible, cruel thing. As insidious and hard to remove as weeds in a garden.

Now that the statement was out there, that Stella was in my arms, a picture was starting to take form. Dim and unformed, the sensual possibilities of it was stealing my good sense and giving my desires far too much power. What little of this idea I saw, it gave me hope that all the impossibilities that were plaguing the three of us had a very simple solution if we were only brave enough to seize it.

*If anyone could handle us...it really is her. Us...both of us...*

I shook my head and released her. This wasn't smart. This would make the mission impossible, a failure that I, and the rest of the world, could ill afford.

*The mission...the mission has to come first.*

Stella stood there for a moment before heading to the kitchen and pouring herself a glass of water. I kept my back to her, focused on the view of the city skyline, on the lingering smell of lasagna, on anything really that might distract me from this insanity.

"Isaac must've been pretty damn worried," she chuckled. "Lasagna *and* banana bread."

I snorted, unable to help myself.

"He muttered the whole time."

"Yeah, that's him alright."

The soft affection in her voice was impossible to miss. She cared for him, wanted him.

And she wanted me too, that was undeniable.

Slowly, painfully, I shut away the longing Isaac and Stella had awakened until my mind was sharp and cold once again. This was right, this was what was needed in this moment.

I took a deep breath and was about to suggest that she go home to shower when Isaac came breezing in.

"Okay, I have an idea of how we can keep Stella safe," he declared, his glamour falling in a second and revealing what was fast becoming my new favorite color of Gargoyle skin.

"Oh, really?" Stella said from the kitchen. "Do tell."

Isaac spun around, eyes wide and mouth agape.

"Oh, I uh...well, um..."

And now he was blushing.

"Bloody hell, you two are going to be the death of me," I whispered, forgetting that though Isaac was half Gargoyle he probably still had very good hearing.

Which was proven when he grinned at me over his shoulder.

*The fucker is actually enjoying my discomfort.*

I leveled a heated glare at him and punctuated it with a growl that sent a new flush of color to his face, and a fire in his eyes.

"So, Stella is the only one that can go into the club right?" Isaac said, doing his best to move on.

"Right," I said.

"Wrong. Ben never said we couldn't go in the club, he said we couldn't stake it out."

"But you two won't get in without a member or an invitation--" Stella began and then her eyes became wide, forkful of lasagna hanging in the air in front of her mouth. "Oh holy shit."

"Yep!" Isaac said, nodding triumphantly.

"Since I don't share your apparent telepathy, will one of you fill me in?" I asked.

"I can get one of you into the club. You'd just have to come as my guest," Stella said. "But we'd have to keep the fact that we're investigating on the down low and sell the story that you're just there as my guest."

"And what would that entail?" I asked.

Stella's smile bloomed as she turned to Isaac and I was instantly jealous.

"How do you feel about being my sub?" she asked him.

Isaac stared at her, the playful bravado gone though he flushed even deeper this time and his dick stirred in his shorts.

"I think we've already established that I like the idea," his voice was husky.

"And what will I be doing while the two of you play?" I asked, the snarl in my voice far more forceful than I'd intended.

But it was hard to hold it back when envy had poisoned my blood in seconds at the thought of Stella and Isaac in that club, playing those parts.

*Except it's not just playing for them. They both want it.*
And that realization made it worse.

"You said you have some really small cameras right?" Isaac asked.

"Yeah."

"Small enough to hide on a collar?"

I knew exactly where they were going with this and I hated how much it stung that I was getting left out.

"Probably," I said, doing my best to put up my walls so they didn't see how this plan was affecting me.

"Use your influence with the department to get a surveillance van," Stella said, voice going into planning mode. "Then you can observe from there and see if you notice anything we don't."

"You can also keep an eye on us."

"You should stay in your glamour," Stella said to Isaac, "just in case the killer really is getting his victims from there, we don't want him getting any ideas about you."

Isaac nodded.

"And you think just being led around by her will be enough to keep Ben away?" I asked Isaac.

"Maybe, maybe not," he admitted. "But it does mean I'm right there if he does anything."

I glanced at Stella, expecting her to protest that she didn't need Isaac there for that. But instead she slipped her hand into Isaacs and gave him a grateful grin.

"He'll be pissed that I'm there with someone as cute as you," she said, bopping Isaac on his nose and getting a dimpled grin in response. "But he also won't be able to get me alone. As my sub you'll be with me the whole time. It's a good plan and it doesn't sideline me. Thank you."

"Any time," he said, puppy dog eyes grazing over her.

I felt like an intruder and as much as I would've liked to shatter this damn moment, I chose instead to retreat to my room while the two of them discussed how the dynamic would play out tonight.

Once the door was closed, I fell onto my bed and put my face in my hands.

How the hell had all this gotten so out of hand? I'd learned a long time ago that there was no such thing as a simple mission since artifacts were often times the very definition of wild cards. But I had thought I'd gotten pretty good at anticipating the possibilities, seeing the curves in the road coming in enough time to compensate for them.

But with Isaac and Stella, my feelings for them had come at me from a blind spot I hadn't even known I'd had. If I really stopped and thought about it, my desire for Stella was easily explained by leftover angst and emotions from our time together. It was the sudden strength of my feelings for Isaac that I didn't have an explanation for. Why was I loathe to use this connection for information? I'd never been squeamish about a honey pot before. Yet the thought of only fucking Isaac to find out if he was a traitor left me cold inside. I wanted more than that, and I certainly couldn't stand the thought of hurting him when he found out I was just using this lust to ferret out information.

And now here I was, longing to force my way into the operation as their Dom. Wanting to explore all the filthy things I never got a chance to with Stella and bringing Isaac in as well. It was tempting to let my mind wander to all the lurid and obscene things I'd do with the two of them, but I'd already opened a fucking Pandora's box of sexual frustrations that was throwing me off my game. I refused to add to it.

So I snagged my tablet off my nightstand and began to assemble all the information we had on Ben into helpful diagrams and graphics so I could create a digital whiteboard and see it all spread out. We'd uncovered the fact that his identity was fabricated, but every attempt to peel away the lies to get the truth about who he used to be was a dead end.

I tapped out a message to the tech team, asking them to look into it. There were firewalls upon firewalls that were far beyond my skill level. I received a response within minutes letting me know that the process was highly involved and could take a day or two.

A snarl wound its way through my clenched teeth. Patience was eluding me on this mission. I wanted those knives *now* so I could put this case to rest and get the hell out of here before I made a mistake that bound me to these two in a way I wouldn't want to extricate myself from.

*Though I fear, it may already be too late for that.*

# CHAPTER NINE

## STELLA

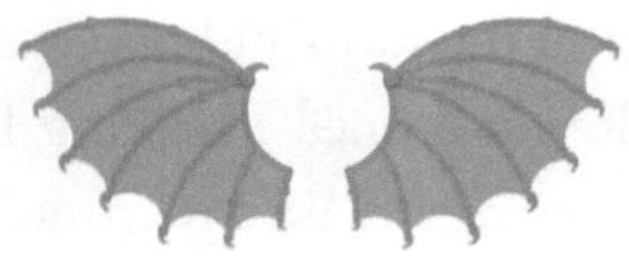

Both of us ignored the way James had fled the room and kept talking over what Isaac thought he'd like, what he didn't and came up with a good plan on what to do at the club. It would be enough to sell the illusion without venturing into one of the rooms unless we wanted to. Isaac had been more than willing to take it all the way if we both wanted that, even if it meant letting James see the entire show.

"I do need to ask you something," Isaac said, not quite meeting my eye. "I am attracted to James and he's made it clear that he's attracted to me too. I know we aren't together but I feel like with everything that's been happening between us lately--"

"You want my permission to fuck James?"

He nodded, guilt and hope shining in those gorgeous purple eyes of his.

I would've been lying if I'd said that there wasn't an ember of jealousy burning away in my chest. I wanted to be the ham in that Gargoyle sandwich, and I was certain that I never would be, which was fine. I'd be a fool to risk letting James back into my life like that.

*Now why the hell does that hurt so much?*

The answer was staring me in the face every time I glimpsed the tenderness in James' eyes when he looked at Isaac. But it was only a small thing, it never stuck around for long, and so I was consoled that maybe Isaac was just a quick fuck for James. They'd get it out of their systems and then it would be Isaac and me again. Still, I had to ask the one question that was eating me up inside right now.

"What does that mean for us?" I whispered, heart pounding at how fucking vulnerable this was.

"I still want you," Isaac said. "So I guess, the question is, would you mind sharing me?"

I took a sharp inhale and clasped Isaac's hands in mine.

"I'd be okay with that," I finally answered.

"You sure?" Isaac asked, eyeing me with concern.

"Am I without any qualms whatsoever about it? No. Am I secure in the knowledge that while you want to get railed by James you still want this ass? Hell, yes."

Isaac snorted out a laugh that had his eyes dancing and me smiling back in spite of how my heart thundered in my chest.

"I need time to get ready for tonight," I said, breaking the moment, "so if that's all, I should get going."

We hugged, an odd and stupidly awkward moment considering what we were going to be doing later tonight. But it had been cute to see Isaac flushed and stumbling over his words as he walked me to the elevator.

I took my time when I got home with a long bath, getting into the right head space and pampering myself in a way I hadn't in a long time. My fridge was pretty bare but I managed to find some fruit and cheese to give me a little something in my stomach so I wasn't hangry later tonight. As I passed the bottle of Jack on my counter, I found myself utterly uninterested for the first time in a long while.

With a flutter of excitement in my belly, it was time to get my Dom outfits out of their case. It had been so very long since I'd worn them, and even though tonight technically wasn't about the kink, I couldn't help being excited to be immersed in the world I loved.

My Dom outfits were about the only things, besides my sidearm, that I was fussy about keeping in good condition. They were in a special garment case that took up half my walk in closet. A smaller case next to it held my toys, floggers, riding crops, paddles, collars, nipple clamps and a variety of other things.

Opening it was like stepping back in time. I ran my hand down the leather of my favorite micro skirt, the one that showed my crotch if I so much as leaned over too far. It was black with tiny red kisses on the hem. I always wore it with a red thong to torment my sub with seeing what they couldn't have. Next to it was my red and black halter and a box of my favorite pasties. I had intended to wear my leather pants tonight but one look at this outfit and I changed my mind.

*Though, where is James going to put the camera...*

An image of James seeing me in this outfit, the way his nostrils would flare, the only outward sign besides his cock that he was aroused, hit me and I clenched my thighs together. He'd been jealous of Isaac, so much so that he'd gone to his room to pout.

I let the soft strands of a flogger run through my fingers and wondered what it would be like to be stretched across James' lap in this skirt, his hand reddening my ass.

*Stop. You need to focus on Isaac tonight, he's your sub.*

I opened the third case. It was a long rectangle and contained some of my most expensive items.

A selection of four high quality wigs.

"Hello, gorgeous," I whispered, and picked one up.

I never, ever played as a Dom with my real hair. The wig was my final piece of costume, the thing that took me from Stella to Mistress Magdalena. And the one I held in my hands was my favorite. A red-brown color, the ponytail high up on my head. Sugar had helped me figure out wigs, how to wear them and what looked good on me.

And while I was a little rusty, the mechanics of putting it on came back to me fairly easily.

I had told Isaac and James that it would take me several hours to prepare and they didn't even blink, for which I was grateful. Putting on my Mistress persona was not something I ever rushed. It was as close to sacred as I ever got, and even though this was for a case, I wouldn't treat it with any less importance as I did any other time I put it on.

By the time I was done, and drove to James' penthouse, there was a certain amount of pride and strength that coursed through me that I realized I'd missed terribly. I took the backbone, the courage I'd learned from Dawn with me every day, that was true. But there was something about becoming Mistress Magdalena again that was different. It was a role, a thing I put on, but that didn't mean it was fake. It was, in some ways, a more real version of me than Stella ever was.

I was wearing a long black trench coat over my outfit, but I was also wearing a shit ton of makeup, a wig that added about four inches to my height, along with thigh high stiletto boots that added another six, so I was well over six feet tall. Usually that meant I towered over any sub I had, but I knew that with Isaac, this should put me at just a little over his height in his glamour.

When I walked into the penthouse I set my bag of things for Isaac down on the absurdly huge couch and started to get down to business.

"I have the collar, though I don't really know how you're attaching much to it," I said just before turning to them. "Were you able to get a backup just in case?"

James and Isaac were standing facing one another with James' hands on the leather harness that Isaac wore. Both males stared at me, Isaac's mouth gaping open. James, on the other hand, appeared unaffected, but I knew better by the way his eyes roamed down my body, the scorch of them when they eventually locked onto mine. I was pleased with the fact that he was pretty damn aroused just at the sight of me.

I smirked at them and slid the trench coat off. I thought Isaac's jaw was going to hit the floor and the growl that rolled up from James' throat had my pussy wet instantly. But, as I was trained to do, I refused to show it. Instead I walked over with a seductive roll to my hips, not caring that both males were ready to eat me alive.

I ran a fingertip down Isaacs spine and he shivered. He was dressed in very tight black lycra shorts that cupped his ass and cock perfectly. In his glamour, Isaac was a fucking Adonis and I wanted to run my tongue over the curve of that ass just before taking a bite.

"Nice," I murmured.

"Thank you, Mistress," Isaac answered, breathless.

I glanced at James over his shoulder and I almost bowed my head at the feral, commanding look that met me.

Isaac was between us, James' hands curled possessively around the leather that crisscrossed Isaac's chest, and my hands were on Isaac's shoulders as he trembled. It all felt so natural, so perfect. I wanted to reach across Isaac's body, draw James closer and beg to kiss him while Isaac was trapped between us.

And from the scorching heat in James' gaze, I knew he wanted something similar.

I gave him a grin instead, to hide the desire and pain my chest. It would take something simple and yet more than a few hugs for James to earn my trust again.

"Is our Isaac ready?" I purred.

Isaac took a sharp breath in at that, and then I saw the back of James' hands graze Isaac's erect nipples.

"Yes," James voice was rough, the deep timber rumbling over my clit like a graze.

"Good," I turned Isaac around, letting the tips of my breasts brush against him but not giving him permission to touch me. "Now, be a good boy and let us figure out which collar to give you."

Isaac bowed his head, cock straining the front of his shorts already.

We hadn't even left for the club and already we had slipped into our roles so effortlessly. I doubted, there and then, that Isaac and I would be able to end the night without getting one of us off.

I followed James to the table where the special cameras were and tried very hard to keep my equilibrium. I was Mistress, I was indomitable. And yet, in his presence the desire to kneel, to worship him was almost overwhelming.

Like a lot of Doms, I'd started as a sub and had found that I could be a switch with the right partner. The catch was that very few these days brought the sub out in me. James was not only bringing it out, he was making me want it deep in my soul.

"James," I whispered.

His sharp gaze swung to me and I had to force myself to hold it.

"Are you sure this is alright with you? Things might get intimate. I don't want you being uncomfortable."

He smoldered as he turned to me, body rigid with self-control, and I wondered if he was like this as a Dom too. Controlled, cold, and imperious.

I clamped down on the thought and forced my lust-addled brain to focus.

"Are you asking me if I'll hate watching the two of you fuck if it comes to that?" he responded.

"Yes."

He hesitated for a moment. And when he answered, his words had me trembling.

"I like to watch. And I think I'd especially like to watch the two of you. So no, I won't be bothered."

I scrambled to get control, to hold onto my power as Mistress Magdalena.

"Should I get you some lube for your time in the van?" I asked, with a smirk.

The bastard saw what I was doing and leaned toward me with a sexy quirk of his lips. His breath skated across my cheek as he whispered in my ear, "No, I'll let Isaac take care of it later."

*Fuck!*

I stepped back, simultaneously more turned on than I'd ever been in my life and furious.

"Not if I exhaust him first." I snapped my fingers, not even looking at Isaac, as he made his way toward me. "Time for your collar, pet."

"Yes, Mistress."

James' gaze stayed locked on mine, cords of muscle standing out on his arms as his hands clenched into fists. It was the only outward sign that he was affected by what I'd done, but it was enough.

I held my hand out for the collar, testing to see if he'd give it to me to put on or do it himself. The tension around us pulsed.

In the end, James placed the collar in my hand, but brushed the inside of my wrist and my palm with the sharp sting of his claws. A concession and a show of what I could have if I wanted it. And god help me, did I want it.

The collar James had chosen was simple at a glance. Black leather with a chrome ring in the front. But there was the most intricate detail of a winding vines on the surface, tiny studded flowers punctuating the smooth design here and there. The design would hide the wire and the camera perfectly.

Next came what I was sure was a microphone, which was similarly hidden on the harness.

"There's a wire in the microphone that will let me get a signal for the security cameras. I'll be tapped into those as well, so we should have very good coverage."

"What powers it?" I asked, trying to examine the tiny devices without touching them.

"It's a trade secret," James said with a wink.

I rolled my eyes.

"Would you have to kill me if you told me?"

"Something like that," the words were simple enough, but the tone promised dark things that made my skin tingle. "Now for yours."

"I don't really have many hiding places, but you're welcome to try and find one."

Even with the nearly foot of extra height my wig and shoes supplied me, James still towered over me as he came up close. He didn't have his wings out, as usual, but his body eclipsed me with the broad expanse of his chest, shoulders and hips. He was so fiercely beautiful up close, a beastly thing of nightmares to some. But to me he embodied the kind of other worldly power that heated my blood, and made my better judgment leave the building. Again, James teased my skin with his claws, but this time it was my neck as he swept the hair off my shoulder and into one of his giant hands.

"I'm going to put it in your wig," he held out a small hair pin.

"Be careful. I'm serious when I say I will take the cost of the wig out on your flesh."

"I wouldn't dare ruin such a masterpiece."

He secured the hair pin at the apex of the ponytail and secured the wire within the thick tresses falling down my bare back.

"There," he whispered in my ear, "no harm done."

I turned, something snarky and brilliant on my lips, but I couldn't breathe, much less speak. He was so close, I could smell the spice of him and the ozone of his innate magic. His hungry eyes darted to my red lips, and I knew he wanted a taste. But, in typical James fashion, he eased himself away and turned back to the dining room table with all its files, laptops and gadgets.

"You're both set," he said. "I'll follow behind you and park on the street but at a discreet distance from the club."

"Got it," I turned to Isaac, "you got a jacket that goes with that?"

He snorted and glanced up at me through his lashes. His smile produced those dimples I loved so much and I swore to myself that tonight I would finally nibble on them if I had the chance.

"I do actually," he said and produced a biker jacket in response.

My laugh echoed through the penthouse as he put it on and modeled it for me.

"What do you think?"

"I think you're almost too adorable and I'm going to have so much fun making you blush tonight," I said.

His blue eyes sparked with heat.

"I'm at your mercy, Mistress."

I blew out a breath and shook my head.

"You may come to regret that."

I'd visited the club just that morning, but that had been the back, which was normal by comparison to the erotic banquet of sights that met me when I stepped through the door of the main room.

Most think sex clubs are dingy places where body fluids coat every surface in a sticky miasma that is anything but conducive to sex. And, maybe some are like that. But not the Hearts and Swords Club. Dawn had this place cleaned thoroughly every single day, every toy was sterilized after use by the staff, every surface scrubbed and polished to a gleam. Most never noticed the scantily clad on-site cleaning staff that wiped everything down behind each person that used a spanking bench, stocks or Saint Andrew's cross. But before I left, I had been one of her right hand Doms, I knew every little secret about this place.

*Except what piece of shit patron is using it to source his victims.*

The main room was wide and deep, with dark red and black wallpaper and gleaming black floors. Booths were scattered throughout, some small enough for only two or three people. Others were huge, meant for groups. To my right was the always well-stocked bar, black and red polished surfaces that looked like diamonds on a playing card. Above us was a vaulted ceiling, black and nebulous. Hanging from the center was a black chandelier with what looked like hundreds of candles set into it. At first glance, it appeared that the twisting black tendrils that made up the chandelier were abstract, nothing more than random pieces. But if one were to study it, they'd see that it was comprised of bodies, hundreds of them grasping and clutching at one another in an orgy of passion. Each fake candle was held by a hand reaching up from the writhing mass of bodies.

Sconces lined the walls, the light partially eclipsed in red shades and providing just enough illumination to barely puncture the darkness of the room. To my left was a hallway, also bathed in red and black, that led to the public playroom. To the back of the room and to the right, I could glimpse a wide staircase that always reminded me of the one in Scarlett and Rhett's house in "Gone with the Wind". It led patrons up to the private rooms, one of which I'd reserved with Dawn, just in case.

I took all of this in, cataloguing who was here, who I knew and didn't. There were far more new faces than I would've liked. I hated to admit that I'd been looking forward to seeing some of my old friends.

*But I suppose I should be glad they aren't here. If they were, they'd be in danger.*

Beside me, Isaac gave a shuddering breath and I glanced at him to make sure he was alright. This could be overwhelming if one wasn't used to it. Earlier today, Isaac had admitted that he'd never actually been to a club like this. He'd barely begun to explore his love of being restrained, of being disciplined. He'd said it all with a deep flush on his face and with shy glances at me. It was so sweet I'd almost fucked him right there in James' penthouse.

I pulled on the shiny leash attached to his collar and he leaned toward me.

"Color?" I asked.

"Green," he whispered.

He didn't have a safe word, so we were using the color system instead. Green was 'everything is fine, I'm good, I want to keep going'. Yellow was 'I need to slow it down'. And red was, of course, 'full stop'.

I ran my fingers through his hair, pulling a little along the way but ultimately it was meant to soothe him. Isaac leaned into my touch and let out a long breath.

"Come on."

I led him over to the bar, slowly, as if I wanted everyone to see the pretty little thing I had on the end of my leash. And, in truth, I very much did.

Isaac's outfit was downright plain compared to most others here, but that was fine. *He* was the real attraction. The perfect tan of his skin, the way his muscles bunched and rolled as he moved. The oddly endearing and vulnerable sight of his bare feet on the floor.

I felt dozens of pairs of eyes follow us. Some were on me, and I felt their desires like a caress along my skin. Others were for Isaac, and I would bet even money that, by the end of the night, I'd have several invitations to some group play. But that wasn't what we were here for.

*And besides, the only one I want to play with us is stuck out in the damn van.*

There was no way to hide an ear piece so we had no communication with James. He would know if we were in trouble though, and that was enough. At least, it better be.

When I stepped up to the bar, I recognized the corset clad bartender and couldn't help my grin or the light feeling in my chest.

"What are you still doing here, Sapphire?" I asked the tall, bald Gryphon.

They turned toward me, vertical slits surrounded by yellow and orange met mine and extended canines shone when they smiled. Fine golden fur covered them from the collarbone down to their feet, their dark claws were painted a blood red and intricate tattoos decorated the light brown skin on their face.

They threw their head back and gave a deep throated laugh as they ran around the bar and took me in a bear hug. Usually, I had rules about touching me while I was in my Mistress persona, but Sapphire was family, just as much as Dawn was so I let it pass.

Gryphons are a rare Supernatural that most don't even know exist. Glamours tended to react oddly to Gryphons, causing enough of their true form to slip through that it made it hard for them to blend in, so they were still forced to stay hidden. Here, Sapphire's appearance was simply seen as eccentric role playing by most, since the Supernatural community generally denied the existence of beings like Sapphire. But I was one of the few that knew differently. Sapphire's magic had been stripped long ago, and their clan had abandoned them. And so they had been near feral and starving when Dawn had found them and brought them in here. Sapphire wasn't interested in the sex aspect of the club so much, though they did partake now and then. So Dawn had put them to work behind the bar.

"You bitch," Sapphire said, pulling away and wiping tears from their cheeks. "I missed you!"

"I missed you too."

Their eyes glanced behind me where I knew Isaac stood, head bowed as I'd instructed him to do before we entered.

"New friend?" they asked.

"Something like that."

They shook their head and laughed again before leaning close and whispering in my ear.

"Why are you really here?"

"Information," I said, running a hand over Sapphire's furry shoulder to act as though we might be hitting on each other. "Someone is killing Supernaturals and Mundanes from here. I need to know who."

Sapphire took in a sharp breath.

"I'll keep an eye and ear out."

"Thank you."

They went back behind the bar to help out the other bartender, but not before setting a club soda with lime in front of me with a wink. Sapphire knew that I didn't drink when I was here, ever. I had a hard time finding the "off" switch when it came to drinking in an atmosphere like this and there was no way it was safe for me to do any BDSM while intoxicated.

I began to take sip of the drink, aware of Isaac still behind me, still waiting for me and still quite aroused. Just as I set the glass down, fully intending to keep Isaac waiting a bit longer, a hand reached out to touch my arm.

The riding crop that I'd set on the bar was in my hand in an instant, and I blocked the unwelcomed touch. I turned to face the person who would dare do such a thing and found myself face to face with Ben. My heart stuttered in my chest and I almost withdrew the riding crop in fear of his retaliation. But then I my senses zeroed in on the feel of the crop in my hand, the way I looked down at him in my stilettos.

I wasn't Stella.

I was Mistress Magdalena. And *no one* touched Mistress Magdalena without her permission.

*Especially not him.*

In spite of the cold sweat that started to break out on my palms, I forced my spine to straighten, and my eyes to narrow. I slipped, at least partially, into that space where my power resided, where I was the one in control. And Ben couldn't touch me.

His jaw clenched and he moved his hand from where the riding crop had stopped him. I could feel Isaac vibrating with rage behind me, but I wouldn't allow him to rescue me. I didn't need it, because I wasn't some wilting flower right now. I was powerful, strong and no one could take that from me.

"That was a bit rude," he snapped. "I was just saying hello."

"Say it with your mouth, standing right there, and keep your hands to yourself."

Red tinged his face and his brown eyes widened.

"This is my club and I--"

"Can't do anything to me," I slapped the ridding crop in my palm and widened my stance. "Do you know what I do to people who touch me without permission?"

"I'm not--"

"No, you're not. You're not my sub and I'm not your Dom. I'm not your *anything*, Ben, and I never will be. And you may own some of this club, but you obviously don't know the rules, so allow me to educate you so you don't embarrass yourself any further."

By now the patrons around us had quieted down and were watching us with wary glances. They didn't know if this was part of a scene or something more serious, and the way some of them wouldn't look at Ben had me wondering how many lines he'd crossed here with people who had found a place of belonging here, as I had.

Rage ran through my blood, burning away some of the lingering fear. I did not lose control in this persona, not ever. I could get mad, but I controlled that feeling, it never ran roughshod over me. Even so, I was definitely having a hard time doing that when faced with the man who had made me feel so damn powerless.

*Not powerless anymore.*

"Consent is everything here," I began, my voice hard, unforgiving. "It is our god, our unbreakable rule. I did not give consent for you to touch me and yet you thought you could. You can't."

He just glared at me, lips pressed so tight they'd gone white. The glint of a silver chain around his neck caught the low light, and a ripple of something passed over my skin but then was gone. I didn't let it get to me though.

I tilted my head to the side, as if I were studying him. And, I was, but not in the way he wanted. I wanted to push him so he left, but not so much that he took anything out on the people around him.

*Just a little more I think.*

"Perhaps a demonstration is in order," I snapped my fingers at Isaac and he came up beside me.

"Yes, Mistress?"

I cupped his jaw, nails digging slightly into his skin.

"Kiss me."

His nostrils flared, pupils dilated. This was the moment we'd both waited for with baited breath all this time.

"Yes, Mistress," his breath ghosted across my face just before he took my mouth.

And I do mean he *took* it. I'd given him permission, and Isaac wasn't being shy now. His hands were fists at his side, but my body ignited as if he were touching me everywhere. His tongue plundered my mouth, delving and curling against mine and I recognized the different texture of a Gargoyle tongue.

*Clever boy, you unglamoured your tongue for me.*

Gargoyle tongues weren't just thicker than a human's, they were longer and very, very dexterous. He twined it around mine, pulling before releasing it only to nip at my bottom lip. I bit him back, hard enough to draw a bead of blood. He gasped but I consumed the sound, my hand clutching his face to hold him in place.

When we parted, I was blissfully unaware of our audience for a moment. There was only Isaac, his red mouth, his piercing gaze of adoration. We'd danced around that kiss for a year now, I'd begun to wonder if we would ever cross the line. Now that we had, I knew that my fears had been right.

If he let me, I'd keep him forever.

"Thank you," his voice was ragged with need and I didn't need to look down at his crotch to see that he was fully erect.

"You've pleased me," my voice was just barely controlled. "You may choose a reward, what do you want?"

"The spanking bench, please."

The request surprised me for a moment. I had thought he'd ask to go down on me in one of the private rooms.

*All in good time, I suppose.*

"Go, choose the one you want and wait for me. Do not do anything to relieve your arousal or I will be very, very displeased."

"Yes, Mistress."

I unhooked the leash from his collar and waved him on toward the hallway.

As if I had all the time in the world, I turned toward Ben. His jaw was clenched hard enough to crack a tooth, chest heaving with fury. There was a time when the look on his face would've had me fleeing his penthouse in fear. But I wasn't that same woman, and this wasn't his domain.

*It's mine. And it's Dawn's and everyone else who calls it home, I don't care what a piece of paper says.*

"Now do you understand? Or would you like another demonstration?"

I knew he understood that I was asking about more than the issue of consent. I was telling him that he would never, ever have me, that I was far removed from him and I would never be at his mercy again.

It was almost entertaining to watch him gather the tatters of his pride around him and act like I hadn't just dressed him down in the most visceral way. With great effort, Ben straightened his button up and gave me a tight smile.

"That was very entertaining. Maybe I'll watch you flog that pretty boy sub of yours."

The last thing I wanted was for Ben to be there at such an intimate moment, but I'll be damned if I showed him that. So I shrugged and turned my back on him. On the outside, I hoped I appeared calm, unruffled because inside, the combination of personal power, fear and anger was making me shake like crazy. My hand trembled just a bit on the club soda and Sapphire came over.

"You good?" they whispered.

"Yeah," I answered. "I'll be fine."

"Dawn doesn't let him harass anyone, if you're worried about that. But..."

My eyes snapped to them.

"What?"

"He got to one of the new girls. Pretty little blond thing, and none of us see her much anymore. She's usually waiting for him upstairs. I've gotten good at keeping tabs on her but he's isolating her more and more."

"Name?"

"Patty."

"I'll see what I can do."

Sapphire nodded.

"If I see anything at all I'll let ya know."

"Thanks."

The conversation was just what I needed. It focused me on the task at hand, on the innocent people I was trying to save. Ben was an unexpected monster from my past, but he was one I could handle. And tonight it was about finding answers.

*And about Isaac.*

I was surprised he asked for the spanking bench, but also excited. It had been a while for me, and I relished the way a good flogging could undo a person. I'd have to pay special attention to Isaac's reactions though. He was new to all of this, and he may not know his limits. It would be up to me to keep him safe. Which meant I couldn't let Ben throw me off.

I didn't know why Isaac felt he needed to be punished but it didn't matter. I would deliver his sweet punishment, and then I'd kiss away the tears.

# CHAPTER TEN

## ISAAC

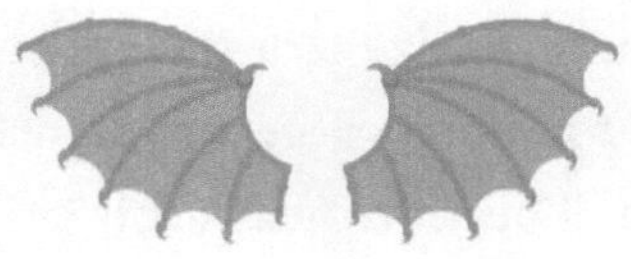

I was surprised that I could find my way to the public play room after watching Stella be a fucking Amazon and then kiss me back like she owned me. The moment she'd walked through the door at James', I was longing to feel the sharp sting of her lash my skin, hear the sinful purr of her voice in my ear, telling me how good I was. When she finally spoke to me tonight I was already half drunk with the relief of it.

I'd always known she was strong, no one could be around her for five minutes and not see that. But Stella as Mistress was something else entirely. It was as if she kept the true breadth of her strength caged and only let it out when she was in this persona. To be the one she paid attention to was intoxicating. I was precious, special and I desperately wanted more.

My legs shook with both unfulfilled need and leftover anger at her piece of shit ex, as I made my way down the hall and to the play room. The second I rounded the corner, I had to stop as sensations flew at me at lightning speed.

The room was bigger than the main bar area, but I suppose it would have to be. The walls in here were a slightly lighter red and the floor was the same shiny black, but there were red hearts scattered into the stone. There was a small raised platform that seemed to act as some kind of stage at the center of the room where someone was being tied with Shibari rope while several couples watched on black leather couches. To my left was a woman cuffed to a Saint Andrew's cross being flogged by a mountain of an Orc with dark green skin and huge tusks. Another man was in a set of stocks as a Harpy pegged him, her razor sharp teeth gleaming in the low light.

It took me a moment to realize that the couches made a ring around the center platform, a row facing the stage area and another row that faced out to the walls. The light was a bit brighter in here, but not by much. My Gargoyle sight allowed me to see clearer than most Mundanes, so I could easily recognize the red stripes on one woman's buttocks as a beautiful female Werewolf striped her with a cane. The room wasn't full, but there was enough going on that I could've stared for hours just watching the unashamed freedom in this room. I wasn't raised with the belief that sex was bad, but there were limits. The first time someone accidentally scratched my wing during sex, and the jolt of pain caused me to orgasm harder than I ever had, I knew that I wanted something different than what was acceptable to my more "traditional" family and friends.

I'd tried to seek it out as I got older, but there was always something missing. Either the partner wasn't really into it, or they didn't listen. I realized, as I finally made my way to a red leather spanking bench along the center of the right wall, that this might be the first time I had ever been with someone like this whom I completely trusted.

Anticipation was a heady drug, warm and brutal as it coursed through my veins. I didn't know if Stella would want my hands bound into the cuffs that were attached to the ring at one end, so I simply waited. And the longer I did, the more I trembled, the more my mind conjured what this could be like. The sounds of people crying out, begging, punctuated by the slap of things against flesh was ramping up everything until I began to grind against the bench, desperate for sensation to take the edge off. I hadn't been touched yet, not really, but everything around me was a caress on my mind, riling up every suppressed fantasy and desire until it was raw and exposed.

A sharp slap on my ass had my body stilling against the red leather.

"Did I tell you that you could get off?" Stella asked, imperious and so damn sexy.

"No, Mistress. I'm sorry."

She walked around to the end of the bench and slipped my hands into the soft cuffs.

"Color?"

I gazed up at her, letting all the adoration I'd hidden, all the longing and desire that had been growing for the past year into my eyes.

"Green."

There was only the flicker of recognition in her eyes to tell me that she saw everything I couldn't say but wanted to. Stella ran her nails through my hair and down my face before stepping away.

On the wall behind me was a variety of spanking instruments. When we'd talked earlier, I had confessed that I wanted to experience this for the first time with her. Stella had been turned on by it, and now here we were; me so aroused that I was shaking while she slowly chose what she was going to use.

When the first kiss of a flogger fell across my shoulders, a sobbing moan flew from my mouth before I could stop it. It was sharp and stung, and yet felt so damn good. She did it again, and again, over my shoulders until I was sure red marks were beginning to appear. I was aware that I was crying out, but it wasn't just about the pain. Something was happening inside of me, a burden started to shake loose from my soul the longer she struck me.

When she moved down to my ass, the tight fabric of my shorts added to the sting and my eyes watered. The longer she did it, the more I longed for her to touch me and yet also didn't want it to stop. I had been holding on for so long; to my fears about the Protectors, to my fears that I wasn't good enough to be Stella's partner. And now, all of that fell away until there was nothing but me and her. I wasn't a traitor, I wasn't a spy. I wasn't the guy that didn't ever really fit in his Gargoyle family or his Mundane family. I was just *me*, stripped down to the essentials of my being with each lash.

By the time Stella stopped, I was hazy, almost drunk from the release. And it wasn't about my cock, no that was still rock hard. This release was something deeper, more profound. I was only a little surprised to find tears on my face as Stella uncuffed me. She squatted down in front of me and raised my head with a deceptively gentle touch.

"Oh, sweet boy," she murmured.

Then she was kissing my tears away, consuming the poison that she'd lanced from me.

A ragged sob escaped me and I started to reach for her, but stopped.

"Please," I begged.

"What do you want?"

"To touch you? Please?"

She gave me a gentle smile and brought my hand to her face. It was a lifeline, drawing me back to myself enough to sit up when she got to her feet. For a second my head spun. If not for her arms steadying me, I would've fallen off the bench.

"Slowly, pet," she whispered, so soft and soothing.

When I dismounted the bench my knees shook but I could walk. Still, Stella's arms were around me, checking in with her eyes. Her hand grazed my back and I hissed at the pain.

"Color?"

I was going to just say 'green' but I stopped and thought first. I was sore, but it wasn't unpleasant.

*And we haven't really had a good look around yet.*

It was almost funny that I'd forgotten the real reason she and I were here in the first place.

"Green," I said, giving her a soft grin.

When she reattached the leash to my collar, I had expected her to lead us back into the main room. Instead, she led us around the perimeter of the play room, her gaze appraising as she watched those in the middle of different scenes. I was surprised to see so many more Supernaturals and Mundanes here than when I'd first climbed onto the bench. There was nearly every kind of Supernatural with the notable exception of Gargoyles. I filed that away, hoping I'd actually remember it in the riot of sensations that were still assaulting my senses.

Each moan, slap, cry, each glimpse of bodies colliding and pleasuring each other, had me feeling a little more out of my body.

*Now I know how Alice felt falling through the rabbit hole.*

At last, Stella led us to a couch near the raised platform in the middle. We were facing the entrance to the room with a good peripheral view of the walls to the right and left. Stella motioned for the seat next to her and I climbed up, legs tucked beneath me. Stella leaned toward me, and I closed my eyes, trembling for whatever she was about to do. Her lips grazed my ear as she whispered.

"Angle your body a little so James can see the back wall in the camera."

*Yes...work, of course.*

My disappointment must've shown on my face because Stella nipped my chin with her teeth and ran her nails down my back. I hissed as pain radiated from the welts there.

"Patience, pet," she cooed, "more to come."

The person who was tied up before was replaced by a different one, who was now suspended above the platform, her face a mask of pure, undiluted ecstasy.

"Sub space," Stella said, idly running her fingers over more of the welts on my back. "Do you know what that is?"

"No, Mistress."

"It's the way you felt at the end of our session on the bench. For some, it's like being drunk and high all at once. For others, an out of body experience where nothing exists but pleasure and pain intertwined," her gaze turned to me and I found myself unable to hide my devotion. "It's different for everyone, but it's a wonderful state of being."

"I very much enjoyed it," I whispered.

Her gaze sharpened and she captured my mouth with hers. I once again unglamoured my tongue to wrestle with hers. Stella's taste was like nothing I'd ever had before. Spicy and wild, addictive. My hands ached to touch her, to know the heft of her breasts in my hands, the wetness of her cunt on my fingers.

But I hadn't been given permission, so I clenched them tight on my thighs and devoured her with my mouth and teeth.

When we parted, Stella was out of breath, shock on the edges of her calm, controlled gaze.

"I enjoyed getting you there," Stella said and it took me a moment to remember what she meant. "I...Isaac, this has all been so...unexpected."

I turned my head as she palmed my cheek and pressed a kiss to her wrist. Then, because she didn't stop me, I ran my lips further up her arm, delighting when she shivered at the nip of my teeth. I glanced at her, waiting for her to withdraw. But instead, Stella quirked an eyebrow and grinned at me.

"Well?" she asked, "are you going to finish what you started?"

I grinned against her skin.

"Yes, Mistress."

I unglamoured my mouth and teeth, nibbled her inner arm with my fangs as I sucked and kissed my way up. When I was at her shoulder, Stella's hands were in my hair, and she gave a sharp tug to pull me up to her mouth. The position was awkward as I tried to keep my body from colliding with hers, but when she pressed a hand to my back and I fell forward into her and groaned. My back was on fire, but it was a delicious contrast to the soft rasp of her skin and the fabric of her halter against my chest. Even with the harness, I could feel so much of her against me and I wanted more. I rubbed myself up and down her body, my cock brushing against her thigh.

"Oh god," my voice was guttural. "Mistress...please can I--"

I didn't even get the words out before Stella seized my wrist and shoved my hand under her skirt.

"Fuck me with your fingers," her voice was deep, hard with command. "And if you make me come hard enough, I'll suck your cock."

I held her gaze as I slid her thong aside and ran the knuckle of my finger through her hot, wet folds. The only sign that she was affected was the sharp inhale as I circled her clit.

"Your *real* fingers," she whispered. "Fuck me with your real fingers, Isaac."

Even though the glamour was essentially me, there was something far more intimate about shedding it as I touched her. My cock strained the front of my shorts, throbbing as I tried hard not to spend myself. There was already a wet patch from the precum that had leaked out of me. But as I shed the glamour on my hand, making sure my claws were retracted, and slid not one but two of my fingers inside Stella, I was sure that I wasn't going to be able to hold out much longer. She was tight and so perfect as I pumped in and out of her.

Stella bit off a whimper as she began to roll her hips, her nails digging into my shoulders. And still, I didn't look away, even though I wanted to see my fingers plunge in and out of her. I wanted to see the look she made when she came more. I wanted to see this strong, indomitable woman undone from being finger fucked by me.

She shifted and was now facing the stage, thighs spread as I pumped faster under her skirt. Whereas I was kneeling on the couch with my body facing the wall to her right.

As her hips rolled and bucked faster, and her nails speared into my skin as she bit her bottom lip, I realized that James was seeing and hearing all of this. And suddenly, that one thought, knowing that the male I wished was here with us, the only other being I wanted with as much ravenous hunger as I did Stella, was seeing us together, made me lose my restraint.

I fell to the floor between her parted thighs and began to bite my way up her thighs as I worked her harder.

"What do you think you're doing?" she panted.

"I want to eat your pussy." Gone was the bashful submissive. I was too lust drunk to care that I was attempting to top from the bottom.

Stella gave me a hazy grin and opened her legs wider.

"In front of all these people?" she asked.

I wasn't sure if it was a test to see if I was sure I really wanted to do this with an audience or not. But I took the question and decided to raise the emotional ante. I lunged forward and whispered in her ear, "I don't care about them. I only care about pleasing you and letting *him* watch."

If Stella's gasp was any indication, she knew exactly who I meant.

When I pulled back, she was biting her bottom lip again, rolling just a little against my fingers still buried inside of her.

"Private room." Then she finally asked, "green or red?"

There was no hesitation when I answered. "Green."

I had no idea if we'd done enough of a, undercover job or not, and I honestly didn't care. As Stella practically dragged me from the room and up the ridiculously wide staircase, I wasn't a detective, or an agent of the Protectors. I wasn't guilty or afraid. I'd been reduced to my base parts, a panting beast who was blind to everything but the promise of getting to run my tongue through Stella's wet slit.

I followed her down a dark hall and through a door with the number five on it. The room itself didn't register, just a space with walls and a bed that was inconsequential to the woman pulling my face to hers and kissing me like I was oxygen.

"Can I touch you?" I gasped out as soon as she let me go.

"I thought you wanted to eat me?"

"Yes, please."

Stella gave me a wicked grin and backed herself onto what I now saw was an enormous bed with manacles hanging from the wall at the head of it. She saw me look at them and chuckled.

"Next time, pet. Right now," she eased her boots and red lace thong off without taking off her skirt, "you have a job to do."

She barely had to pull her skirt up to expose a closely trimmed mons and a pink, glistening cunt. I fell to my knees between her legs, which she draped over my shoulders.

My thumbs parted her, exposing her clit peeking from its hood, begging to be tasted. Just before I dove in, Stella's voice stopped me.

"Take off your glamour."

I glanced up at bright eyes, intense with longing. We were in private, though I wondered if there were cameras in these rooms. It would be dangerous if the killer was in the security rooms and they could see in here. But I understood the request, why it was important. And I didn't want anything between us either, not even something as thin as my glamour.

As quickly as I could, I slipped off the tight shorts, because they wouldn't fit my Gargoyle form, and let out a throaty whimper as my cock sprang free.

"Don't even think about it," Stella demanded just as my hand was about to grab a hold of it. "That is *mine* and you don't come until I tell you."

"Mistress..."

She lunged off the bed and grasped me, and I cried out at the contact. It was too tight, bordering on pain, but I didn't care, my hips bucked of their own accord, desperate for anything to relieve the ache.

But Stella held me fast, only letting her thumb rub the tip where a thick layer of wetness was smeared over it.

"Glamour off. Pussy eaten. And then, if you please me, you'll have earned my mouth around your cock. Do we understand one another?"

I whimpered when she let me go but managed to whisper, "Yes, Mistress."

"Now," she sat back on the edge of the bed, pulled her skirt up once more and crooked her finger.

The glamour shed in a moment and the perspective of the room shifted as I grew taller. Suddenly Stella wasn't the same size as me, but smaller physically. Still, I was in her power, no matter my size, and I knelt again. This time, however, I pulled her legs over my shoulders and relished the sight of her open to me.

*To me and James. I hope he's enjoying himself.*

I had a brief, sharp wish that he was in the room with us, commanding us both. I decided to keep him in mind as best I could, to try and give him a good show and hope that next time, if there was one, he would be here with us.

How often had I imagined kissing her most sensitive spot? Making her cry my name as she let down her walls and let me see what no one else did? Not her body, though that was a god damn treat. I wanted to see her heart. And as I looked into her eyes I saw it there, shining just for me, the beauty that she so closely guarded.

My beautiful Stella.

*Mine...oh god...that's what it is.*

That pull in my chest was sharp, bright and it indeed was a string of sorts that bound us together. But before I could truly comprehend what it all meant, Stella had grabbed one of my horns and guided my mouth to her slit. The moment her scent hit me, nothing else matter but drinking my fill of her.

With a growl of hunger, I dragged my tongue through her in one long swipe, from her taint to her clit, and was rewarded with a trilling cry from Stella. My tongue dove through her folds again and again until I was fucking her with my tongue, which I was able to plunge deep inside of her and undulate, until I found her G spot.

"Fuck...oh my...god," Stella let out an obscene groan on the last word.

Her grip on my horns tightened and she rode my face hard. I was beginning to think that I'd be able to handle feasting on her without grinding myself against the bed, when her toes grazed the soft, sensitive membrane of my wing.

The groan that exploded from my mouth was the most obscene thing I'd ever heard.

"Color?" she asked, breathless.

"Green...green, please."

"Do I need to put a cock ring on you?"

"No...no I can-- ah!"

Her toes grazed my wing again. Up and down, up and down. Cold fire raced from my wings to my cock, a gloriously overwhelming sensation that made me start to sob.

"I haven't come yet," she purred.

I dove in like a man possessed, needing Stella to come as much for her pleasure as to speed my own. My hands dug into her hips to keep from grasping myself, my claws puncturing the thin fabric of her micro mini. I was about to burst from the taste of her, the screams and cries I was wringing from her as she writhed against my mouth.

"More...more, Isaac."

My fingers crooked against the spot I found inside of her and my tongue pressed and twisted against that pearl of hers. I was helpless, a supplicant in thrall to his goddess. Mistress was too small of a word for what she was to me in this moment. I would give her the beating heart from my chest if she asked it of me, flay the skin from my bones. I would burn the world down for her.

Her cries became more like sobs, and a moment later, a rush of wet hit my fingers as her pussy clenched around them. At that moment, I almost shot my load against the mattress just from how unhinged I'd made Stella.

When her whimpers quieted, Stella sat up on her elbows and looked down at me, her skin red and eyes wide as I licked her off my fingers. She watched with hungry eyes as I cleaned her completely off my skin and I waited with bated breath for my reward.

"You please me once again," her voice was ragged.

She slid off the bed and motioned for me to stand.

"Put your back against the wall, as tight as you can with your wings out."

I rushed to do as she said and hissed at the contact. The welts of my back were sore, but instead of the pain distracting me from pleasure, it only seemed to amplify the aching in my dick.

By now, the tip of my cock was dripping strings of liquid onto my thighs. When Stella dropped to her knees in front of me, it was the most erotic, most incredible sight of my life.

She'd been larger than life all night, demanding my obedience and submission with one look from those bright eyes of hers. I'd given it gladly, drunkenly. And now, Mistress Magdalena was kneeling at my feet, running her hands up my thighs, slow and possessive.

And still, I was in her thrall. I was at her command.

When her fingers grazed my cock, I almost came out of my skin.

"I'm going to suck this pretty cock of yours, Isaac, and I'm going to play with your wings while I do it. And when you come, I'm going to drink you down to the very last drop."

I whimpered out a "Please" and waited, trembling on the edge that she'd held me at since the moment we got up here.

A Gargoyle dick wasn't like a Mundanes. It was ridged like our tails and our foreskin was a series of small rings that expanded when inside a partner and locked us together for breeding. Then, there was our horn. It was a small  protrusion at the base, about an inch long and about the thickness of a pencil. It was more sensitive than our cock, and was the perfect placement to hit the clit on Mundane female partners. It also secreted a mild aphrodisiac.

I expected Stella to start with the tip, like all my other partners, too unsure about my horn to play with it at all. But I should've known better.

Stella took the horn into her mouth and sucked on it.

"Holy fuck!" my back bowed and I saw stars. "Oh fuck, oh fuck, oh fuck."

A dark chuckle rumbled against my skin as she released it and licked her way down my cock to the weeping head.

"Poor baby," she crooned, "you've been waiting a long time."

"Yes," I hissed, thrusting up just a little. "Please Mistress, please can I have your mouth?"

"Mmmm...."

Her tongue ran through the white liquid on the top, licking me like an ice cream cone. One hand grasped my base, just at the horn, while the other snaked around and grazed the outside of my wing. I went up on my toes, keening at the intensity, only to have the sound choked when the pain from my flogging was added to the mix.

And then her lips finally closed around me. I had no words for this, no sound came from my gaping lips as she worked her way further down my shaft with each pass. I was way too big for her to take fully, but that didn't matter. Not when she was sucking me to the back of her throat at each pass, caressing my wing with gentle touches. It all combined into thousands of tiny pin pricks of fire that raced down my body. I was lost on a sea of sensation, pleasure from her wicked mouth and gentle hands. Pain from the welts on my back rubbing on the wall as I thrashed.

Forgetting the rules, forgetting my place in this game, I reached down and wound my fingers in the pony tail of her wig as I began to fuck her mouth. She moaned, a sound of pure, filthy enjoyment as saliva dripped down her chin.

"You're everything," I panted, hips snapping faster. "I want...you...oh, fuck!"

A string of incoherent syllables poured from my lips as I spent myself down her throat. She took every single ounce until I was a wrung out, weeping mess.

When she released me, my knees buckled and I fell to the floor in front of her.

"Stella," I reached for her, desperate with need to feel her against me.

She wrapped me up, holding my head against her chest as sobs wracked my body. I didn't understand it. How something that was so powerfully intimate, the best orgasm of my life with someone I loved could make me feel so raw.

"I've got you," she whispered, pressing tiny kisses to my horns and forehead, "I've got you, Isaac."

I clung to her, our bodies completely entangled with one another. As the sobs began to fade, a peace began to descend over me. Never, in all of my life, had I ever felt so safe, so cared for and wanted.

*I love you, Stella. I love you.*

# CHAPTER ELEVEN

## JAMES

The damn van was too small to pace in, and between the security camera feeds I'd tapped into and the two cameras on Stella and Isaac's clothes, I could see the two of them from every fucking angle.

I could see the spreading dampness on Isaac's shorts.

The flush of Stella's skin on her throat and chest as she got close to coming from Isaac's damn fingers in the public play room.

The rush of need when he told her he wanted to eat her pussy.

And, maybe worst of all, I could hear it when Isaac told her that he wanted me to watch while he pleasured her. I could've found distraction in the words if they'd been said with malice, with the intent to make me jealous. They hadn't.

Isaac wanted me to watch because he was getting off on the idea. And Stella wanted a private room for the same reason.

"Bloody hell!"

I ran my hands over the short hair of my glamour and tried very hard to distract myself with scouring the feeds for anything suspicious. It took dimming the audio in Isaac's collar mic to be able to concentrate on anything other than the two of them breathing heavy.

I was almost able to do it until Stella commanded him to shed his glamour.

My eyes widened at the sight of her, spread out on the bed, welcoming pussy on display. I had been forcefully ignoring their feed since they went into the room while keeping the audio open in case of an emergency. But this?

I couldn't look away from her, pink and glistening, her folds so full and ready to be plundered. It was Isaac's point of view camera I was looking through, using him as a proxy for this experience. I stared in aching wonder at the way she commanded him, at the way she gripped him, wishing the entire time that it was me she had her hand around, that it was my tongue that was about to drink from her.

I watched transfixed as Isaac paused in front of her, spreading her wide and it hit me with a surety that I wanted to deny but couldn't. Isaac was doing this small act for me, inviting me into their moment. My breath rushed out in a groan and my dick was in my hand before I could stop myself. It didn't escape my notice that this was getting ridiculous. I'd jacked off more in the last day and more than any man my age had a right to. I needed a person to fuck. I needed...

*Isaac. I need Isaac.*

I ignored the whisper in the back of my mind that I needed Stella too, and decided then and there that I'd have Isaac's mouth around my cock tonight.

But in the mean time I wasn't going to walk around with an aching dick.

Staring at the feed as she rode his mouth, writhing and crying out, I almost came from just two strokes. She was even more beautiful than I remembered when she sat up, eyes glittering like stars, skin flushed. I wanted to lick the sweat off her, to carve my name in both their flesh, mark them as *mine.*

*Shit. I'm in deeper than I thought.*

It was a fleeting thought, because Stella was sucking on Isaac's cock horn and I gasped at the filthy audacity of the act. I had never considered asking her to do it but now I was jealous of Isaac, that he knew what her lips felt like on that most sensitive part.

I ran my claw over my own, desperate for an approximation of what he was feeling and knowing that it fell woefully short of the truth.

When she closed her mouth over his cock, I stopped holding back. I worked myself mercilessly, just as she did him and when Isaac cried out his release, mine shot out all over my pants and hand.

I sat there, sweating and panting, achingly lonely as I watched Stella give Isaac after care. I wanted to burst in there and wrap them both up in my arms, to wash them up and then put us all to bed together. But this wasn't the plan. First of all, I couldn't even get in there without Stella, and second, I was pretty sure Isaac had wanted me there, but I had no idea how Stella really felt.

Would she ever trust me again? I had mishandled the situation in the worst possible way when she was emotionally vulnerable. I had told myself it was best to just rip off the Band Aid, to make it a clean break. But I saw now, that had been about me and not wanting to confront her, more than it had been what was best for Stella.

I sighed and looked down at the sticky mess I'd made and swore. I'd packed an emergency bag full of different things before I left in the van, including baby wipes. It took half the package to clean me up, and even then I had to glamour away the giant wet spot in the front of my pants.

When I looked up at the screen, Stella and Isaac's cameras were looking up at the ceiling and there was the faint sound of a shower going. I forced my mind away from the image of the two of them cleaning each other and decided to take the reprieve to study the footage we had collected.

It was damn difficult to review it without falling back into lust but my release helped to keep me from doing it. I watched Stella dress down that piece of shit, Ben, my claws coming out at the way he glared at her. I knew what a predator looked like, especially when they were angry, and Ben definitely fell into that category. Cold raced down my spine at the way he looked at her, and I switched to the security feed to watch him after she left him at the bar. There was something about the way he followed her as she walked away, the slithery way he moved through the space. He had definitely shed any kind of mask he'd been wearing when he first walked up to her.

*But there's something else...something familiar that I can't put my finger on...*
I slipped into a space that a former partner once called "investigator hyper drive" as I scoured the tapes for every single angle and shot I could find with Ben in it. After he'd done a circuit around the main room, not speaking to a single person, he made his way to the public play room. He hadn't been there five minutes when he zeroed in on Stella and Isaac.

If he'd looked angry before, the look on his face as he watched them was something else entirely. It was cold fury and hatred so intense that it chilled my blood. As I continued to observe him, something happened to his eyes, a shadow eclipsed them for a moment and was gone. I had to rewind the footage three times to make sure it wasn't a trick of the light. And when I was sure that it wasn't, that cold sensation intensified.

*What does that mean? Is he a demon? An ephemeral? Is he something else entirely?*
Ephemeral's were a mystery to most of us. No one really knew the extent of their abilities or where the hell they came from because the bastards were so secretive. But the few I had known never exhibited that trick with the eyes.

*Doesn't mean they couldn't though. And with as many Supernaturals as there are in there, I wouldn't be able to distinguish him from all the others. Damn!*
But the longer I thought about, the more I observed Ben, the less I was convinced that he was Supernatural. Something didn't fit, something I needed to discover because the way he watched Stella...

*It's hungry...not just jealous it's...hateful, possessive. He's never gotten over her. And now here she is, in his sights again. But this time she's taunting him with someone else. Shit. He's more dangerous than we anticipated.*

I was so absorbed in the footage that I almost didn't see it when Ben's face appeared in the cameras on Stella and Isaac's clothing.

"What the fuck!"

Alarm bells rang in my head and my blood ran hot with panic. They weren't there, possibly still in the shower or the soaking tub since Isaac had never been flogged before. My claws and fangs broke through the glamour. A low, rumbling growl tore up from my throat as I watched him rummage in their discarded clothing. I needed to see what he was doing. If he opened the door, I'd get in there even if I had to break heads to do it. But until then, I had to watch and observe.

He was searching for something, that was obvious and when he found it my vision turned red.

In his hands was Stella's red lace thong. He grinned at it and stuffed it into his pocket before leaving. If I ever got my claws on this man, I would shred the flesh from his fucking bones. How dare he take *anything* from Stella! She wasn't his to own, wasn't his to get anything from!

*He doesn't deserve a god damned trophy from her! ...wait...trophy...*

I tapped into the security feed again and watched him leave the room. He went down stairs and into the public play room again, taking a seat in a corner where shadows made it very difficult to see him. Before now he'd been constantly moving, like a shark in water. But now, he was still, utterly so, as if he wanted to be invisible.

"Who are you looking at?" I mumbled to myself.

I switched through the feeds until I found one that was closest to the same angle that Ben was looking toward. But by now the play room was quite full, and it could've been one of about a dozen people that he was studying. Still, I took note of them all, just in case.

I was wrapping up the list when the door to the van slid open and in came Stella and Isaac, both in street clothes and wearing stupidly relaxed grins on their faces. Jealousy spiked through me and I tamped it down. There were more important things to talk about, to think about. And I was damn happy about it.

"Where'd you get those?" I asked, gesturing to their clothes.

"I asked Dawn to stash a bag for us in the room and we slipped out the back."

I wondered if I should tell her about the thong and realized that it was important. She had to know that Ben was still a threat, maybe a bigger one than we'd first thought. When I was finished, Isaac bared his teeth and snarled, about to rip open the van door when Stella stopped him.

"Not the time or place," she said.

"I'm going to rip out his fucking throat!" Isaac's voice had dropped several octaves and his eyes were glowing.

"Not before I have the chance," I said, my voice also having dropped.

"Will you two stop it?" Stella demanded. "I appreciate the protective thing, really. Ben isn't someone I want to tangle with alone, but we have to be smart about this. We're here to catch a killer. We'll deal with Ben the Creep after. Now, what did you find?"

"Not much," I said, letting the reason why hang in the air between us.

Isaac blushed and wouldn't meet my eye, which only made me want to grab him by the back of the neck and kiss the shit out of him. While Stella gave me a slow, teasing grin that had me holding back the instinct to pull her over my knee and spank her ass until it was cherry red.

"Would you like us to review the footage?" she asked.

I leaned in, enjoying the sight of her pupils flaring and her breath picking up.

"No, I think I'll do it on my own," then I glanced up at Isaac, who was watching us with an intensity I hadn't seen before. "Unless, of course, you'd like to join me."

Isaac's lips curled up into a grin.

"Maybe."

Stella crossed her arms and glared at us both.

"I'm kinda tired, can we go back to the penthouse and work, or do you two want to fuck in the bushes?"

Isaac and I exchanged a grin, mutually delighted that we'd gotten under her skin. It was turning into a kind of addictive foreplay.

*But between Isaac and me or Stella and me?*

I cleared my throat, pushing all of that aside. Tonight's footage needed to be scoured and I wanted to get as far from the club, and Ben, as possible right now.

"I'll meet you two at the penthouse," I said, and met Stella's annoyed gaze. "You should stay there. Who knows what Ben will do after your little show tonight."

Her lips tightened and the muscles in her forearms rippled as she made fists.

"I'm not hiding from that asshole."

"It's not hiding," Isaac interjected, "it's being smart. He stole your fucking underwear. And I don't know if you noticed, but he was watching us like a hawk. It was fucking creepy."

She huffed out a string of swear words and grunted.

"Fine! But just for tonight."

I nodded, secretly hoping that it wasn't. After what I'd seen, I was aching to have both Stella and Isaac in my bed. But how to overcome the twelve years of hurt and anger that separated Stella and me? That was something I had no answers for.

# CHAPTER TWELVE

## JAMES

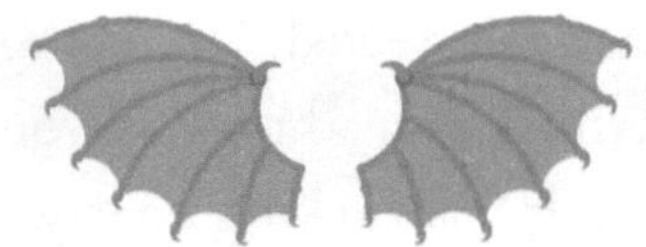

In two hours, we were all three in my penthouse, the footage uploaded to my computer and running on the three monitors I'd requisitioned from the Archive supply warehouse in Seattle. Stella and Isaac had gone to an all night greasy spoon by the name of Minnies and ordered pancakes, french toast and the biggest omelette I'd ever seen to go. Now takeout containers littered the counters of my kitchen and the place smelled of breakfast foods. Usually that kind of clutter would drive me nuts, but I was too distracted by Stella's nervous pacing.

She was trying to play it off as being angry at Ben, but I could see the fear simmering below the surface. We'd poured over the footage, all three of us analyzing the strange shadow that passed over his eyes but none of us had any clue what it was. I'd put out feelers to the Archive and hadn't heard back from the Librarians yet.

"That's an honest to god Gryphon?" Isaac asked, munching on one of the last pancakes

"Yep," Stella replied. "Sapphire is very private about it though."

"I thought they were a myth."

"We've got one as acting Arch Librarian at the Archive," I said, typing in a search into the database.

Isaac's gaze swung to me and Stella stopped mid stride to stare at me.

"What?" I asked. "We do. He's pretty private too but he doesn't seem to leave the Library much so that works for him."

"You have a Gryphon?" Isaac's voice was incredulous. "As a *librarian?*" I snorted.

"Librarians are high ranking in the Archive, practically untouchable. And the Arch Librarian perhaps especially. They are the guardians of all the knowledge the Archive has amassed. In the days of the previous director, Francesca, they were the only thing standing in the way of her gaining some truly terrible powers. Max Dearborne was the Arch Librarian then and he risked a lot to keep that knowledge from her."

"Where is he now?" Stella asked.

I shrugged.

"Retired, or so I've heard. His mother is the new director but she's understandably tight lipped when it comes to her children."

"And so you now have a *Gryphon* in that role?"

"Yes. He's...interesting."

"Sapphire offered to keep an eye out for us," Stella said, flopping onto the couch and laying down. "They're very good at observing and listening without looking like they are. So hopefully we'll get some additional information before the bastard strikes again."

She yawned and curled onto her side.

"I need a nap."

"You can have one of the guest suites," I said, purposely not looking at her.

I didn't want her in a different room. I wanted her in my bed, soaking the sheets with her scent and cum. But I knew that wasn't happening and so I'd settle for at least having her under my roof.

"Thanks," she waved at us, tight ass swaying as she walked down the hall to the far guest room.

Isaac and I both watched her walk away and he laughed at me when the door closed and I let out huff.

"Am I just going to have to lock you two in a room until you fuck it out?" he asked.

"One night with her and suddenly you're an expert about what she and I need?" my voice had an unexpected bite to it. "You really want to share her?"

"Yes, actually," he leaned toward me from where he sat at the table, his purple eyes glinting in the light. "You don't think I thought of you in that room with us the whole time? That I imagined what it would be like to have you there? I want to share her *and* you."

"And you got her buy in on that?"

"Not on all three of us, no. But on you and me? Yeah."

I launched myself out of my chair, but not at Isaac as I wanted to do. Now it was me that was pacing, trying to get a hold of the undeniable truth that I was hurtling toward something that would forever change me.

Fucking Isaac was one thing.

Fucking Stella was another.

But the two of them together? The *three* of us?

It was different than just the casual dalliances that had been my default all these years. I knew, without a doubt, that they could satisfy me, be what I had been searching for all this time. It wasn't logical, it didn't make sense in my mind, but my gut knew this to be true.

Isaac's hand on my shoulder stilled my steps and I let out a long breath when he embraced me from behind. We hadn't done more than tease one another, and yet this also felt *right*. He soothed me and I had no idea how.

"I'm sorry if I pushed," he said, his breath ghosting along my back. "It was just so clear to me that even though tonight was amazing, it was missing something. And I think that something is *you*."

"Stella and I have history. Painful history. She's not just going to let me in again so easily."

"Yeah, she's prickly," Isaac's voice was thick with affection.

I turned around and Isaac let me go, but we were still very close together. He really was so beautiful, more so in his true form than with his glamour on. And he was also half foot smaller than me, which gave him an added appeal.

My hand ran down his back and he hissed.

"Sensitive?" I asked.

"Yeah."

"The welts will heal in a few days."

His face fell a bit at that, and I chuckled.

"I'd be happy to give you new ones."

His purple-gray skin flushed and I couldn't help but lean in and kiss him. He moaned into my mouth and I was rock hard in seconds. There was still the question of Isaac's loyalty, the dark specter of betrayal peeked around the corner in my brain and I almost stopped. This was much more than a simple fuck for information, I was risking my own heart this time, not just a mark's.

*But there's something that doesn't fit with Isaac. He's not the type to betray the people in his life, especially not Stella. I don't think he's the enemy here. And if he's not, then what's his story?*

I broke off the kiss, squeezing the back of Isaac's neck because I couldn't bear to let him go. Isaac was panting, I knew he wanted to kneel at my feet, wait for my command. But I didn't want him kneeling. Not yet anyway.

"Let's go for a flight," I said.

Isaac frowned, questions swirling in his eyes. Instead of asking, though, he just nodded. Stella would be safe here with all the extra security, both Mundane and Supernatural I had installed in and around my penthouse. Nothing could get to her here, but I still went down the hall to check on her.

The thin sheet molded to her body, revealing the fact that with the exception of a pair of panties she was naked. Moonlight streamed in through the tall windows and lit her up in a pale glow that had my heart catching. She'd always been beautiful, but when I'd last been with her, Stella wasn't the confident women she was now. Her soul had been bruised. She was unsure of herself and her personal power. Yet, in spite of everything life had thrown at her, she'd become this strong, intelligent woman. She bowed to no one, unless she wanted to, and I found myself longing to earn that right.

I brushed a hair out of her face and she stirred.

"What's going on?" she asked.

"Isaac and I are going for a flight," I said, sitting on the edge of the bed. "You'll be safe here."

Maybe it was the vulnerability of being half asleep, but the fear she'd been holding back was front and center in the way she looked at me, the few seconds she held my hand.

"Sleep, Stella," I pressed a light kiss to her forehead. "We'll be back."

"James," she cupped my cheek, running her thumb along my temple, "I...tonight, between me and Isaac..."

"We'll talk about it later. Not now."

She bit her bottom lip and nodded.

"Okay."

I tucked a blanket around her just in case she got chilly and watched her eyes flutter closed before I left.

Isaac was already out on the balcony, wings flared at his back. The first time seeing a Gargoyle's wings was special. We didn't show them that often even among our own kind. Being our most vulnerable part, it was a matter of extreme trust for a Gargoyle to show their wings when it wasn't a battle situation, much less have their back to someone with their wings out like that.

His wings weren't as large as mine, but they were perfect for his frame. I always bristled at the description "bat-like", no matter how accurate it might be at its core. We did have a similar structure, but our wings were far more beautiful. Iridescent in the right light, with shades of blue, silver, green, purple. Isaac's were mostly a dark purple that bordered on black but when the moonlight hit them, I saw glimpses of blue. The upper most arc ended in a small claw, hooked and sharp, it was this top part I ran my finger down and he shivered. The purple and blue membrane that made up the majority of the wing was leathery and looked thin, but was actually quite strong.

Warmth spread in my chest at the sight, at what it meant. Isaac was telling me, in a way that would only mean something to me, that he trusted me completely.

*I truly hope he's not a traitor. I don't know if I'd be able to kill him if he was.*

"I haven't flown with another Gargoyle in a long time," he said.

His boyish excitement was contagious and I returned it.

"Well, I hope you can keep up."

He snorted.

"Pretty sure you're older than me. Maybe I should be worried about you."

"We'll see."

I stepped up onto the ledge of my balcony and looked back at him as my wings flared. Isaac's eyes widened and his jaw tensed. I didn't have to glance down at his groin to see that he was hard at the sight.

"Wanna make it interesting?" I asked.

"What do you have in mind?"

"If I race you around the city and win, you suck me off right here after."

Isaac's breath picked up.

"And if I win?"

"I'll suck you off first."

"Deal."

With a lascivious grin, I jumped. My wings snapped out to catch me and I worked them so I that rose in the air. Isaac met me as I climbed, and laughed.

"C'mon, old man!"

I snarled with a laugh and tore off after him. We'd gotten high altitude fast and it would've been freezing to anyone else if they were in the clouds with us. Instead of the cold affecting me, it glanced off my body as my temperature dropped to protect me from the chill. I hadn't been flying just for the fun of it in years. Isaac's pure, uncensored joy was contagious and I let loose a roaring laugh as I zoomed past him.

"What were you saying, little Isaac?" I asked over my shoulder.

His grin turned competitive and Isaac put on a burst of speed that I matched in seconds. He was younger and more agile, but my age gave me experience at racing in this way. I spun and dove down to catch the better wind currents that carried me faster with less effort. I took a moment to look out to my right, where the lights at the waterfront twinkled. A ferry was in the distance, the warm glow from it's lamps was idyllic, calm. I could almost forget about what stalked the night in this city as I took in the city. But I had a race to win. I could take in the view later. When I popped back up into the clouds, Isaac's shocked yell was more satisfying than it should've been.

He closed the distance fast, showing little signs of fatigue. I realized that even though I was in the best shape of my life, my stamina might not be a match for a young Gargoyle like him, even a half Mundane one. And while losing to him wouldn't be so bad, I really wanted to see him on his knees in front of me.

So I dove back down, but Isaac, being a quick study, did the same.

Now we were neck in neck as the wind currents aided us. At this rate, Isaac could win so I dipped down, as if I were once again finding a faster way. When Isaac followed this time, I jumped back up and put on a last burst of speed. My wings pounded the air, and I whipped between the buildings and power lines. I could hear Isaac's wings behind me, gaining fast.

I grunted as I forced more from my own wings and saw my balcony ahead.

I landed with a pant half a second before Isaac. The race had heated my blood, and one look at Isaac's flushed body, his shining purple eyes and I couldn't hold back.

I gripped the back of his neck and pulled him forward, crushing his lips with mine.

It wasn't a kiss so much as our mouths and teeth and tongues wrestling one another, seeking the next pinnacle of sensation as I clawed his chest, leaving a trail behind to mark him as mine. Fat raindrops started to pelt us as we stood, exposed to the elements on my balcony but neither of us cared.

"I won," I gasped as I pulled his mouth off mine. "And I want my prize."

"Yes," he answered, eyes glazed.

My claws bit into his neck where I still gripped him.

"Yes, what?"

He swallowed.

"Yes...Daddy?"

Thunder rumbled through the city, and lightning ran a jagged line through the night as his words flooded my mind in desire. I chuckled, a cruel and seductive sound, as I slipped into the Dom Isaac wanted.

"That's right," I traced his bottom lip with one claw, "and your Daddy wants his cock sucked. Now."

Isaac fell to his knees, wings flared out to the side and I had to bite back a moan at how damn beautiful he was; a dark prince kneeling at my feet and about to offer me worship. I crossed my arms and stared at him with a stern expression as he unbuckled my pants and pulled them down with shaking hands. Outside, I appeared unaffected by the way Isaac's breath stuttered, the heat of his mouth as he licked and bit his way up my thighs. Inside I was on fire, my heart raced and something else pulsed in my chest, right next to that jagged piece of myself that longed for Stella. It scared and thrilled me all at once and I had no idea why.

By now it was raining in earnest but I barely noticed how drenched we were. Not when Isaac was working my cock like a fucking artist. When he came to the base, where my horn was, he glanced up at me with a silent question in his eyes. It was exactly what I'd wanted sitting alone in that van, looking in on the two of them.

"Do it," my voice rasped, a roll of thunder punctuating it.

"Thank you," he whispered.

For a new sub, Isaac was falling into his role as if he were made for it, which only made me want to explore him more; see how far I could push him, what his limits were. But I didn't have much time to think about that when Isaac took my horn between his lips and sucked.

I let out a soft roar of shock, head thrown back before I could stop myself. It was exquisitely overwhelming. Light exploded behind my eyes and I worried that I'd spend right there, like a youth. Even though I wanted him to keep going, I pulled Isaac off my horn by grabbing his hair.

"That's enough playing," my voice was hard.

He was panting, his glittering eyes illuminated by lightning as he gazed up at me. I realized then that he must've ingested some of the aphrodisiac from the horn. The front of his shorts was tenting, his hips bucking just a little, as if he were seeking friction.

"Please, can I just..." he begged, hand going to his crotch.

"If I let you touch yourself, you'll be greedy and forget all about taking care of your Daddy."

"I'll suck you so good, I promise."

"Hmmm..."

My tail snaked out between us and I tapped the end on his lips. Isaac's eyes widened and his cock quivered in his shorts. He knew exactly what I was asking.

Holding my gaze, Isaac opened his mouth and I slipped it between his lips. A thousand tiny pin pricks of sensation raced up and down my tail and through my body as I slid it in and out, in and out. It was only by the slimmest margin that I kept my expression dark and commanding, when all I wanted to do was let my jaw go slack and let loose an obscene snarl.

"Shorts off, now," I demanded.

They were gone in a blink and I grinned down at him.

"I'm going to put my tail around you, and if you're a good boy, I'll let you come. But if you get distracted, if that pretty little mouth of yours doesn't do its job, then I'll turn my tail into a cock ring and keep you on the edge of coming for hours. Understand?"

Isaac swallowed and nodded vigorously. As I wound my tail around his erection, I wondered if Isaac would purposefully disobey just for the pain part of the pleasure. My tail tightened around his cock, and he let out a throaty groan.

"Oh god, it's..." he grunted as my tail slowly ran up and down him.

But when he didn't put his mouth on me a few seconds later, I stopped and simply gripped him very, very tightly. His eyes flew open and he grabbed my thighs with his hands. I loosened it, but not enough to let him come.

"You're not doing what you're told," I said.

"Y-yes, Daddy, I'm sorry."

Isaac's mouth was wide, but he still struggled to take me and a perverse thrill shot through me watching him try so hard.  There was the faintest scrape of his fangs along the sides of my shaft and I hissed as the hint of pain and pleasure were entwined.

"Take it like a good boy," I grabbed a hold of his horns and began to move him up and down my cock. "Slap my thighs if it's too much."

I was easy at first, letting him adjust to my size. As a reward, I began to move my tail up and down him again, tightening at the top of his shaft just as I bottomed out in the back of his throat. Thunder boomed above us and the next lightning bolt was so bright that Isaac's body glowed in perfect erotic beauty. When he began to buck his hips, I slowed down and a gurgling sob rolled up from his throat.

"I want my cum dripping from your pretty little mouth, Isaac. When I get what I want, I'll give you what you're begging for . But not until then."

He looked up at me, equal parts pleading and adoration in his eyes, as his mouth strained to contain my dick. I'd had plenty of beautiful beings go down on me, but staring at him caused a sharp stab of longing to burn through me. This wasn't going to be enough, I knew as sure as I knew my own name. This was just a taste of what I wanted, *needed* from Isaac. I wanted his ass, I wanted him panting and moaning under me, I wanted him to wind his tail around me until I painted his chest with my cum. I wanted his tears of release, just like he gave to Stella tonight.

In other words, I wanted his soul.

"You're so beautiful," I murmured, running a claw down the side of his face but not breaking the skin.

He shivered, pausing on my cock. I wanted to say so much more, but the words stalled in my throat. So I decided to show him instead.

I drew him down my cock, to just shy of my horn, and bucked at the same time, bottoming out and making him gag. I eased off for just a moment, and then went again. He gagged again, chin wet with saliva. I eased back and looked down at him.

His eyes were closed in ecstasy, precum dripping off his tip and coating my tail as I moved slowly over his length. Isaac was enjoying this as much as I was.

And so, I unleashed.

I fucked his mouth without mercy, pulling on his horns as I thrust up and bottomed out again and again. The sound of him gagging on my cock, the slurping of his sucking, knowing that I was making him crazy with arousal as he gave me such pleasure, it drove me to a place I hadn't been in so long. Wild abandon took over, an animal side of me that I'd rarely let out began to break free. Thunder rolled and snapped above us as lightning cracked and the sky drenched us in rain, the world just as primal as we were.

I snarled and gnashed my teeth as I fucked his mouth harder and tightened my tail around his cock, just like I imagined Stella's cunt might feel. I was no longer the buttoned down agent, the man in control of himself and everything else. Isaac had unhinged me.

I was aware enough to know that I wasn't hurting him, on the contrary. His hips bucked in time with my tail and he moaned around me. I could tell that tears leaked from his eyes and mixed with the saliva on his chin.

"I'm gonna make a mess of you," I gasped. "Would you like that, little Isaac? Where do you want your Daddy's cum?"

Isaac's trembling hand touched his chest and I let out a dark chuckle.

"That's right. You want me to mark you. You want to be my little cum slut, don't you?"

Isaac's moan was so deep and throaty that it nearly had me unloading right there. But I held on, just a little longer, until he was sobbing around me, cum shooting in white ropes from his cock onto my feet.

I yanked him off me and it only took two pulls to have me painting his chest in my release. Before I'd even finished, Isaac batted my hand away and took over. Fire engulfed my balls and shaft as I roared and spent more than I could remember in a very long time.

When I was done, we both remained still, panting while the rain rinsed the cum from our bodies.

Isaac's head nuzzled my thigh and a tremble went through him. My insides felt like I'd run for miles uphill, weak and shaky, but I knew that Isaac needed to be taken care of.

Gently, I used my pants wipe to up any fluids the rain hadn't taken care of and then I guided him to the bathroom in the master suite.

*I don't want to run away...I don't even want to stop touching him.*

My mouth went dry and that pulling sensation in my chest became stronger.

*It can't be, can it? And if it is, does that mean the more painful one is for Stella?*

Gargoyles could have more than one mate; we weren't especially monogamous as a species. But if I'd formed a mating attachment to Stella all those years ago and broke it without realizing it...

*That would explain why I've never been able to form any kind of attachment to anyone else, why it all felt so empty.*

I was well and truly fucked if this was the case because Stella didn't trust me and may never again. Still, I'd been able to form a mating attachment to Isaac, which might've only been possible because I was near Stella.

*None of which will matter if he's a traitor. Bollocks! Can I fuck up this mission any more than I already have?*

Isaac grinned up at me as I guided him into the hot shower, so trusting and sweet that it made the attachment ache.

"You okay to stand?" I asked.

He nodded and I reached for the soap. But he was there first.

"Let me."

"I'm supposed to be taking care of you," I said quietly.

"Says who? Weren't you in there with me? Don't you need some after care?"

My throat became tight, tears itched my eyes and I brought Isaac in for a tender kiss.

"It's been a long time," I said.

"Well then, all the more reason to let me."

We'd just had dirty fucking out on my balcony, but this moment, Isaac cleaning my skin with gentle swipes of the cloth, massaging my body where the muscles were tight, this was more intimate. It tore away any kind of walls I'd built up for myself after I'd run from Stella, leaving me truly naked.

I braced my hands on the wall and shuddered. Isaac didn't ask me anything. Instead, he pressed his front to my back and held me tight. I clasped his hand and held on. He was my buoy in the storm that tossed inside me, the one solid thing that would make sure I didn't drown in all this.

"You feel it too then?" he whispered against my shoulder blades.

I stared at him over my shoulder, unable to speak.

"I didn't think I'd ever get one," he continued, "being half Mundane. But...it was so fast with you. Hours, and there it was, right next to..."

He cut himself off and looked away.

"Right next to Stella," I finished for him.

"Yeah."

I turned around and pulled him to me, indulging in a long, kiss that shattered me and put me back together all at the same time. When I eased back, Isaac's gaze had turned glassy again, but there was also a hint of worry there.

"I don't know how this is all going to work," I admitted, "but I can share you with her."

"And I can share you with her too."

I snorted.

"Kid, that's never gonna happen."

His crooked grin sent heat through my veins.

"Old man, never say never."

There was still one thing that I needed to know before I could really accept this bond with Isaac. One last awful question I needed an answer to. And I didn't want to ask it. I wanted to ignore it's existence and go on happily fucking Isaac's brains out.

But I knew if I didn't dig this out now, it would fester and rot what we might be able to have.

We toweled off and dressed in silence, Isaac continually wearing the most adorable, dimpled grin I'd ever seen. It was bloody infectious, and in spite of how afraid I was, I found myself smiling back at him as he took the lasagna out of my fridge.

"It's pretty good cold, or I could heat it up," he said.

"Dealer's choice," I replied, uncorking a bottle of red.

I let Isaac put two pieces into the microwave and take the glass of red before I dropped the bomb on him. If I was more patient, I'd wait until he'd had a glass or two, but there was no way I was going to be able to eat lasagna across from him with this hanging between us.

"Are you a spy?"

He choked on the vintage and set the glass down on the counter. His skin turned a very dark purple and he wiped his mouth with the back of his hand.

"Shit," he said, his voice hot with anger just before he slammed his hand on the counter. "Shit!"

"I'll take that as a yes," I drained the glass and poured another. "I'm asking because it doesn't make sense. You don't make sense as a spy. You are loyal, good. And the Protectors, if that's who you're working for, are not. You're not vicious enough to be one of them."

I expected a lot of different reactions. Isaac laughing wasn't one of them.

"I think they know that," he said.

My stomach dropped at those words and I went to him, my hand cupping the back of his neck tenderly.

"What happened? I asked.

His shoulders sagged.

"I didn't know who they were when I joined," he began. "That's no excuse. It's actually a sign of naiveté and stupidity."

"No, it isn't. It's what they do. Lie and coerce to get people to do what they want. It's not your fault."

"I thought I was joining the good guys. It's in their fucking name! I wanted to make a real difference but...I know the truth now."

Tears glistened on his cheeks and I couldn't help it. I wiped them away with my thumbs and framed his face with my hands.

"They want the knives," he said. "And... they're willing to kill anyone in their way. *Anyone*, James."

"Stella," I whispered, mouth dry.

He nodded, face hard with determination.

"I can't allow that," he continued. "I won't."

"I know," I answered him.

"I'm sorry. I should've told you, but I... I wanted *this*, what we have. And it all felt so fragile and new and I thought if I told you that you'd reject me and I... fuck, James. I've never felt this way before, the way I feel about you and Stella. I was just afraid of it all going away."

I should've been angry, or at the very least, this should've been the thing that would cut me free from this bond. But perhaps acknowledging it, even in the frightened way I had in the shower, was enough to make it stronger. Because instead of pushing him away, instead of calling for a prisoner extraction, I wrapped Isaac up in my arms and held him tight. The moment he let out a long sigh, his muscles relaxed, and a dark corner of my heart flared bright.

*Mine.*

The one word sang out in my blood, quiet and sure, much like Isaac himself.

I kissed the top of his head and held him tighter.

*Alright then. If he's mine, that means only one thing.*

"No one is going to touch you," my whisper was hard, growly. "We're getting you out of there. I swear it."

# CHAPTER THIRTEEN

## STELLA

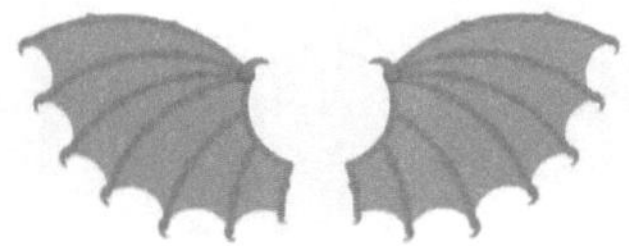

I woke to the buzzing of my phone and slapped my hand where my nightstand should've been to grab it. Instead, I managed to topple over a clock and lamp that shouldn't have been there. I sat bolt upright and looked around, my sleep soaked brain taking a moment to remember where I was.

The room had that weird light that wasn't moonlight, but not quite sunrise either, though after a minute I realized that it wasn't far off. Soft sheets wound around my legs on top of the most comfortable mattress I'd ever slept on. The room was beyond huge, perfect for a Gargoyle.

*Or two.*

The thought had me simultaneously jealous and aroused as I imaged Isaac and James tangled up with one another in here.

But the phone buzzed again and cut off any further exploration of that complicated fantasy.

I stared down at the text and swore, tearing the sheets from around my legs.

*"Two more bodies. Same MO as others. Get down to fifth and Bell right away."*

I threw on a tank top as I ran out of the room and opened my mouth to call for the males, when I heard soft sounds, like someone chuckling or kissing. My gaze swung to the kitchen, landing on Isaac and James tangled together in a tender embrace. The look on James' face choked me.

It was happy, sweet, full of things that haunted my most lonely nights with what could've been if he'd just cared enough. I'd longed for that look to be directed at me again, to feel the warmth of it blooming in my body. And here it was, but not for me.

The two of them must've seen me out of the corner of their eyes, standing there like an idiot with my feet rooted to the damn floor. They didn't jump apart, after all why would they? I'd said I was okay with this. Except I'd fooled myself into thinking it would just be fucking. Not James and Isaac staring into each other's eyes as if their whole world revolved around one another.

And once again on the outside of James' affections.

"We got bodies," I whispered, my voice raw.

"Stella--" Isaac said, taking a step toward me.

I couldn't stand the look on his face and I certainly didn't want his words right now.

"Save it. We have a job to do so put on some fucking clothes and let's go."

I turned on my heel and made it into the bedroom before the ripping sensation in my chest was too much to bear. Everything hurt; I slid down the wall and buried my face in a pillow, the closest thing to me, to try and muffle the sounds of my crying. I hated to give in to this, to let myself be affected by James *again*. Hadn't I learned anything from the last time he'd left me a broken shell? Why did I think this time would be any different just because we weren't fucking?

Loneliness seared through me, and I felt my heart crack, causing me to curl up into myself.

It was true what I said. We did have a job to do, but right now, I couldn't seem to get off the floor.

I kept telling myself that I had to put this all away, just like last time. That I had done it once, I could do it again and come out the other side stronger. But was that true? I had become more mature, more powerful after James left me, but that had been a near thing. If not for Dawn and what she'd taught me, who knows what would've happened to me.

I could say that I had Isaac, but did I really? And was it even fair to put that on him?

No, I couldn't do that. I had to do this myself this time. I could and I would.

There was a case to distract me, people to save. And once that was done, there was plenty of Jack in the world to keep me comfortably numb until my heart knit itself back together.

And Isaac...

*For all I know he'll want to go with James. Everyone leaves at some point.*

It was a stupid lie, told to harden my heart and make me capable of surviving this. I knew that Isaac cared for me, deeply. But right now, it was somehow easier to believe that he wanted James more. The impenetrable shell that I'd created around my life was familiar, safe, even if it was horribly desolate.

"Stella?" Isaac's voice was worried on the other side of the door. "Can I come in?"

"No," I barely managed to get out. "Just give me a minute."

"Okay."

Deep breaths and some extreme focusing on the feel of the hardwood floors under me, the cool air against my skin had me able to think in a few minutes. After that, I could get to my feet with only a little shaking in my legs.

"Okay, you can do this," I said to myself, pulling clothes out of my overnight bag.

With each item I slipped on, I reconstructed my internal armor, piece by piece, until the burning pain in my chest was distant, and I could ignore it enough to pretend like nothing was wrong. When I walked out of the room, with my side arm secured in my shoulder holster, my game face was firmly planted.

James and Isaac were in their human glamours, both of them sliding firearms into similar shoulder holsters. It was fucking ridiculous how sexy they both looked in slacks and button downs that hugged their muscular physiques, the sleeves rolled up to reveal forearms covered in dark hair and ropes of muscle. Where Isaac's body, both in and out of his glamour, was boxier, James' was long and broad. The contrast between them was beautiful, arousing and I didn't want it to be.

They both looked up at me, but where Isaac gave me a shaky smile, James turned away with barely a glance my way. It felt like proof of what I'd thought in that room. He may feel a little bad about hurting me this time too, but that was it.

A broken chuckle escaped my lips and both males frowned at me.

"C'mon boys," I said with a grim smile, "time to do our jobs."

We all three got into the elevator, Isaac a strange kind of buffer between James and me, as we awkwardly refused to look at each other. A few seconds of this and Isaac let out a long breath through his nose and hit the elevator stop button.

"What the fuck?" I asked.

"Damn it, Isaac!" James said at the same time.

"Spit it out," Isaac demanded of me.

My heart gave a sharp lurch of panic.

"Fuck you."

I reached for the button and he got there first, blocking me. While he'd left a huge space open next to me, James and I still remained stuffed into our separate corners.

"You two," Isaac pointed at both of us, "are driving me fucking crazy, and not in the way I'd prefer you did."

"I'm not unpacking all our shit in a fucking elevator while two dead bodies are cooling on the ground," I spat out.

"Fine. Save that for later, but whatever has the two of you pretending the other one doesn't exist, that needs to be said. Right now."

We eyed one another and I crossed my arms across my chest. The longer we stared the more it became apparent that we were each waiting on the other to speak first.

*This right here is why we would never work. We're both Alphas who don't bend easily.*

Isaac's hand fell on my shoulder and then on James', a bridge between us that had my heart hammering.

"C'mon you two, time's a wasting."

James glanced at Isaac and then back at me, his gaze turning soft. It threatened to knock the air out of me, and I had to grit my teeth to keep from letting it show.

"I care for Isaac," James finally said. "And I assumed that you would be alright with us. But if you aren't--"

"I'm fine with it, Isaac should've told you that" I whispered. "While I want Isaac, I see the way you two look at each other. I'd be selfish to say you two can't have that and keep him all to myself."

"So you're alright sharing?" James asked.

There was no way I was letting him off the hook *that* easy. I gave him a feral grin and shrugged.

"As long as I get to watch next time. I mean, turnabout is fair play."

Isaac sucked in a breath and I snaked my arm around his waist.

"Oh, I think something can be arranged," James said, his gaze searing.

I refused to show all the emotions his reaction created and simply smiled wider.

"Good."

He snorted and turned away. I let go of Isaac and pressed my back to the wall of the elevator, arms crossed once again.

"Well, I guess that went well, " Isaac murmured and pushed the button to get the elevator moving again.

We were all silent on the ride to the crime scene and I was grateful for it. We needed to get our heads out of our genitals and solve this fucking case. Sunrise was teasing the horizon, the sound of seagulls and the smell of the water drifted to me through the open window of the car. I loved this time of the morning in Seattle, when the sky was just starting to wake up, pink and peach tinting the puffy clouds. Often it would be raining or had just finished so there was a clean feeling in the air. And if it was timed just right, there would be the faintest hint of coffee under the sea salt. But often the only reason I was up was because there was a crime somewhere. When we arrived, I thought I was ready for another gruesome scene.

I was wrong.

The look on the faces of the uniformed officers who had cordoned off the area was scared, disgusted, and I saw one of them dart off down an alley to puke. This part of Seattle was the scene of many a crime, usually the victim was one of the homeless in the city. Sometimes a person walking back from a dive bar without a friend would get mugged, sometimes it was worse. But this time, it was the serial killer, so I steeled myself and ducked under the yellow tape, wondering what Supernatural victim we'd be faced with this time. When I rounded the corner, my feet refused to move and Isaac collided with me. James stuttered to a stop beside me and we all three just stared.

Splayed out in the middle of a dark alley that stank of empty beer kegs and an overflowing dumpster were two bodies, if they could be called that anymore.

I swallowed back the bile and took a step forward, careful to avoid the blood that had run and pooled on the filthy pavement. Someone had set up lights to give us and the Supernatural CSI enough light to work since the alley was completely dark without them. Every slash, every gaping hole was disgustingly gaudy. It felt wrong to so brightly illuminate these two naked and mutilated bodies, as if we were putting them on display. But we weren't. We were trying to see all of the horror they went through so we could find the evil that had done this to them.

That's what I told myself anyway as I visually examined the bodies, doing my best to stay out of CSI's way and push down the revulsion creeping up my throat.

*Clinical...detached...what are the basics? Species...gender...*

"Another Orc male, at least I presume," I said, gesturing to where his genitals used to be. "Mun....Mundane female..."

I swallowed hard and stepped away from Isaac, who had tried to reach out and comfort me. I couldn't show weakness in front of the other cops, I'd learned that a long time ago. The only thing to do was keep it simple and examine the facts in front of me.

"Male is missing both eyes," I began again, my voice rough, forceful. "Lips cut up the face to the cheekbones on either side...neck...neck cut deep enough that head is nearly detached."

I couldn't keep talking, no matter how much it helped me process. It was all too much. I'd be here all night just cataloguing wounds because this time, the female victim had also sustained extensive trauma. So I just wrote it down. Every knife slash I could, every organ that lay on the ground beside this poor Orc.

If all this wasn't proof enough that the killer was escalating, then the woman would have been.

Up to this point, the Mundane victims were barely touched, but this unfortunate woman was now the exception.

Her throat was cut, like the others, but this time, the killer had slashed her face up so bad that I knew the coroner would have to use dental records or fingerprints to identify her. Her hair was soaked in blood, I had no idea of the color right now. Her hands had been cut off and...

I turned away and ran out of the alley, losing the meager contents of my stomach around the corner. I heaved in breaths, trying hard to gain back some control as I leaned against the building. Strong hands clasped my shoulders and rubbed them. I knew without needing to turn around that it was Isaac.

"It's okay," he whispered. "Take your time."

"You know I can't."

Police work at this level wasn't without it's sexism, and if I showed even a glimmer of anything that could be deemed "feminine weakness" then the questions would start about my fitness for this kind of duty. Especially considering my record for pushing the limits with my superiors.

"The uniformed officers puked plenty before we got here, and the only reason that CSI isn't running away is because those guys are a whole other breed. No one is going to think twice about you needing a minute."

"Did you see the Mundane?" I asked, unable to stop myself. "He...what he did to her chest and vulva?"

"I did. He's escalating."

"It's not just that. The slash marks...they were disorderly, some deeper than others..."

I wanted to take a moment to just calm myself but my mind wouldn't let me. I pressed the heel of my palm to my eyes, wishing I could press the images out of my memory. It took a minute, but soon I could think past the horror of what I'd seen to find the clues hidden in the gruesome spectacle.

"He was furious," I whispered. "This was different than the others. There isn't the careful, methodical feel to it this time. It was chaotic...hacking. What changed? What made him do it *this* way?"

James rounded the corner, face stormy as he stalked toward us. It was odd that the sight of him, visibly shaken and yet also angry, would be comforting but it was. He was like a tall avenging angel and it made me believe, just for a second, that things would be alright.

"We can't really do anything here," he said, voice hard. "The bodies are too badly torn up. I told CSI and the coroner that we would want whatever they have by noon and updates on anything new as soon as they have it confirmed."

I nodded, latching onto the logical way James was approaching this.

"I assume you noticed--"

"The escalation," I said.

He gave a short nod.

"We need to look back over the footage from tonight, see if we can find the two victims and who might have been stalking them," Isaac said.

"I think I might already know," James said, purposely not looking at me.

I wasn't psychic and to the best of my knowledge, Gargoyles did not possess telepathic abilities. Yet, the way he said that one sentence, the fact he couldn't look me in the eye, told me everything.

"Ben?"

"I think so. I saw him at the end of your time there. He changed on a dime and was just staring at a group in the public play room. The look on his face...it was chilling."

"But I thought you said it was this other guy, the one whose family died?" Isaac said.

James rubbed his forehead and let out a long breath.

"I know. Either I was wrong and it's not the child that survived that massacre. Or Ben is that man. You said yourself Isaac, his back story doesn't add up, it reads like someone made it up."

"Wait, you two were investigating Ben?" I asked. "Since when?"

"Since you told us about him," Isaac answered. "We thought maybe we could find out something that would be useful, get him to bend the rules. Or at least something that would help us protect you from him. And yeah, his back story is a little too perfectly benign."

"Speculating isn't going to help," James said, "we need to get back to the penthouse and look at all the evidence side by side. I also need to check on something with the Archive Librarian, there was a weird kind of shadow that--"

"Stop! Stop talking!"

I couldn't breathe. Their theory, the very real possibility that I'd fucked a *serial killer* was suddenly choking me. I sprinted down the street to the corner, desperate to get my mind to clear, to shed the panic that was about to overtake me. I hated Ben, but he'd always been a known quantity. He had been obsessed with me, stalked me, threatened me. I could handle a piece of shit like that.

But this? Using evil knives to carve people up? He could possibly be the kid that my dad had kept tabs on for years, the one that he'd dragged me to visit a few times. If that was the case, had he been obsessed with me from then? Did he know who I was? Who my father was?

"No, stop," I told myself.

I needed to remove the emotion from this, to lay out all the evidence clearly and see if those lines really did connect. I closed my eyes and breathed deep. In and out...in and out. Once my heart started to slow down, and my hands stopped shaking, I saw the path forward clearly. I could do nothing for the victims other than bring their killer to justice. And that was exactly what I was going to do.

"You're right, James, we need to go back to the penthouse," I said to my partners, who had followed me at a small distance. "If Ben really is that guy, if he is the one stalking these people then we need to know that because it might give us some answers on how to draw him out. We also need to compare the list of Supernatural victims with the list of those involved in the attack on his family. If this is about revenge, then he's checking them off the list and we need to see how many and what kind are left. And we need to look at the footage again, specifically whatever you saw with Ben, see if those two could be in that group."

Isaac squeezed my hand and gave me a lopsided smile of encouragement. He knew better than to get all mushy with me out here where everyone could see. James just studied me for a moment, the barest flicker of movement made me wonder if he was about to hug me and if he shut it down.

"Let's go then," he said.

We walked back to the crime scene to confirm that there wasn't anything left for us to do and collect any information that the CSI had found so far. It was scant at best, but when I asked them to turn the bodies over, the same sigil from the previous bodies was carved into the Orc's back. This time it was the only knife work that appeared precise, unemotional, and showed the sigil as complete.

*Why do I get the feeling like he's been practicing?*

Disgust welled up inside of me and I pushed it down. Emotion was fine, and there would be time to feel all of it later. Now was the time to investigate, to seek answers. I needed to channel my feelings toward that and not let it sideline or blind me.

It was a short drive back to the penthouse, my mind preoccupied with the unbelievable possibility that Ben was the killer. I examined every interaction with him, both in our relationship and in the club tonight. He'd never confessed to me that he knew about Supernaturals when we dated, but he would've had to be somewhat comfortable with the fact of their existence since he invested in the club.

*And if he did, and he is the killer, then that means he bought it specifically to source his victims.*

Fury heated my blood and I clenched my jaw. That club was supposed to be a place of safety, a place where people could be themselves in a way they couldn't anywhere else. And he'd corrupted it, made it dangerous, a farm to feed his sick need to mutilate and kill. It was far too easy to see Ben as the killer in this moment and I worried that it was because of our past. I needed to calm down, find clear evidence that was irrefutable. Only then could I proceed with taking him down.

On the ride up, I may have been able to calm down a bit if not for the spike of fear that lanced through the small space seconds after we entered the elevator.

One moment James was leaning against the wall, frowning in thought, the next he was in front of both Isaac and me, a fierce, low growl coming from his throat.

Suddenly, Isaac's claws came out and he pushed me behind him.

"What the hell is going on?" I asked.

"Something is wrong," James' voice was unnaturally low and he transformed in front of me. "Isaac, watch her."

"Okay, seriously I can take--"

"Magic," Isaac hissed.

"*Dark* magic," James replied.

The elevator doors opened and both James and Isaac's claws fully extended, razor sharp and gleaming in the light.

"Stay here with her," James ordered.

Isaac visibly bristled but shuffled me into a corner and blocked off any escape with his body. In his human glamour, I might be able to see over his head, but in his true Gargoyle form, Isaac was just tall and wide enough that I couldn't glimpse what was happening.

"Talk to me," I demanded. "What's wrong?"

"Someone broke into the penthouse," Isaac snarled. "That should've been impossible but they used magic to break his wards."

I swallowed at that. If Ben could wield magic...

"Who would do that?"

Isaac stilled and huffed out a breath.

"I have some things to tell you once we know it's safe."

"Well, that doesn't sound good."

He groped behind him for my hand and I gave it to him. He squeezed, as if he were trying to hold onto me, keep me not just hidden and safe, but with him. Isaac being scared brought out a need to comfort him, to take care of him, which was more than a little surprising. While I wasn't an unfeeling bitch with my partners, it was rare that my protective instincts flared so fast and hot.

"You can trust me," I said, pressing myself against his broad back and winding my arms around his waist.

He was warm, firm and already familiar in a way that surprised and pleased me.

"I'm afraid you'll hate me."

"It would take a lot for me to hate you Isaac. And I'm pretty sure that while I may get angry, I'm not going to hate you."

"I hope that's true."

I heard the claws on James' feet click before he rounded the corner and filled the doorway of the elevator.

"It's clear of traps or anyone that shouldn't be there. But they've taken our evidence and research."

"What?" I screeched, pushing against Isaac so I could get out.

He moved after a shocked moment and we ran into the penthouse. I skidded to a stop in the main room and stared, mouth hanging open.

They hadn't just stolen things, they'd demolished the place. The furniture was torn to bits, the stuffing pulled out. Pictures were torn off the walls, glass lying all over the floor in bright shards. The table was overturned, monitors and laptops smashed to bits. The kitchen was disaster, with every cupboard emptied, and I was sure if we went into the bedrooms, those would be wrecked too. Among all of this, the part that didn't make sense was that the containment unit for the knives was utterly destroyed, the smoldering ruins of it wreaked of ozone and sulfur. The floor boards had been torn up at odd intervals as well, revealing openings as if there had been things stashed there. When I looked closer, I saw that actually, they hadn't been torn up, but blown to bits, as if someone had blasted an explosion to make each hole.

"I assume that's where the wards were," I said, pointing to them.

"Yes," James said. "The good news is that everything we had was scanned and backed up onto the Archive's private servers. The bad news is that the Protectors now have all the same knowledge we do. They'll be closing in on the knives."

I frowned at him in confusion.

"The who?"

James glanced at Isaac who scowled as he stalked around the place.

"I haven't had the chance to fill her in," he replied.

"Fill me in on what?"

Isaac heaved a sigh and told me about being recruited into the Protectors, who they were, what they wanted from him, what they were threatening him with. All of it.

Of course, I was angry about losing all of our evidence, about some other assholes being out there more concerned with some damn magical knives instead of the people who were getting hurt by them. But more than that, I was angry at these Protectors, at how they'd used Isaac, how they'd scared him and how they'd used me to do it.

Yes, he'd lied to me, nearly betrayed the investigation and had definitely put it all at risk. If James hadn't backed up the files we'd be up shit creek without a paddle.

*Speaking of James...*

I glanced at him, worried that this would make him throw Isaac out of the investigation, not that I'd allow that. But instead of the closed off cold scowl I'd expected, there was just as much concern for Isaac as I had. And a fierceness that I recognized as the mirror of my own desire to protect Isaac.

If James, whose trust was about as difficult to win as the lottery, could put his faith in who Isaac was, then that was pretty convincing evidence to go with what my instincts were telling me.

"Say something?" Isaac whispered, his voice trembling.

"I'm not happy, " I admitted. "You should've told me before now, you should've..."

"I know. I was afraid, but you're right. If I'd told you, then maybe we wouldn't be in this situation now. And I know asking you to trust me is going to be hard, but I am trying to leave that damned organization. I've been putting them off about what's going on in the investigation but they must've followed me here and taken matters into their own hands."

He shook his head.

"I was stupid to think that I could out smart them."

"Beating yourself up won't help," James said.

And then it hit me. Why he may have wanted to be spanked tonight, why he looked like he'd let something so heavy go when I'd finished.

"You've felt guilty for a while," I said.

Isaac's purple eyes swung up to mine and he knew exactly what I was talking about.

"Yes."

I walked up to his back and ran my hand down the wide expanse. Isaac stiffened and sucked in a breath, the welts of my flogger faint on his skin. I pressed a kiss between his shoulder blades before circling around to face him.

"You wanted forgiveness, absolution?"

"Yes," his voice cracked.

Bracketing his face between my hands I planted a soft kiss on his mouth. This was Isaac, my Isaac. The one I trusted with parts of myself that I hadn't shown anyone else in so long that I'd forgotten what it was like to be seen in that way. My partner, my best friend. He'd made a mistake. A big fucking one, but he'd tried to fix it and failed. Now he needed help, not recrimination.

*And it will only keep us from stopping the killer to fight among ourselves over things we can't undo anyway.*

"Given," I said, and pressed another soft kiss to his mouth.

Isaac groaned against me and pulled me tight.

"Stella...I don't think I deserve you."

"Oh, you don't," I chuckled. "But I don't deserve you either so I guess we're even."

Isaac let out a breathy laugh and I kissed him again.

"Where do we go from here?" I asked James once I'd slid my arm around Isaac.

"I've contacted the Archive. We can use one of their bases here in the city. A couple members of the tech team will meet us there to get us set up with access to the servers and new equipment. When anyone is in residence on a base, the Archive has around the clock staff for security. This won't happen again."

"This wasn't an option before?" I asked.

"I wanted to keep a low profile and..."

"What?"

James pinned me with his eyes and I gulped down a breath.

"I didn't think you'd come with me if I was working out of one of the safe houses."

I could fall into those dark eyes and never want to crawl out. I'd done it before, and it was the most exhilarating and terrifying and heartbreaking experience of my life.

That's why I had to look away, to protect myself.

"Next time, ask," I said. "Now, let's see if there's anything worth salvaging and get the hell out of here."

We fanned out in the destroyed penthouse, sifting through shredded Italian leather and possibly original edition art work that most museums would weep to be able to own.

James carefully rolled those up while he also looked around for anything else of value. Under the destroyed remnants of his coffee table, I spotted a small case that would fit a few file folders and wondered if the idiots who had raided this place had left something after all. As I bent down to pick it up, a pressure pushed against my ears, as if I were changing elevation. The stinging stench of sulfur hit me moments before James roared and his body collided with mine.

A bright flash of light blinded me at the same time something else pushed me through the air, and I landed on my back.

"Stella! James!" Isaac screamed.

I could barely hear him over the ringing of my ears. My vision was so fuzzy that I couldn't focus my eyes. Was I lying down? What was that sticky stuff under me?

"James..." I whispered just before my heavy body fell into darkness.

# CHAPTER FOURTEEN

## STELLA

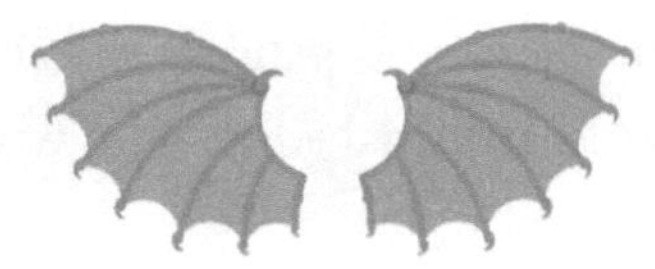

Everything rushed back.

An explosion.

James jumped in front of me.

Blood.

Ben.

Ben was a killer.

Maybe.

Mutilated bodies.

More blood.

James jumped in front of me to save me.

*James...no.*

"James!" I screamed and sat up.

Wires snaked out from my arms and some kind of heavy blanket was draped over me. The room was dark and my heart pounded from the nightmare and the unfamiliarity around me. As my eyes adjusted, I recognized a kind of hospital room. I was lying in a very large hospital bed. Monitors beeped beside me and the lights were off except nearby where someone was staring at me, a clipboard in their hands. Once my eyes focused more, I recognized that she had smoke curling off her dark red skin, eyes that were completely black and a smile that showed two sets of fangs.

"Well, well, well, you're awake early," she said, her voice husky, seductive.

"Where am I? Where's James?"

"You are in an Archive hospital, although you'd know it as the old Queen Anne High School. James is down the hall, likely arguing about not needing anymore medical attention." She came toward me and I saw that she was clothed in a tightly fitted vest over a light blue button up, fitted black slacks and one long braid dangled down her back. Slim red and black horns curled on either side of her head.

"What are you?" I asked before I could stop myself.

Her mouth widened and she laughed.

"You *are* a spit fire, aren't you? That's good, James needs someone like that in his life. I'm an Ephemeral. My name is Delphine."

"Stella, " I said.

"Nice to meet you."

"What happened?"

"You were almost incinerated with a very nasty, cursed item," she said, pulling the heavy blanket back to expose pink skin on my upper thighs. "The blanket has been accelerating your healing. You'll need about another hour before I can discharge you."

"What the...?"

The blanket glowed as she put it back on me and that's when I noticed a tickly kind of itch over the area that had been burned.

"Susan LaFlesche Picotte's blanket," Delphine said.

"Okay..."

She smiled at my confusion.

"She was a female physician in the eighteen hundreds who traveled thousands of miles to care for Indigenous people. This was a blanket she often carried with her to soothe those she cared for. It absorbed her gift for healing and comfort."

I wasn't at all sure I should be touching such an artifact of not only cultural significance, but obvious power too. It made me uneasy to have one James' magical items on me.

"It won't hurt you," she handed me a glass of water.

"Is James alright?"

"He put his stone skin up in time, but even that couldn't protect him from the explosion completely. He's got a few burns on his back but he'll be fine. Gargoyles heal pretty fast."

"Maybe he should have the blanket."

"I suggested that, and he refused. Said he wanted you to have it."

"Oh."

Delphine chuckled.

"Yeah *oh*. Gotta say, never thought I see the day James fell to cupid's arrow once, much less twice."

"What...I mean, it's not like that between us. He's just a friend...colleague, that's all."

"Sure. And that other Gargoyle is also just a friend to both of you?"

I flushed and looked away.

"Look, it's none of my business but I'm going to give you a piece of advice anyway," Delphine sat on the edge of the bed, her smile fading. "Working for the Archive can be rewarding, exciting, it can even feel like a life's purpose. But the danger that comes with it...well, let's just say that those of us who have been here long enough, we know that when we see happiness, we grab it and hold on for as long as we can because something, or someone, is always around the corner to take it away from us. Happiness in this life isn't just fleeting. It's rare, and fragile. If you find it, if he does, don't push it away. It might not come around again."

"Why are you dropping these truth bombs on someone you barely know?"

"Because James is a friend who helped me at a very low time in my life. I might not be here without him. And I owe him a debt. If I can nudge him toward the happiness I was denied, then my debt will be repaid."

Her voice was thick with sadness and regret. It pierced through the flimsy barriers I'd been holding onto around James and Isaac, around what I knew we all wanted and could have. I couldn't escape the truth of her words, no matter how much I wanted to. This experience proved what she said. I'd thought that we just needed to get through this case, come out the other side and then I could figure out what these feelings for James meant, how they could live side by side with Isaac.

But that was bullshit. There were forces that wanted us dead, that almost had accomplished it. What would I have done if James hadn't been able to use his stone skin protection in time? What if it had been Isaac, whose stone skin wasn't as strong as James'?

"Get some rest," Delphine said, getting to her feet.

"I can't. There's a killer out there."

"Well then, at least give that blanket another hour or you'll be in quite a lot of pain from those burns."

I nodded, her words swimming around my mind in confusing soup. Exhaustion hit me hard and I laid back, intending to just rest my eyes for a moment, and think about what she'd said, even though I didn't want to.

But I must've drifted off because when I opened my eyes, the blanket was gone and the blinds in the room were open to let in some of the Seattle afternoon summer sun. I winced at the brightness at first and then my eyes adjusted. In the corner, standing there like a sentinel, eyes wide with unmistakable worry, was James.

He took a step toward me, a half lunging movement that he halted in the middle of and just continued to stare at me. Usually I would've given him shit for being such a worrywart, but not this time. Not when we had come so close to losing one another.

He rubbed his enormous, clawed hand on his ridiculous black slacks, tail lashing behind him.

"How are you feeling? Are you hungry? Thirsty? You know, the blanket can cause a little bit of dehydration, that's why we had you on an IV but they disconnected it about an hour ago. I can get you some water or Gatorade, I know how you like those carbonated waters. Maybe--"

"James," I said, before he could recite the entire menu of whatever passed for a cafeteria around here.

He stopped, swallowed and continued to stare at me with those big sad eyes.

"Stop feeling guilty," I said.

"Can't. I should've swept the place more thoroughly. I should've kept you both out of there altogether. I wasn't thinking clearly enough!"

I reached out for him and snagged his hand when he got close, which dwarfed mine. He stared at our hands, and ran his thumb over my knuckles.

"You could've died," his whisper was ragged. "You'd be gone forever and I'd be here, in a world without you."

The torture in those words snagged on my heartbeat and pulled. I used to think that James wouldn't have cared what happened to me, that his leaving the way he had meant that he was done with me. And for twelve years, that's exactly what it had been.

And now, here he was, tormented at the thought of losing me. He hadn't really gotten over what had been between us; we'd both just shoved it to the side and tried to forget about it, like a ghost in an attic. But, like all ghosts, it got tired of being ignored and was now screaming to get out. Even though I wanted to face it all, fear locked me in place.

"I'm sorry, Stella," he whispered.

"Don't," I tried to pull my hand away but he wouldn't let me. "You can't just...You're just saying that because you almost got me blown up."

"No, I'm not."

I pulled again and he tightened his grip.

"Will you stop trying to put up a wall between us and listen?"

"No," my voice broke. "I can't let you hurt me again. I won't."

James winced at that and I thought he would stop holding onto me, but he came closer instead.

"I'm sorry I ran that night," his voice was rough. "I'm sorry I lied to you. I said it was a mistake, but it wasn't."

Tears coursed down my face, hot and terrible. My chest was hurting again, cracking and burning as he lanced the wound he'd inflicted all those years ago.

"Stop," I sobbed.

He took my face in his hands, and his thumbs wiped the tears away, but more just took their place.

"Stella, I wasn't prepared for you, for what you meant to me. I hurt you and I ran and by the time I realized what I'd done, I thought it was too late so I stayed away. But now that I'm back with you I realize what I did. You are my mate, you always have been. That's why it hurt so bad to leave you."

"No," I tried to shake my head but he held me fast. "Isaac, you and him--"

"Gargoyles can have more than one mate."

The full implication of his words hit me and I could only stare at him. Isaac...Isaac was his mate.

*But so am I.*

My body was a mass of confusion as it all sank in.

I wanted to run.

I wanted him to hold me.

I wanted to kiss him.

I wanted to hit him.

In the end, I knew that this reunion could not be gentle. There was too much shit that had piled up. James had to earn my submission; he had to break not me, but the scar tissue that had accumulated over the wound he'd inflicted on my soul.

I slapped him hard across the face. Shock and anger, lust and arousal warred, all in equal degrees in his expression and he let me go.

"You threw me away that night," I spat at him, all the pain filling my throat and dripping from my words. "You told me it was a mistake, that I was a mistake!"

"I was wrong."

"And so that's supposed to make it all better?"

"No, of course not but--"

"You broke my fucking heart!"

I drew back to hit him again when he seized my wrist.

But I do have two hands, and I began to raise that one when he grabbed it too. With a sharp push, I was flat on my back on the large bed, arms pinned on either side of my head. James bared his teeth at me, so close that his breath was hot against my face.

"I wish I'd never met you," I cried.

*I missed you.*

"Liar," he snarled.

"I wish you'd never fucked me."

*I wish you'd fuck me right here.*

His pupils flared.

"Liar."

"Fuck you!"

*Fuck me!*

I don't know which of us moved first, maybe it was both of us, because our mouths smashed onto each other, all teeth and tongues, as we sought to dominate one another. The burn of my broken heart flared into a full-on inferno, consuming my body and incinerating any reservations. It turned me into an animal when he released me, grasping and tearing my nails into his shoulders. I wanted to rip him to shreds while I rode his face, I wanted to tear his heart out while he filled me with his cum.

He wasn't exactly gentle either. The claws of one hand shredded the thin hospital night gown with one swipe and I was completely naked underneath. His claws stung my flesh where he raked them down my body, as if seeking the part of me that would give in to him.

"I'm going to fuck you," he growled against my throat. "Make you come over and over again on my cock until you're screaming my fucking name, *mine* Stella! This pussy, these tits, this ass, your goddamn soul. All of it is mine!"

I wanted to tell him to shut up and just do it already when he simultaneously bit my shoulder and shoved two of his fingers into me up to the knuckle.

I screamed and grabbed one of his horns to hold him in place. The pain of his teeth and the insane way my body hungered for him mixed into one hell of cocktail. I wanted the beast, I needed him as wild as I was. I wanted his marks all over my body, to feel the ache of him for days. Only this pain, mixed with acute pleasure, would begin to heal what he broke.

"Big talk," I gasped as he worked me mercilessly, "but I don't see your cock anywhere."

He pulled his mouth off my flesh, dark eyes glowing. When he grinned, a spike of fear hit me.

He was ferocious, dark and powerful, and he was about to take twelve years' worth of sexual need and pain out on me.

*At least I hope so.*

His pants dropped and I groaned with hunger when I saw his massive cock.

Dear god, he was magnificent.

So thick that I knew without a doubt he would split me but I did not care. Veins ran under the bulging ridges that began at his base and ended at the bulbous tip, where the rings were swollen. His horn dripped a golden liquid along his shaft, thick like honey. I licked my lips, longing to taste him.

"You want this," slowly he ran his hand over his dick while he pumped me with the other. "You want me to fuck you dirty and bare? Fill up that cunt of yours?"

"As if I don't have another Gargoyle on retainer," I spat at him.

He laughed, the dark sound skittering across my skin and I shivered.

"Oh, baby girl," he crooned, still working us both deliberately, his fingers starting to crook inside of me. "You are so fucking sexy when you fight me. Safe word."

I bit my lip to stop a moan from erupting, and grinned up at him. This was going to hurt, and I was going to savor it.

"Wings."

The savage confidence he'd been wielding began to weaken and he slowed his movements, staring at me with thinly veiled shock. I'd thrown him off, taken the upper hand of control. I should've been thrilled at that, but instead I just felt more raw and exposed. I didn't want his tenderness right now, I didn't want him to suddenly stop trying to win this battle. I needed him to overtake me, to wrestle control from me, to earn it.

"What, lose your courage?" I challenged, rolling my hips against his hand. "Should I just finish the job myself since you're not up for it?"

It was like I'd slapped him again. His lips curled up into another snarl, and my pussy clenched at the sight of those fangs of his. He withdrew his hand and yanked me up from the bed. His claws dug into my hips, and I knew I'd have the marks of them on my body for days. It made a rush of heat and wetness fill me. When he slammed me against the wall so hard my tits bounced, my legs wrapped around him of their own accord. James ran his cock through me, up and down, up and down.

My nails sank into his shoulders as the sensations ripped through me. Not enough though, not nearly enough.

"Beg," he commanded.

"No."

He bit and licked my throat and down to my rock hard nipples. When he sucked them between his teeth, the sharp bite of his fangs had me trying to roll myself down onto him. I was aching to be filled, to be stretched to the point of pain and beyond. But all he did was let me feel the tip of him, pressed it to my clit in tiny circles that teased and put me on the edge of release.

"Beg," he said again against my skin.

I whimpered this time, my own need to be in control slipping.

"N-no."

He chuckled and continued to torture me with sharp bites and tiny intrusions of his cock at my entrance.

"Beg me to fill this pussy," his dark voice made me quake, his teeth scraping against my breast as he talked. "Beg me to fuck away the last twelve years, Stella, and I swear we'll never be apart again."

*Crack* went my heart, and I started to sob again.

"James," I could barely get the word out.

My chest was caving in and my heart was splintering. I needed him to help me shed everything I'd surrounded myself with, but I did not expect it to hurt like this.

He looked up at me, and there was tenderness there, but that wasn't all. There was fire in his eyes, illicit promises in the way his tongue darted out onto my skin. He was the dark god of all my fantasies, all my broken-hearted desires. He was the only one I would submit to, the only one who had ever, and would ever, earn it. Whether or not he broke me all over again, whether or not I should trust him, that truth was clear to me in this moment.

So I let the jagged pieces he'd splintered start to come back together. I let my heart begin to beat with the warmth I had denied it, and tasted tears on my lips when I whispered, "Please, James. Please fuck me."

One moment he was pulling me into those dark eyes of his and the next I was drowning with the sudden hard thrust of him up into me.

"You feel so fucking good."

He pulled out and pistoned back in.

"I never want another woman Stella. Never. This is my pussy."

He kissed me, drinking my tears and my screams of dual pain and delight as he fucked me hard. At first, all I could do was cling to him as he pushed me to the cliff's edge of sensation.

His cock-horn hit my clit over and over, each time spreading fire through my body as the aphrodisiac flooded my system. I began to grind down to meet his every thrust until I was riding him as much as he was fucking me. Our bodies moved in time with each other as if we'd been doing this all our lives. I could feel his every ridge, scraping along my walls, hitting my G-spot with brutal efficiency.

"Beg me to fill this cunt with my seed," he panted.

"Yes, yes, please."

"Please what, baby girl?"

"Fill me up, I want you dripping out of me for days."

"Fuck!"

His hips picked up to a punishing pace that was wringing me out with unending pleasure. Every time I thought I was about to finally come, there would be another peak, and another. I was so aroused, so sensitive that I was now crying for a different reason.

"Please, James," I sobbed, "make me come."

He thrust into me completely, and I threw my head back into the wall as I bit down on another scream. I was so full, it was almost too much. But then his hips swirled, his horn pressing and circling my clit, again and again, and I couldn't hold it back. Obscene sounds rained from my lips, punctuated by nonsensical words, pleading and begging him.

"C'mon baby," he crooned, "let go and milk my cock like a good girl."

*Crack* went the last bit of my armor and I let it all go.

Stars burst behind my eyes and my toes curled as everything exploded. I choked out a rolling sound that was half mewling half exultant as my entire body lit up and pulsed. Warmth rushed up into me and I realized that James was coming now too. That only pushed me onto another one and we trembled through the onslaught together. The rings on the head of his cock expanded and I gasped, mouth hanging open as I was stretched yet further.

In the back of my mind I wondered what my cunt would look like after James' savage fucking. But even if it was a gaping hole, I couldn't care less. I was boneless, drifting along on a sea of warmth, and the sense of being completely cared for, wanted.

James' arms circled me and drew me against him. I was cradled against him as he carried me to the bed. We were locked together until his rings deflated and I wondered if the bed would even hold the two of us. But as he positioned us onto it, the hospital bed didn't so much as creak.

I let out a long breath, not even self-conscious that I was drenched in sweat and hadn't showered for at least a day. James turned onto his back and nestled me against his chest, pulling up a blanket when I shivered and covering us both. His claws played with my hair while his other arm held me tight.

I planted little kisses on his chest, unable to help myself as I drew circles on his huge arm with my fingernails.

"Are you alright?" he asked.

"I'll be sore, but I'm fine," I looked up at him with a grin. "Next time maybe we could try a bed or the floor."

He chuckled.

"We do seem to have an affinity for the wall, don't we?"

The memory dimmed my joy, and his too. James' claw carefully traced my jaw and he shook his head.

"I was an idiot. Can you forgive me?"

I took a deep breath, unsure of what to say or do. I wanted to say yes, to put it all behind me and pretend like it was just a bad dream. But it wasn't. It was one of the defining moments of my life, for better or worse.

"I will," I said, my words slow. "But it's going to take time for me to trust you again."

"I know. And I'll do whatever it takes to earn that trust. I just need you to know that I can't go back to not having you in my life. You or Isaac. I can feel you both, here," he put his hand over his heart. "You're both connected to me. And our connection, I broke it when I left. Now I need to rebuild it because I don't want to live without you, Stella."

I let out a long breath. It was everything I wanted to hear when I was twenty. And everything I was afraid to grab hold of now.

"I don't expect you to feel the same," he continued. "But I hope you will in time."

"I... James, I never got over you," I admitted, though it terrified me. "I want all of this, but I'm scared."

I cringed and shook my head, fearing this vulnerability as much as I knew it had to happen.

"I'm sorry," he cupped my cheek. "I'll do anything to earn back your trust. Whatever you need."

I wasn't sure exactly what that would be, with one exception.

"You," I swallowed the tightness in my throat. "I need you and Isaac. I don't how it will all work, but I want you both in my life."

James sighed and then gave me *that* look, the one that had been on his face with Isaac, the one I thought I'd imagined when we'd been together before.

And I gasped out a sob.

"Don't cry," he whispered, kissing the tears away again. "My heart, my mate."

I let out another sob that turned into a giggle and I was shaking my head, beaming at him as James looked at me with a confused frown on his face.

"You don't understand."

"You're right," he said.

"That look," I ran my hand over his broad face, relishing the fact that I could. "It's...it's everything I wanted. It's you loving me. You love me."

I laughed and cried and peppered his face with kisses as he chuckled under me.

"Well, of course I love you," his sinfully deep voice sang over me. "You think I'd form a mating bond with someone I didn't?"

James kissed me, languid and slow this time as his hand squeezed my ass.

"I missed this," he smacked it and I flushed. "Next time, maybe I put you over my knee, make this pretty ass all cherry red."

"Next time?" my eyebrow quirked up. "Someone is very confident of a repeat performance."

"Oh, baby girl, I'm just getting started with you."

My grin turned devilish.
"I should hope so."

# CHAPTER FIFTEEN

## ISAAC

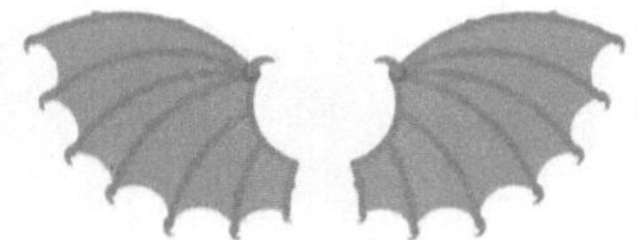

I could smell the two of them down the hall, and decided to guard the door so no one disturbed them. This was a long time coming and I'll be damned if anyone ruined what might be the one chance we all had to be happy together.

The sounds they made, snarling and growling, crying out and banging against the wall had me painfully hard but I tamped down on it. Hopefully they would want me with the two of them at some point. But even if they didn't, I had them both individually, and that was enough for now.

Once things quieted down, my mind again replayed the terrifying moments after the cursed object went off.

James had stayed conscious long enough to call for the Archive to come get us all and then he collapsed. I'd never been more conflicted and terrified than I was trying to make sure both of them were alive. The Archive got there fast, but for me, it felt like forever before James and Stella were loaded into an ambulance and taken to a hidden Supernatural's hospital. The facility was actually the former Queen Anne

High School but a glamour made everyone believe it was an apartment building. The Ghosts here were a bit intrusive, but they also helped keep too many Mundanes from snooping around by giving off some very uncomfortable spectral vibes. I was a Supernatural and even I found it a bit much while I'd been here.

Once we arrived, it had taken hours for both Stella and James' treatments to be completed, and even then, Stella had slept through the night and most of the next day due to the extent of her injuries.

I knew that I would never be able to forget the sight of her lying on the rubble-strewn floor of James' penthouse, burns running from her torso down her legs, cuts from debris on her face. Then James staggering against the injuries that had gotten through his stone skin. His entire back had to be treated as well as the backs of his thighs.

*Thank god he didn't have his wings out or it would've been much worse...not that it was great to begin with.*

"Okay, are they done?" the Ephemeral doctor asked with a fangy grin.

"Probably, though I'm pretty sure he knotted her."

She sighed.

"Fucking Supernatural males and their dicks. Alright, I'll be back, but you don't need to stand guard you know. Go get some rest, you look like shit."

"Thanks."

She chuckled and walked away.

I ran a hand over my face and realized that she was right. I was exhausted; I had barely slept since we got here.

*Maybe I'll just rest my eyes in the waiting room.*

It was a small private room that they'd shoved me into when we all first arrived. They wouldn't let me see either of them, so I was left to pace and worry until one of the doctors recognized that I needed to see them or he'd have one out of control Gargoyle on his hands.

Once I knew they were alive, I was given security clearance and the use of a laptop to take a look at the files James had uploaded to the secure server. It was the best distraction I could've had, telling myself that Stella would want an update when she woke up.

*Because she will. And she'll be fine...she has to be.*

If there had been any doubt that I was head over heels for her, it was destroyed by the gaping ache that erupted inside my chest at the mere thought of never seeing her again. And then I'd think of losing James and something similar would happen. It wasn't unheard of for Gargoyles to develop mating bonds to more than one being, but I never thought that I'd have that, being half Mundane. Even though my experience was milder than some I'd heard of, I had no doubt that my nature was indeed bonding to both James and Stella, just in different ways.

With Stella, the bond was wild, fiery and without hesitation.

And with James it was quieter, slower, almost contemplative.

*Just like the two of them.*

I snorted as I packed up the laptop and legal pads I'd been making notes on.

"Something funny?" James asked, from the doorway.

He smelled like her and him, mingled and fucking perfect. My nostrils flared and I took a deep breath. James' grin widened when he noticed and he shook his head.

"So, I guess you know."

"Are you kidding? I had to stand guard to keep security out of there. They thought someone was killing her."

James chuckled darkly.

"Oh there was plenty of death, just not the kind they were thinking of."

I smirked.

"So I don't need to navigate the snappish sexual tension between the two of you anymore?"

"I wouldn't say that," he answered, crossing his arms. "It's Stella's preferred method of foreplay so..."

"Fuck," I ran a hand over my face.

"You alright?"

James came up to me and put his hands on my shoulders.

"You look exhausted."

"I am, but it can wait. I was doing work, trying to find those connections that Stella wanted before everything blew up."

"Yeah, I know."

"Wait, how?" I asked, frowning at him.

"I've been checking on what you've found, putting together a presentation. You weren't the only one that needed a distraction while Stella healed."

"Oh, well...thanks for the heads up."

He massaged my shoulders and kissed my forehead.

"I thought you needed some space, I'm sorry if I misread."

"You didn't. I just...it's not good, James."

"No, it isn't. And we can't keep it from her."

What I'd found was disturbing in the extreme and, while I agreed with James, I still wanted to protect Stella from all of this. Especially since I knew she'd want to charge in and take care of Ben before he could harm anyone else.

"You two cuddle buddies ready to get out of here?" Stella asked, smiling at us from the doorway.

The second I saw her I broke away from James and wrapped her up in my arms. Some of the new security detail we had went to our places and packed up several weeks' worth of clothes for all of us and instead of the thin hospital nightgown, Stella was in her usual jeans and a faded band T-shirt.

"I thought I'd lost you," I kissed the top of her head.

"Can't get rid of me that easily," she grinned up at me and pressed a gentle kiss to my lips.

James came up to us, hesitant but obviously wanting to be a part of this. When Stella reached out for him I let out a breath of relief. He gathered us both against him, being so much larger than either of us and we both curled into his torso. It was so peaceful, so *right*, but still, I was shocked when the mating bonds in my chest snapped tightly into place. I gasped and James jumped.

He'd felt it too, and we stared at one another.

"What the fuck was that?" Stella asked, staring down at her hands.

"Did you feel that?" I asked.

"I felt something. It was like electricity zapped into me."

"That's the mating bonds," James answered. "Looks like you're stuck with us."

"You okay with that?" I asked.

She pursed her lips and looked up as if in thought.

"I don't know. Does that mean I get both your cocks at once?"

James threw his head back and laughed as I pulled her to me for a hard kiss.

"Baby girl, if you want to be stuffed full of Gargoyle cock, who are we to deny you?" James said.

Her grin was pure sin as she looked at both of us.

"Then I think I'm just fine with it," she said.

Once we'd packed up the laptop and any other supplies the Archive wanted us to have from the hospital, we were led to a back room that held a huge old fashioned elevator.

"Um," Stella glanced around, "someone want to explain the murder elevator?"

James snorted.

"They're taking us through the underground, in case we're being watched."

A tall, willowy framed woman with light brown skin and wavy dark brown hair darted into the elevator. Her shoulder holster held a pistol, and her hip holster a gun that looked straight out of a science fiction movie. Right behind her ran one of the most beautiful men I'd ever seen.

His brown skin was dusted with some kind of glittery powder, his short hair dyed in a light blue that faded to pink and then white at the tips, which were purposefully tousled. His long hands had bright pink nails that were impossible to miss as he waved at us, flashing a grin with his pink glossy lips. He wore a flowy kind of peasant blouse that was off the shoulder and a pair of very short shorts with pink gladiator sandals.

"Marcus?" James asked, shaking the man's hand. "This is a long way from London."

"Orders from Director Dearborne, love. She wants you to have the best and that's me."

"Sprite with you?"

"No, they had to get some things ready for a different mission. Just me and my dangerous colleague here."

He gestured to the woman who was closing up the elevator and pushing a few buttons to get us moving.

"Andromeda Kane, Head of West Coast security," she said, "call me Andy."

James introduced us all. Marcus gave me a playful once over and then glanced at James, whose frown clearly said that I was not available.

"Shut up!" Marcus' jaw dropped. "Did someone finally snag mister tall, dark and enigmatic?"

"We need new computers," James said instead of answering, "immediate access to the servers, holographic screen ability and level four security clearance for hacking."

Marcus whistled.

"That is a tall order. Lucky, I already figured you'd want all that. It's set up and waiting for you. But I've got a few more surprises."

He studied me before turning back around and making a note on a large tablet. Then he turned around again, gave me a slow once over and made more notations. James didn't seem especially phased by all this, but Stella and I exchanged confused frowns.

"What was that about?" she asked.

"Taking your measurements, dear," Marcus said.

"Without even touching me?"

He turned around and tapped his temple.

"I have special contacts. Lets me scan your body and upload it to my design suite"

"That a Sprite invention?" James asked.

"Of course! They're adjusting it to make threat assessment easier, lots more goes into it than what I use it for but they're hoping to have it ready for field testing in a few months."

"Wait," I said, mind racing to comprehend what I was hearing, "you have technology that can scan a person and get their measurements and you're turning it into..."

"A comprehensive way to scan an area and send the information to an AI that will assess possible threats, entry points and other issues in an area using a sophisticated algorithm."

Marcus answered like it was an everyday occurrence while Stella and I stared at James with open mouths.

"You work here?" Stella asked him.

"With this type of technology?" I marveled.

James shrugged.

"Yeah?"

Marcus snorted and shook his head as we stopped, then Andy began to open the gates and doors of the elevator.

"Only you would be so blasé about our work," he said. "Mr. Stoic, this one."

We stepped out into an area that was made to look like an old fashioned waiting room, with huge comfy chairs and a reception desk, where a Ghost hovered, dressed in old fashioned western garb.

"Hey there, Cap," Andy said, "we need a guide to four-ten-twenty."

The Ghost nodded and disappeared. Instead of reappearing, another one materialized at the door. This one was a young woman in flapper dress who winked at James.

"Okay, how is it you can see them and I can't?" Stella asked Andy.

"I've got a special charm that enables me to interact with them," she said. "But it's limited. I can only see them and talk to them, I can't hear them or interact with them past that."

"I gotta get me one of those," Stella muttered.

"Been a while, James," the Ghost said with a lustful grin.

James cleared his throat while I arched an eyebrow at him.

"Yes, well...shall we?"

"A Ghost?" I whispered, as we followed the guide out of the receiving room.

"Ever tried it?"

"Nope."

James grinned at me.

"Then don't judge."

The Ghost led us out into one of the many tunnels in the Supernatural network. They were all different depending on the Ghosts that kept them in shape. This one had small rooms every few feet, where Ghosts went about their daily existences. The tunnel itself was paved with a mixture of old stone and brick. The ceiling was more than sufficient in height for us, and James and I could walk side by side without touching the walls. It was nice not to feel claustrophobic in my true form. It wasn't as dark as other parts of the tunnel I'd been in, and I noticed that the lighting above us was an odd collection of antique chandeliers and lighting fixtures that looked like they belonged in a speakeasy. There was a musty smell that tickled my nose, not unusual for the tunnel system. But every once in a while, a sharp tinge of incense or something else would creep up from the Ghostly residents.

Marcus chattered on with James as we made our way, while Stella and I tried to digest just how incredible the Archive really was. I had assumed that it was all just people running around tracking down old relics and dropping them off at a warehouse. But from what I gleaned, while Marcus was divulging what had to be secrets, the Archive was a worldwide organization with several different sub organizations within that helped the agents and those in charge of storing artifacts. The one that Marcus and this person named Sprite worked for was the Magical Sciences Department. The name alone had my brain short circuiting for a full five minutes.

Marcus named a few others, including the apparently mysterious and super classified Library, but I was still stuck on the fact that people were combining science and magic and that it was helping to save the world.

*That's where I should've gone, that's where I want to go! If they'll have me after this, maybe...who knows though. First, I have to survive getting out of the Protectors.*

By the time we came to another receiving room with another elevator that would take us to the surface, my brain was bursting.

"Stay here while I, and my team, secure the area," Andy said, going into the elevator and slamming the doors closed.

"She's in a bad mood," Marcus said when she left. "Not any of your fault. She was pulled off security for the transport of the Hope Diamond."

"Jesus, they finally got it?" James asked, envy dripping from his tone.

"Oh my god, James! It was a shit show. That thing has so many curses on it. I recommended a portable dark vault storage unit, which we just got approved for field use, but Sprite was all 'No, we need to try and unravel the curses, it's too powerful blah blah.' First curse breaker comes in and guess what?"

"They get disintegrated," they both said at the same time.

"Took five Witches and a shit load of counter artifacts just to neutralize it," Marcus said.

"That's too bad about the curse breaker," James shook his head, "anyone I know?"

"No. Unfortunately, it was one of the new recruits, really desperate to prove herself."

James winced.

"Hate to see that happen."

"Yeah, but at least it happens less these days than before."

"Before what?" Stella asked with wide eyes.

Marcus opened his mouth to speak when James cut him off.

"Ancient history, right, Marcus?"

His mouth snapped shut and he mimed locking his lips.

"Well, now I'm really curious,' I said.

"Later," James said as Andy came back down and gave us the go ahead. "We have other things to focus on."

With a start, I realized that I'd actually forgotten about the case as we walked through the tunnels. It was a nice break, but James was right. We needed to finish this before anyone else died.

"Don't be a stranger, James," the flapper Ghost said with another wink.

I smirked at him while James grunted and gave her hasty wave goodbye.

"One of these days you're going to have to tell me how that works," I said.

"Okay, this is really annoying," Stella groused as the elevator took us up. "I can't see a damn thing."

"I'll tell you later," I said.

"That's not necessary," James cut in.

"Oh, from the way you're blushing, I think it is," Stella said with a wicked grin.

"Fuck me," James muttered.

"Only if you ask nicely," she replied with an eyebrow waggle.

Andy made a choking laughing sound and turned away, though Marcus just outright chortled.

The elevator let us out inside a large shed at the back of a property. We followed Andy out across a ridiculously manicured yard and through the back door of the house, which was a three story mini-mansion. The horns on my head buzzed as I detected more Supernaturals on the grounds, though I didn't see anyone else.

"There's security up and down the street and on the grounds," Andy said, leading us through the simple but elegant kitchen, down a short hall and into what had to have been a library or den at one point and was now our working space. "You'll have an Archive-approved chef but that's the extent of the household staff. The Director deemed this operation level five classified so I was limited to who I could bring into the house."

"A *chef*?!" Stella said with a clap of her hands, at the same time James said, "We don't need a chef."

The two of them frowned at each other and I saw the power struggle coming from a mile away. Which we did not have time for, and I certainly didn't have the patience to let play out.

So I put a hand on each of their shoulders and smiled at Andy.

"Thanks, that's just fine."

"No problem," she said with a chuckle. "I'll be out back in the mother-in-law if you need anything. Otherwise, the house is yours."

James scowled at me while Stella beamed and kissed me slow and seductively before shooting James a playful smile and darting into the new work space.

"Would you rather someone was on sight to feed her every four hours or deal with delivery?" I asked just as James opened his mouth to likely take me to task.

He pressed his lips into a line and let out a sharp breath through his nose. Without a word I knew I'd won, so we both followed Stella in to the room.

It was easily the size of the main room in James' apartment. The wall to my left was mostly windows half hidden in heavy blue drapes. My feet sank into thick blue and brown carpet as I took in the room we'd be working in. The walls were some kind of dark red wood and the bookshelves that lined the wall to my right were made of the same stuff. The ceiling was more than high enough to accommodate a Gargoyle's true seven and half foot height, so James and I shed our glamours. Not that I needed anything that large but James did. I was pleased to see that extra-large chairs and sofas had been provided for us, as well as what looked like a heavy dining room table where three laptops, four monitors and a strange black box sat in the center of the table. There was a fireplace on the far wall that was cleaned out and empty, and a sideboard held sodas, water and sports drinks to the side of that.

"This is...cozy," I said.

Stella laughed and plopped onto one of the oversized chairs at the table. It dwarfed her to the point where I had to stifle a laugh at how adorable she was, with her stern game face, in a chair that made her look like a child.

James, on the other hand, saddled up to the table, crossed his arms and grinned down at her. This time, I decided to just let them go for it while I set up the laptop I'd been working on at the hospital.

"What?" she asked, crossing her arms too. "This your seat? God knows it's perfectly portioned for you and your ego."

I snorted.

"Still with the smart mouth," James said. "Do I need to take you over my knee?"

And just like that, my cock was hard and I didn't give a shit what was on my laptop.

The only sign that Stella was affected was the flush in her face, otherwise she sat there, legs and arms crossed now with a shit eating grin as she stared up at James.

"You're all work and no play. There's no way you'd actually take a break to teach me some manners."

James caged her in with his hands on each of the arm rests and leaned down. His nostrils flared as he smelled her arousal, which was flooding my own senses as well. Just watching this little bit of their flirting had me bursting with want.

*I really want them to tie me up and make me watch them.*

I clenched my hand to keep from going to my dick and forced my attention back to the laptop even though the two of them were sucking all the air out of the room with their staring contest.

"Maybe that's because you'd like it too much," James murmured in that low, dark tone of his. "It's called a punishment for a reason."

"Excuses, excuses," Stella countered with her own sultry, mistress voice.

"If you two could decide whether you're going to work or fuck, that would be great," I finally burst out.

Their eyes slid to mine and I knew right then and there that the next time either of them played with me, I was in for it.

"Someone is feeling left out," Stella purred.

"We'll just have to make it up to him," James agreed.

I groaned and jumped to my feet, ready to just leave the two of them to wreck one another so we could get some work done after.

"Oh, all right," Stella huffed, pushing James away and getting to her feet, "party pooper."

Stella gave me a hard kiss and smacked my ass hard enough to echo through the room and make me bite down on a moan.

"You're really mean, you know that?" I whispered.

"Denial of desire is an effective tool," her breath caressed my ear. "Also it's pretty fucking hot to watch you get aroused by me and James. We'll have to find a way to include that."

I turned to her, some of the playfulness gone, which deflated her grin a bit too.

"Are you really okay with this? The three of us? Are both of you on board with that?" I asked them both.

"I thought our little hug in the hospital already answered that," Stella said.

"I think I need to hear you both say it."

James wrapped his hand around the back of my neck and pulled me in for a hard kiss that stole my breath and made my head fuzzy.

"It's what I want," he said.

Next Stella pulled my face to hers and plundered my mouth.

"Me too."

I was glassy eyed at this point and unsure what the hell to do. I'd wanted to get all the shit I'd discovered out in the open but now I was horny and exhausted.

"What do you want to do?" Stella asked me.

I let out a long breath, because being fucked senseless by both of them sounded pretty damn good. But the case was weighing on me, and the sooner we got that out of the way, the sooner I might be able to actually enjoy being utterly destroyed by these two.

"Work first, play later," I said.

"You always were the good one," Stella said with one last quick kiss.

James started getting the laptops synced while I started a pot of strong coffee.

"So," Stella said, sitting on the edge of the table once I got back, "what did you find while I was recuperating under the magic blanket?"

I took a deep breath, and nodded at James to bring up the files I'd sent him earlier.

The black box thing in the middle of the table dinged and in front of us a large box appeared, much like the outline of the white board we'd been using to tape up pictures and write notes on. This, however, was holographic, just like something out of a movie.

"That is the coolest thing I've ever seen!" Stella squealed, and leaned over to snag the box off the table.

"Careful!" James said.

Stella waved it around, and I wondered what the hell powered it since there was no cord.

"Is it Bluetooth?" she asked, holding it up high, and then down low.

"Yes," James snatched it from her and set it back on the table.

"I wasn't going to break it, sheesh."

"Isaac," he growled, "don't you have some evidence to share with us?"

"Ah, why yes, I do."

When the images and notes that I'd compiled suddenly appeared on the holographic board, I stared at it wide eyed.

"Is that what you were doing while you were recuperating?" I asked James.

"Yep."

Stella, who was suddenly a lot less distracted by the tech than by the images it was projecting, frowned up at the holographic board.

"Walk us through it," she said.

I slipped into that space in my mind that had always helped me dispassionately look at a case. It was harder than ever before, and I knew it was because Stella was so damn close to all of this. Even so, I wouldn't do her the disservice of thinking she was too weak to handle this. If she did have a hard time, James and I would be here to help, but until then, I was going to treat her as my partner, an equal, just like she deserved.

"I went through the footage that James had tagged from our night at the club," I began putting the stills up on the holograph. "Here's Ben, after coming downstairs."

The footage took up the entire projected screen and we watched Ben make his way through the public play room. No matter how many times I'd watched this, the way his entire demeanor went from visibly furious to a strange kind of predatory calm made my skin crawl. I was sure some people did have the ability to compartmentalize in such a way, but there was something about the way Ben did it that didn't seem natural. As if something else was influencing him in that exact moment.

"Show it again," Stella said, her voice distant, hard.

She had her game face on, all trace of playful seductress gone as she slipped into detective mode.

*Still sexy as fuck though.*

I shut down the thought and rewound the footage. We all watched it twice more and I paused.

"Show me the group he's staring at," Stella asked.

I pulled up the next section, paused and minimized it so that I could pull up driver's license pictures of the latest victims.

"These two," I motioned to the latest victims, "are here and here."

I showed where they were in the crowd; one was dead center, the other on the edge of the group.

"They don't look like a couple," James said.

"That doesn't mean much at the club," Stella said. "It could be part of a scene or maybe they're poly. But it does make Ben look like the killer."

"It certainly does. But we don't have hard evidence to tie him to the murders," James said. "We do, however, have enough to know that he's the likeliest person to have the knives."

"Maybe, but I doubt spooky cutlery is admissible evidence in a court of law," Stella said.

James looked like he wanted to say something and stopped himself. It set off a red flag in my head, but I ignored it. There would be plenty of time to figure out all of James' moods and expressions once this asshole was behind bars.

"I took the liberty of calling him," I said, earning dual scowls from James and Stella, "under the guise of informing him of the new murders. In a not subtle turn in the conversation, he alibied out. I checked on it, and the club member confirmed he was with her at the time of the murders."

"Who was it?" Stella asked.

I pulled up the photo of a Mundane female with blond hair, dressed in leather with a submissive collar. Stella shuddered, noticing the horrid similarities in their appearance.

"I don't recognize her," she said. "But Sapphire did mention that Ben had a sub under his thumb."

"I would have remembered a Stella doppelganger if she'd been there that night," James said.

"No, you wouldn't," Stella answered. "Also, according to Sapphire, Ben keeps her locked up tight..."

I brought up the time stamp that showed him coming down the stairs the next morning with the submissive in question.

"Do we see him go up the stairs on that night?" Stella asked.

"Yes."

I pulled that up too.

"How does the time stamp match up with when the Orc and Mundane left the public play area?" Stella asked.

James typed something on his laptop.

"He went upstairs at the same time the victims were leaving the club, according to security footage."

She bit her bottom lip and fidgeted with a pen.

"What are you thinking?" I asked after a few minutes.

"There are exits that most people don't know about," she said, "Dawn keeps them a secret from most of the staff and all of the guests. They're supposed to be for security to get to different areas quickly in the case of an emergency. What if Ben used one of these? They aren't monitored in any way. If he used one to leave, we would never know it."

"And if this woman was afraid of him or in a relationship with him she might feel compelled to cover for him," James said.

"I don't think Ben was keeping her in that room as part of Dom play," Stella said, her voice a little shaky. "He never liked other men looking at me, talking to me, nothing. If this woman is a stand in for me..."

"He's controlling her too," James finished.

"And using a Dom-sub relationship as cover," I said, anger burning through me.

"There's something else too," James said. "That strange shadow across Ben's eyes? I heard back from my contact at the Archive Library. There are no reports of the knives causing anything like that. But, there are magical mind control items that do that when activated."

"Maybe that's how he gets the victims where he wants them," Stella said. "I've been wondering that for a while. We know how he subdues them, but not how he gets them to the locations. If that's the case then he may not be choosing actual couples, just putting two victims together who fit whatever he's looking for at the time."

"What would the item look like?" I asked.

"It's usually a charm, about an inch or two in diameter," James answered. "The person has to wear it on them to use it. It's also not all powerful. If Ben isn't a Witch, and there are no signs that he is, then the charm would have a limited number of uses and limited strength in terms of who he could and could not influence. So he'd have to choose his victims carefully because the charm isn't going to last very long."

"Wait," Stella snapped her fingers. "Ben was wearing a necklace that night."

"Okay, skeezy but not unusual," I said.

"No you don't understand, Ben hates jewelry. He wouldn't even let me wear earrings when we had sex."

"That's a weird line to draw," James said.

"Yeah, well, he is a psycho stalker. And now probably serial killer," Stella swallowed, looking a little pale.

"You okay?" I asked.

She shook her head.

"No, but working this makes it better. If it's him, and I'm thinking more and more it is, then catching him and bringing him to justice is going to be a hell of a lot more than just closing a case. It's going to feel like justice for me too."

I rubbed her back and she leaned into my touch.

"The one question is," she continued, frowning at the screen, "how is he tied to the Pacific Heights massacre? Is that the right track or is it a false lead?"

I glanced at James as he scowled at the table, arms crossed.

"Fuck," Stella said, glancing between us. "You're not done dropping bombs, are you?"

"Afraid not."

She pinched the bridge of her nose.

"God I wish I drank during a case. Okay, just give it to me."

The list of assassins from the Pacific Heights murders popped up on the holographic screen next to a list of the Supernatural victims.

"A perfect match," I whispered. "And--"

"Oh my god," Stella covered her mouth and stared at James and me. "The last two on the list--"

"Gargoyles," I breathed.

"Two of them," James said.

Stella swore a blue streak as she pulled her hands through her hair. It was the way she looked when an idea she hated came to her, and I could guess exactly what it was.

"I know how we may be able to draw him out but...it's risky," she said.

"Use me as bait," I said, "with you at the club."

She nodded.

"No fucking way," James said, glowering at us. "Besides, he already saw you both there."

"But I was in my glamour," I said. "I'm the next Supernatural on his list. It could work."

"He already seems to want to get to me," Stella argued. "If he is the killer, then the combination of Isaac in his true form and me might be enough to push him over the edge. He'll make a mistake and you can catch him."

"Stella, you're underestimating his obsession with you," James said through gritted teeth.

"I know the stand-in thing with his new sub is creepy but--"

"Not that!"

James almost broke the laptop as he beat the keys. Instantly, driver's license photos popped up on the holograph showing the Mundane victims.

Every single one of them were blond, over five feet six inches tall, and within five years of Stella's age.

"Do you see it now?" James growled, eyes blazing. "He's not just choosing the Supernatural victims to check them off a list. He's finding ones that pair with stand-ins for you!"

Stella stared at the images, eyes wide, mouth gaping. Her skin paled and she looked like she was about to puke. I pulled her in for a hug but her eyes wouldn't leave the screen.

"How did we miss that?" she whispered.

"The first victim had dyed her hair the day before, but he must've been committed already because he went ahead with it," James answered.

"Oh my god...the most recent one," she began to shake, "what he did to her...he was angry at me that night at the club. He...oh my god, what he did to her, that's my fault."

"No," I pulled away enough to cup her face in my hands and make her look at me. "Fuck that. None of this is your fault, not one thing! It's his choice."

"But I antagonized him, I pushed him and then he...Isaac, what he did to her..." the last few words ended on a sob.

James came up behind her and engulfed her shoulders with his hands. Stella reached up and clasped one of them, her knuckles turning white with how hard she held on.

"Isaac is right," he said. "Ben's escalation isn't your fault. It would've happened regardless."

Stella was one of the strongest people I knew, but she also had one of the softest hearts. It was why she had to be so strong, so hard most of the time. And also why the fact that she showed this side to me at all was such a precious gift. But in times like this, when I needed her to see past the crushing grief and guilt, it was hard to know how to help her.

I was about to suggest that she take a rest, maybe see what the chef was making for dinner, when James' stern voice cut through the moment like a searchlight through the dark.

"Stella, this is not your fault."

She let out a shuddering breath, swallowed and half turned to look at him over her shoulder while my hand went to her waist. James and I held her like this, between us, a safe harbor for the tumult of emotions that threatened to sweep her away.

It felt good.

It felt *right*.

When she looked back at me, her eyes were red from crying but there was a stubborn set to her jaw that made me smile.

*There's that sexy as fuck strength.*

"I'm done letting him use me to hurt others," she said. "Let's nail the son of a bitch."

# CHAPTER SIXTEEN

## STELLA

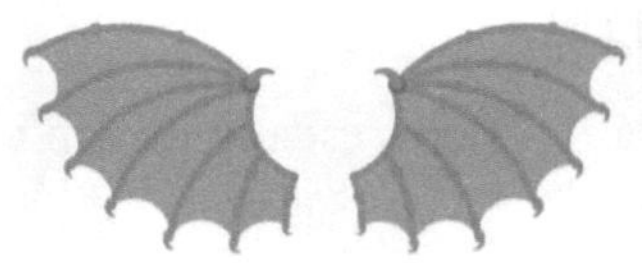

I t turns out that finding out that your psycho ex has become a serial killer, is targeting women that look like you and might be exacting revenge against the community that murdered his family when he was a kid, combined with almost dying, really takes it out of a girl.

After formulating a plan for Isaac and me to go back to the club tomorrow night and tying myself up in knots with worry because I couldn't get ahold of Dawn, I ended up stripping off my jeans and sleeping on one of the huge couches while Isaac napped on the other one. When I woke up, twilight had conquered the daylight and the room was quiet, devoid of Gargoyles. But from the amazing smell in the air, I assumed they were eating.

I stretched on the couch, my stomach rumbling, but I didn't want to get up right away. For the first time in so long, I woke without a dull ache behind my ribs, without my mind mired in a fog of loneliness. Instead, there was a warmth inside of my soul, and I was...

Content.

The word rang through me, dragging fear behind it. If life had taught me anything, it was that there was always something, or someone, waiting to shred your happiness to pieces. It could be a malignant tumor, or an asshole ex. Maybe a car crash, or a serial killer. Maybe just one's own stupidity. But the possibility was always there; a grim reaper waiting for its opportunity.

And if that was the case, I had a choice, didn't I?

A preemptive strike at the parts that depended on others, and hurt them before they could hurt me too bad. It was something that my more cowardly instincts liked, probably because it had been my modus operandi for the last twelve years.

Or, I could do the brave thing, the thing that made my pulse hammer, and trust James and Isaac to love me back.

I pressed the heels of my palms to my eyes and let out a long shaky breath. How could something I wanted so bad that it hurt make me so terrified? A jagged sob welled up and tears leaked out from under my palms and down my cheek.

The couch shifted and I didn't have to look up to know who was sitting at my feet. His hand skated up and down my bare legs, not seductive but soothing. James didn't say anything, knowing me better than I knew myself as he always did. When I could finally speak without breaking down, I took my hands away and looked at him.

"I'm afraid," I whispered.

He nodded, twining our fingers together.

"I know. It's hard to think of being open when you've spent so long closed off."

I frowned at him and ran my thumb over his bulging knuckles.

"You're not talking about me, are you?"

"No. I closed myself off after I left you. Afraid that I would hurt others, afraid of opening myself up to what I glimpsed with you that night. It wasn't until Isaac, the dimpled little fucker, that I felt that shell break."

I laughed in spite of myself at his description of Isaac and sat up.

"He is scary good at breaking down barriers, isn't he?"

James snorted.

"It's his super power, but don't tell him. I don't think he knows."

I let loose a full throated chortle that ended on a very unladylike snort. James' eyes danced as he looked at me, a relaxed grin on his broad face. I couldn't help reaching out and tracing the line of his mouth with my index finger.

"I can't promise I won't try and sabotage this at some point," I said.

"Alright."

"But I can promise that I'll listen if you call me on it."

He leaned forward and grazed his lips across mine.

"Deal."

James' kiss deepened, his tongue tangling with mine in slow, tempting strokes. I pulled myself into his lap, legs stretching to straddle him. A wonderful ache made itself known between my legs and I grinned against his lips like an idiot.

"I don't think I'll ever get used to feeling small in your arms," I said.

"You're not, though."

"Not for a Mundane, no. But it's kinda nice for once to know what it may be like to feel dainty compared to a partner."

He chuckled and stood, his hands cupping my ass as my legs wound around his waist.

"I like that I don't have to worry about snapping you like a twig when I fuck you."

"Ooooh, planning on getting rough with me?"

He growled before nipping my bottom lip.

"Would you be opposed to that?"

"Depends."

He began to lick and bite along my jaw, and down to my throat.

"Handcuffs?"

"A little pedestrian, but okay."

"Saint Andrew's Cross?"

"Now we're talking. Yes."

"Rope?"

"What do you want to do with it? I don't like suspension."

His grin was hungry, dangerous and my clit quivered in response.

"I want to tie you up with Shibari rope," he whispered, "make you into an obscene present for me to open. Maybe make sure the rope rubs that sensitive little clit of yours so every time you move it makes you wetter...and wetter."

I groaned, hands clasping the horns on either side of his head.

"You'd like that wouldn't you, baby girl?" he purred. "You want me to tie you up? Make Isaac watch while my tail jacks him off?"

"You better not be bluffing," I breathed, my pussy so wet I was sure I was leaving a trail along his bare stomach even through my underwear.

He groaned and took my mouth in a hard kiss while I reached down and palmed the bulge in his pants.

"You need dinner," James said, licking my jaw.

"You are dinner."

His chuckle sent vibrations through my body, the sound so dark and dirty that I whimpered.

"Patience," he said. "Dinner first."

When I had been a sub, I was an especially bratty one. So the admonition to be patient did nothing but wave a red flag to my tendency to be a disobedient child.

So even though I allowed him to set me on my feet, I made sure to slide my body down his so that he felt the way my nipples pebbled under the thin T-shirt. When I turned to go into the dining room, my fingertips grazed his hard cock and I shot him a wicked grin over my shoulder at the way his breath hitched.

"Coming?" I taunted.

He growled at me, frowning deeply before following me.

I wonder how far I can push him before he has me back against a wall while Isaac watches? Or...maybe he'll command Isaac to take care of me.

I shivered at the lurid images that were being splashed across my brain. Horny didn't even begin to describe it.

Someone could sail a fucking toy boat in my panties right now.

Isaac was sitting at the massive table, which was spread with chicken in peanut sauce, a delicate shrimp dish, and several different kinds of rice. My mouth watered, but I was not about to be deterred. What the pussy wanted, the pussy generally got.

*Doesn't mean I can't eat a little bit though.*

With a grin, I sashayed over to Isaac, my skin burning with the heat of James' gaze. He knew that I was about to test all the limits. But I wondered if that thought had him as turned on as it did me.

"Hey there," Isaac started, "have a good--"

I cut him off by shoving my tongue in his mouth and without missing a beat, Isaac's claws were tangling in my hair as he held me to him. I tasted the peanut sauce and wine on his tongue. By the time I was done, both our lips were a little swollen.

"I'm starved," I said, letting as much heat as possible into the words.

"Um...well, the, uh, the food is...ah, fuck!"

I sat on his lap and wiggled my butt.

"Go on," I said looking over my shoulder, feigning innocence. "What's good?"

"Uh..." he took a deep breath, a flush creeping up under his purple-gray skin. "The um...chicken, that's pretty good."

I made sure to grind as much as possible before I stood up and leaned forward so my boobs strained the t-shirt, and held out my plate for James to fill.

He scowled at me, arms crossed and I grinned up at him.

"James, dear," I said, "could you put some food on my plate?"

He hesitated for a second until I swished my hips, and Isaac let out a hissing grunt behind me.

"Better hurry before poor Isaac makes a mess in his pants."

"Bloody hell, Stella," James huffed as he dished out the food for me.

I sat back on Isaac's lap, letting his poor cock have a little break as I began to shovel the food into my mouth. Isaac took several long, slow breaths, but it didn't help deflate him any.

"This is good," I said, and let a dribble of peanut sauce fall on my shirt.

Both males had their eyes glued to the spot and I made a show of licking the fork before running a finger along my chest to catch the mess, only managing to smear it.

"Oh, dear," I said. "I think this shirt is a hopeless case."

I sat up, pulled it over my head and dropped it to the floor, holding James' increasingly heated gaze the entire time.

I managed a few more bites before more of the peanut sauce just happened to fall across the top of my breasts, which were currently spilling out the top of my bra.

"I'm very clumsy tonight," I cooed. "I may need some help cleaning this up.

Isaac laughed under me and covered his eyes with his hands. James just stared in that stern, domineering way of his, but I could tell by the bulge in his pants that he wasn't as unaffected as he'd like us to believe.

I looked over my shoulder at Isaac and let my tongue trail slow over my lips.

"Could you assist me detective?"

His cheeks flushed and he shifted in his seat, clawed hands tight against my body.

"Well, if it will help my Mistress, how could I refuse?"

I set the plate on the table and leaned back to give him better access. His thick, long tongue darted out between his fangs and he gave the top of my breast a light lick that did very little to mop up the peanut sauce. I grabbed one of the horns on the top of his head and pressed him down harder onto my skin. He groaned and his fangs scraped my neck, along with his tongue.

One of Isaac's hands clasped my hip, while he ran a claw down the side of my body and continued to lick and nip me. I arched my back, pushing my tits out, and let my head loll back onto Isaac's shoulder as I stared into James' eyes. He was still frowning at us, but now there was an unmistakable tension in his body, in the way his hands were clasped into tight fists at his side. He was holding himself back. Maybe because he wasn't sure he was welcome or what we wanted.

Whatever the reason, I didn't mind letting him stew a little.

My grin widened as I opened my legs so that they were now on either side of Isaac's, my body draped over his and open.

"Tear my clothes off with your claws," I commanded him.

"Wait," James' hard voice cut through my growing lust like a knife.

We both looked up at him, held perfectly still by his command.

"Stella, today has been a hard day, are you sure this is what you want. What you need?"

Only James would see past my horny exterior to the frightened, reeling woman underneath. He was right, I'd been shaken by almost dying two days ago and by the revelations today. Down to my very soul. The threat wasn't just a faceless being anymore. It was someone I knew, someone who wanted *me*. Someone who could rip my life apart in a moment.

And that was why I needed to feel safe. To be held with the orbit of the two males I trusted most, a place Ben could not touch me. Why I needed to feel alive, to celebrate what we still had in spite of the explosion and in spite of Ben's threats.

I let all of this into my eyes as I looked at James, and said, "Yes."

Everything I couldn't say was encapsulated in that word, in the air between us, in the way he knew the deepest parts of me. It all passed between us in a moment. He gave a tiny nod, imperious but also full of love and I let out a slow breath.

"Proceed little Isaac," James said, his voice deeper now.

Isaac snarled against my shoulder as his claws tore the bra from my torso. My breasts were free, and the cold air hitting them made me gasp. But then Isaac's hot mouth was there, drawing one nipple into his mouth with a sharp bite. My grip on his horn tightened and I arched my back more.

"Underwear," I gasped, still keeping eye contact with James.

The rip of the cotton was unnaturally loud in the dining room and the next thing I knew, something long and sinuous was teasing the outside of my cunt.

I looked down to find Isaac's tail at my entrance, my thighs wet from arousal.

"Please, Mistress," he panted against my breast.

"Yes," I said.

"No," James said at the same time.

The quiet command in his voice stilled us both. I didn't see him take his slacks off but when he rounded the table toward us, James was completely naked, his perfect, engorged Gargoyle dick arched toward his hard stomach, honeyed liquid dripping off the base of him where his cock-horn was shedding its aphrodisiac. Bulbous, twin sacs swung between his thick thighs and I longed to cup them as I sucked his cock as deep as possible.

He stopped a few feet from us.

"Safe word?" he demanded of me.

"Wings," I breathed, loving the flare of his pupils at the word.

He looked at Isaac.

"Color?"

"Green. Fucking green."

James gifted Isaac with the tiniest of smirks before snapping his fingers and pointing at his feet.

"Isaac, put Stella on the table and kneel."

His claws grasped my hips and plopped me onto the table, the cool surface causing a sharp sting to my nethers that wasn't altogether unpleasant.

James caressed Isaac's hair and tilted his face up.

"Do not touch yourself or do anything until I tell you. I want you to watch as I teach our Stella a lesson in obedience."

"Yes, Daddy."

I sucked in a breath at the name, my fingers sliding down to my dripping center. Fuck me, that was the hottest fucking thing.

James' hand snagged my wrist before I could reach my clit, and he shook his head.

"I haven't had dinner yet, and since you clearly don't want food, but you want to be licked and bit, you're going to be my plate."

My lips parted on a gasp, my body going hot even as my nipples hardened to stiff peaks, as if it was freezing.

"Lay back," his voice was dark as sin and I helpless to obey.

He positioned me so that the back of my knees hit the edge of the table, my pussy right where a plate would be.

"You also are not allowed to come until I tell you," he clarified as he sat in the chair and laid a napkin across his lap as if he were about to eat at a five-star restaurant. "Arms over your head, legs apart."

"Yes, sir," I smirked, as I made a show of opening my legs to either side of him, and balancing my feet on the arms of his chair.

James shook his head.

"Such a brat."

I was not prepared for the warm peanut sauce on my stomach and gave a hiss of shock as it hit my skin. I stared down at James, who very calmly leaned forward and barely let his lips graze my skin as he plucked a piece of chicken off of my body with his teeth. Again and again he teased me with the merest sensation of him. Soon I was whimpering with frustration, the sight of him bending over me and not touching me as he ate food off my skin was oddly erotic.

"Damn it, James, either touch me or-- Ah!"

He slapped at my mons, then ran a finger through the leftover sauce on my stomach. I watched as he sucked it off his finger.

"Isaac," he drawled, glancing at Isaac.

"Yes?"

"Come here."

Isaac jumped to his feet and stood beside James, who snagged the back of his neck and pulled him down for a kiss that was slow, savoring. I could do nothing but watch, my thighs kept apart by James. I wanted to touch myself as they kissed, to smear the peanut sauce over my breasts and beg them to lick every drop off of me. And as I tried to sneak my hand down, just for a little friction at the top of my clit, James broke off his kiss and intercepted my hand.

"You just can't seem to obey, can you?"

"But I'm hungry," I said, flashing my teeth at him in a frustrated smile. He tsked at me and shook his head.

"Isaac, since Stella can't be good, will you please hold her arms above her head so I can finish my meal?"

He was so infuriatingly calm, his voice so even. He dabbed the corners of his fucking mouth like this was a leisurely supper and not a full blown erotic fantasy that was leaving me aching.

I huffed out a frustrated breath and saw the ghost of a smile tease James' lips. Isaac scrambled around to the other side and climbed up onto the surface by my head. His cock was weeping precum, a large pearl of it hitting the perfectly clean table. How he was managing not to let his tail rub against his dick was a mystery to me.

*Hell if I had a tail like that I'd probably never leave my fucking bedroom.*

When Isaac's hands pressed my wrists to the cool table I smiled up at him, relishing the way he flushed, the pant of his breath across my face.

"Gimme a kiss?" I asked.

"No," James said, taking a sip of wine. "You haven't earned it."

"What do I have to do? You've already eaten peanut chicken off my stomach."

James sighed.

"Perhaps you're right, perhaps I need to give you something else to do besides laying still and quiet. Obviously that's too difficult a task."

James leaned down and dragged his tongue through the sauce on my stomach as he speared me with...

Wait...his hands are holding my thighs open so what...?

"Oh fuck-- Ah!... fuck me!"

My back bowed off the table as I realized that it was his tail that had entered me and was now filling me with a spiral of ridges. In and out, curling and undulating inside of me. I strained against Isaac's hold, my hips bucking and obscene mewling cries pouring from my lips. Heat built in my core, spreading in a wildfire of sensation as his tail fucked me hard and fast.

And then it was gone.

I grunted deep in my throat and whined out a "no".

James chuckled against my skin, the peanut sauce almost completely gone now.

"You haven't earned it yet."

"What do you want?"

He hummed against me as he licked up my torso and around one of my nipples.

"Isaac," his voice vibrated against my breast, "you may feed Stella your cock."

I looked to the left and saw Isaac's dick, the head purple from being so damn hard, ridges bulging. It looked so good, the honeyed fluid of his cock-horn dripping onto his balls. I wanted those in my mouth too but first things first, I needed Isaac's dick.

He transferred both my wrists to his hand, they just barely fit. And with the other hand he held the back of my head. I licked the tip of his dick, the salty thickness of the liquid was so good, I groaned.

"Someone is hungry after all?" James asked me with a grin.

If I could've, I would've flipped him off. Instead, I moaned as I took Isaac deeper, his hand fisting my hair.

"You may come down her throat," James said, "Stella, hit his thighs if it's too much. Otherwise, hold still so I can start my dessert."

He was so infuriatingly calm, as if having me splayed out, naked, as his own personal serving tray, while Isaac fucked my mouth was an everyday occurrence.

But as he leaned over and began to bite and suck strawberries off my tits, I glimpsed his cock dripping with fluid.

Isaac grunted and gasped above me, his cock-horn not quite hitting my lips as I deep throated him over and over. The ridges of it were so strange and erotic against my tongue. Even though James' claws were now digging into my hips as he held me down, his rough tongue and fangs scraping just along the outside of my areola but never latching onto my aching nipples, I knew I could hold on, handle all of this.

And then his fucking tail teased my opening.

I sobbed around Isaac's cock as James' tail once again filled and fucked me. These two already had me wound so tight that it didn't take long before I was at once light and heavy, my skin too tight to contain so much and yet, I was also about to break apart.

But just as Isaac was spurting hot streams of cum down my throat and I thought I'd surely go right with him, James withdrew his tail. Tears poured from my eyes, due to more than the deep throating. I was raw, my body one live nerve that was coiled and unable to release. I was desperate, I'd do anything for James to give me that orgasm.

I realized then, as Isaac withdrew his cock and pressed a devastatingly tender kiss to my mouth, that I'd never been more vulnerable in my life. But I was safe here, with them. Safe from the world outside those doors. Safe from being broken and bruised. Utterly, and serenely, safe.

"You're so beautiful," Isaac kissed away my tears. "I love you so much Stella."

As Isaac withdrew, James was there, done with his strawberries.

"You're so pretty sucking his cock," James purred against my skin, "so sexy taking him like a good girl."

I'd never had a praise kink, but the second those words were past James' lips, my walls spasmed and I let loose another sob because I had nothing to clench around.

"I think it's time for me to finish dessert."

"James..."

But he wasn't reaching for another dish. Instead, he was holding my gaze with a heated one of his own as he licked and sucked his way down my body. When he got back in his chair, my clit was at the perfect height for him to press a kiss to. I hissed in a breath as his thumbs parted me and he dragged his thick, hot tongue through me.

"You taste so good. Do you know how jealous I was of Isaac when he was feasting on you in the club?"

"Yes, I could smell it in the van."

He chuckled against me.

"Still so bratty. Gonna have to do something about that."

"Sorry, sir," I said. "Please don't stop."

"There's those manners," he licked through my folds. "I'm gonna eat this pussy, and fuck you with my tail while I do it."

"What about you?" I asked.

"Can I... please?" Isaac asked, his voice rough with need.

James smiled.

"You want more of your Daddy's cock? Come get it. Stella, touch your tits and don't stop."

"Yes, sir."

I wished I could see Isaac kneeling at James' feet, but I knew the moment he took him in his mouth because James' breath stuttered on my skin and his tail did a wild, flippy thing inside of me.

"Oh my god," I groaned, rolling my nipples between my fingers.

And then there was nothing but the wet sounds of James devouring me and Isaac sucking James off. They groaned and grunted as I writhed on the table, my skin sticky with the food residue and James' saliva, but I didn't care. He was eating me like I was the main course, his tail curling and spasming in ways I'd never felt before and would never be able to forget. I screamed out, the sound choking on the end, as light burst behind my eyes. I felt my skin catch fire as an orgasm ripped through my body, obliterating any sense of space or time.

I heard James let loose a roar and Isaac growl. I felt a rush of wetness flood from me, claws broke the skin on my thighs and I tore a fingernail as I scraped them against the table.

But all of that was from a great distance. I was lost, utterly and completely on this cloud of bliss and I didn't want to come back down to earth. It wasn't until warm arms had picked me up and soft lips caressed my face that I opened my eyes.

James was carrying me, Isaac beside him and we were going up the stairs to one of the bedrooms.

"Think the shower is big enough for us all?" Isaac asked.

"Don't care," James grunted, "I need to be with you both."

I could walk, but I liked being carried against his body. I snuggled in and James chuckled.

"Greedy little thing."

"Just because I like rubbing up against my two hot Gargoyles?"

Isaac smacked my bare ass and I let out a squeal.

"Save that for next time," I winked at him.

We stopped outside what had to be the master suite's bathroom, which had a giant tub that would still probably not be big enough for all three of us, and a large shower that was a little sunken and completely open withou a shower curtain or door. It took up the entire back wall and had three shower heads.

"I think that will do," James said and set me on my feet.

James got the water warmed, while Isaac and I got towels.

I had always enjoyed after care, but never this much with James and Isaac not only washing me but one another too. Even flaccid and laying against their thighs, their cocks were magnificent. Isaac's was more thick than long, which I greatly appreciated. But James' was both long and thick, even bouncing softly in the shower.

"You are insatiable," Isaac said when he caught me looking.

I licked my lips and shrugged.

"What can I say, I like dick."

"Me too," he said.

James laughed behind us and pulled us each in for a kiss.

"Let's get cleaned up and then have an actual dinner while we work."

It was so easy to just slip into things with these two. I had no worries about whether or not I fit with them, no desire to keep an eye out for signs that they were annoyed by who I was. For the first time I could remember, I wasn't operating with one foot out the door. It felt good, peaceful.

And yet, as I threw on some comfy summer jammies, that voice of fear hissed in the back of my mind, reminding that someday, everyone always leaves. Everyone.

Not this time. Not them.

I had more conviction than I'd ever had before, but it still wasn't enough to silence that voice completely.

# CHAPTER SEVENTEEN

## STELLA

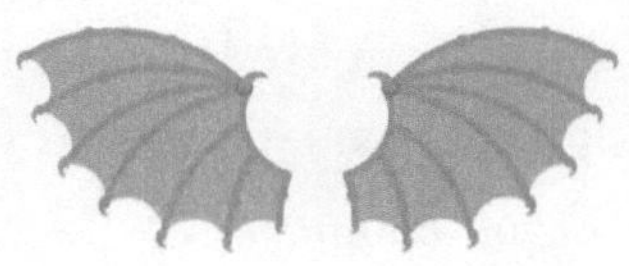

I stared out at the backyard, which was small with the mother-in-law house back there, but still impressively groomed. A water feature gurgled away somewhere to my left, where lush green and blooming bushes created a feeling of privacy. Two small fruit trees were to my right, their blooms starting to fade into fruit. Roses, lilacs and something that I thought was honeysuckle was spread out around the whole perimeter of the yard. A well-trimmed and watered lawn was laid out in front of me from where I stood on the back porch, a cup of coffee between my hands. It was good coffee, way better than the precinct's, but I couldn't really enjoy it.

For the last two nights, we'd been parading Isaac in his true form through the club, but with the exception of Ben keeping a creepy eye on us, there had been no movement from him at all.

I was starting to wonder if we'd have to try some official channels with what scant evidence we had, which was not a route I was looking forward to since it meant dealing with the Seattle police chief, who hated my guts.

*But we can't keep going like this. He may already have a different victim picked out for all we know. And I'll be damned if I go to another crime scene like the last one.*

I gripped the handle on the mug hard and took a sip as Isaac came out onto the porch.

He didn't ask if I was okay, and I wondered if that was because he could feel me through this mating bond thing. James had told me that, as a Mundane, I'd have a more muted experience with the bond, but now that it was firmly in place between the three of us, I'd be aware of it. So far, beyond a very subtle sensation of tugging just behind my left ribs, there was nothing. I was trying not to let it get to me, not to let myself think that it may be a sign that something was wrong.

*Maybe this is what he means by muted.*

"Nothing huh?" I asked Isaac as we heard James grousing in the kitchen.

"Nope. He's been over the footage from the last two nights at least a dozen times. Nothing actionable."

"Fuck! What are we going to do? We need a lead, something, *anything* that will let us search his place or the club or both."

As if whatever gods existed heard me, my phone buzzed in the pocket of my sweats. When I dug it out, Dawn's number appeared and my heart leapt into my throat.

"What happened?" I asked as soon as I answered.

"It's Ben's sub. Her family says she's missing, hasn't been seen in two days. I don't know what to think. She's not upstairs, I've looked, and I don't know where Ben lives."

My stomach twisted and I forced my mind to calm down. I had to think, see this clearly.

"Have you reported it?" I asked.

"No," her voice lowered, "you know how the police are about anyone associated with my club. And since she's a submissive you know what they'll say."

I sure as shit did.

"Is she a Supernatural in any way?"

"No."

I sighed and ran a hand through my hair. If she had been it would've fallen into my murky jurisdiction and I'd have some strings to pull. But since both she and Ben were Mundanes, this would fall in with the Mundane cops at the downtown precinct.

*Oh joy, this will be fun. But it could be one way to get Ben, find the knives and end this.*

It wasn't the way I wanted to take him out. There was nothing tying him to the murders that would be enough to hold him. But if this got him put in jail, then it didn't matter.

"Okay," I said, "Isaac and I will go to the precinct, see what we can do."

Dawn let out a long breath.

"Thank you. I... Darling, you know how I feel about guilt, but right now, I am having quite the hard time following my own rules."

The vulnerability in her voice struck something deep inside of me. She was scared for this woman and feeling guilty because she couldn't protect her. For Dawn, there was no greater sin than not keeping her employees safe.

"I'll find her," I said. "I don't know how, but I will. And Ben won't hurt anyone else."

"I know that you have your hands full with the serial killer case, but if you could make this a priority, I would greatly appreciate it."

On the surface, the request was understandable enough, but there was something about the way she asked, as if she were trying to push me off the case on purpose...

*Don't be stupid. Dawn is just worried about her and rightly so. Who knows what Ben has done to the poor girl.*

"I'll use everything at my disposal."

"Thank you, darling. Be careful."

Isaac tensed next to me as we walked into the enormous downtown precinct. James was at the safe house, working on the surveillance footage from last night, while we tried to get permission to submit a search warrant for Ben's penthouse. This whole situation was technically both mine and the Mundane precincts jurisdiction in different ways. Mine, because Ben was a person of interest in the Supernatural killings, and theirs because they were both Mundane. I had brought as much evidence as James would let me have to tie Ben to the killings, hoping it would convince the captain to release the sub's disappearance to me as an adjacent issue to my case.

It was thin at best, but it was all I had.

As I passed the desks of the idiots I'd tangled with a few weeks ago, one of them flipped me off while the other one leered.

"What are you doing here, freak fucker?" one of them asked.

"What did you say?" Isaac asked, lunging for him.

"Not today," I said, putting a hand on his chest. "Remember the stakes."

Isaac pulled back, eyes blazing as he eyed them.

Both officers snorted and laughed as we walked past and into the captain's office.

The man was a thin balding snake who had replaced an addiction to cigarettes with an addiction to nicotine gum, which he was chewing away at. His desk was pristine, not even family photos marring its surface. The office was just large enough for his desk and two chairs; enclosed and claustrophobic with the tinge of sweat and old cigarette smoke hanging in the air. I hated this place for lots of reasons, but this man was high on the list.

"What the fuck do you want?" he snarled. "Didn't I give you something to keep you out of my hair?"

I frowned at that and plopped a file down.

"What's this?" he flipped it open and began taking the pages out.

"That's what we have to tie Ben Harper to the Seattle Supernatural killings."

"Ben Harper?" he said, and snorted. "You want me to let you pursue charges against one of the wealthiest men in the city? Based on what? Magical nonsense? The word of some guy from London who supposedly works for Scotland Yard?"

"No, based on that," I tapped the file.

"And the fact that his girlfriend is now missing," Isaac interjected.

For the first time, the captain's gaze landed on Isaac and he shook his head.

"The two of you are a pain in my ass."

"We want a search warrant for Ben's penthouse," I continued, ignoring the way my skin itched with warning.

The captain dumped the file into the trash can.

"Denied."

Isaac was vibrating with rage next to me and I had to take the lead before he lost it. So I leaned forward, hands braced on the desk, and forced the captain to look me in the eye.

"Why?"

I hadn't expected him to be intimidated by me, no matter how much taller and broader than him I was. But I didn't expect him to laugh in my face either.

The captain stood, his chuckle dripping with sarcasm and hate.

"You actually think I give a damn that someone is carving up the freaks in this city? It's good riddance as far as I'm concerned. We should've never let them live here, much less give them their own fucking police branch! You stir up shit storm after shit storm when you don't get your way and now you want me to piss off Ben fucking Harper over nothing? The only reason you're not collecting unemployment is because I wanted that snooty asshole from London off my back so I tossed this to you and your 'Supernaturals'. I don't give a shit if you solve it or not. The guy that you're working with is only concerned with whatever magical item is involved, so find it and get the hell out of my office!"

"And the victims?" Isaac asked through clenched teeth. "The Mundanes he carved up, what about them?"

"Well, according to your report, they're sex workers so...wrong place, wrong time, I guess."

One minute Isaac was turning away toward the door, the next he was spinning around and gripping the captain by his throat and lifting him off his feet.

"Fuck! Put him down, Isaac!"

The captain's face was turning red and he was desperately trying to pull Isaac's hand off him.

"You're supposed to protect them!" he snarled. "You're supposed to be different, to give a fuck when people are carved up like sides of fucking beef!"

I put my hand on his arm and squeezed hard.

"This isn't the way, remember?" I said, my voice calm in spite of how my heart was beating its way out of my chest. "You're always telling me that we need to be patient, to find a way. This isn't it."

"It won't matter if he just set us up to fail."

Now the captain's face was turning purple.

"Don't let him win," I pleaded. "He thinks you're all monsters, don't prove him right."

With one last growl, Isaac dropped the captain, who fell on his ass, choking and coughing.

"You deserved that you piece of shit," I said.

"You both...are finished," he wheezed as he scrambled to his feet. "Badge and gun, now!"

Before the captain had even finished, Isaac had thrown them both down on the desk.

"Fuck you and your badge," Isaac spat. "Someday, your bill's coming due. I hope you choke on it."

I knew this was coming, deep down I knew, but where Isaac seemed perfectly resigned to having his badge taken, I couldn't bring myself to place mine on the desk. I stared down at it, remembering how proud I'd been at my graduation, how much shit I'd eaten to make detective and then mountains more to become head of the Supernatural Branch. I saw the faces of the males I'd worked with, my friends. They'd be fine without me, they were all fine detectives who wouldn't take any shit. But that wasn't the point. I'd always taken as many of the hits from this office as I could so they didn't have to. Now I wouldn't be there to protect them, to make sure things were pushed through when they needed to be.

And I wouldn't be a cop anymore.

"Stella, are you deaf?" the captain demanded. "I said you're finished."

"I heard you," the words stuck in my throat.

"What, you thought you could just do whatever the fuck you wanted and you'd never see any consequences?" the captain chuckled. "First your father flushed a good career down the toilet to work with those freaks and now--"

My fist crashed into his face and cut off whatever else he was going to say.

"You can say whatever you want about me, but don't you dare talk about my father."

"You get out before I charge you with assault, you crazy bitch!" he screamed, wiping blood from his nose.

I took one last look at my badge before placing it, and my gun, onto the desk. Isaac didn't touch me as we turned and walked out, knowing that I couldn't show any weakness here, even if it was the last time I'd walk through this place as a cop.

There were whistles and laughter as we made our way to the door. Several of the men I'd made life hard on glared at me with murder in their eyes and I was suddenly grateful for the safe house that none of them knew about. But all of it added up to one thing that was painfully clear to me now: My life in Seattle was over.

I'd just about made it out of the precinct when the very last person I wanted to see strolled through the doors.

"Well, this is an unexpected surprise," Ben said.

Isaac took a step forward and I held him back.

"What are you doing here?" I asked through clenched teeth.

Ben's face transformed into a mask of concern that made me sick with its insincerity.

"Well, you see, my new girlfriend has gone missing and I'm very concerned."

His words acted like alchemy, transforming the pain of losing my career into something hard and hot. And then I realized that I'd been set free; I was no longer beholden to working within the law to bring Ben to justice. The only rules were the ones James had, and I was pretty sure those were bendy as fuck.

Even while my skin crawled being this close to him, I didn't say or do anything. Instead, I let him think he had me right where he wanted me so the moment I made his entire life collapse like a house of cards would be all the sweeter for how surprised he would be.

"Be seeing you, Stella," he said, his fingertips brushing my arm.

"Touch her again, and I'll rip your fucking head off," Isaac snarled as we walked past.

"Not if I rip yours off first," Ben said, rage leeching through his concerned expression.

I gave Ben one last look, meeting his eyes with my head high and swallowing down the sick feeling of his skin against mine.

"Let's go, Isaac," I said, "Mr. Harper has a report to file, don't you?"

He nodded and turned away. I could see claws start to seep through Isaac's glamour and I pulled him after me into the sharp Seattle sunlight.

Fury vibrated off of him as we climbed into the SUV where Agent Kane was waiting for us. She didn't say anything, for which I was grateful. Both of us needed to process the complete upending we'd just been through.

My mind spun with the fact that for the first time since my early twenties I was without a job, with nothing ahead of me other than just this one goal: to bury Ben.

I closed my eyes and tried to process it all, sift through the burning rage and pain to find the logical place I would need to formulate a plan, but it just wasn't there. By the time we pulled up to the house, I was no calmer. If anything, I was more off balance, my muscles jumping with the release of all the adrenaline that had no place to go. Isaac stalked in ahead of me and charged into the den.

"What the fuck happened?" James barked as a greeting. "I just got off the phone with the King County Sheriff and the police chief, both of whom told me that my investigation is no longer connected with them in any way."

"We were fired," Isaac snarled, making fists with his hands as he contemplated punching the wall.

"What?" James asked.

"You heard him," I replied, my voice low. "We're not cops anymore."

My voice broke on the last part and I did start to punch the wall. But James was there instead, saving me from breaking my hand as I connected with his.

"I'm sorry," he said, fire in his eyes instead of pity. "This might be a good development though."

"Yeah, I thought of that too," I admitted. "We aren't hindered by the rules of the police force anymore. We can go in and just end this."

James nodded.

"Agreed. Get the knives and get out. I've already contacted London and told them that we will likely be done here in a few days."

"Wait," I said, as his words sunk in. "What do you mean 'get the knives'? You're not just going to let Ben go."

James swallowed and crossed his arms.

"Stella, Ben was never my mission. The knives were. And now that things have escalated the way they have, his obsession with you, the Protectors targeting both you and Isaac, this is far too complicated to wait around so we can catch Ben. We have the chance to get the knives, and leave Seattle. We need to take it."

"James, you can't be serious," Isaac said.

Red clouded my vision and my heart pounded in my ears. I must have heard him wrong, James couldn't be saying what I thought he was. I stood there, frozen inside the wave of everything that was crashing down on me, for maybe an hour or a minute, it didn't matter. Because once everything came back into focus, I ran up to James and punched him across the face.

"You son of a bitch!" I screamed.

"What the fuck?" James asked.

"Stella!" Isaac seized my arms and pulled me back.

"You'll let him go? After all this?" I raged, spit flying from my lips. "You don't give a shit about the victims, the ones he carved up like an animal!"

"Of course I do! But I care about you more!"

"Fuck you! You'll just let him keep killing?"

"If the knives were the catalyst, removing them should stop his blood lust."

"Listen to yourself," I shook my head. "*If* and *should*. What kind of person are you to be okay with that level of chance when it comes to something like this?"

James grit his teeth and looked away from me for a moment. When he looked back there was a fierce savagery in his eyes that gave me pause. Isaac drew in a sharp breath behind me, and his hands tightened on my arms as if he were now preparing to drag me away from James in case he became a risk to me.

"The kind that has waited a lifetime for a mate," his voice was ragged, strained, "and now I have *two* that don't have enough sense to see a chance at safety and happiness when it's handed to us on a silver fucking platter!"

"Could you really live happily ever after knowing that he's living free, terrorizing women? Because we both know, even if he doesn't kill anyone else, he's still a fucking predator."

James growled and turned away from me. It was all the answer I needed.

"Let me go," I shrugged Isaacs hands off. "I need to punch something and if I stay here much longer it's going to be his face again."

"I think I can help with that," Andy said from the doorway. "Come on. Let's leave Mr. Knives Only to stew in it for a bit."

Before I turned to follow the agent, James swept his hand over the table, sending dozens of files flying, as he roared out his frustration. I hoped that he'd realize how fucked up this was and change, because with or without his help, I was taking Ben down.

# CHAPTER EIGHTEEN

## ISAAC

"**W**ell you sure know how to stick your foot in your mouth," I said as I picked up the files James had scattered.

"She's the one being stubborn!" he snarled at me, eyes blazing.

"No, James, you both are! Fuck's sake, being the reasonable one with you two is going to kill me."

"I was never here for Ben. I was only ever here for the knives."

"Yeah, well, that's not how she or I operate, and you should know that."

I stacked the papers on the table and swore at the mess.

"She's just upset about losing her job," James shot back.

"Yeah, that and the fact that Ben was at the precinct, playing the part of the worried boyfriend."

James whipped his head around and snarled but that was all.

We settled into a quiet tension as we both cleaned up and sorted everything back into their proper files.

"She always said she'd die in this city," James said, his voice calm, sad. "That it was the only place on earth she'd bleed for. That's why she became a cop."

A stab of guilt hit me. If I could've held it together during that meeting maybe she wouldn't have this hanging over her now. But no, that wasn't really true, either. Too many people were gunning for Stella at this point, it was only a matter of time before someone, at some point, gave them an excuse to get rid of her. Instead of beating myself up more, I slapped the last file onto the table and faced the situation clearly.

"I know, she's said similar things before. And now, all of that's been taken from her."

"She can still live here."

I snorted.

"Every single cop she's pissed off is going to come for her. She can't stay here and she knows it. You didn't see her face when the captain asked for her badge," I shook my head and swallowed down the sadness eating me up. "It was like he was cutting off a piece of her."

"That's what I'm saying. This is really what's eating her up. When she's able to move past it--"

"James, stop! This is foolish and you know it. Is she sad about her career, yeah. Is that the only thing that's got her beating the shit out of your security chief right now? No, not even close, and you know that. So, do us all a favor and face that fact because when you do, you're going to let go of this stupid 'not my mission' bullshit."

James' jaw worked as if he were trying to stop himself from saying something, and I saw tears glimmer before he turned away from me. I wanted to reach out to him, to hold him and soothe whatever had him so wound up. But the mating bond was getting stronger and I sensed that wasn't what he needed. So I stood still, and waited for him to figure out what he wanted to say or do. When he finally spoke, his voice was tattered, hesitant.

"I'm not used to being consumed with others as I feel myself consumed with the two of you. My heart beats for the first time, Isaac, and I fear that, if something were to happen to one or both of you, it would stop and I'd have to live a hollowed out existence. I am driven by the need to protect what is *mine*, and the two of you are more mine than my own flesh. I-I cannot lose you...please, beloved, do not ask me to...please, Isaac."

His shoulders shook and I could no longer stand there and let him hurt. I drew him tight to my chest, the sting of tears hitting my own eyes as his pain ripped into me. James was a towering male, yet he curled into me and clung to my body as sobs wracked him. My claws ran through his hair, scratching along his shoulders in light circles as I became his shelter in the storm of his emotions. Our bond pulsed, bright and beautiful inside of me. I realized then that James may appear so strong and imposing, but it hid a heart terrified of love and loss. I could help him heal, and I would, but only if he let me.

"You can't lock us up to keep us safe," I said after a few minutes. "This has to be a give and take. I admit that Stella can be impulsive, but that's where we come in. We can all balance each other, but not if you insist on controlling us. You have to trust us, just like we do you."

"But what if pursuing him costs me the two of you?" he wept against my neck. "Isaac, I couldn't survive it."

I pulled his face up so I could look him in the eye, my hands on either side.

"You listen to me," I said, pushing as much compassion and steel into my voice as possible, "there's no way in hell the three of us can't do this. Not if we work together. And if the worst should happen--"

His face crumpled and just about ripped my heart out.

"--it will hurt, but you will survive. You *will*."

A ragged sob welled up between his lips as I pressed a tender kiss there, tasting the salt of his tears. The sweet kiss became hard and demanding so fast that my head spun. Before I knew it, I was groaning as James pulled me hard against him, ravaging my mouth. His claws dug into my ass, piercing and insistent as he bucked his hips into me.

"I need you," he panted.

"Yes," I gasped. "God, yes."

His claws tore through my shorts and before I could process the cool air on my cock, James had my ass pressed against the table we were working on.

"Look at you," he purred, "gods above, you are so beautiful."

His tail rubbed against the length of my shaft, slow and torturous as his nails dug into my back, marking me as his, as surely as Stella had with the flogger. I hissed, pain and pleasure mixing a heady cocktail that shot straight to my dick. James' mouth pressed hot, thorough kisses to my throat, owning me with each suck and pull of his teeth. I held onto his horns and tried to bring his body closer to mine.

"Your tail," he whispered, "give it to me."

I brought it around until James could reach for it. When he sucked it into his mouth I let loose an obscene moan that ended on a string of incoherent syllables that may have been my attempt to speak. No one had ever played with my tail during sex, much less sucked on it.

James let it go with a dark chuckle.

"So many things I'm going to teach you, little Isaac, because we will have those days and nights."

I sank into his eyes staring back at me with such fragile hope, and I wrapped my hand around the back of his neck.

"You're damn right we will," I kissed him hard, devouring his groan.

"Wrap your tail around me," he gasped when I'd released him, "jack your Daddy good."

I was shaking in the fiery space between want and need as I wound my tail around James' cock. If I'd thought him sucking on my tail was the pinnacle of erotic, seeing his tail wrap around my own cock at the same time and start to move as mine did was enough to send me out of my mind. Our hips bucked, cocks and tails brushing against one another in a symphony of moans and gasps. I didn't care that anyone could walk in, that my entire career had just gone up in flames, or that this wasn't solving the chasm that James had opened between himself and Stella.

All I knew was the rasp of our mingled breath as we gave one another waves upon waves of pleasure, as I drank in the sight of James becoming undone by my actions even as he broke me wide open at the same time. He snagged my neck and pulled me in for a brutal brush of his lips, teeth grazing my tongue as I plunged it deep into his mouth.

"Give me everything," James breathed, his tail picking up speed around my dick, "all of you."

"Yes," I matched his pace with my own tail. "All of me is yours."

"Say it again."

Faster, harder.

"I'm yours, James!"

He roared out a strangled breath as white streams of cum flowed between us. My mouth dropped open in a silent growl as I followed him seconds later, marking James with my cum as thoroughly as he did me.

Our tails stayed wrapped around each other as we dragged claws and lips over one another, licking and biting in an attempt to devour one another.

"I can't get enough of you," James breathed. "I want to take you all day. Want to touch you, mark you."

"I know," I pressed my face to the base of his throat and nipped at the hollow there. "I feel that way about you too. Both of you. You're both my world, James."

"As you are both mine. But you're right," he cupped my face and pressed our foreheads together, "I cannot rule you both to keep you safe. We have to trust one another. I'm sorry, forgive me. I'm not good at relationships."

My lips grazed his and I ran my hand down his hard shoulder.

"Forgiven. Although, you may have to do more groveling to get that out of Stella."

He blew out his lips and nodded.

"Yes, I think you're right."

Slowly, we untangled ourselves and ran up for a quick shower, that turned into James teasing my back entrance with his tail, slick with soap.

It was just playing around at first, and then it turned serious fast, with both of us panting under the shower heads. We weren't lying when we said we couldn't stop touching one another. Even when we were done in the shower, we found reasons to caress each other as we toweled off.

*When this is over, I want months of nothing but taking James' cock.*

"We should get dressed and see about Stella," James said, giving me a good view of his perfectly sculpted naked ass as he walked out of the bathroom. "I hope she left something of Andy intact."

I snorted and followed him into the bedroom to get some fresh clothes.

Just as we were walking back into the den, Stella came marching in, covered in sweat, her face red from both exertion and what looked like a couple of punches to the face. Right behind her came Andy, equally sweaty and showing signs of their sparring session.

"I'll see you later, if these two idiots are smart enough to listen to you," Andy said.

"Yeah, and thanks for the session," Stella said.

"Any time."

Andy sauntered away, shaking her head at the two of us.

"Okay you two," Stella said, hands on hips. "I've got a few things to say."

I opened my mouth to give her the update on what James told me, hoping it might curtail a potential argument when James waved me off.

"Let her say her peace."

"Damn right I will," she said.

James crossed his arms and smirked at her while Stella paced. She was nervous, and James, the sexy bastard, was enjoying it.

"I know you want to protect us," Stella said, her words halting, "and that you may only be here for the knives, and I respect that. But," she whirled around, index finger pointed at him, "you need to remember that a relationship isn't just about the biggest asshole in it."

"It's about all the assholes," he said.

"Yes. No!" she smacked him on the bicep. "I'm not the asshole here."

"No, you're not."

"Stop arguing with..." she stopped and faced him, her arms now crossing as well. "So you agree that *you're* the asshole here."

"Yes. Enjoy the moment, it won't come around very often."

She snorted, face softening.

Watching the two of them like this, it was easy to see why they burned so hot and fast before. They were like flames without anything to keep them contained, running loose and destroying any chance they had at a relationship. But me...

*I'm like that circle of rocks around a campfire. I can help them contain it, feed it but not let it destroy anything.*

Pride swelled in my chest as I saw my place here with the two of them. I loved them both so completely and yet differently. I loved them for myself and for what they could be together.

They turned to look at me and I realized that I had been telegraphing my feelings down the bond between us.

"You're cute when you're waxing romantic," Stella said, twining her fingers with mine.

"He's just plain cute," James grinned.

"Well, on that we can agree. But," Stella turned serious, "that doesn't solve all of this."

"He knows that," I said. "And I have a feeling that you have some kind of plan."

"I do and I need you both to just shut up and listen before you go judging it."

"Well, that's not a good beginning," James said.

I arched an eyebrow at him and he huffed.

"Continue."

"Why, thank you. I was going to anyway," Stella said to James. "We all agree that it's time to take the fight to Ben, and that Isaac and I not being cops anymore frees us up to do just that."

We both nodded and my grip tightened on Stella's fingers. She may be putting forth a brave face, but I could feel her jumble of emotions clearly down our bond. She was heartbroken about her career, but determined to see this through the end regardless. And I loved her all the more for it.

"He needs two more Gargoyles," she continued, "and he's obsessed with women that look like me. So...I propose we all three go to the club tonight, that I don't wear a wig and that we play a scene in the public room. We tempt him with everything he wants, and he'll let his guard down, I know it."

My heart kicked up at the suggestion. While I wanted nothing more than to play with both Stella and James, doing it for the sole purpose of luring Ben out into the open made the whole thing feel wrong.

*Still, I can't deny that it's a good plan and that it would work.*

"I'll do it," James said, his eyebrows furrowing together in a deep frown, "but only if we agree that it's more than a ploy. I will not sully our connection like that. We do it in sincerity or not at all."

I expected Stella to make a sultry joke, or to roll her eyes at his seriousness. Instead, she reached up and cupped James' cheek.

"As if I could fake anything with you," she whispered. "You've always been able to see right through me and it terrifies me."

"Because you can't trust me?"

"No, stupid. Because I know I can and what that means is that I don't have an excuse not to give my heart to you."

James pulled her close to him and kissed her forehead.

"Forgive me for hurting you earlier," he whispered. "I was afraid to lose you. Both of you."

"I know," Stella hugged him tight, fingers still holding onto me. "To be honest, I am too. This is all pretty fucking terrifying."

James chuckled.

"Yes," and then he looked at me, "but I think we'll all get through it."

"I meant this relationship stuff," Stella said.

"Me too."

I couldn't take it any longer, so I put my arms around them both and kissed them each in turn. If we all made it through this, the first few years might be pretty rocky, but as I tightened my arms around them both and basked in the warmth of our mating bonds, I knew they were both worth it.

# CHAPTER NINETEEN

## STELLA

I'd never before experienced the sensation of walking into a room and everyone stopping whatever they were doing to stare at me, but that's exactly what happened to us when we walked through the door of the Hearts and Swords club.

The three of us had spent the rest of the day talking out what we were and were not comfortable with, what the scene would be like in broad strokes, and what we'd do if Ben attempted to attack us.

Andy was on standby, in case we didn't check in by a certain time, though she didn't seem entirely comfortable with the situation. When I'd told Dawn what we wanted to do, she'd tried very hard to get me to rethink this.

"You're poking the bear and I'm afraid of something happening to you, my darling," she'd said.

"I know, but I really do think this will be the thing to make him show himself. I promise, no stupid chances."

She'd given us permission but it had been grudging at best.

Now, I saw her lounging in one of the VIP booths, her light eyes focused on us with a hint of frustration.

Isaac's leash in my hand was a little slippery with sweat, but I didn't show how nervous I was. My blond hair fell in waves down my bare shoulder and while it felt strange not to be in my usual persona, it was minimized by just how *right* everything else felt. Isaac next to me in his usual tight shorts and collar, looking all the more erotic with his true form, while James towered behind me, holding a red studded leash attached to the collar he'd gifted me with this afternoon. I was in my red leather boy shorts and silk halter that hid very little when the right light hit it. I glanced back at James and couldn't help a breathy moan at the sight of him. His dark purple bare chest, the flex of his muscles when he raised my leash just a little, displaying the fact that he, and only he, had collared Mistress Magdalena. His usual black slacks had been replaced by black leather pants and that hugged his ass and package to perfection. Everyone in here would be able to see what he was packing and I hoped they appreciated the view, because that was all they were getting. A possessive heat took hold of me and I bared my teeth at a woman who reached out to touch James.

"He's taken," I hissed.

The woman shrugged, eyes trailing over James.

"For now," she purred.

James claws stroked my scalp and his lips brushed my ear as he whispered, "Easy, baby girl. After all, we're here so they can look."

"Yes, sir."

I ran my hand over Isaac's head and he leaned into my touch, even as I leaned into James'. It wasn't all that surprising that we'd slipped so effortlessly into these roles, as if we were created to be this for one another. I could easily become addicted to this dynamic, the push and pull of switching with these two males who had conquered my heart and body. I would give them anything, submit to James' demands, fulfill Isaac's most base fantasies and neither of them would ever abuse it. That was a kind of trust that I never thought I'd find in this world, and here I was, surrounded by it in the form of two males that every person in this room wanted to fuck or be fucked by.

I snorted in delight, lips curled into a grin.

"Something funny, baby girl?" James asked, his claws just barely scraping the skin on my back.

"Just thinking of how lucky I am. One of you on my leash," I kissed Isaac, "one of you holding mine."

James' deep chuckle skated down my body.

"You look so pretty with my collar on, I may just never let you take it off."

He slammed his lips to mine, fucking my mouth with his tongue and leaving absolutely no doubt at all who I belonged to.

When he stopped, I was panting, chest hot from the sudden spike of desire.

"You want something from me tonight?" he asked.

"Yes, sir."

"Hmmm..."

His claw ran along my red bottom lip and when he withdrew, I lurched forward, chasing just a little more contact.

Without a word, James led us down the hallway and toward the public play room. I followed him with a dozy kind of smile on my face and glanced back at Isaac, who stared at me with longing.

"Sweet boy," I crooned, "is this too much for you?"

"No, Mistress," he whispered.

We were supposed to be working, and I'd thought it may be challenging to keep focused, but I had no idea it would be so impossible not to be dragged under by the power of James as *my* Dom. He was like a drug, reaching in and numbing anything but the need to please him, to give him what he wanted. It had been a long time since I'd been on the submissive end of things, but even then I'd never felt so completely taken in by a Dom. And yet, I wasn't scared.

*Because I know, in my soul, that he cherishes me. Which is why I'm drunk on this already.*

When Isaac and I were here before, with the exception of that first time, we were able to keep a sense about us. We may have looked lost in our moments, but both of us were aware of the room and the people in it. But when we'd planned tonight, none of us had considered how the mating bonds would have changed things. Even my muted sense of it was humming in my chest by the time James had completed the circuit around the room. As we sat on one of the leather couches, I began to worry that we would lose ourselves in all of this and prove far too easy of a target.

*Andy has our back...I hope.*

My worry must've telegraphed because James ran his hand over my hair and pressed a kiss to my shoulder.

"Safe word?"

I licked my lips as he continued to press biting kisses to my skin.

"Wings."

"Do you want to use it?"

"No."

He studied me, making sure I was alright before sitting back. His massive arms were spread across the back of the couch, and with Isaac on one side of him and me on the other we took up the entire thing. Isaac sat on his knees, head down as I lounged against James, red high heel hanging off one foot.

We'd arrived late enough that the room was getting quite full. A symphony of cries and moans were punctuated by the slaps of a flogger or the wet sound of fucking. It was a lurid concoction that aroused me enough that I started to touch myself without thinking.

James seized my wrist before I'd slipped my fingers under my waist band.

"What do you think you're doing?" he demanded.

I nodded at the people around us.

"They're just so...stimulating."

"Hmmm...they are. But you aren't getting off on your own fingers here tonight."

I put my bottom lip out in a pout.

"Can I ride Isaac's cock then?"

We both glanced at where Isaac knelt so lovely and so hard that the waistband of his shorts was pulled away from his stomach.

"No," James said, running his finger along the length. "You haven't earned that either."

Isaac trembled as James idly played with his erection.

We'd all agreed that in order to make this work, we had to make the biggest possible spectacle of ourselves. And the stage in this room was the way to do it.

No one was using it at the moment, and while we could've gone up at any time, James kept us waiting long enough that he had to tear my hand away from my cunt three times, and Isaac's shorts had a large wet spot in the front.

James shook his head and gave a disgusted huff and I breathed out a little sigh of relief.

"Baby girl, you have such a hard time listening, don't you?"

"Maybe you should teach me a lesson."

"You'd enjoy it too much."

"So would you."

"That's true."

James frowned at the stage and ran a hand over his chin, as if thinking. Then he stood in a fluid, sensual motion and pointed at an extremely large chair that was made just for a Supernatural of James' size. It looked like some kind of dark throne, and it took four staff to wrestle it onto the stage. When they got it in place and James climbed up, he snapped his fingers and pointed to the foot of it. Isaac scrambled up to the platform and knelt where he pointed, but I was still down on the floor, arms crossed and I wicked grin on my lips.

"Baby girl, get your ass up here," he commanded with a direct glower.

"Yes, sir."

I'd never, in all my years coming here, heard the play room become so quiet. Everyone stopped what they were doing and turned their attention to us. Now, I'd had plenty of sex in the public room; I'd been spanked, fucked by dicks and with strap ons alike while people watched. But not once had I ever felt the tremor of anticipation and nerves that went through me when James took my hand and sat on that throne. I looked down at Isaac, nerves ricocheting down our bond.

"Color, my pet?" I asked.

"Yellow," he whispered. "I'm sorry, I..."

I cupped his cheek and turned his head up to me.

"Stop. It's alright. And if all you can do tonight is watch, that will be enough."

I tasted his lips slow and gentle and felt him begin to calm down.

"Do you understand?" I asked.

"Yes, Mistress."

James put his hand on the top of Isaacs head and stroked his hair.

"Remember, this isn't for them. It's for us, no matter why we're here."

Isaac nodded.

James' expression hardened again and he pulled me across his lap.

"I once made you a promise," he said kneading the flesh of my ass.

"Did you? Was it to fuck me in a bed?"

Even though I was expecting it, the smack took me by surprise.

"Such a mouthy little thing."

"You like it."

Another smack and I bit my lip against a moan.

"You're damn right I do."

Then he began to spank me in earnest. The tightness of my shorts only added to the sting and soon I was writhing around on his lap trying to get some friction for my throbbing clit.

"Does this arouse you?" he asked with a chuckle.

"You know it does."

"See, you enjoyed it too much."

I squirmed just right over his rock hard cock and grinned up at him.

"And you didn't?"

He growled and stood with me in his arms. I gave a squeak of shock just before he turned and dumped me onto the chair. With a hard yank he tore my shorts off, leaving my glistening pussy visible to everyone in the room. When I tried to bring my legs together, he held them apart, but otherwise refused to touch me.

"Isaac, color?" he asked.

Isaac stared at my folds, wet and just begging for him.

"Green," he replied, voice ragged.

"Then lick her cunt, but don't let her come. Not yet."

Isaac spread my legs more until one was draped over each arm and went to work eating me like a starved male. I gave a cry as something hot and bright lanced through me and then settled into a warm thrum. I wasn't just aware of my own arousal; suddenly, I could feel a glimmer of Isaac's too as he sucked and licked me. Right behind it was James' adrenaline-soaked lust as he stood there and watched us with more love than I ever thought possible. The moment our eyes connected, he knew that I could feel him and a rush of pride swelled in both of us.

And if it had been difficult to not get swept away by how well they could give me pleasure before, it was impossible now. But just before the damn broke over me, Isaac backed off. A keening whine escaped my lips and I tried to reach out for Isaac, to bring him back, when James snagged my wrist.

"I'm your master tonight," his voice was rich as sin and twice as beautiful. "I'll give you everything you need, but you have to be patient. Isaac needs a taste of his reward now."

James snaked his tail around and slipped it into Isaac's shorts. His eyes grew wide and his mouth hung open as he panted. I could see James' tail undulating around Isaac, pushing him higher and higher, only to back off and leave him in unfulfilled agony.

*At least I'm not suffering alone.*

"Isaac," James' voice held a hint of a tremor and I loved that he was as affected as we were. "Our girl's cunt looks neglected. Would you take care of that for me?"

"With pleasure."

He dove in, sucking and licking like he'd been away from me for a lifetime. I grabbed one of his horns and started to fuck his face with sharp, unashamed cries as an orgasm coiled at the base of my spine. When it burst, Isaac lapped up every drop until I was a shaking mess.

"You see, when you're a good girl, you get rewards," James said, his voice pitched loud enough to be heard by others. "Whose slit is this?"

"Yours," I whispered, glassy eyed.

"And yet, it's been days since I fucked it. That doesn't seem right, does it?"

With a whimper, I shook my head.

"What about little Isaac? He's been so good, how should we reward him?" James asked.

"What do you want, my precious pet?" I asked him.

He stared up at me with adoration even as his hips gave tiny thrusts forward, searching for friction.

"I want you to suck my cock while you ride him," he answered in a hoarse whisper.

I was dimly aware of the sound of moans from below us, the slapping of bodies fucking, but none of it mattered. I didn't care if Ben was out there fuming at us, I didn't care that the entire club had likely come into the room and started fucking the second Isaac's face was in my pussy.

All that mattered was my two males, this moment with the three of us, taking and giving in a perfect union of trust.

Both of them took a hand and helped me to my feet, then James sat on his majestic throne, arms lazily set on the arm rests as I unfastened his pants and pulled his cock out. A string of precum fell onto the leather and I licked it off him with a groan.

Before I could wrap my lips around his shaft, Isaac's hands lifted me by my hips and set me on James in a reverse cowgirl. My drenched opening was lined up with the wide head of his dick and I was about to lower myself when James stopped me, claws digging into my hips.

"Whose pussy is this?" he demanded.

"Yours."

He lowered me past the head and I threw my head back onto his shoulder at the delicious stretch of him.

"Who gets to fuck this wet slit tonight?" he asked, louder.

"You!"

I had to earn each little bit of progression, answering his demand about who I belonged to, until he was fully sheathed inside of me.

"You're so tight around me," he rasped, pulling my head back by my hair. "This cunt is mine. But your mouth, that belongs to Isaac tonight."

I turned to see that Isaac had shed his shorts and was stroking his cock, panting as he approached me.

"If it's too much, slap his thigh," James whispered.

I licked my lips and nodded.

"Fuck her mouth and don't stop until she's drunk every last drop of cum from you," James said, voice carrying, though at this point I wasn't sure there was anyone really paying attention.

Isaac now gripped my hair, tall enough in his true form that I barely had to sit forward to line up his dick with my mouth. I opened as wide as I could and let loose a hungry moan as I took him as deep as I could. His eyes rolled back on a breathy cry and I knew this was not going to last long. Which was good because James angled his hips up, fingers coming around to play with my clit.

He must've ran them over his cock-horn before touching me because fire raced down my spine as the aphrodisiacs stripped the last shred of control out of my grasp. I rolled my pelvis down onto him, as Isaac thrust himself into my mouth. They worked in tandem, filling me and leaving me starved for them in perfect unison. Just when I thought this couldn't get any filthier, Isaac's tail came around and began to tease my tight nipples under my halter, ridges rough against my sensitive buds at the same time that James' snaked around my waist and dipped between my ass cheeks. The moment the ridged tip penetrated my tight hole I let loose a howl just before falling into a blissful state of oblivion. Around me I was just barely aware of a crescendo of orgasms, of beings caught in a feast of carnality that we had created.

I clutched and clawed at both of my mates, a savage craving taking control as I became wonderfully, painfully aware of every sensation James and Isaac were also experiencing. I knew what it felt like to find pleasure from penetrating and being penetrated by their tail, to have my cock sucked while I sucked it. As we drove each other higher and higher, I began to cry. That fire that I'd run to had started to consume me. But then, just when I was about to crumple with ecstasy, the storm broke over us. My body spasmed as I drank down Isaac's release and James roared and filled me with his cum and knot.

With a sob, Isaac's cock slid out of my mouth and I fell forward onto Isaac's chest. His arms held me tight just as James pressed his lipst to my back. I was cradled secure and safe between them as I began to shake.

James crooned soft words into my ear, and then Isaac's, as he too began to cry softly into my hair.

"My beloveds," James whispered, holding us both now. "My dearest treasures."

I'm not sure how Isaac managed walking after that, but I didn't have a choice; I had to be carried since James' knot was securely inside of me. He took me up to one of the private rooms, Isaac trailing behind us as he stroked my legs.

"Are you alright?" he asked as we sat on the bed.

I nodded against him, Isaac's face nuzzled into my stomach, his arm slung around my hips.

"That was...I've never..." I said, my voice hoarse. "Is that normal with bonds?"

"No, I don't think so," James said, "I've never felt anything..."

He shook his head and pressed a gentle kiss to my head.

It was then I became aware of two different sensations under my ribs, like I had two additional heartbeats. It startled me at first, and then I calmed myself and really focused on them. One was gentle, warm like a perfect day in spring. The other was a bit stronger, rougher, as if it had seen some shit and was tougher for it.

My breath caught on a sob and I raised my head to look at James.

"It's you, both of you. I feel...the bonds. You're both here."

"That must be what happened," Isaac said, raising his head enough to lay it on my shoulder now. "It solidified while we were up there."

"You mean I won't always feel myself being penetrated by my not-my cock?" I asked.

They both chuckled.

"Not sure," James said, "maybe, but it probably won't be quite this strong."

"That's good because as much as I enjoyed that I'd probably die from it after a while. I mean, it would be one hell of a way to go but..."

Isaac huffed out a laugh against my skin, planting little kisses while he did. We all hadn't stopped touching this whole time and it calmed us enough that soon we were ready to shower and get out of here.

"I'll go get the spare clothes out of the car since I'm the only one who managed to keep his clothes with him," James said once his knot had decreased.

"You should wear those instead of the slacks," Isaac said.

"Definitely."

His only answer was a little smirk over his shoulder.

Isaac and I held each other as we got the shower ready and once James returned, the three of us took our time, soaping and soothing one another.

"I wanted this," James said, rinsing the shampoo from my hair. "I was so jealous that first time when I knew you were in here, giving each other after care. I wanted to be the one to do it and I couldn't."

Isaac ran his hands over James' shoulders.

"You're here now."

"And I always will be."

We held each other under the warm water until my skin turned pruney. It was simple and beautiful and everything I'd ever wanted. I hoped that we'd get the chance to have more of this without the worries of a case hanging over our heads. I wanted time with these two males, quiet moments and loud ones. Fights and making up. I wanted a life with them and it should've scared me but it didn't. How could it when I knew from the way these bonds pulsed and tugged exactly how they both felt about me? Neither of them wanted to cage me, or change me. They just wanted *me.* I was enough as I was and that brought happy tears to my eyes.

"Come on," James said, kissing the top our heads, "we need to get out of here, see if Ben took the bait."

"I'd almost forgotten about him," I confessed. "I didn't see him, not that I was really looking. I wonder if he was there."

When we got to the car, my feet skidded to a stop and the three of us stared in shock.

"I think he was there," Isaac said, a low growl punctuating his statement.

In red paint, across the hood of the SUV, was written "whore" all in capital letters. And then around the car, looking far too much like the slash across the throat of his victims, was a line of red paint, wet and dripping.

# CHAPTER TWENTY

## STELLA

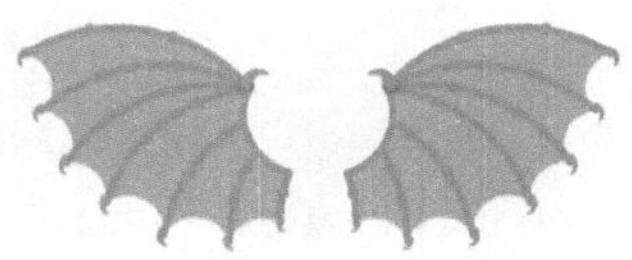

I'd fallen asleep wedged between James and Isaac, none of us having wanted to stop touching, even in our sleep.

This morning, warm and held by both of my Gargoyle mates, I had never been more light, more peaceful. It was true that the risks to our lives were still out there, that the Protectors still wanted us and the knives, that if Ben's fury last night was any indication, he was going to come for us. We walked on the edge of being torn apart by death more than most people. And still, it didn't stop me from snuggling closer, from offering up my soul to James and Isaac last night, free of any hesitation. They were mine and I was theirs for as long as we were gifted breath. And I wasn't about to waste a second worrying about the day death came for one, or all, of us.

I stretched my arm overhead and Isaac groaned behind me.

"You keep wiggling that ass and I might just have stick my dick in it," he mumbled against my shoulder.

"Tease," I said with a roll of my hips.

"Jesus, Stella."

He bit and licked my skin, his cock hard and poking at my ass. I only wore a pair of lace panties, so it wasn't long before the wetness of his precum reached my skin.

"Are my beloveds not sated?" James rasped as he ran a claw down my breast.

I was about to say something sassy but it died on my tongue the second James' mouth latched on to my nipple at the same time Isaac's hand dove beneath the waist of my panties and found my aching clit. I'd always had a bit of an insatiable libido but with these two around the damn thing was perpetually on overload.

Not that I really minded.

Both of them worked my body in slow licks and circles, our panting breaths filling the air of the master suite. I was caught between these two powerful beings, their warm, hard skin caging me in from the front and behind and yet I'd never felt more safe, more treasured.

My stomach tightened as the two of them wound my body tighter until warmth spread like syrup through my veins and I cried out a brief release. Isaac leaned away from me and I was vaguely aware of the side table being opened as James kissed me slow, his tongue stroking mine with languid motions as I took his cock in hand and began to spread the precum from his tip down his shaft in deliberate, slow strokes.

When Isaac's hand slid my panties down, I had a half second to realize what was about to happen before James rolled my back onto Isaac's front.

"Baby girl," James whispered, loathe to take his lips from my skin, "you had both our cocks last night, but I think Isaac wants your ass...what do you think? He takes your ass while I take care of your greedy cunt?"

My breath stalled in my throat at the thought of them both inside of me like that. It was a little strange, considering that last night their tails, tongues and cocks were all inside me at one point, but this felt more intimate.

I reached back and trailed my fingers over Isaac's cheek, then over James'. Taking in the love shining in their eyes, the trail of fire James' mouth carved on my skin, while Isaac's claws sent shivers. Want was too small a word for what was beating in my chest as I lay here between them. Our mating bond burned inside of me, and always would. I'd never get enough of them and I was very okay with that.

"Yes," I whispered, "I want that."

Isaac notched the head of his cock at my back entrance and I tensed at the girth of it.

"Shhh," Isaac whispered in my ear, "relax, Stella, I won't go any further than you want me to, okay?"

I nodded.

"I trust you."

He kissed and bit my shoulder as he eased me down onto him, a little at a time before withdrawing. All the while James' tail was rubbing against my clit as he teased my core with his cock. The orgasm from earlier had been nothing, a mere appetizer compared to the blaze they were both stoking inside of me.

When Isaac withdrew, James pushed in further. I was never empty, increasingly full, until Isaac was seated completely. I let loose a throaty groan, the muscles on my neck standing out as I strained to contain so much pleasure.

"You like that, baby girl?" James voice was brimming with filthy promises, a smile lifting the corner of his mouth promising more.

He thrust in more as Isaac held himself inside of me.

"You want us to stuff you more, paint you with our seed?"

I whimpered, clutching at his shoulder.

"James...Isaac, I...god!"

They began to move together, filling me enough to burst and then almost leaving me empty, only to fill me again. Our obscene symphony rose on the early morning air, wet slapping as flesh met flesh, illicit moans and groans followed by my whimpering cries. I was floating in the sky, yet also held down by them as they pressed me between them. I was their willing plaything, they moved me as they wanted, wringing pleasure from my body as they raised their own into a crescendo.

I mewed and cried out as they whispered my name against my skin, fucking me with sharp thrusts that sent tremors through my body.

"You're so fucking tight," Isaac gasped, his hip thrusts become erratic as he began to lose control. "You take me so good, Stella."

I reached down and cupped his balls, squeezing just a little and he let loose a string of incoherent syllables that ended with him coming across my ass and back.

His strong arms banded around me, his fluids sticky between us as he brought our skin flush and took my mouth in a bruising kiss. James braced his hands on either side of us and began to fuck me in earnest.

"Mine," he growled above us. "Mine!"

James' cock-horn was hitting my clit so hard and so perfectly that it was now painfully sensitive. I wept, pleading and begging him stop one moment and then not to stop another.

Isaac's teeth bit down on my shoulder, body squirming under mine as James roared up at the ceiling and filled me with ropes of hot cum. When his knot swelled inside of me, the sound of cracking wood reached my ears through the torrent of my own release and the next thing I knew, the bed collapsed under us.

At first it didn't quite register, my senses too overwhelmed with my mates to really take in what had just happened. Then the fog started to lift for all of us and we laid there, gasping for a moment before a bubble of laughter welled up in my chest. I tried to stifle it but one look behind me at Isaac's wide eyes and it burst to the surface. Then he was chuckling, shaking my body with the deep tremors. And then James lowered his forehead to mine and let loose a throaty laugh that only whipped Isaac and me into more laughter.

"Well, I guess we won't be getting this bed in our apartment," James said.

I wasn't sure what apartment that would be, or where he was thinking we would live after all of this and I didn't care. It was pointless to fight the fact that I would follow the two of them anywhere.

*I could get a PI license, or maybe join the Archive.*

Neither of those options really fit if I was being honest, but there was no way I could dwell on it with the way James was cuddling me against his chest, running his claws through my hair and laughing with Isaac, who was laying on his side next to me, cleaning the cum off my back with a warm washcloth while he told some joke.

*Yeah, as long as I've got my boys, I'll be fine.*

The bubble of peace we'd found that morning didn't last long. As soon as we'd showered and were settling in with our coffee and morning pastries, my phone buzzed. It was an unknown number and alarm bells went off in my head. I snapped my fingers at the two of them and they immediately stopped talking.

"Hello?" I answered.

"A-are you Stella Wright?" asked a small, female voice choked with tears.

"Yes, who is this?"

"This is Patty, I'm B-Ben's g-girlfriend."

My eyes widened and I put the call on speaker.

"Patty, thank god are you okay? Where are you?"

"I-I'm at the club. He's got me locked in a back room and he left his phone and your number is one of the only ones in there. Can you help me please? He's going to kill me, I know it."

She was sobbing on the other end and I had to push through fury to get to logic and think straight.

"Patty, listen to me, you need to stay calm and tell me where in the club exactly you are."

"I don't know! He's kept me drugged and moved me around. There's no windows here and it smells musty."

I frowned. The only place that could be is the storage shed out back, but when I'd been there, it had been the least secure place I could imagine.

*Unless Ben turned it into a murder shack.*

"Okay, you just hang on. I'm coming for you."

"Thank you."

Her cries were cut off as the call ended and I stared at my phone for a second.

"You know that's a trap, right?" Isaac asked.

"No shit," I replied. "Still doesn't negate the fact that we need to get her out of there."

"No, it doesn't," James agreed. "He chose the perfect bait."

"But it's weird, right?" I said, pacing in front of the kitchen island. "He's just reaching out to *me*, not the two of you."

"Maybe he assumes that one or both of us will come with you," Isaac said.

"Maybe. But it's also a severe departure from his usual MO. Which suggests that he won't act like he has been."

"Which means we need to be extra careful," James said. "And there's one thing we haven't discussed. Even if we get the knives and manage to take out Ben, the Protectors are still after both of you."

Isaac ran a hand through his hair.

"I've had a thought about that, but neither of you are going to like it."

My eyes widened half a second after James snarled out a "No fucking way!"

"Are you out of your mind?" I demanded.

"If I have Andy's help and lure them to the club while James backs you up with Ben, then we take out the Protectors and close the case. It's the easiest way."

"And just how the hell are you going to lure them there?" James demanded.

"I can contact my handler. I memorized the emergency number."

"And you think they'll believe you?"

"Oh no, not at all. But I'm betting on them at least being desperate enough to both catch me and the knives that they'll take the bait anyway."

James growled and clenched his hands so hard against the granite countertops that his claws gouged the surface.

"No matter what we do, we'll be at risk," Isaac said, running his hand down James' bicep. "I can either have them running after me the rest of my life, or we can take a stand and get rid of them now."

"It will only be temporary," James answered. "They'll never stop coming for you, Isaac."

He smirked, dimples on full display.

"Then I guess I'll just need a new identity. But at least this way, I can prove my loyalty to the Archive and we can get rid of the group here in Seattle."

"It's a smart plan," I said, even though I didn't want to. "We need to coordinate with Andy and her team fast because if I wait too long, Ben is going to get suspicious. If he isn't already after last night."

James nodded but he didn't move. I could see the fear rippling off him, even if I didn't get a bitter taste from my bond to him.

"Hey," I moved his face to look at me, "we're all going to make it out of this. So stop worrying."

"How do you know?" his whisper was heartbreaking in its vulnerability.

He needed reassurance, proof that this was all going to be okay. And I couldn't give him that, as much as my heart broke and I longed to. So I just kissed him, as Isaac and I held him.

"I don't know, I just do."

He let out a long breath.

"I guess that'll have to be enough."

In the end, everything came together quickly and within two hours, we had Andy's team assembled at the safe house. Maps and schematics of the club were spread out onto the table in the den, a group of about half a dozen agents looking on. There was one Orc and a Werewolf. Everyone else was Mundane and I silently hoped it would be enough to combat whatever the Protectors threw at them.

"I'll go in to the shed," I said, pointing at the map she'd drawn of the property for the club. "There's only one way in or out and it sits in a spot that isn't well covered by plants or trees, so there's no way he can take me anywhere. James, Isaac and the rest of you will arrive fifteen minutes after me to secure the knives and get ready for the Protectors."

"I still don't like leaving you there alone that long."

"Too bad, you need to get the knives out of there before the Protectors show up. And we can't risk Ben getting spooked. Now Isaac--"

"I know," Isaac said. "I need to time this right, and hopefully those bastards don't show up too early. Andy's team and I will keep them out front as long as possible and try to minimize the impact to the building itself. Have you been able to get a hold of Queen Dawn?"

"No," I frowned, worry creased my forehead. "But we'll just have to go ahead anyway. She'll understand, she wants this over as much as we do. Now, if we still don't have Ben or the knives by the time the Protectors show up, James and I will split up and scour the inside of the club itself. If the fighting should reach the interior, try to keep it to the bar area, that's the first place we'll search and clear. Any questions?"

Everyone shook their heads.

"I don't have any supplies for you two," Andy said, "apologies for that but the director wasn't keen on letting artifacts out into the open with the Protectors in play. I do have a couple of stingers though."

She drew out two of those guns that looked like a prop from a Steampunk cosplayer and I snatched it up.

"What's the deal with this?"

"It's non-lethal," Andy said. "Works pretty much like a regular side arm but the recoil is a bit more. A regular charge can stun up to three men at the medium setting, or kill one man at the high setting. After that, it will take up to three minutes to recharge, so think before you use it."

I nodded and slipped it into my hip holster. Isaac took the second one and did the same.

"Stella, can I see you for a moment?" James asked.

I stifled a sigh and followed him out of the den. He'd been on edge ever since Patty's phone call and I couldn't blame him. I was too, but if he was going to try and talk me out of this, we were about to have a very uncomfortable discussion.

"Here," James handed me a green and gold bug made of some kind of hard substance.

"Um...thanks?"

"It's an Egyptian Scarab. It's one of the few artifacts that I'm allowed to keep for missions. You breathe on it and whisper 'help friend', then point it at the person you need killed. When it's done, say 'return friend' and it will come back to you."

"You don't need this?"

James shook his head.

"I'd rather you had it. After you've given the first instruction, don't touch it again until you've given the second command or it will start to eat your flesh."

I swallowed down a rush of sick at that and forced myself to slip it into the pocket of my jeans.

"I don't need to tell you that I'll rip him apart if he touches you," James continued, cupping my cheek with his hand.

"No, you don't. But I get first blood on this bastard if it comes to that."

He huffed out a laugh.

"Deal."

James pressed a desperate kiss to my lips and held me tight against him, claws pinching my hips.

"I'm coming back to you, no matter what," I whispered.

"You better."

# CHAPTER TWENTY-ONE

## JAMES

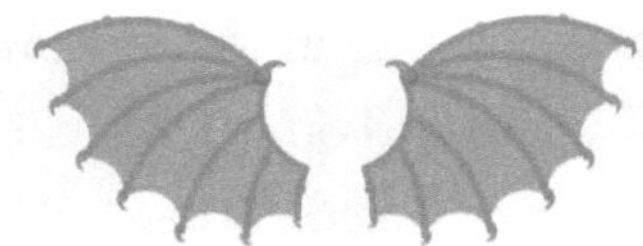

I hated watching Stella leave. It went against every single instinct I had to let her go to that sick bastard without me. But it's what needed to happen. She had to convince him that she was there alone, get him to expose the knives so we could get them into containment.

"She'll be okay," Isaac said, his voice calm even though his body was tense.

I could only nod, my mouth too dry to speak.

"We're a go in ten minutes," Andy said to her team, and then she turned to us. "I don't want to add to your stress but I've got a bad feeling all of the sudden. Do we know for sure that the Protectors are going to fall for this?"

"Nothing is a for sure, you know that," Isaac said, "but their behavior up to this point indicates that they will do whatever it takes to secure these knives. Even risk walking into a trap."

Andy nodded but the tense frown remained on her face.

I was about to suggest that maybe I should shadow Stella sooner, when the phone in my phone buzzed in my pocket. This was an Archive only phone so if someone was calling me on it, there was no way I could ignore it. The caller ID said "M" and my stomach tumbled.

"Marcus, what is it?"

"We finally cracked that firewall for Ben's real identity. James he's--"

"I know, I mean we suspected but we really don't need the proof anymore."

"That's not all we found. His aunt, James. She's not dead, she's been in Seattle this whole time."

Everything inside of me tensed, because I knew what he was going to say. The horror of it had me in its grip and I couldn't do anything other than stand there, shock and terror ripped through me when he said, "It's Queen Dawn. She's his aunt. And not only that, we have proof that she joined the Protectors. James, you've been compromised you need to get the fuck out of there!"

"Stella," I croaked and dropped the phone.

"What's wrong?" Isaac demanded.

"Andy, we're moving out right now, the whole thing has been--"

The windows in the den exploded, sending all three of us back and onto the floor.

Everything went dark and quiet. For how long, I had no idea.

When I came to, my ears were ringing and smoke filled my vision. For a second, confusion wracked my brain as I tried to remember why I was flat on my back. Then everything came rushing to the forefront and my ears popped.

The room flooded with people in tactical gear, all of them pointing guns at us. To my left, Isaac groaned and I tried to roll over to get to him, when someone shoved a barrel in my face. I bared my teeth and growled, but the asshole just laughed.

"Look at this ugly fucker," he said, "growling like an animal."

*Oh, he wants to see an animal? I am happy to oblige.*

I grinned at him, without any humor, and got to my feet. My body ached as I slipped my stone skin into place, sealing in the dozens of cuts and bruises from the explosion. I could sense Isaac down the bond, and he was more wounded than I was, but not grievously, much to my relief. The man in front of me took a half step back while two others tried to get Isaac to his feet.

The moment Isaac's roar of fury broke through the room, I reached out and gripped the man by the throat. The crunch of his windpipe collapsing barely registered as I gave myself over to the primal rage that coursed through my veins.

My mates were in danger, and I had to protect them at all costs.

Isaac's claws ripped the throat out of one of the men that had dragged him to his feet, while the other one attempted to use a cattle prod to stun him. His stone skin wasn't as thick as mine, but it still managed to protect him from the worst of it. Isaac roared again, and punched the man so hard that his head turned at an odd angle, and he dropped to the ground.

A shot behind me had me spinning around to see Andy standing there, one arm hanging useless at her side. Cuts decorated one cheek, and she held her gun out with her good arm as she shot two others in the face.

"We need to get out there and see what's happening," she said, swaying on her feet.

"You're in no condition," I replied.

"And you are? All you can think about is Stella, I can see it on your face."

I hated that she was right, and guilt seared through me.

"It's okay," Andy said, spitting blood out onto the floor, "I get it. I used to be in love once too.

"What the hell happened?" Isaac asked, clutching his side.

"Are you--" I lunged for him and he waved me off.

"Fine, just a bruised rib I think."

"No time to explain," I said as more gunfire sounded outside.

I wanted to get to Stella, to protect her from the shock of finding out that the woman she saw as a mother figure had betrayed her. But there was no way I could leave Isaac in this situation when he was wounded and the Archive agents were likely outnumbered. The love I had for both my mates warred inside of my chest, aching so bad it felt like someone was ripping my heart in two.

*I have to think tactically and trust Stella. This needs to be contained. She knew she was walking into a possible trap but...*

A sharp pain cut through me and I hissed at the same time Isaac did.

"Stella," he said, eyes wide. "What the fuck is-- ah!"

Red exploded on Isaac's shoulder seconds before another bullet tore through his thigh.

The tenuous hold I had on my protective instincts were shredded at the sight of my mate bleeding on the floor. My roar shook the walls, Andy's voice telling me to calm down was distant as if she were miles away. I only saw the man in front of me, now shooting his rifle at me. The bullets bruised when they hit my stone skin but that was about it, and when he realized that I wasn't backing off, the man tried to turn and run.

I grabbed his arm and pulled, relishing the sound of the tendons snapping as the arm was pulled from its socket. His screams were delicious as I crushed his hand. I the shoved the barrel of his rifle into his mouth so hard that I broke teeth and pulled the trigger, the back of his head blown out in a shower of bone and blood. The warmth of it as it trickled down my hand, the wet sound his body made as it slid to the ground was all something I knew I'd think of later, after the fog of rage was past. But right now, it merely drove my bloodlust higher. I would slaughter these petty Mundanes who dared to shed the blood of my beloved. I would make such a bloody mess that they would tremble in terror at the thought of putting their hands on Isaac ever again.

I stepped through the hole in the wall, where the windows used to be, tore the rifle from the first man I saw and hit him across the face with the butt of it, smashing his nose completely. I pressed the rifle point blank to his face and, without a second thought, shot him.

"James, stand down!" Andy screamed at me from behind.

I didn't even turn around. She was likely afraid I wouldn't recognize friend from foe, but I wouldn't hurt those on my side. I could distinguish that much in my current state.

Bullets pinged past me, the painful bruises I would have from the impact of them against my stone skin was not something I was concerned with right now. I ripped through the two men who were coming at me, distantly aware of the other Archive agents fighting for their lives.

"James!" Andy called.

A man came at me with a monstrous knife that I proceeded to tear from his hand, ripping off two fingers in the process, and shoved it through his throat. I didn't bother to wait for the light to fade from his eyes before I dropped him to the ground.

I snarled and roared and gnashed my teeth at anyone who dared come at me, anyone who pointed a gun at me. My hands were coated in slippery blood and mangled skin by the time I realized that I'd made it across the street and there weren't any more men in my path.

A sharp smell of ozone hit my nostrils seconds before a burning tear of pain ripped through me and I fell to my knees. It hit me again and again until I was face down on the grass, panting.

My eyes went in and out of focus as I tried to locate the person who would hit me with such a weapon. I stared up into the eyes of an old man who crackled with power. His hands were covered in rings, a medallion around his neck.

"Agent Carmichael," he said with a thin-lipped grin. "We meet at last. Where are the knives?"

"Go fuck yourself," I spat at him as I tried to get onto my hands and knees.

Another blast hit me and I collapsed.

"Where are the knives?"

Another blast and my vision started to retreat.

"I don't want to kill you," he said, "but I will if I have to. And then I will torture Isaac. And then I will torture Stella. And then I will resurrect them and make them into my personal servants. Until they decay too much, of course."

My heart stuttered in fear as I realized that I was facing a Necromancer. That kind of magic was outlawed, but something told me the Protectors really didn't care about that.

"Now where are the knives!"

He didn't wait for an answer before he hit me with that electrical pulse again. I know I passed out for a few seconds because when I opened my eyes, the Necromancer was staggering, a red hole in the center of his forehead. When he fell to the ground in front of me, Isaac was standing there lowering his gun.

"Isaac," I croaked out and forced my arms to push me up.

My mate fell to his knees and that's when I saw just how wounded he truly was. His shoulder was covered in blood and the leg he'd been shot in gave out under him so he listed to the side. More blood was dripping from his mouth and he coughed as if he were having trouble breathing.

I caught him just as he fell to the side, ignoring the way my entire body cried out in anguish.

"Stay with me," I begged.

His usually vibrant skin was too gray and his eyes fluttered closed before opening back up sharply.

"Stella," he whispered, a wet sound that made my heart squeeze in fear. "You have to...get to her."

"You need help first. Someone help me! I need help!" I screamed as I looked around.

There was no more fighting but in the state I'd been in, I hadn't paid any attention to who was winning. Were the Protectors in control? Would anyone come save Isaac or would I have to hold him as he faded away.

"Don't die," I pleaded, running my hands over him. "Please my Isaac, stay with me, please don't die."

I kissed his forehead and looked around for anyone to help.

Isaac grabbed my face with surprising strength and pulled me down to look at him.

"Stella," he insisted, more blood on lips. "You...have to...save her."

He pressed a hand to my chest and there, behind the fear of losing Isaac, was a throbbing beat filled with more terror, more pain.

"Go," he pleaded. "I'll...be fine. Promise."

"Help me!" I roared, my entire being torn.

I had to hold him, to make sure he lived. But I also had to save Stella from whatever she was going through right now.

Andy limped up to me, two men trailing behind her that were far too fresh looking to have been here for the whole fight.

"He needs help, please," tears fell down my face.

"You two, stabilize him," Andy ordered before glaring down at me. "Let him go and come with me, right now."

I didn't want to let Isaac go but I had no choice.

"I'll be back, and I'll have our girl."

"I know," he gave me a weak smile before I placed him on the stretcher the two men had laid out on the pavement.

I followed Andy into what was left of the house, bodies and blood covering the floor. I wasn't sure how much of that had been from me because the memories were still foggy, but from the way the bodies were torn apart, I could glean that I'd done quite a bit of the damage.

"If we weren't in the middle of some shit, I'd recommend you for immediate leave and relieve you of this mission," she snapped. "But as it is, the Ghosts in the tunnels are having fits, they say that there's some kind of dark energy and it's driving all of them into different sections of the tunnel. We're about to have spectral spikes all over the damn city, which the ghost tours are gonna love, but the Mundanes not so much when their walls start bleeding and their electronics start to smoke. I'm guessing the dark energy is your knives, and that Stella is likely in the shit down there. So go and resolve this situation before I have the West Coast Archive Chief up my ass about all of this."

I took two steps toward the backyard, where the closest tunnel entrance was, before glancing back at Isaac.

"I swear that I'll look after him," Andy said, her voice just a little gentler. "Now go."

"Thank you."

I tore off through the house and to the shed in the back where the tunnel entrance was. When I pushed the elevator button I realized that I was covered in dirt, blood and bits of bone and flesh. There wasn't time to do anything about it and I hoped Stella wouldn't be too badly traumatized seeing it.

*I'm coming, just hold on. Both of you, just hold on.*

# CHAPTER TWENTY-TWO

## STELLA

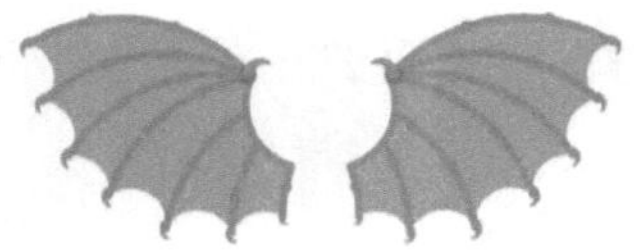

My eyes were unimaginably heavy, as if a weight sat on the lids. As I swam to the surface of consciousness, the sensation of something holding down my entire body had panic burning through me. My eyelids took forever to open and when they did, my vision refused to focus right away. The smell of dirt, mildew and perfume hit my nostrils, making me gag. My mouth was so dry that it hurt to swallow and I wanted desperately to turn my head, raise my hand. Hell, at this point I'd settle for wiggling my finger.

But no matter how much I tried, I could only move my eyes.

*Okay, calm down. This isn't good but I need to remember how the fuck I got here.*

I took a few deep breaths, pushing through the horrible smell and forced my cloudy mind to think.

I'd gone to the club, the place eerily quiet after I'd called Sapphire and Shug and told them to make sure no one was there since I couldn't get a hold of Dawn.

*Dawn...something...what is it about Dawn?*

That question felt incredibly important but I couldn't find the answer so I kept going down the murky path of my memories.

I'd made my way to the shed out back, checked it but other than an old bag of fertilizer, I'd found nothing. I was just about to leave when...

*Shit! The bastard stuck a needle in my neck. And I'd bet even money it's that paralytic shit he's been using. I'm lucky he didn't overdose me.*

I moved my eyes as much as I could, now that they were better focused and recognized the mish-mashed style of one of the underground tunnels. I was in a sort of sitting room that looked like an opium den and a Victorian sitting room had a very confused baby. Red lanterns and a small crystal chandelier were above me, a faded rug on the floor that felt rough where my hands rested on it. I could just barely glimpse a sideboard with crystal decanters and a pipe collection of all things to my right. To my left I could see the clawed wooden feet of what could be a couch. The walls were an odd mixture of faded pink wallpaper and brick.

*There must've been an entrance in the shed. Are all sheds in Seattle equipped with a tunnel entrance? A little obvious but...not important. Where the fuck is that psycho?*

Not that I wanted him to be around, but not knowing where he was didn't exactly make me feel better either.

A sudden bloom of pain across my forehead had me taking a sharp inhale through my nose. A second later, I could move my head a little. If pain preceded the ability to move, then this was going to really suck.

The turn of my head was more like a clumsy flop and I spotted a sign to my right with directions to two different tunnel entrances near a door way.

The knowledge came with a terrible sinking feeling. Even if James and Isaac knew I was gone by now, they'd have to scour miles and miles of tunnels to find me. And by the time they'd done that, would I be in one piece? Would I be here?

*I have to get out of here. If I could just move my fucking body...*

My jaw suddenly ached, as if someone were drilling into my teeth and then, miraculously, I could slowly move my lips.

Voices drifted to me from my right and I closed my eyes quickly; better to make them think I was still out then reveal too soon that I was awake. Maybe I could buy the guys more time.

As the voices became closer, I could distinguish male and female. Was Patty here?

*No her voice is higher this is...no.*

My stomach twisted as betrayal dragged a whimper from the back of my burning throat.

I suddenly remembered what it was about Dawn that I should know and it *hurt*.

Just before the injection flooded my system fully, I'd hit the ground and looked up, conscious enough to make out her face holding the needle.

"Why couldn't you leave well enough alone, darling?" she'd asked just before darkness had pulled me under.

Tears leaked from my eyes before I could stop them and I prayed they wouldn't notice.

"She's mine!" Ben whined. "You told me I could have her."

"And you will, dearest," Dawn's voice floated on the air. "But the knives must be satisfied, and that whimpering idiot you had on a leash wasn't sufficient. Not enough guilt and shame. We must give the knives what they want. After all, they showed us the path."

"Yes, Aunt, but I thought that's why we were killing the others. They deserved it, they were terrible beings, remember? But Stella is for me!"

"Hush now," Dawn admonished, her voice getting closer. "I never said you had to kill her. Just bleed her a little, a few cuts here and there."

A chill raced down my spine at the words. I was more than awake enough to feel every fucking thing, but my body wasn't coming back under my control fast enough to fight back, or reach that little bug thing James had given me. I needed at least my hands to wake up so I could dig it out of my pocket but considering how my neck was just now starting to ache, I had a bad feeling my hands wouldn't wake up fast enough.

I narrowly avoided flinching as the sound of someone's feet came close to me on the gritty floor.

"She's still so pretty," Ben's voice was now nauseatingly close. "A little bit of strict dieting and I'll have her thin again. And then I'll tie her up and fuck away the memory of those filthy beasts' hands on her."

*Fuck you if I'm too much woman for you to handle, you limp dicked--*

His hand caressed my cheek and bile rose up in my throat. I thought I hid the tremor that coursed through me as his fingers traced a line down my jaw to my collarbone but the sudden sting of his fingers digging into my face as he grabbed my chin made my eyes fly open in surprise.

"Awake so soon?" he grinned down at me, and then nuzzled my cheek with his mouth. "Good, I wanted to look into your eyes as I did this."

Of all the terrifying things I'd been through in my life, this was the worst of them; unable to move or struggle as Ben leaned toward me, getting ready to put his lips on my skin. But before they made contact, Dawn's voice stopped him.

"That's enough, Jacob," Dawn didn't raise her voice but it still struck through the air like a whip.

He pulled away, shooting daggers at Dawn, and stood up.

I turned my head to look at Dawn standing behind him, arms crossed, face drawn into a tight frown.

"Why?" my voice broke.

She actually had the good grace to appear upset for a moment before her cold exterior returned.

"You stuck your nose in something that was not your business, darling. I tried to make you stop, to distract you with that pathetic girl's disappearance. But you and your Gargoyles wouldn't take the hint."

"You...had the knives?"

"Yes," she nodded. "Jacob and I found them at an auction in San Diego. They called to us, promised us that we could right the wrongs of the past. The wrongs done to my brother and his family."

"But you...your club...you're not this..."

"Oh, darling," she knelt down and wiped my tears away with her fingertips.

And god help me, I longed for the comfort her touch had once afforded me, even as repulsed as I was by it now.

"I know that not all Supernaturals are evil. They're just...well, rutting beasts really. I provided a safe place for them to explore their true natures. And over the years, as I got to know them, I realized just how much of my clientele had dark, brutal pasts filled with deeds they would never see justice for. Every one of those creatures deserved the death that Jacob gave them, I can assure you."

"No," I tried to turn away from her but she gripped my face and made me look at her.

"My poor nephew needed peace after being denied it all those years. And I needed to find some kind of justice for my brother. The knives simply showed us the path to justice, healing."

"How did you...know about them?"

She smiled at me, a look that had once been so precious, like the rays of the sun after a storm. It hurt so much to have her look at me like that, and a broken sob leaked from between my lips.

"You think the Archive is the only group that knows about artifacts? The Protectors have gone by many names over the years, and I have been among their ranks ever since my dear brother's death. You see, your father had every chance to bring the killers to justice, but the moment it was revealed that my brother had stolen artifacts, well, the Archive came in and hushed everything up. They didn't care about capturing the creatures who had tortured and killed my brother and his family. All they cared about, were their precious artifacts. So when the chance came to strike a blow against those self-righteous wind bags, I took it."

"And now? They want the knives."

"Oh, I know. I tried to distract them with false clues, with the inevitable betrayal of your pretty boy partner, and it worked. They think I'm abroad, searching for some stupid book. And by the time they realize it, I'll be long gone. But since I couldn't have them bursting in *here*, I threw them a bone. The location of your safe house. Now they'll be far too busy killing your Gargoyles and the other agents to come looking."

"No...no! How did you even know where we were?"

Dawn stood up with a giggle.

"Did you think I'd let you have a peek at my security footage without creating a way to spy on you, as well?"

Dread coiled in my stomach and spread to where the mating bonds beat under my ribs. I didn't know if it was the paralytic that had made me unaware of them, or if I had been too scared, but one of them was weak, barely pulsing, and the other was filled with so much pain it stole my breath.

"No...Isaac," I whispered my shoulders suddenly on fire as the drug began to wear off there.

"We have one thing that must be taken care of before we can leave," Dawn snapped her fingers and Jacob walked up beside her carrying an old fashioned surgeons kit.

"No...no!"

I tried to squirm, to move, kick, *anything*. But I could only thrash my head side to side.

"Calm yourself," Dawn soothed. "The knives merely need a little bit of blood. I've agreed to let Jacob keep you, but you must pay a price. You cost us our justice, and now we must begin again in a new city."

Ben or Jacob or whatever the fuck his name was knelt beside me and unrolled the knives. A sickly sweet smell rolled off them and suffocating terror struck me, oily and thick. I began to yell and scream, sobbing as I begged Ben not to do this.

"It will only hurt a little," he smiled at me, voice so calm, as if he were talking about a flu shot. "I won't go too deep, and soon you won't even remember that we were apart. Isn't that right Aunt Constance?"

Dawn caressed his cheek with maternal love.

"That's right, dearest Jacob. Now, obey the knives, we mustn't tarry too long."

"Please don't...*Dawn,* please don't do this!"

I screamed as Ben held my head and drew out the first knife. He dragged the blade along my cheek bone and red hot pain scorched through my face. A dark tendril rose up from the blade as Ben watched my blood drip from it and I began to cry harder.

Cramps coursed up and down my arms but I hardly noticed as Ben drew the blade along my other cheek. Another dark tendril, and a harsh whisper grated against my ear.

"You sick son of a bitch," I snarled as he set the knife down. "I'll gut you, I swear to god I will!"

I thought at first that he hadn't heard me, but then he drew back and slapped me across the face. His blow snagged on the cut on that side and opened it even more. But the pain was becoming distant because I noticed how bad my hands ached. I was getting movement back, I would have to time it just right; I may be able to move my arms soon but I was still pretty damn weak from that crap they injected me with.

"You will need more punishment than I thought," Ben said, and ripped my shirt down the front.

Fiery cramps were now racing up and down my torso as he took a larger knife and began to cut my chest just below my collarbone. I endured the pain, the humiliation of having him this close to my nearly naked body. After he'd carved three, careful lines in my flesh, Ben turned to replace the knife and I slipped my fingers into my pocket where the Scarab was.

Dawn seemed to be paying more attention to the knives than she was to me, her head cocked as if she were actually listening to them. I had a moment to wonder, if the knives had never come to her, would she had simply gone on being the woman who had given me a home and love when I'd needed it most.

*It doesn't matter, I have to survive this. Even if it means she doesn't.*

I turned my head and brought the scarab to my mouth, breathing on it as I whispered "help friend". When Ben came back with a different knife, I flung the thing, though I really didn't have to. It came to life and flew straight at him. Ben stared in shock and the scarab flew into his mouth.

Dawn gave a shout of warning but too late. Ben staggered to his feet and began to swat his body, as if he were trying to kill the scarab. Then he convulsed, blood seeping from his mouth and eyes.

"*What have you done!*" Dawn screeched.

Ben collapsed, gaping holes opening up all over his body and I sat up as best I could with the lower half of myself still unable to move. When he stopped twitching, the scarab flew out of one of the holes on his torso and aimed straight for Dawn.

She snarled and shot at it with confiscated Stinger Andy had given me earlier. The scarab stopped in midair and tried for her again. I went to reach for the knives but remembered James saying they corrupt anyone who touches them. I silently hoped that didn't extend to those who had been sliced up by the damn things, and began to drag myself over to a nearby table.

Behind me Dawn was screaming at the scarab, a series of fizzes and pops accentuating her rage. I focused on the table, hopeful that it would have something I could use as a weapon when the smell of ozone and sulfur burned my nose. When I looked back, the scarab lay in a burnt heap on the floor. Dawn's eyes had taken on a murderous gleam that sent cold terror through my body. I pulled myself across the cement floor so fast and hard, ripping my fingernails, but it wasn't enough. Dawn was on me in a second, and her body pinned mine to the floor.

"You murdered him!" she screamed in my ear. "All he wanted was to love you!"

I reached back and raked my torn fingernails down her face. She wailed and I bucked the upper half of my body up enough to throw her body off mine.

I grabbed for the table leg and pulled it down, shattering a glass vase and candy dish. Just as my fingers closed around a large shard of pink glass, white hot agony ripped through my leg. I looked down to see Dawn with one of the knives shoved through my calf.

"Let's see how far you run without your Achilles tendon," she spat.

I'm not sure when my lower half had started to wake up, but my uninjured leg jerked away from her and I flung myself at Dawn's exposed thigh with a grunt.

The shard of glass sank into her enough to piss her off but not do any serious damage, and she backhanded me, throwing me to the floor. My head hit the hard surface and I saw stars just before Dawn jumped onto me, her hands coming to my throat and choking me.

"I gave you a chance to do some good! To be with us!" Her eyes widened, lips pulled back into a snarling look that rendered her unrecognizable.

This wasn't Dawn, this was a being of pure murderous rage and evil that stared down at me.

Her grip tightened and my lungs burned for air. My hands scrambled through the broken glass, searching for a weapon.

"I loved you like a daughter, and you have been nothing but a disappointment!"

Tears leaked from my eyes, both from being strangled and from the pain of her words. I kept telling myself that I didn't have a choice, that the woman I once knew was already dead, and finally, my hand clasped what felt like a large enough piece. I swung my arm up and at her throat, the jagged piece of glass sinking deep into her pale skin, just below her jaw line, and her hands fell from my throat.

I coughed and rolled as she toppled off me, blood running in a thick stream down the front of her.

I laid there on my side, throat on fire, as I gulped down air in between sobs that shook my injured body. I could barely feel Isaac's soul and the thought that he was dead or dying made me curl into a ball in agony. But then, through that haze, came something bright and strong.

"James," I whispered moments before he came barreling around the corner and into the chamber.

His eyes latched onto mine and I reached out to him as broken cries rolled from my body.

"Stella," his voice was harsh with emotion.

For such a huge Gargoyle, James picked me up with exquisite tenderness and held me against him as he set me on a nearby couch.

"Wait right here," he kissed my forehead.

All I could do was nod and continue to let tears drip off my chin.

He came back with a strange box that was silver, gold and purple. As I watched, he doused the knives with a thick pink solution and then placed them in the box. Everything blurred around me and I wondered if it was the drugs or something else. It scared me, the thought of being unable to move again.

"James," I whispered just before the darkness took me over.

# CHAPTER TWENTY-THREE

## ISAAC

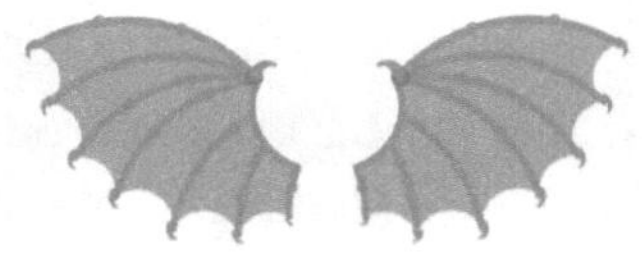

I woke to the sensation of heat on my body, not unpleasant but comforting. Beside me, someone shifted and I managed to open my eyes enough to see that it wasn't really a body as much as James' arm, which had my hand in a firm grip.

It was then that my sleep addled brain cleared enough to take in my surroundings.

We were back at the hospital, the room much larger than the standard one Stella had been in. The lights were dimmed and the violent shades of red and orange from a Seattle sunset, or sunrise, was seeping through the small cracks where the curtains weren't closed all the way. Beside my bed was another one, in which James rested. And then beside him was yet another bed where Stella slept, bandages covering both sides of her face and peeking from the top of her hospital nightgown. The sight of the wounds had a growl emanating from my lips before I could stop myself. James' eyes opened and took me in, a devastating smile lighting up his face a moment later.

"You're awake," he whispered, sitting up in the bed.

"Are you alright? Is she?"

"I'm a little banged up, my stone skin protected me for the most part. And Stella is going to be fine. Some scaring, but nothing life threatening."

My jaw hardened as I took in how fragile and pale she appeared, swathed in blankets and bandages. Two IVs curled from her arm, and I now saw a bruise along her jaw line.

"She's going to be fine," James reiterated. "Believe me, I would know if Delphine were lying. They called in their best healers for you both."

"What happened? How did they even find us?"

James took a deep breath.

"I got a call from Marcus just before the attack. I'd asked his tech team to cut through the firewalls protecting Ben's true identity. They finally did and confirmed that Ben was actually Jacob Marcone, the only survivor of the Pacific Heights massacre. But they also discovered that Queen Dawn was his aunt, Constance Marcone. She'd joined the Protectors under a different name two years after the death of her brother and his family. She and her nephew took Stella down into the tunnels with the knives. I don't know everything that happened, but they used some of the knives on her."

I gripped the blanket on my lap aggressively, my claws ripping the fabric.

"Easy, she's okay."

"They hurt her," I growled, "they put their hands on our mate."

James ran a hand down my arm with one hand and turned me to look at him with the other.

"She's going to heal. They didn't take her from us, and when it all hits her, she's going to need us to listen, not pummel things."

"This coming from the male who went into a rage when I was shot."

"Yeah, I, uh, got a little out of control."

I snorted.

"How are your wounds?" James asked.

It was only then that I noticed the sting of pain in my shoulder and thigh.

"Sore but not too bad. I wish my stone skin was thicker, these bullets might not have been able to penetrate if it was."

"Marcus says they're developing some kind of nanite armor and they're looking for Supernaturals to test it on."

My eyes widened, shock parting my lips.

"You mean, join the Secret Archive?"

"Well, I don't make the decisions but I think you'd make a pretty damn fine agent."

I looked down at my hands and choked back my tears.

"If it's not what you want--"

"It's what I want," I said. "There are just things we need to talk about. But first, did you get the knives?"

"Yeah, we got 'em. And Ben and Dawn are dead, thanks to her."

I glanced at Stella, my heart breaking for what she must've gone through.

"Are you going back to London?" I asked, barely able to get my mouth around the words.

I dreaded the answer and what it may mean for the three of us. Now was when the hard work started, the questions about how we were going to proceed. And instead of the confidence I thought I'd approach it with, I was finding myself painfully nervous.

"Actually, I had a debriefing while the two of you were being looked at," James said, his thumb running over the back of my hand.

"Why doesn't that sound good?"

"Well, it was...interesting. Director Dearborne is grateful that I snagged the knives. But as you pointed out, I lost control at the safe house when you were wounded. My primal side took over and I killed ten men. While it saved the mission, she feels that I may need some time off. Especially since I'm newly mated."

I swallowed. James and Stella were both ambitious, they both needed purpose and a challenge. What would happen now that neither of them had that.

*Shit, none of us have a job now it sounds like.*

"I haven't taken time off in over ten years," James said with a chuckle. "So I have quite a lot of vacation time coming at me. I was thinking, maybe when you two are healed up, we go traveling? Just for a little while? Too long and I'd go stir crazy."

My pulse sped up, as I took in what he was saying.

"We could start in Hawaii," he continued. "I've always wanted to see Stella in a bikini and I bet you'd look amazing in those low slung swim shorts. Then maybe hit Spain or Italy."

"Are you...are you taking us on a honeymoon?"

His gaze turned heated and he claimed my mouth in a gentle, yet hungry kiss that left my head spinning.

"I guess I am," he murmured.

"And after that? Is your leave permanent?"

"No, but Director Dearborne isn't going to let me do extensive field agent work with you two. She says my instinct to protect you is too much of a liability and she's right. I could've completely lost control and injured agents. That's not something I'd be able to come back from. But, rumor has it that the field office Chief in New York is retiring soon."

He gave me a sly grin, that I gladly returned.

"Oh yeah?" I asked.

"Lots of really old buildings in New York."

"Perfect for perching on."

"And doing other things."

This time James kissed me like he hadn't seen me in years. His tongue tangling with mine, fangs biting my lips as he gripped the back of my neck and took what I gladly gave.

"I love you," I whispered against his lips. "And I'd follow you wherever you went."

"I love you too," James said with one last nip at my bottom lip. "You could train to work in the field office there, though I wouldn't be able to go on any missions with you."

"And Stella?"

James' grin turned playful, like a little boy on Christmas.

"I've also heard that the Head of the Supernatural Branch in New York is looking for an experienced officer to take his place when he retires in a few years. With a letter of recommendation from Director Dearborne, no one is going to care that she got fired here."

"Oh my god," I glanced over at where she still slept, "she's going to flip out. Better not tell her until at least after Hawaii, or you're not getting that vacation."

"Yeah, that's the truth."

We both stared at her, our girl, so brave and fierce and all ours.

*This is my family. The three of us, together, no matter what is thrown at us we're going to weather it, every time. If we survived this, we'll survive anything.*

I'd never hoped to have this, two mates that I adored, that adored me back, looking forward to a career I could be proud of in a city I'd once thought I'd never see again.

"You okay?" James asked, wiping a tear from my cheek.

"Yeah, I'm...I'm just really fucking happy."

James chuckled and grazed my forehead with his lips.

"Me too, beloved. Me too."

A half asleep voice interrupted our increasingly passionate kisses and I snorted on a laugh.

"Ugh, you two done groping?" Stella asked, eyes still closed. "I want to hear more about this job opening."

**Three Months Later**

"Oh my *god,* this pizza!" Stella crammed a slice of New York's finest into her mouth, sauce leaking from the sides of her lips.

"You've said the same about the food in nearly every city we've been to," James said with a smirk.

She mumbled something around a mouthful of pepperoni, cheese and olives and then moaned.

James received a commendation from the Archive for retrieving the knives, which made it safely to the newly constructed Dark Vault. And as soon as Director Dearborne awarded him the special medal in our hospital room, she announced that James was going on a well-earned vacation for the next three months.

Stella and I were discharged from the hospital after a week, in which she drove every single doctor and nurse to the brink of sanity. It was absolutely no surprise to any of us that she was the worst patient. Delphine had said that normally she'd have kept someone with Stella's supernatural injuries for another week of observation but "I don't think the hospital would survive."

So we left with a long list of instructions on what to watch out for should her wounds from Jack the Ripper's Knives prove to have left anything behind. James and I watched her like a hawk, only aggravating her all the more but thankfully didn't see any side effects beyond the scars.

"I can't heal them," Delphine had said, "but if that's the only thing the knives left behind, she should count herself lucky."

And we did, count all of us lucky. I had no idea how close we'd come to losing one another until later, when James and Stella had divulged what had happened to each of them during the whole crisis. I'd held Stella tight all night and it was proof of how shaken she still was that she didn't even complain. From the time I woke up in the hospital, the three of us hadn't been apart, sleeping in the biggest beds we could find in ridiculously expensive hotels until James booked us a flight to Hawaii. We island hopped, spending hours on white sand beaches, drinking and eating and fucking and laughing. James and I flew over the islands at night and made love on the cooled lava beds of a volcano. We took Stella for several flights as well, and had a midnight picnic on a private beach after getting permission from the locals.

I'd never known such a sense of belonging, of peace as I did the weeks we spent there.

True to James' word, we toured Spain and Italy, and even took a trip to France to see the Eiffel Tower and treat Stella to real French pastries. We spent so much time on beaches that now Stella's blond hair was nearly platinum and her skin had the most beautiful golden hues to it. The white scars on her cheeks and chest stood out in sharp contrast, and there were times I saw her touch them as she cried. It was in those moments that hate curdled the beauty I was experiencing. I wished I could tear Ben apart for what he'd done to her, but that was in the past. The present was what needed my attention, and so I held Stella in the moments when the memories hurt. I told her how much she meant to me, how I'd never been alive until she and James had come into my life. How I'd kiss it all away if I could.

She would smile at me, sometimes we'd fuck it away, sometimes we'd just quietly hold one another until James noticed what was happening. Then the three of us would cuddle, or distract her with a movie. I never thought I'd be the kind of male that enjoyed nights in with Netflix but, settled on the couch with James and Stella, I found myself deeply content.

"So where is this wonderful place you found us?" Stella asked, licking the grease from her fingers. "Let me guess, some old as fuck building?"

James grinned at her and kissed the tip of her nose. We were both in our glamours, since we were walking around New York in broad daylight, and the sight we made had people turning their heads and staring at us. We didn't even try to hide the fact that we were all three together with Stella between James and me, our hands entwined now that Stella was done with her second slice of pizza.

"I'm actually quite curious too," I said. "You haven't told me anything other than I'm going to love perching on it."

"It's a surprise."

We strolled along in the gorgeous fall weather of New York, which would soon fade into the bone chilling cold of winter. The trees in Central Park still held their rich autumn foliage and we took our time, letting Stella buy an ice cream at a vendor while I gave in and purchased a pretzel.

"The chief called me," Stella said around a lick of double chocolate fudge. "He wants me to come in tomorrow to meet the crew. I won't be the only woman this time, thank god. A little estrogen would be great."

"Really? Do you know what species she is?" I asked.

"Orcish, actually."

"No way!"

"Yeah, blew me away too, you know how Orcs can get about their females. Apparently she still has an Orc shadowing her, but only one. I've never met an Orc female, I'm excited!"

"What about you?" I asked James.

He shrugged.

"Director Dearborne still hasn't taken me off leave officially but unofficially, I'm supposed to check out the field office this week once we get settled. It's going to be a quiet transition. You, however," he kissed me over Stella's head, "better promptly be at the office Monday morning at eight sharp."

"Yes, sir. Or should I call you Daddy?"

James' eyes flared with lust and a growl rolled up his throat.

"You do that and I think we'll get a reprimand for keeping the bathroom occupied all day."

"Hmmm...that sounds like an interesting problem to have."

"You two better not spend it all at work," Stella said, tossing her empty cone in the trash, "I expect some after work orgasms from at least one of you."

"Yes, mistress," I said, kissing her.

"That's better," she replied with a grin.

We walked for a bit longer until James pulled us to a stop in front of a gorgeous pre-World War II building with three fantastic towers at the top. It was a light cream color, not a spot on it, as if the birds knew this place was far too expensive for them to shit on.

"Here we are," James said with a broad grin. "Home sweet home."

Stella and I stared up at The Beresford building, mouths hanging open.

"How the fuck did you afford a place here?" she asked.

"Well, funny story. Being paid very well, and being friends with a lot of Witches who have the gift of foresight, meant I invested my earnings wisely and lived pretty cheaply for the past hundred years."

I knew what he really meant; he'd never settled anywhere because he'd never wanted to, until now. And it warmed my heart that at last James had found a home with Stella and me.

We followed him inside, the doorman nodding to us as if we had every right to be here. I'd not grown up poor, but we definitely hadn't been anywhere near this zip code. I half expected someone to throw us out, but the concierge simply nodded at James, and smiled at the two of us in turn.

I consciously closed my mouth but Stella almost collided with the front desk as she walked backwards in an attempt to take in the gorgeous lobby.

"Coming, dear?" James asked with a wicked smile on his face.

"Yeah," she said, drawing out the word.

We were silent in the elevator, Stella and I staring at one another while James wore the biggest grin I'd ever seen. When the doors opened, we walked just a few feet to the door of what was going to be our home.

*Our home...the three of us.*

It hit me then, the fact that the three of us were going to make a life together. The last three months had been a whirlwind of sex and gorgeous locations. None of it was real life, just an extended vacation that we had more than earned to heal and find some peace before we were thrown back into the dark world of Artifacts and killers. But now we stood outside the place where we'd live and love one another for the rest of our lives.

"You okay?" James asked.

I realized then that I was crying, but I laughed as joy broke over me in an inescapable wave.

"We're home. The three of us...we're home."

Stella's eyes shone with tears too and she hugged me tight.

James just kissed us both and drew us into his arms.

"I love you both so much," I sniffled.

"Should we see what James bought us?" Stella asked. "See if it's up to our standards?"

I snorted at that and nodded.

"I had some work done, interior design changes," he said, sounding just a little nervous. "It had been a three bedroom but I thought we'd want to share, so I had them combine two of the bedrooms into one."

"And the other?" Stella asked.

He grinned over his shoulder.

"That's a surprise."

The entry way was simple, white and black tiled floors and a huge mirror with a small table underneath to my left. He led us to a living room that was also simply decorated in blues and whites, large windows opening up to a perfect view of Central park and the towering sky scrapers beyond.

"Oh my god," Stella breathed.

"You should see it at night," James said. "All I could think about was the three of us sitting here, drinking wine and watching the lights come on across the park and the city."

"It's perfect," I said.

We explored the rest of the penthouse, my breath stalling when I saw the brand new chef's kitchen James had installed for me. The bedroom was indeed huge, though in our true forms, it would fit us perfectly. Stella bounced on the bed, frowning.

"What's wrong?" James asked.

"Do you think it will hold?"

We'd broken more than our fair share of beds on our vacation, so it was a fair question.

"It's steel reinforced and cost me a fortune, so it better. But, I'm not sure how often we're going to use the bed for sex."

"Oh, really?" she asked with an arched eyebrow.

He led us out to the last door at the end of the hall.

"So, when I had the master suite enlarged, I also had some changes made to the left over bedroom."

He opened the door to a white and gray room with red and pink accents. It was airy and bright, with candles everywhere. It took me a moment to really understand that James had designed us a--

"Sex room?!" Stella squealed, running in.

"Holy shit," I gasped.

It was gorgeous. A huge Saint Andrew's Cross was against one wall, flogging instruments, handcuffs, and a variety of sex toys sat in gorgeous racks and shelves near the Cross. A spanking bench was in the corner to the right of an inset wall fireplace. A tantric chaise sat in the opposite corner, a soft red blanket half draped across it. A white leather couch was to my left, perfectly positioned if James ever just wanted to direct us and watch. The wallpaper was a swirl of what looked like pencil drawn naked people in various sex positions but you'd have to look very hard to figure it out, otherwise it just appeared to be random swirls. Black and white nudes were in red frames on the walls, a red and white lighting fixture made of what looked like blown glass feathers was above us and black sconces dotted the walls.

"Well? What do you think?" James asked.

Stella ran her hands over the floggers before picking one up and caressing it. When she looked up, the grin she gave me shot straight to my cock and my knees trembled.

"I think we're going to be very busy for the next few nights," she said.

James chuckled, and ran a hand down both our backs.

"I think you're right."

WANT TO SEE WHAT SHENANIGANS THEY GET UP TO IN THEIR NEW SEX ROOM? CLICK HERE FOR THAT LITTLE SCENE OR COPYING AND PASTING THIS INTO YOUR BROWSER: http://trishheinrich.com/secrets/bbc/

AND IF YOU CAN SPARE A MOMENT, PLEASE BE SURE TO LEAVE A REVIEW WHEREVER YOU GUSH ABOUT BOOKS! THANKS FOR READING BOUND.

READ ON FOR A SNEAK PEEK AT THE THIRD BOOK IN THE MONSTERS & ARTIFACTS SERIES, ABANDON: AN ORC MONSTER ROMANCE

# CHAPTER TWENTY-FOUR

## ANDROMEDA

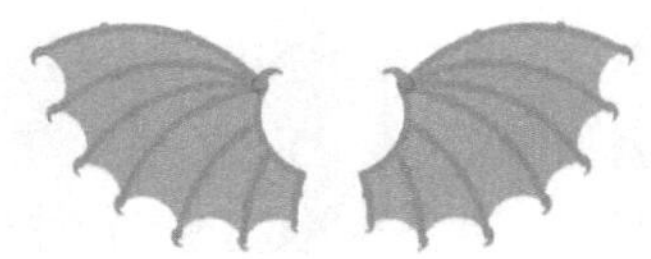

It had been over three months since the incident in Seattle, and I'd received no word that I was being censured or that I was receiving a commendation for it. So I had no idea why Director Dearborne wanted to speak with me. I hadn't been assigned to the main London office since my marriage went up in flames. That was four years ago and I hoped I'd never lay eyes on this place again. Back then, the Director of the Secret Archive was a raging psychopath by the name of Francesca and I was lucky to get out of her office with my skin intact. I got my reassignment, far away from my ex and never looked back.

Or at least, that's the narrative I believed.

Over the years, I had ignored the constant ache in my chest at the dissolution of my marriage long enough that it was a distant murmur, a slight inconvenience. I forgot the nights I'd spent curled into a ball, sobbing myself to sleep. Or the gnawing loneliness that seemed to eat me alive. I had drowned all of it in work, and faceless one night stands until the pain of my failed marriage was a distant memory that belonged to a different woman.

But now here I was, back in the one place that held constant and brutal reminders of the male that had promised me forever and didn't deliver.

I paced the waiting area outside of Director Dearbornes office, the yellow and gray surroundings were intended to be calming compared to the red and black of her predecessor, but it was wasted on me. As the minutes dragged on my palms started to sweat and my mouth became dry. There was no reason to expect Luke to come sauntering around the corner, stupid grin on his handsome Orc face.

Right?

A rich, low voice started to filter through the hallway to my right and my pulse jumped.

Was that him? Was I going to have to come face to face with him after all these years?

*You can do this. Nut up Andromeda! He's just your ex for crying out loud.*

I took a deep breath, squared my shoulders and slipped into the stone faced mask I'd gotten very good at wearing. Underneath it, my heart was beating so damn hard it hurt, and my nails dug into the palms of my hands. There was no way to avoid this so I was going to just have to accept that and move on, like I'd done with things before.

But when the owner of the voice came around the corner, it wasn't the six and half foot Orc I'd expected. Instead, it was a very handsome Korean man with odd tattoos on his arms and backs of his hands.

"Ah, Ms. Kane, we're so sorry to have kept you waiting," he said, reaching his hand out. "I'm Trey Park, Liason to the Council."

I shook his hand, which was inordinately hot and noticed his tattoos shifting on his skin. One look in his eyes told me that it wouldn't be prudent to ask about it, so I let it go without a word and followed him into the office.

"Can you tell me what this is about?" I asked as I crossed the threshold.

"Now that Trey is finally here, yes," said the pretty white woman in front of the desk who could only be Director Angelica Dearborne.

The office was warm if in a very beige way. The colors much brighter at least than Francesca's with the cream walls and blue furniture. It was nice not to have a sense of terror and foreboding hanging in the air as I shook Director Deaborne's hand.

"Madam Director," I said.

"Ms. Kane, it's a pleasure to meet you in person," she gave me a smile and eyed Trey as he poured a cup of coffee. "Would you like anything?"

"No, thank you."

She nodded and accepted the cup from Trey. There was a crackle of energy between them that I recognized as attraction but also caution. And if the rumors about Angelica Dearborne were true, she had every reason to be cautious about loving someone. The end of her marriage made mine look like a month at a spa.

I shoved those thoughts aside, and folded my arms across my chest.

"Now down to business," she said, setting the cup on her desk. "We've called you back from the west coast United States because we have an asset that has gone missing and we need you to find him."

Unease prickled along my spine. I wasn't usually sent in for extraction. Bodyguard maybe, security detail certainly. But getting someone out of a scrape was not my speciality.

"Why me?" I asked.

"To the point, I like it," Trey said.

Angelica's blue eyes sparked but it was the only indication of her irritation with the man.

"The asset is someone you know and we believe that you're the only one that can find him."

She handed me a file, but I already knew what I'd find.

"Luke," I whispered, staring at the picture in his file.

His beard had a bit more gray, as did the hair at his temples. His glasses were square now, and he had a ring on one tusk, a sign of respect in his clan. The reason he may have gotten it twisted in my gut and I swallowed.

"You should know," I said, snapping the file shut, "that we are supposed to never work together again."

"I read that," Angelica said.

"We don't mix well since our divorce."

"I read that too."

"So you know sending me in is a fools errand. If you want him out of there, you need to send an actual extraction team."

She let out a long breath and folded her hands in front of her. I held her gaze, determined not to look away.

"We sent in an extraction team," Trey said, "and they disappeared."

My eyes snapped to him, dread starting to spread through my body.

"Before they did," Angelica said, "they were having trouble finding Professor Turner. They thought they'd zeroed in on his location, but then they missed their last three check ins. I'm afraid of what that means, for the team and for Professor Turner."

"So," I swallowed, controlling the tremble in my voice but just barely, "you're sending me in to find a body essentially."

"I hope not. But you are the only one who worked closely with Professor Turner in the field. You know his habits, how his mind worked. No one else does, at least not like you. We need you to use that knowledge to find him and bring him back."

"And the artifact?"

"It's in your briefing, as is the team going with you. Whatever you need from the supply ward is yours."

I realized then that the file they'd handed me wasn't on Luke specifically, it was my assignment.

"You were so sure I'd say yes?" I said.

"Actually I had even money you'd quit," Trey said with a grin. "I was at the charity benefit the night—"

"That's enough Trey," Angelica said, her voice hardening to steel.

My face burned with embarrassment at the memory of that night but I'd be damned if I let it show any more than I already had. I opened the file again, scanned the preselected team, all men and women I'd worked with before and tried to come up with a compelling reason to say no.

I couldn't, because while I'd imagined dozens of ways to make Luke suffer after our divorce, I didn't want him to die. If I was the only one that could save him, which had a nice bit of poetic justice to it, then I had to do it. No matter what I felt.

"Alright," I said, closing the file again. "When's the departure?"

"As soon as you can be ready."

"I'll meet with the team and requisition supplies. Can we be out tomorrow?"

"Yes. And thank you," Angelica said, "I know this isn't going to be an easy assignment for you."

"Yeah well, he doesn't deserve to die out there. Even if I do hate his guts."

Trey chuckled and shook his head.

"Poor Luke."

**GET YOUR COPY OF ABANDON: AN ORC MONSTER ROMANCE BY CLICKING HERE OR COPYING AND PASTING THIS INTO YOUR BROWSER:** https://www.amazon.com/dp/B0BDPY4VKP

# ALSO BY

Craving more books by me? You can find all of my books on Amazon and read free with your Kindle Unlimited subscription! Check out my backlist below!

**The Silver City Celestials**

Devil's Temptation
Devil's Desire
Angel's Awakening
Angel's Agony

**Monsters & Artifacts**
Feral: A Werewolf Monster Romance
Bound: An MMF Gargoyle Romance
Abandon: An Orc Monster Romance

**Monsters & Artifacts: The MacDonald Werewolf Clan**
Coming 2023

# ABOUT AUTHOR

Trish Heinrich's dark and dirty romance is fueled by caffeine and panic. A lifelong geek, she's thrilled to at last combine two of her favorite things: kissing books and fantasy/sci-fi. When not daydreaming about the latest book boyfriend she's creating, Trish is geeking out with her two kids about the latest superhero movie, cuddling with her husband or binge watching Lucifer...again. You can find her books on Amazon and Kindle Unlimited. You can also keep up with her on Instagram and Tik Tok where her handle is @trishheinrich on both.